D0909746

UNNATURAL CAUSES

MARK OLSHAKER

UNNATURAL CAUSES

WILLIAM MORROW AND COMPANY, INC. / NEW YORK

HOUSTON PUBLIC LIBRARY

R0154510730
HUM

This is a work of fiction, any similarity to persons living
or dead is purely coincidental and exists solely in the
reader's mind.

Copyright © 1986 by Mark Olshaker

Lyrics on pages 35 and 39 by Graham Nash.

© 1970 BROKEN BIRD MUSIC (ASCAP) Used by permission. All rights reserved.

All rights reserved. No part of this book may be reproduced or utilized in any form or by
any means, electronic or mechanical, including photocopying, recording or by any information storage and retrieval system, without permission in writing from the Publisher.
Inquiries should be addressed to Permissions Department, William Morrow and Company, Inc., 105 Madison Ave., New York, N.Y. 10016.

Library of Congress Cataloging-in-Publication Data

Olshaker, Mark, 1951–
    Unnatural Causes

    I. Title.
    PS3565.L823U5   1986   813'.54   86-8468
    ISBN 0-688-05896-5

Printed in the United States of America

First Edition

1   2   3   4   5   6   7   8   9   10

BOOK DESIGN BY RICHARD ORIOLO

FOR MY BROTHER, ROBERT

AUTHOR'S NOTE

This is a work of fiction, and aside from obvious historical references, all characters and situations are fabrications of my imagination. There is no *Men of Action* magazine, and there is no intended or implied similarity to any actual publications.

Novel writing is, by its very nature, a solitary pursuit. Yet writers do not write in a vacuum; at least this writer does not. My gratitude and appreciation go out to many people. My editor, Lisa Drew, and my agent, Jay Acton, were unfailing in their friendship, support, insight, and enthusiasm. They were the ones who saw this through from concept to actuality, and I am unendingly grateful to both of them.

Larry Klein was always there with ideas, suggestions, and an uncanny ability to straighten out twisted or missing logic. And as always, A. E. Claeyssens pushed me to come up with the best book I was capable of producing.

I want to express both my thanks and admiration to all the members and former members of the United States armed forces in various fields and specialties, who guided me and shared their experiences and their expertise, especially Captain Fred Sanford, Medical Corps, USN, and Captain James Lea, Medical Corps, USN (retired).

Claire V. Broome, M.D., of the National Centers for Disease Control in Atlanta was a gracious and fascinating host and provided invaluable help in my understanding of the excitements and mysteries of epidemiology. Here, in Washington, Drs. Ronald Kurstin and Brian Mullin patiently explained and elucidated complex surgical and pathologic procedures. As with everyone else, they gave me the facts. Any excesses and liberties I have taken are solely mine.

For their various and sizable contributions, I also want to thank Deborah Baker, Ken Chaletzky, Ray Hubbard, Ann Merz, my parents—Thelma and Bennett Olshaker—my brother Jonathan, and Stephen Phillips.

Then there are two other people—my wife, Carolyn, and my brother Robert. It would be difficult to convey properly the effect each has had on me and the inspiration each has been to me. So I will say only that for all the general reasons, and all my specific reasons, the last book was dedicated to Carolyn. And this one is Robert's.

Humanity has but three great enemies: fever, famine and war; of these by far the greatest, by far the most terrible, is fever.

—SIR WILLIAM OSLER, M.D.

But if the cause be not good, the king himself hath a heavy reckoning to make, when all those legs and arms and heads, chopped off in a battle, shall join together at the latter day and cry all "We died at such a place"; some swearing, some crying for a surgeon, some upon their wives left poor behind them, some upon the debts they owe, some upon their children rawly left. I am afeard there are few die well that die in a battle; for how can they charitably dispose of any thing, when blood is their argument? Now, if these men do not die well, it will be a black matter for the king that led them to it.

—WILLIAM SHAKESPEARE,
  Henry V

Ah, love, let us be true
To one another! for the world, which seems
To lie before us like a land of dreams,
So various, so beautiful, so new,
Hath really neither joy, nor love, nor light,
Nor certitude, nor peace, nor help for pain;
And we are here as on a darkling plain
Swept with confused alarms of struggle and flight,
Where ignorant armies clash by night.

—MATTHEW ARNOLD,
  "Dover Beach"

PROLOGUE

NEAR BINH THUY, IN THE RUNG SAT SPECIAL
ZONE, MEKONG DELTA.
FEBRUARY 14, 1966

The mission was like all the others. A three-man hunter-killer squad from Navy SEAL Team One had been sent to "interdict" Vietcong forces harassing riverine traffic in the delta. Only this time it didn't work out. The VC encampment was right where intelligence said it would be. But on the way in Donovan had stepped into a sling snare attached to a bent-over sapling. It flung him through the air like a rag doll and impaled him on a bed of sharpened bamboo punji stakes. He was dead before he had a chance to scream. The springing of the trap was enough to alert the enemy, though. They'd opened fire with everything they had. McNeely had taken the better part of a B-40 grenade square in the thigh, and Thorpe got an RPD round in his shoulder. Now he was the only one left standing; guards from the camp would be on them in minutes, and McNeely was bleeding to death.

There was one slim chance: somehow reach Stanway's squad at the prearranged landing zone about four kilometers away and hope like hell the three of them were still alive. Long odds all the way around, but absolute zero on any other possibilities.

Thorpe knew he had to clear at least a couple of seconds for analytical thought before he moved. After that it would be all instinct and reacting. Now began the drill—the drill to maximize efficiency and at the same time to crowd out fear. The human mind can accommodate only so much at a given time, and if fear is allowed to take up part of the capacity, it will soon have all of it. And then the survival odds do drop to zero.

He tried to suppress the racing, pounding pulse between his eyes, the loose, queasy feeling in his stomach and bowels. They were just dangerous distractions. The seering pain where the RPD had ripped into his shoulder was more useful. It would focus his attention and drive him on, like a jockey's whip on the flank of a racehorse.

Analyze. Prioritize. But for God's sake, hurry up. He struggled to control his breathing. The thoughts raced through his mind. They had to get out fast. But he couldn't move McNeely in the condition he was in. And he couldn't leave him alive for the Cong. They'd take his eyes first, and then his balls, and only then would they offer him the opportunity to divulge the SEALs' position. No. Thorpe either had to take him along to the LZ or kill him here himself.

How could he carry him with that gaping leg wound? Again, only one possibility. Damn. He opened the small first-aid kit on his canvas belt pouch and took out two sixteen-milligram morphine Syrettes—all he had. He knelt and tore away the shredded tiger-stripe camouflage cloth from the area around McNeely's thigh. He unscrewed the transparent needle cover of the first Syrette and pushed in the wire stylet to break the seal. Then he jabbed the Syrette into the leg just below the buttock and slowly squeezed the tube until all the liquid was gone. He did the same with the second Syrette. McNeely uttered a low moan. It sounded more animal than a human.

Jarring him as little as possible, Thorpe unhooked his web belt and removed the pouches and grenades. He looped it around McNeely's upper leg, as far from the wound as he could get. He pulled the belt tight, until the skin around the belt turned white. He waited an instant. It wasn't enough. The blood was still gushing.

Now there was no choice.

"Forgive me, Jerry," he whispered.

He extracted his Ka-bar survival knife from its leather sheath and quickly examined the blade. The Ka-bar is specially selected by the SEALs because of its ability to hold a fine edge. It would have to do.

He should sterilize it, he thought. But his only source of fire was a lighter, and the petroleum fuel would just make it worse. He stripped away the remaining fabric of the pants leg. He aligned the Ka-bar blade perpendicular to the thigh, right above the wound. Then he pressed down with all his weight. McNeely opened his mouth wide in agony. Thorpe jammed in his fist to stifle the scream, but McNeely mercifully passed out before making a sound.

The knife sliced easily through the torn flesh and stopped when it hit bone. Thorpe wrapped both hands around its hilt and, with his knee hard down on the other end, forced it through with quick, jerking thrusts. He felt the vibrations from the cracking bone travel up his arms. He turned his head away to retch. A little added pressure guided the knife out the other side of the leg.

Quickly then he pulled the belt tourniquet as tight as he could. As gingerly as possible he wrapped the pulpy stump in gauze, with an outer covering of the material he'd torn from McNeely's pants. He wiped the bloody knife off on his own shirtfront and replaced it in its sheath.

He was ready to move out when he heard the rustling. He crouched, listening intently for the exact direction and nature of the sound. After a few seconds Thorpe could tell he was not alone.

Then he saw him: a single Charley scout off in the dense bushes; probably the point man of his patrol. In a moment the gook would find him and McNeely. He couldn't outrun the guy under these conditions. He would have to take him out . . . before he alerted the rest of his patrol.

SEAL training emphasizes precision and surprise. He would need both. He left the unconscious McNeely lying on the ground as bait. Then he positioned himself behind the nearest thick tree. He judged the distance. Every foot would be critical. Even with the silencer the Smith & Wesson 9mm would make too much noise. He'd have to do this job by hand.

He withdrew the length of concertina wire from his utility pouch. He uncoiled it and formed it into a loop. He tossed a stone over near McNeely's head to draw the Charley's attention. When the scout came sniffing up, Thorpe could see a smile of delighted surprise cross his face. He knelt over the body. Instantly Thorpe sprang the entire distance from the tree. In the same motion he reached the wire garrote over the scout's head. Bracing his landing with the scout's body, Thorpe immediately pulled the wire tight. Regaining his full balance, he drove his knee up into his adversary's back while at the same time grasping his Ka-bar knife, bringing it up above his head, and slicing down through the Charley's neck. A fountain of blood gushed out the carotid artery as the body slumped silently to the ground.

He stopped and listened again. It had been a clean kill. He had not alerted the rest of the VC. Thorpe figured this gave him about three minutes of grace. He quickly evaluated McNeely. Confident that the bleeding had now stopped, he checked his compass, then hoisted McNeely up on his back and waded through the swampy forest in the direction of the landing zone.

With his eye continually on the lurking dangers of the treeline, he slogged through the soft muck of the tidal ponds and the shallow water of the mangrove swamps. His knees buckled. He stumbled and struggled to keep his balance. He could feel leeches slithering up his legs and attaching themselves to his skin. One grabbed hold near his groin. His body convulsed. He wanted to rip them off, but he couldn't let go of McNeely. He vomited into the water. His shoulder had gone numb, and he was starting to feel lightheaded from loss of blood. The green number dots on his Rolex diving watch had gone fuzzy, and he had no idea how long he'd been traveling. But the ground was getting gradually more solid, and if he was going in the right direction, the LZ couldn't be more than half a click away.

Just then something whizzed by his head and impacted on the tree ahead. Another. The bullets flattened against the wood. AK-47 rounds. The Cong had caught up with them.

No chance to duck. He'd have to make a run for it, dart between the trees on the firm ground. Don't give Charley a steady trail.

He ran with all his might and stamina, trying to cushion McNeely from the shock as best he could. His chest heaved from the exertion. His heart tried to break out of his rib cage. All the while he kept glancing down at the leg stump below the tourniquet. No new bleeding.

The shots kept whistling by him. Closer and closer. Soldiers always talk about the bullet out there with your name on it. Couldn't think about that now. Just had to keep going.

Then he saw it. Like a vision out of the Bible. The landing zone. A packed-earth clearing in the midst of this green ooze, just as Recon said it would be. The chopper was there, waiting, its rotors turning leisurely and its door gunners poised for any attack. Nothing in his life had ever thrilled him more.

As soon as he reached the clearing, he saw Stanway emerge from the chopper and run toward him. A medic came out and took McNeely from his shoulders. Thorpe collapsed in Stanway's powerful arms. The other two SEALs from his patrol helped the medic lift McNeely into the chopper as the door gunners laid down covering fire. Within seconds the Huey was airborne.

They laid McNeeley out on the floor, and the medic felt his neck for his carotid pulse. He placed his cheek right next to McNeeley's nose and mouth and held rigidly still.

"How is he?" Thorpe demanded.

The medic only shook his head.

It couldn't be. He couldn't be dead. Thorpe's mind was whirling. It was a clean amputation. He had stopped the bleeding. Maintained respiration. What had he done wrong?

The medic turned McNeely on his side, more quickly and roughly now, as delicacy no longer mattered.

"This guy saved your life," he said to Thorpe.

"What ... how?" Thorpe managed to say through the haze of his exhaustion and grief.

The medic pointed to a small, jagged, round hole slightly below McNeely's shoulder blades. "If you hadn't had him on your back, you'd have taken that bullet."

The drumming, pulsating whir of the chopper blades rang in his ears as Brian Thorpe finally allowed himself the luxury of unconsciousness.

The memory of that day never ceased to haunt him. It changed everything from that point on and led him to his new career.

1

The drumming, pulsating whir of the chopper blades rang in his ears as Brian Thorpe waited with the rest of the trauma team on the edge of the United States Naval Hospital's landing pad. In a few moments the helicopter would be on the ground, and the furious stuggle to save a life would demand every element of his skill and energy.

Perhaps it was his SEAL training, but Brian found he could often reach down to a certain level of calm and stillness within himself just before a period of maximum stress. It wasn't a relaxation technique so much as simply the ability to step back out of the situation for an instant or two. Then, when the challenge did come, he could face it with all his consciousness carefully directed and focused.

Brian's gaze traveled up the strong vertical lines of the hospital's main building, the twenty-two-story tower rising high above the gently rolling hills of Montgomery County. Too stolid and fortresslike to be considered pure Art Deco, the structure was nonetheless an impressive example of what might be termed late WPA *moderne*. Like its contemporary the Pentagon, Bethesda Naval was constructed out of white reinforced concrete that looked as if it could withstand anything the forces of nature or the imagination of man could throw at it. How strange it must have seemed in the 1940s: this military citadel ascending toward the sky to dominate the rural farms and cow pastures ringing the nation's capital.

Despite its overwhelming profile and bearing, within a short time the hospital had somehow managed to blend in with its improbable surroundings. And it was not until a pleasant afternoon in May 1949 that the institution burst onto the public consciousness. For it was on that day that the first secretary of defense, convinced that his many perceived enemies were finally closing in, quietly looked out over the lovely Maryland countryside from his window on the sixteenth floor, then calmly jumped. Of all the many souls who had lived and died in this building, for some reason this was the one Brian thought about most often.

The helicopter landed. Crouching low to avoid the rotor downdraft, Brian and the rest of the team dashed for the door as two paramedics piled out with the stretcher. One of them held two IV bottles with feed lines running into the comatose patient.

"What is it?" Brian yelled above the helicopter din.

"Gunshot in the chest," the paramedic shouted back. "Heavy bleeding. Unconscious when we got there. Started decompensating on the way and pressure just bottomed out"—all this said as they raced along the concrete path from the landing pad to the emergency room's double swinging doors.

Once inside, the anesthesiologist forced an endotracheal tube down the victim's throat and with his knife, started a third intravenous line, this one a cutdown directly into the saphenous vein in the leg. Brian ripped open what was left of the victim's shirt, poured Betadine over his chest, picked up a scalpel, and slashed from the bottom of his neck to just below his rib cage. The tissue layers separated as tiny fountains of blood spurted forth.

"I want two units of O-negative stat and a cross match in case we make it into the OR," Brian ordered. "Spreader!"

The nurse instantly slapped it into his hand. Just as instantly he fitted it between two indentations on the exposed sternum and jerked down. The breastbone cracked, and the two rough-edged halves flew apart. Blood cascaded out the sides, obscuring the entire field.

"Suction! And let me have those units now!"

The resident immediately penetrated the blood-filled chest cavity with suction catheter tips. As soon as the fluid had been cleared away, Brian could see the source of the bleeding. The bullet had ripped into the ascending aorta and left a gash big enough to put a thumb through.

Brian grabbed the two pieces with both hands, then worked feverishly to cross-clamp the artery so it would hold long enough to get the patient into the operating room.

"I'm finally getting a weak pulse," the anesthesiologist reported.

"Okay. Let's move."

As one coordinated unit the entire trauma team surrounded the patient's gurney and traveled the short distance to OR-1, already prepared for such circumstances.

Brian emerged four hours and thirty-seven minutes later. His mind and muscles were weary; his surgical greens, caked with blood. But his patient was still alive and on his way up to intensive care. To Brian Thorpe, decorated veteran of three combat tours in Vietnam, the surgeon was society's single combat warrior against death. He'd gone one-on-one for almost five hours this afternoon, and this time he'd triumphed.

As he left the operating room, one of the medical students who'd been watching came up to him excitedly. "That was brilliant surgery, Dr. Thorpe. Really inspiring." He stopped when he realized other people were listening and looked around, slightly embarrassed.

The circulating nurse came to his aid. "It was good," she said. "Too bad the man came in for a gallbladder."

"Any fool can do a gallbladder," Brian retorted. "I thought I'd do something really dramatic!" He put a friendly hand on the med student's shoulder and walked out.

He was in the scrub room, stripping off his latex gloves, when he felt a powerful hand lock onto his elbow. For a split second an ancient reflex conditioned by survival in a foreign combat zone seized hold of him, and he tensed to strike. But then a newer, stronger instinct suppressed the first and allowed him to turn around calmly.

A man in worn marine fatigues stood in front of him. A ward nurse and hospital security officer were rushing up behind him through the scrub room doors.

"Do you realize how close you came to being my next patient?" Brian commented as he turned.

The man removed his hand immediately, and the pleading expression on his face clearly stated that he meant no offense by the action. "Commander Thorpe?"

"That's right."

"I tried to stop him, Doctor." The nurse broke in. The guard stepped forward and grabbed the man by the arm. "How did you get in here?" the nurse demanded.

Brian waved her off. "I'll take over interrogation of the prisoner," he said. "Let's at least give him credit for his infiltration techniques. The military spends a lot of money trying to teach that." At this the intruder even smiled slightly. Brian was trying to figure a way to end the whole scene and politely get rid of this guy when he noticed the black metal insignias on the man's jacket.

Flat black instead of shiny brass. It could mean just one thing. There was only one situation in which the marines didn't want their emblems gleaming: combat, where they could be spotted by an enemy.

"You were a medic with the Third Marine Division at Dong Ha in 1969," the man stated urgently. He was probably about Brian's age, maybe a year or two younger. But he had that sort of wild, slightly spooked look in his eyes that already betrayed a lifetime's worth of hard living and harder luck. The clinical description would have been that "the subject presented himself in a state of high anxiety and emotional excitation."

"Yeah, I was with the Third Marines," Brian confirmed, and it instantly brought him back to another time and place, a time of unceasing horror, yet a time when he felt closer to people he'd hardly known than practically anyone he associated with today. "Were you?"

"Yes, sir, I was."

Brian studied him carefully. "Do I know you?"

"No reason you should remember me personally. But you saved my life, and the lives of a lot of my buddies, too."

This altered the equation again. "Is that a fact? Well, I am delighted to see you after all this time." Brian smiled and extended his hand.

"Sir, Davis is my name, Radley Davis." There was an awkward moment during which Davis nervously shifted his weight and twisted his rumpled camouflage cap from one fist to the other, trying to decide whether saluting or accepting the hand would be more appropriate. In the end he did neither.

"How do you do? I appreciate your coming to see me"—he glanced around the room and made a gesture to take in the surroundings—"like this. Now, how're you getting along? What can I do for you?"

"I heard you'd become a real doctor, and that's what I need—a real doctor ... someone I can trust. I knew I could trust you 'cause of what you done for me already." He glanced warily at the blood-covered front of Brian's surgical garb. "So I tracked you down to here, sir."

Brian instantly decided he didn't particularly relish the idea of being tracked down anywhere. Both tracking and being tracked were aspects of his life he preferred to leave far behind, within the jungles and swamps of his young manhood.

"God, I wish I saw some of those guys more often. Are you still in the corps ... Mr. Davis?" Brian asked.

"No, sir, I'm not, I'm most sorry to say. Staff sergeant when I left. Mustered out in '73, though I wish to God it'd all been different."

"He shouldn't even be here!" The nurse broke in again. "He should be at the VA hospital if he feels he needs medical attention."

"Right, and let them make me into another vegetable like they done to my buddies. No, ma'am, no, thank you, far as the VA is concerned. I want someone who's looking out for me, not trying to clear their damn desk." The lightly buried hysteria was rising rapidly to the surface.

Brian put up his hands. "Hold on! Let's take this one step at a time." He turned to the nurse. "Lieutenant, please show Mr. Davis to my office, would you?"

"But, Dr. Thorpe," she protested, "he really should be seen by the VA."

"I know. But we're just going to have a little talk about the old days. He's going to get me caught up." He turned back to Davis. "Sit tight for a few minutes, okay? I'll be back as soon as I get out of this bloody stuff. Then we can talk."

"You saved my life," Radley Davis related. He looked down at the floor and spoke haltingly, tightly clutching the sides of the orange plastic chair as if he were afraid of falling off. "It was the morning we took Hill Eighty-four. I was in the first assault wave, and the dinks were trying to bury us for good. We were completely pinned down by mortar fire. The lieutenant had already bought it. I took a load of shrapnel in the gut, and I was just laying there on the ground, puking blood and trying not to look at my intestines through the hole in my belly. And all the time I'm thinking to myself this is one shitty place to die." There were tears in his eyes, and his hands were trembling. He sat silently for a moment.

Finally he looked up. "You pulled me out of there. I don't know how you did it. But I do know you could have easily got yourself killed trying."

Brian listened solemnly, elbows propped up on the scuffed surface of his gray metal desk and chin resting heavily on his interlocked fingers. At first glance it might have seemed a casual, restful pose. But it was in actuality one that provided him the degree of physical stability he suddenly felt in need of.

His mind raced back to that time. After completing college, Brian had gone back to Vietnam as a corpsman to assure himself he really did want to make the commitment to medicine, the way a novitiate might choose to serve a time in some famine-stricken missionary outpost to make a true test of his faith and vocation for the priesthood. He had come back absolutely certain.

Radley Davis was bringing it all home to him again.

A barrage of images assaulted him. The dreamlike, surrealistic feel of the whole thing: nostrils burning from cordite, every muscle cringing, then recoiling as machine-gun rounds whiz by just above your head, dodging across a stretch of blood-soaked earth, praying you can find some magical potion among your standard issue supplies to keep the life of the moaning nineteen-year-old kid from leaking out onto the mud. The cosmic illogic: You aren't supposed to carry a weapon, and the Geneva Convention clearly classifies you as a noncombatant. But they're shooting at you just the same. And most of all, the futility. On one side there's the entire enemy force, geared up for the sole purpose of causing death ... and expert at it. On the other side, there's only you, single-handedly trying to prevent it, after they've had the head start.

"So anyway," Davis went on, "after that I knew you were the kind of guy who would never let another guy down—the kind you could trust with your life. And that's why I'm here."

Normally a simple recitation of symptoms and the chronology of their onset establishes the common ground in a first meeting between doctor and patient. But Brian had the feeling that whatever Davis's complaints turned out to be, they were better set in the context of a more thorough and wide-ranging history. It was already abundantly clear at this stage that the man's current condition was very much a product of his past.

Slowly, painstakingly, Davis laid out his life for the physician. For the most part he kept his eyes cast downward, looking up occasionally with a mixture of timidity and disbelieving gratitude which said he surely hoped he wasn't boring Brian or taking up too much of his time. Brian made a show of picking up a pencil and squaring a pad of paper in front of him to reassure Davis that this was not the case.

Davis, Brian learned, was a rural North Carolina boy. He was known to everyone simply as Rad. He had proceeded directly from his high school graduation ceremony to the Marine Corps recruitment office, and the day when his parents drove down to Parris Island to watch him graduate from boot camp was the proudest of his life. He wanted nothing more than the distinction of defending his country from the Communist threat, despite the fact he'd never in his life come across a Communist or even more than vaguely knew what they stood for. But he knew an important rite of passage awaited him, and he knew he wanted to serve. And in that way he was like so many other southern boys, who, regardless of generation or the passing social fancies in the rest of the nation, consider it their privilege and duty to take up arms for the flag and the old values.

He was assigned as an infantryman to the Third Marine Division, stationed at Dong Ha, seven miles from the demilitarized zone, and became a member of Colonel John Winthrop Blagden's legendary Seventh Marine Amphibious Unit, the same one in which Brian came to serve as a medical corpsman. He was known in-country as a true "Semper Fi" marine—fearless, aggressive, loyal, and unquestioning. He was awarded the Purple Heart for his wounds on Hill 84 and a Bronze Star for bravery during the celebrated and controversial Eagle's Talon raid, debated over for so long after the end of the war.

It was only after the war that things turned sour for Davis, he recounted. The military made it clear it had no further use for him. He went to computer school on the meager post-Vietnam

GI Bill because he'd heard that that was where all the jobs were going to be. But his reception in the civilian job market wasn't any better than his welcome back from Vietnam had been. Several years, several jobs, and several failed relationships later, he had nothing more to show for himself than a minor police record and a growing feeling of worthlessness and despair.

"Why, specifically, have you come to see me?" Brian asked, careful to affect the physician's objectivity. It wasn't a role that came easily to him in this particular case. *There, but for the grace of God . . .* he thought, and kept thinking it the entire time Rad was talking. For Brian, most of the memories had been at least partially healed by the scar tissue of time. For Radley Davis, it was clear that time had provided little more than tender scabs, easily ripped open by the slightest contact.

"I been having these pains, sir," he explained.

"What sorts of pains?"

"All kinds, a lot of different ones. In my stomach, my side . . . Lately, it's been getting worse."

"Right or left side?"

This question seemed to throw him. "Ah, both, I guess."

"You're sure."

"Yes, sir. Ah, maybe my right. Yeah, my right side mostly."

"Are you having these pains now?"

"Ah, well, sir, some of them, yes, I'd say I am."

Rather than take any notes, as he'd set out to do, Brian found himself rhythmically tapping the pencil on the edge of his desk, as if this would lead him to a pattern in the symptoms. "You say you were wounded by shrapnel?"

"Yes, sir."

"How long have you had these pains?"

"I'm not sure."

"Weeks? Months?"

"More than months, I think."

"Do the pains increase with movement or exercise?"

"I—I think so."

"Have you ever had blackouts or amnesia?"

"Not that I can remember."

Brian tried to suppress a smile. "Fair enough. Do you have any idea when the symptoms began?"

"A long time. But now they're getting worse. I have trouble sleeping. I wake up in the middle of the night. I'm always tense, just thinking about it. I think that's maybe why I can't hold a job no more. And nobody listens when I try to tell them. You're my last hope, Doc." He was openly sobbing now. The way his hands shook when he tried to light himself a cigarette could have been used as a classic study in nervous tremors.

Brian's heart went out to Davis. His physical complaints were certainly worthy of follow-up, but the primary diagnosis could be made across the desk, or even across the room, for that matter. "PTSD" was the abbreviation the military doctors had assigned to it—for post traumatic stress disorder. It was as serious as any personal consequence of the Vietnam War and a lasting national legacy of our adventure over there. By the last official estimates, between 500,000 and 700,000 men were still suffering the effects of PTSD.

It had been bad enough over there for the specialized forces, the Rangers and the SEALs. But at least they'd had the odds in their favor, Brian recalled. Whenever they went out on an operation, it wasn't just to ditty-bop around. They were backed by careful intelligence and had specific objectives in mind. The infantry grunts, on the other hand, were most often just thrown into the maw, with no specific targets and no clearly defined missions.

It was worst of all for the marines. They were often given the same job as the army, a role they weren't set up, equipped, or supplied for. One way or another the marines always seemed to get the raw deal in Nam. But they lived up to their image and reputation. They were tough people who didn't complain, no matter what was thrown at them, and always made do. Brian had come away from Vietnam with an undying respect for the Marine Corps.

"Any other symptoms you can think of, Mr. Davis?"

"Well, I don't know if you'd call them symptoms, exactly, but . . ."

That was when it came out.

First, Davis craned his neck around, looking to every corner of the tiny office, as if he could visually sweep the place for listening devices. Then he stood up for the first time since he'd been there and went over to close the door. He sat down again but pulled the chair close enough to rest his forearms on the front of Brian's desk.

"Buddies of mine," he began, almost in a whisper, "other

grunts. Sonny Lofton, Maxie Craig, Tyrrell Jefferson, Chris Schuyler—he's the one they used to call Princeton. You might have known some of them."

They were only names to Brian. Familiar, one or two, but only names. "What about them?" he asked, again resting his chin on his clasped hands.

"Dead," Davis intoned. "All of them dead."

"In Nam, you mean."

"No. Recently."

The room went suddenly cold.

"How?" Brian leaned slowly back in his chair.

"Different ways," said Rad almost casually. A tone of resignation had crept into his voice, as if it no longer mattered what he said, because the people he was talking about now were far beyond hope or fear.

He opened up his green fatigue jacket and carefully extracted a tan manila envelope. It was one of those oversize ones used for interoffice routing, with a piece of string on the top that wound around two little cardboard disks to secure it closed. The envelope was so fuzzy from wear that it had a soft, sueded texture, and it had been doubled over to fit into his pocket. He opened the envelope and produced about a half dozen newspaper clippings, which he passed across the desk to Brian.

Brian read grimly. One of the articles detailed Anthony "Sonny" Lofton's death when his automobile careened over an embankment on the San Bernardino Freeway at high speed. The Los Angeles county coroner's report noted a blood alcohol level high above the legal limit. Two of the pieces referred to Tyrrell Jefferson's suicidal plunge off Washington's Calvert Street Bridge. Though the officer on the scene didn't come right out and say it to the reporter, the strong implication was that drugs were involved.

The remaining articles were from smaller-town newspapers, where the deaths of ordinary citizens have greater weight and impact, and so provided more details. Christopher Schuyler had been lost in a sailboat off Sakonnet Point, a waterway he had sailed often. The coast guardsmen who boarded the craft after receiving several visual reports found the boat undamaged, but no sign of its owner. Blood and shreds of skin along a five-inch section of the backstay line were evidently from Schuyler's hand and clearly indicated the force of the wave or storm, or combination of the two, that had swept him overboard. The only anomaly was that Schuyler's green marine rain poncho was lying on the deck near the stern, while logic dictated that he should have been wearing it if the weather was inclement at the time of the accident. It was the only personal effect found on board.

And Maxwell Craig died in a hunting mishap near Lake Wallenpaupack, Pennsylvania. He was hunting alone, as he usually did, among the familiar mountain streams and steep, rugged hills he had known since his early boyhood. He was found with a single bullet through his brain and his scope-mounted Remington M700 by his side. Apparently another hunter in the area had mistaken him for a deer in the dense thicket. There were no witnesses to the accident, the other hunter never came forward, and the game wardens were unable to locate him.

Each of the stories—from both the large city newspapers and the small local journals—dutifully noted that the deceased was a veteran of the United States Marine Corps with service in Vietnam, winner of the Purple Heart and other citations.

Brian looked up at his trembling visitor. "These are all accidents," he said.

"Yeah, accidents," Rad repeated, carefully gathering up the newspaper clippings and putting them back in the tattered envelope.

Perhaps one or more of the others was also suffering PTSD, Brian considered to himself. Becoming "accident-prone" was part of the well-documented symptomatology of the disorder.

"You can call them accidents, Doc," Davis said. "But I've tracked four buddies who've died within a couple of weeks of each other. Doesn't that seem a little strange? All guys from the Third Division, all from the Seventh Amphibious Unit. And the next one could just as easily be me."

To the list of other symptoms Brian now felt safe in adding acute paranoia. It was going to be difficult separating the physical stuff from the head stuff in this case. He tapped the pencil once or twice to collect his thoughts. "Look, Mr. Davis . . . Rad. The nurse you spoke to was right. You actually should be seen in a Veterans Administration hospital. But I think we can get around that. I'm going to order up a series of tests, and we'll see what they tell us. In the meantime, I'm writing you out a prescription for Valium. They'll fill it for you at the pharmacy downstairs. Follow the directions on the bottle. I think it'll help you relax. And that should help you more than anything."

"These tests—will you be doing them?"

"No, I'm a surgeon. But I promise you, as soon as they're back, I'll go over them myself."

Rad shrugged with an air of resignation.

Brian stood and ushered him to the door when it became obvious he would have preferred to remain in this refuge indefinitely. Their eyes met when he turned to go, his searching for some further promise or token of commitment from the doctor. Brian put his hand on the ex-marine's arm and escorted him down the hall. When they got to the corner where the two corridors came together, he pointed out the direction Rad should take. Rad nodded. Then Brian made the pledge he'd found over the years that seriously afflicted patients most needed to hear: "I'll stay with this. We'll find out what the problem is. I won't abandon you."

He watched Davis walk down the corridor until he reached the elevators. Then he closed the door and settled into the first solitude he'd had since early that morning. He penned a quick memo ordering Davis's tests and deposited it in his outgoing basket. The workup would reassure the guy there wasn't anything physically wrong with him. And in the next couple of days Brian would look into finding out who could take care of the other side of the problem.

The meeting with Davis had gotten him thinking about the past and what he'd lost. And that made him think about Lizzie. He'd found himself doing that a lot since the split. Not only Lizzie herself but the void her leaving had caused. He'd saved a photograph of them together, still mounted in the dark rosewood frame in which she presented it to him. It was the one taken back in San Diego—on the beach in front of the Hotel del Coronado, just up the Silver Strand from the naval amphibious base where he'd taken his SEAL training.

The picture showed two young, attractive people, both California beach blond though both were in fact from the Midwest: the man lean and trim and looking somehow taller than his six feet; the woman shapely and bouncy and slightly freckled—everyone's dream cheerleader. They were kind of clowning around, affecting silly poses, but what Brian had always liked about the image was that it was obvious, even to a casual observer, how much the two people in it loved each other. He still had it in his office, tucked away in the lower drawer of his file cabinet. But he preferred to remember it rather than look at it. Memory seemed more appropriate at this stage.

But there was another photograph, standing at the far corner of his desk where he could always see it, and this one would never be put away or relegated to memory.

Katie.

It was a recent likeness. Five glorious years old. Cute as the proverbial button, in her blue sailor dress and white tights, smiling that radiant dimpled smile that said "I love you" unquestioningly and unconditionally. Since the breakup he had measured his life by the times he got to spend with her.

He and Lizzie had ultimately put off most everything between them until it was too late. Thank God they hadn't ultimately put off Katie. Out of the darkest moments of their marriage had come the brightest light of his life.

Whatever their problems with each other, Lizzie had never tried to influence Katie about Brian or turn her mind against him. Nor would she; he was sure of that. And for that alone, he would always love her.

The two men who waited by the elevator as the ex-marine came out of Dr. Thorpe's office were dressed in nondescript civilian clothing. Some thought had initially been given to putting them in hospital maintenance uniforms or possibly even enlisted men's khakis. But each of those options involved readily apparent name tags and the possibility of challenge by some superior; whereas in any large hospital "ordinary" visitors elicit no special notice.

Photographs had been discreetly obtained before the subject's consultation with Thorpe, using a Minox LX, modified with an Ickow Z-12 chromatically corrected telephoto lens. The corroborating fingerprints (actually, one would be sufficient) involved a somewhat more delicate procedure, which is why the two men were now following him into the elevator.

As expected, he pressed the L button, and the three of them rode silently down to the lobby. The two men stayed on for the return trip back up and were not overly concerned that other passengers came on as well. None of them was likely to touch the lobby button during an ascending trip.

When the final passenger had left the elevator cab, the two men immediately went into their drill, spreading the white powder over a strip of cellophane tape and lifting a perfect print from the L button. The operation had been carefully rehearsed to require no more time than the interval between two floors.

As it turned out, they had four seconds to spare.

ATLANTA, GEORGIA

There was a large magnolia tree growing just outside Diana Keegan's window, and as she thought back, it was probably the main reason she had taken the apartment. The logic at the time was that if she were going to live in Atlanta at all—a city which she knew primarily from *Gone with the Wind* and which seemed such an unlikely location after Washington, Palo Alto, and Boston—she ought to get the full effect.

But now, every day, as she turned off Houston Mill Road and walked up her building's flagstone path, its borders neatly lined with little painted white stones that separated it from the carefully ordered flower beds on either side, the tree continued to remind her of her own strangeness in this strange land. And for some reason, today the feeling was worse than usual. As she approached the front door, she sensed herself suffocating in the thick, sweet, aromatic complacency of the brightly colored flowers.

To be honest, she had never been overly thrilled with the prospect of living in any southern city—liberal, progressive reputation or no. The South was still the South. The Emory area was a nice section of town, she could walk to work, and it had the advantage of being near the university, so there should be some intellectual stimulation. Yet for a young woman nurtured on the liberating politics and social consciousness of the late sixties and early seventies, Atlanta was one giant step backward. But she had come here for a purpose, she kept telling herself. And if she believed in it, nothing else should matter.

At least so the logic went. Ever since she was a little girl, Diana had wanted to be a doctor. It hadn't seemed quite so important for a while, back in college, when she and just about everyone she knew were busy building for a new world. But then, as the anti-war movement ended and the civil rights struggle waned, it started to become clear that there wasn't a new world coming after all. That being the case, she had to do whatever she could to make the old one better.

Which, by a labyrinthine route through medical school, internship, residency, and the Public Health Service, had brought her here to Atlanta—to the Epidemic Intelligence Service of the National Centers for Disease Control. Maybe the rest of the life's plan hadn't worked out exactly as she'd figured it would, but at the CDC she was convinced she was again doing something useful. The location was a small price to pay. After all, hadn't she lived for two or her Public Health Service years in that tar-paper shack in Salinas, ministering to the migrant lettuce pickers? Still, it had been California, and only a short drive to Monterey at that.

To get into the apartment building, Diana had to dial a security code. She hated this ritual. More than anything else it was a daily reminder that she was now on the "inside." She knew the system was supposed to make residents feel more "comfortable," and most of them considered it a requisite for city living. But Diana had come through the wars and spent a sizable portion of her adult life decrying "comfort." And here she found herself embracing it. It made her feel ridiculous.

As she came through her door and into the small foyer, Diana briefly glanced at the mail, then went into the kitchen and evaluated the meager contents of the fridge. Nothing exciting enough to bother swallowing, much less chewing. She kept promising herself she was going to get it together soon to go do a proper shop. Maybe this weekend. She would spend all day at the Emory Village Kroger. This weekend for sure.

Sharon wasn't home yet. She almost never was when Diana arrived. Young associates in the big law firms worked longer hours than interns. Sharon practically lived at the King & Spaulding office for weeks on end. In a way, that made her the ideal roommate. But she was much more than that, and Diana was sorry they didn't get to spend more time together, especially on days like this, when Diana was feeling lonely and detached. Sometimes lately she would go through an entire Saturday or Sunday and then realize at the end of the day that she hadn't had to use her voice once.

It had never been like that back in the old days—in college and med school. There was always someone around, and there was always something happening. She found herelf thinking about that a lot recently: about GW and Stanford. And even that hellish, bleary-eyed intern year at Mass General was now tinged in her mind with nostalgia.

Diana went into her bedroom to change. She slipped out of her skirt and panty hose and dropped them haphazardly on the bed, then ventured into the walk-in closet in search of a semiclean pair of jeans. One thing about these new condos: They might be put together with spit and chewing gum and you might be able to hear your neighbor through the wall tweezing her eyebrows, but every unit she'd looked at had these incredible closets, each with a built-in shoe rack. Her generation now was supposed to be into clothes. Dress for success, and all that. Not exactly what the revolution had promised.

Despite the fact that she'd been here for more than a year now, Diana still considered the move to Atlanta a temporary sojourn. She hadn't been to the High Museum of Art. She hadn't walked along the banks of the Chattahoochee. She hadn't even been to the Martin Luther King Memorial; she felt bad about that.

And she hadn't really bothered to unpack. So even though she lacked a power wardrobe, the nice thing about these spacious closets was that there was plenty of room in them for all the cardboard boxes she'd never dealt with.

Before she found the jeans she wanted to put on, Diana's eyes fixed on a large corrugated box resting on the middle of the top shelf. She'd packed it the day after she graduated from George Washington, and she'd dragged it with her from place to place, never opening it but knowing she would never get rid of it either.

Today felt like the day to open it.

Standing on her tiptoes and stretching, she managed to pull the box down and set it on the closet floor. It was still sealed with the original plastic strapping tape. Sitting cross-legged on the floor beside it, she peeled off the tape and pulled up the top flaps. She coughed as she breathed in thirteen years of sealed-in must and dust.

Instantly a flood tide of wistfulness and longing enveloped her. The box contained what at one time Diana had considered her most treasured possessions, her most personal and least practical, yet the things that in her more reflective moments defined an era of her life and gave it meaning. They were the touchstones of her various ages—what she had held of value in the world.

First, there was the yellowed plastic hospital bracelet with her name printed on it from when she'd had her tonsils taken out—her first in-depth experience with doctors and medicine. She brought out the string of tiny little-girl pearls her aunt Josephine had given her for the junior high school prom. It was the first time her mother had let her wear stockings.

The blue and white varsity letter from Briarcliff Manor High still held her field hockey and swimming pins. And of course, she'd saved her high school ring (all the girls said it was a real diamond) and the yellow tassel designating membership in the National Honor Society from her graduation cap.

Perhaps one object more than any other symbolized the rapid and crazy transition from high school to college sensibility during that turbulent era. It was a gray plush kitten with the sweetest face ever, and to its pink ribbon collar was attached the black button with the white "STRIKE!" fist. She laughed as she remembered she had named the animal Che.

Next came the report from the Washington Free Clinic certifying she was free of all embarrassing diseases (a great relief) and a newspaper photo of her in front of the White House with the name of a dead GI on a card around her neck from the 1969 November Moratorium march. Her roommate, Pat, who had been marching right next to her, complained that it was always the pretty girls who got their pictures in the paper. There was also a snapshot from Greg Valliere's costume party where Mike had gone as Richard Nixon and she'd dressed up in knee socks and some awful party frock as Tricia.

Wedged against the side of the box was her George Washington diploma; at least she assumed it was. It was still sealed in its blue cardboard mailer. She hadn't gone to graduation, so it had been sent to her.

And one final memory: Inside a metal Band-Aid box were two

joints, tightly rolled in the red, white, and blue flag papers favored at the time. They'd been a gift—for what, she no longer remembered—and she'd been told they were a blend of Colombian Gold and fine-shaved Moroccan hashish. Diana had pledged to save them for some special occasion, the way her neighbors would have stocked away a bottle of vintage port.

She had needed to see all these things again. But now she really did feel like a foreigner—both to the environment in which she currently lived and to the person she used to be. It wasn't the late sixties or early seventies any longer and hadn't been for what seemed like centuries. She wondered sadly if she'd ever fit in again as completely as she once had.

Diana stood up, padded barefoot out of the bedroom and into the living room, where she went over to the record rack. There was a select number of groups she chose from whenever she felt the need to conjure up the ghosts of the past and reclaim herself. Tonight, she wasn't up for anything too heavy, so she chose Crosby, Stills, Nash, and Young. She settled back in the sofa with a glass of red wine and let the hauntingly unreachable voices blend over her.

I'll light the fire . . .
You place the flowers in the vase that you bought today.
Staring at the fire, for hours and hours while I listen to you
Play your love songs all night long.
For me . . . only for me.

The ringing of the telephone jarred her out of her reverie.

"Hel—hello?"

"Diana?"

"Yes?"

"Diana, it's Bill."

Bill. Her mouth went suddenly dry, and there was a hollow feeling in her lungs.

"Bill Eschenberger."

Could this really be happening, or was it just a mental segue to the next phase of her longing for things past? Was he actually calling, or had she simply fabricated him from all the magic totems in the box?

"Diana, are you all right?"

She took a deep breath so she'd sound normal when she spoke.

"Yes. Yes, how—how are you?" Exactly how many years had it been? What should she say? "Ah, where are you calling from?" "Houston." So he was still there.

"Listen, Diana— Oh, I guess I should ask you first. How are you? How're you getting along?"

"I'm okay. Great," she lied. Of all the nights in all the years since they were together for him to call—tonight, when she would have gladly forgotten everything that had gone down between them just to have him there next to her, touching her and loving her again.

"God, it's good to hear your voice. Are you as beautiful as I remember you?"

"I don't know how you remember me."

"Still the same old Diana."

And probably still the same old Bill. That was what she had to force herself to keep in mind as that voice transported her back to quiet and blissfully intimate weekends at Big Sur, pizzas and subs in the interns' lounge at 3:00 A.M., and a thousand mornings when only the thought of the man lying there beside her had given her the courage to get up and face the day. Forget all the summers of roses and the Krug Pinot Chardonnay she had always loved, Diana told herself, and recall the long, bleak winter of their parting. Think hard, and remember all the arguments, the intractable positions on both sides, the petty power plays, and the public humiliations. And then there was the time he'd actually hit her.

But that was not an easy thing to do because while college had been the dawning of her awareness, medical school was where she had grown up and come alive to the concept of true commitment. And William Eschenberger, M.D., had been her guide and companion, partner and adversary, for the last two of those critical years. They had met in her third year, when she was still going crazy. He was an internal medicine resident, and she had rotated through his service at Stanford Medical Center. From that point on she'd given herself wholly over to him. Aside from being her lover, he had been her mentor and her guru—a term that was quite popular back then—and was he completely to blame for the fact that she had finally outgrown the need for such a relationship?

"Listen, Diana, as it turns out, I'm going to be in Atlanta for a conference two weeks from this coming Saturday, and—and I'd love to see you."

She let this sink in for several seconds, until she became aware of the awkwardness of the silence and had to come up with something—anything—to break it.

"Where will you be staying?"

"Well, that depends. I don't know what your setup is like now, whether you're living by yourself or what . . ."

"Will you be coming with . . . your wife?"

This time the silence came from his end. "Ah, no. We're separated, Diana. Have been for months now."

"I'm sorry."

"Thanks. But it's okay. It hasn't been working out for a long time. Even at its best, there was never the passion there that—that we had."

Why was he telling her all this? she wondered, but not for long. *Come on, Diana, you're a big girl now. You know exactly what's on his agenda.*

"I have a roommate," she explained. Not that that would have mattered, but she wanted time to think. How could she even consider taking up with him again? On the other hand, the best of it was better than it had ever been with anyone else. That was the problem with Bill. There was always the other hand.

He obviously knew what was going through her mind, just as he always had. "Well, look, why don't I call you back in about a week? Meantime, I'll book a nice room. What's a good hotel?"

"Oh, the, ah, Ritz-Carlton, I guess," she said distractedly.

"And can you get any Krug Pinot Chardonnay?" She could imagine one of his characteristically self-satisfied winks on the other end of the line.

"We'll see," she said as noncommittally as she could manage. How seductively easy she found it to be drawn back into his orbit. Was it just that she was lonely? Was it having to face that modern cliché of the biological clock ticking away? Or, she wondered as she hung up the telephone receiver, was there something more? Something she'd been too stubborn or too shortsighted to recognize in her mid-twenties?

Their final argument flashed back through her memory. It had happened right after his acceptance letter had come from Baylor.

"You're not happy for me?"

"Of course, I'm happy for you. That cardiology fellowship is what you wanted."

"It's extremely prestigious. What every resident in my position in the whole damn country wanted. And you mean to tell me you're going to stand in my way?"

"No, I'm not going to stand in your way. I'm just not going with you."

"Why not?"

"I don't want to live in Texas, for one thing. And for another, why should I have to be subservient to you? I have a career, too."

"You're not being subservient to me. It's just that I have this terrific opportunity, and you're finishing school this year, so it's no big deal for you. I'm sure I could help you get an internship in Houston."

"I don't want an internship in Houston. I want to be able to lead my own life and make my own choices."

"I keep forgetting I'm living with a radical feminist."

"I am *not* a radical feminist! I *was* a radical because the times forced anyone with a conscience and a mind to become one. And I *am* a feminist for the simple reason that I happen to believe in equal rights for everyone."

"Okay, fine. Have it your way then."

"Don't you see? All I want is to have it *our* way. Did you once ask me how I felt about your applying for the fellowship? Did you once ask me how I felt about moving to Texas? You just assumed that sweet little Diana would go along with whatever wise, strong Bill decided was best. Bill, I'm not your disciple any longer. I'm your lover and your friend."

"Fine. Well, when you aren't so busy balancing that chip on your shoulder, we'll talk about this some more."

But they never did.

In the years since, she often thought about whether she'd made the right choice. By the time the string was finally played out, it hadn't been any different with Jeff Harmon, who'd been in the Public Health Service with her and who had been as "dedicated" as she. So maybe the fault was within her. Maybe she should just stay away from other doctors altogether. Well, the real "maybe" was maybe it was time to finally make some compromises, to realize you can't have everything just the way you think it's supposed to be. Time to join the rest of the world.

The record was still playing.

You, who are on the road . . .
Must have a code . . . that you can live by.
And so, become yourself . . .
Because the past . . . is just a good-bye."

Graham Nash, you made it all sound so simple, and in our youth it was so easy to believe you.

. . . And feed them on your dreams . . .
The one they pick's, the one you'll know by. . . .

Why was it always the woman who had to give in or give something up? Why couldn't he have called up and said, "I know how uncomfortable you were about simply following me, and I realize now I love you so much, and always have, that I am giving up my lucrative cardiology practice and my position on the Baylor Medical School faculty and moving to Atlanta to be with you"? *Dream on, Diana. That ain't the way of the world.*

Then another thought struck her, and it threw her for such a surprising loop that the only thing she could do was laugh out loud: What would she have done if he *had* said that? It was so beyond the realm of reality, but what if? Was this actually what she wanted? "Be careful what you wish for," her mother had always told her. "You may get it."

When Sharon finally came home, she found Diana still sitting on the living room sofa in her blouse and panties, clutching her empty wineglass with both hands. She listened attentively as Diana related the events of the evening and her ambivalence and uncertainty about them, then said, "You're not thinking of letting him get away again, are you?" for Sharon was very much in the market herself.

But then, when Diana went on to relate the events leading up to the events of the evening, she offered, "Men are all shits, aren't they?" In her own eccentric way Sharon could be very supportive.

"So what are you going to do if he asks you back into his life?" she asked.

"I don't know," Diana replied, pensively running a hand through her dark, wavy hair.

"Well, you're going to have to decide something before he shows up on your doorstep."

"Maybe I'll be out of town," she said, blowing an errant wisp of hair from between her eyes.

Sharon looked at her as if she were a child who'd just been naughty but then quickly relented. "I guess this is kind of what we used to call an existential moment for you, huh? Want to go out and get drunk?"

Suddenly Diana's large blue eyes lit up. "Actually I've got a better idea!"

Sharon watched her as she bounded up and scampered into her bedroom. She came back shortly with what looked to be an old Band-Aid box. And her eyes were twinkling with charm and mischief as she said, "When was the last time you got really ripped?"

3

"I'm dying. I can feel it." The voice was weak and raspy. The hands were shaking. The face was ashen and dripping with sweat. The room had become a fuzzy white haze with no edges between walls and floors and ceilings. "You're responsible. It'll be on your conscience." And between gasps, as he lay on the floor, he said it again: "I'm dying."

"You are not!" Brian Thorpe retorted. "Now get up and stop whining."

Slowly, and with a maximum of labor, Gregory Cheever took Brian's extended hand and picked himself up off the racquetball court. "Why do you keep doing this to me?" he panted. "I'm a doctor. I know what happens when you make too many demands on the body."

"And I know what happens when you don't make enough of them."

"Sure, easy for you," he said as they walked back toward the locker room. "Everyone knows SEALs are crazy anyhow. But while you were squandering your youth, running and swimming and jumping out of airplanes, I was refining my mind into the highly developed and sophisticated entity you see before you."

Gregory Cheever was in his late thirties, a few years younger than Brian. He was of medium height, with thick, curly hair and even thicker glasses, and just sufficiently overweight to be considered cuddly by the young ladies he inevitably and—to some—inexplicably managed to attract. The service's annual physical fitness test was invariably his worst day of the year. Other than that, the navy gave him little to complain about. And except for those times when a particularly perverse mood struck him, he generally returned the favor.

Gregory was a peacetime naval recruit who had never seen combat or sea duty. Like most of the educated middle-class members of his generation, he had managed to circumvent the Vietnam draft when he came of age in the late 1960s. After college and an amateur vocation of antiwar protesting, he went on to Columbia's College of Physicians and Surgeons, where he distinguished himself with a minimum of effort. To anyone who would listen, he readily admitted the rationale behind the two major career choices that shaped his life from that point on. Gregory joined the navy to avoid the rigors of private practice and because, "unlike the army, they can't stick you anyplace too out of the way." He chose to specialize in radiology for its intellectual challenge and to avoid the stresses of ongoing patient contact.

By the time they reached the locker room and stepped into the showers, Gregory had come back to himself. "Guess I had you going for a while back there, huh?"

"Right," Brian said.

"It's a dirty job, but somebody's got to keep testing you. Otherwise you're gonna lose it. Then all that expensive commando training the taxpayers scrimped and saved for just goes down the toilet."

"Just pass the soap," Brian said.

"Oh, no, you wild man. I've heard that kind of come-on before. By the way, has anyone ever told you you look kind of cute without your clothes on?"

They both dressed in front of the mirror. Gregory pulled himself up to his full height, sucked in his breath, and pulled the officer's shirt flat against his stomach. It was a well-intentioned but fairly futile effort. Unlike Brian's, Gregory's body was not designed for uniforms. He never looked sharp.

He smoothed down his collar, pausing to run his fingers contemplatively over the stylized brass-plated oak leaf on the left point. While the overall symbol of the military Medical Corps is the caduceus—the winged, snake-entwined staff carried by Mercury according to Greek mythology—naval officers in the corps have the oak leaf as their insignia, with zero, one, or two silver acorns accompanying it.

"Y'know," Gregory declared, still gazing into the mirror at his oak leaf and its single acorn, "I understand why the nurses don't get any nuts, and I can even accept the fact that we doctors get one nut, but why in the name of everything that's fair and honorable would they give the dentists *two*? I mean, how much balls does it take to yank out a fucking tooth?"

"Maybe they need the reassurance," Brian offered.

"Yeah, maybe. But I don't like the whole idea. It perverts nature."

"A lot of things pervert nature. Try not to let it get you down."

They finished dressing. "I'm going down to the radiology reading room," Gregory said. "I'll go as far as the elevator with you." They both headed for the door. "Oh, hang on a minute." He went back to his locker and took out a pack of cigars from the top shelf. He held out the pack to Brian. "Want one?"

Brian shook his head.

By the time they were halfway down the hall, Gregory's head was enshrouded in a cloud of gray smoke which Brian kept trying to fan away from his own face. Everyone they passed gave them a wide berth. "Why do you smoke those things?" Brian demanded.

"I like 'em," Gregory answered, savoring another puff. "Think they make me look sophisticated or important?"

"I think they make you look stupid," Brian stated. "I don't understand it. You're a radiologist. You deal with chest films every day. You know exactly what that stuff does to you."

"No, it's not like cigarettes. I never inhale, so the smoke doesn't get into my lungs."

"Yeah, well, it gets into my lungs."

At this Gregory stopped walking. He took another powerful drag on the cigar and stared at Brian with obvious amusement. Brian, for his part, had failed to detect the humor in what he'd said and prodded his companion along toward the elevator.

"Bri, don't you get it? Back when I was in high school, squeezing my zits and trying to figure out how to get into Mary Ellen McGuire's pants, you were in Vietnam playing SEAL—sea, air, land, finest elite troops in the world. Then, when I was in college marching in antiwar protests and trying to evade the draft and get into every other girl's pants—with marginal success, I might add—you were back in Nam with the fucking marines in he DMZ, trying to put them back together every time they got bull-dozed, with people shooting at you twelve ways to Sunday. You've got two Purple Hearts and enough ribbons on your dress uniform to make it look like goddamned Chesty Puller's. All the times you risked your life for God and country and all that you been through, I can't believe you're worried about a little smoke."

"Maybe I figure I've used up my chances," Brian replied as the elevator door opened.

They stepped inside the cab. Since they were in a hospital, the doors had been set to remain open for several seconds to accom-modate wheelchairs and stretchers. As they waited for the doors to close, a tall figure clad in the dark green tunic of a Marine Corps officer strode toward the elevator.

"For God's sake, ditch the cigar," Brian whispered to Gregory. "You know we can't smoke in the elevator."

Gregory looked around quickly but saw no receptacle. "Well." He shrugged and dropped the smoking butt on the floor by his feet. The marine reached the elevator just as the doors were clos-ing, and once he was inside, Brian saw the three stars shining on his lapel. As soon as he saw the man's face, a jolt of recognition stabbed at his gut. Memories came flooding back.

The marine sniffed, glanced down at the foor, and shot the two doctors an expression often copied by Parris Island drill instruc-tors.

"Is that your cigar, Lieutenant Commander?" he snapped, pointing to Gregory's feet."

"No, General," Gregory shot back. "You saw it first; you take it."

The elevator came to a stop, and Brian pulled him out the door before the general's glare had a chance to develop into anything more audible.

"You are certifiably insane!" Brian grinned.

"Do I detect a note of admiration in the commander's voice?"

Brian made sure they were out of earshot. "Don't you know who that was?"

"Yeah. Some marine general."

"Right. Some marine general. General John Winthrop Blag-den, to be specific."

"Well, that explains that strange, faraway look in your eyes back there. Your unit commander in your last tour of Nam, right?"

"He's the man."

"So that's old Black Jack Blagden," Gregory mused. "The one certifiable strategic genius of the Vietnam War. Or so they say. They also say he may be the next commandant of the Marine Corps."

"I wonder why he's here at Bethesda," Brian said.

"Not for hemorrhoids, I'll bet."

"Why do you say that?"

"Medically speaking, the condition hardly ever presents above a certain rank. By the time they make general, most of those brass hats are *perfect* assholes."

Brian grinned in spite of himself but then felt obliged to say, "A lot of marine grunts who served under him would take issue with you."

"A lot more who came home in body bags won't be asked for their opinions. What about the guys at Eagle's Talon?"

Good old Gregory, who could speak with the luxurious certitude of one who had not gone, in much the same way a childless couple always seems to know the best way for parent friends to tame their cute little hellions.

"You weren't there," said Brian tersely. "You don't know exactly what happened. None of us does." He always felt slightly uncomfortable talking about the war with people like Gregory. With more than ten years of twenty-twenty hindsight, it was easy for them to say it all had been a mistake, that they had been right all along. But what bothered Brian about that particular "analysis" was that it always seemed to leave something out. These people always talked in lofty sociopolitical terms about the wrenching experience and horrible price paid by the "country." But that was an abstraction. Having been personally spared, hardly ever did they focus on the specific sacrifice and courage of the individual men and women who *actually* paid that price. And now he was on his way to deal with someone who had.

Radley Davis was as nervous and jumpy as the first time Brian had seen him. He shifted his weight constantly, unable to find a comfortable position in Brian's orange plastic chair. He kept scratching his forehead and running his fingers back through his

hair. And he gazed at Brian with eyes focused 10,000 miles beyond him—back, no doubt, to the shores of that luckless land of
jungles and swamps.

"How have you been feeling, Rad?" Brian asked.

"I think it's getting worse," he replied.

"Well, I'm happy to tell you that things look pretty good here."
He glanced down at the reports clipped to the file folder on his
desk. "Your test results are all encouraging. Lab work fine. Normal urine and blood values; your cholesterol's a little high. I'd
watch that, but it's nothing a lot of men our age don't have. Blood
pressure's fine. Normal EKG—no heart problems. Nothing indicated by your chest X ray. It shows up some shrapnel, fragments,
but we already knew about that." Brian looked up from the file
and clasped his hands together. "All in all, I'd say you were a
pretty healthy guy."

At the mention of the "good news," Rad had shown some signs
of animation. He had straightened up in the chair, and his eyes
had come back into the room. But when Brian elaborated all the
findings that led him to the pronouncement of good health, Rad's
expression once again sank. He looked as if he'd been deflated.

"Well, if I'm so healthy, why do I feel so shitty, Doc?"

As he stopped to think about it, Brian didn't know why he had
expected Davis to be different from any other patient, to be convinced that he felt good by figures on paper rather than the messages of his own body.

"There can be a lot of reasons," Brian explained. "We use lab
tests to try to screen out what we call organic causes of distress.
Then, after we do that, we can begin thinking about—about other
causes."

Rad stared down at the floor. "So you think I'm crazy; that's
why I'm feeling this way."

"No, not at all. I don't think that way, and I don't want you to
think that way."

"What about my side? The pain's there all the time."

"There are several possible explanations. But you've got to remember that the human body is a very complex and sophisticated
organism. And it's controlled by the most sophisticated organism
of all—the brain. Now the brain gives us all kinds of messages.
First, it tries them through our thoughts and feelings; we all know
about that. But then, if we ignore those messages or for some reason don't recognize them, it'll often try again, this time through

the body in the form of aches and pains, stomach all tied up in knots . . . you name it. As I say, that's why we did the tests first."

"How do you know they're telling the truth?"

"Tests aren't foolproof," Brian admitted. "Unfortunately, nothing in medicine is. But with as complete a workup as we did on you, I think probably something would have shown up if there were anything wrong of, ah, a major nature. Look, I know how you feel. I've dealt with a lot of patients. And sometimes it would be a relief to find something physically wrong that could be taken care of, and that would be that. But I just don't see anything like that here." He handed the lab reports themselves across the desk as a sign of good faith.

But Rad didn't take them. "Look, you can show me as many of those things as you want, but I'm telling you how I feel! Look, Doc—Commander, I came to you because I thought you'd listen to me. If I just wanted to hear someone in a white coat check off boxes on a form—'His blood's red, his piss is yellow, he knows how to breathe'—I could have gone to the VA, just like your nurse said. I thought you'd be different. I thought you'd help me."

Brian fought hard not to become irritated. *This is a stress disorder*, he kept repeating to himself. *You can't expect him to be fully rational.*

"I'm tring to help you," he said. "And I think the best way to do that is to get you to talk about what's bothering you. God knows that from what you've told me so far, you've had to deal with enough to throw anyone."

"Then you do think I'm crazy!" Davis shouted. " 'We'll just have a nice little chat and his pains will go away.' "

"No, I didn't say that," said Brian sternly. "But I was over there, too. I may not know exactly what you went through, but I know what I went through. And a lot of it was pretty goddamned grim. When I got back from my second SEAL tour in '66, I wanted desperately to go to medical school and become a doctor. But I couldn't even consider it until I'd done a lot of thinking, and a lot of talking, and found a lot of ways to deal with my own feelings about what happened over there. And let me tell you something: I haven't resolved it all yet. Don't know if I ever will. That's why I feel and ache so much for guys like you. Because we're all in this together."

This seemed to make some impression. "And what about my

buddies?" Rad went on. "Those other guys I told you about from our unit?"

"That's all really unfortunate—one of those things that make you wonder if there's any justice in the whole damn universe. But what do you think it has to do with your problems? Unless, did you maybe start having your pains and discomfort *after* you read those stories?"

Davis considered the question seriously for a moment. "No," he finally replied. "I'm sure I had them before. Maybe not as bad, but they were there."

"Then I'll ask you again. What is the relationship between them and what you're going through?"

"I don't know. But I know there's something. I'm not smart enough to figure it out. But you are. You're a doctor."

Brian leaned back in his chair until he heard a prominent squeak. "Listen, Radley, I appreciate what you say, but we do have to be reasonable about this—"

Radley shot up from his chair, shoved his hands into his pockets, and began pacing a tight circle in front of the desk. "I've been reasonable long enough," he said explosively. "And look where it's gotten me. Nowhere!" He stopped cold in his circular tracks and, pressing down heavily on his knuckles, leaned forward over the desk toward Brian. "If it was just for me, I'd forget about it." He tried to explain. "Nobody really gives a shit about me. Why should they? But it isn't just for me. It's for all those other guys, too. They're dead and can't stick up for themselves, so someone's got to stick up for them. I was hoping you'd be the one. I thought I could trust you." There were tears in his eyes, but they were tears of frustration.

Brian's stab of irritation was quickly replaced by a smothering wave of depression. Ultimately this case was going to the shrinks, if it went anywhere at all. That much was now painfully plain to see. In a civilian hospital, or under any kind of normal circumstance, Brian would have had this guy out the door in a second. But this wasn't a normal circumstance. This man was owed something, even more than the attention and concern every patient is owed by the doctor. Before he abandoned Davis to the VA's appalling psychiatric refuse heap, before he consigned him to being one more ugly little statistic of the war, Brian had to convince himself he had done everything he could. Even if he couldn't convince Radley, he needed to prove to himself that he had gone the last mile for this man, just as Rad had done for the Marine Corps—and for his country.

"Let's keep on it and try a few more tests," Brian said, "take some more detailed X rays. We have a very good radiologist here. If there's anything there, he'll help us find it."

A few moments later they were standing in the doorway. Brian was bracing himself for an awkward parting when something in the corridor caught Radley's eye.

"Is that . . . ? I can't believe it!" he exclaimed.

Brian looked out and saw John Winthrop Blagden striding purposefully down the hallway.

"Did you know he was here?" The nearly equal stress on virtually every word in the sentence had more than a hint of the Second Coming about it.

"I just saw him in the elevator," Brian said.

"Now there's an honest-to-God blood-and-guts marine for you. Would I give anything to be like him." Then he shifted into a slightly minor key as he said, "Could have been, too, if things had just worked out a little different."

WASHINGTON, D.C.

In Andrey Stoltz's opinion, the best thing about the new Soviet Embassy building was the view. Even though the darkly tinted windows were little more than glass-covered arrow slits, from his office he commanded a spectacular panorama. It stretched from the National Cathedral to Embassy Row, to Georgetown and the Potomac waterfront, to the rolling green hills of northern Virginia. The worst thing about the new building was the offices themselves—sterile little cubicles with no warmth and less character. Despite the view, Stoltz missed the old building, with its high ceilings and elegant details.

For many years the Embassy of the Soviet Union had been on Sixteenth Street, a few blocks north of the White House, in a stately stone-faced mansion built by the railroad magnate George Pullman. The irony that the American headquarters of the pioneering nation of world socialism had originally housed one of the pioneers of predatory capitalism was lost on none of its inhabitants. Shortly after Stoltz arrived in Washington, the embassy had moved into a huge marble block at the peak of Wisconsin Avenue, just before it begins its descent into Georgetown. The site is known as Mount Alto. There had once been a Veterans Administration hospital on the spot.

All in all, the complex reminded Stoltz uncomfortably of EUR, the citadel Benito Mussolini had constructed just outside Rome as a monument to the Fascist movement. But Rome had been a plum assignment for Stoltz: beautiful country, friendly people, excellent food, and nothing terribly important happening that the committee had to worry about. When he thought back on his previous posting, it was like a two-year holiday.

Dmitri Stepanov had asked to see him first thing this morning. There was no telling what the "information attaché" (a title which continually amused both of them) wanted to discuss. Knowledge is power. Information leads to knowledge. Therefore, any information is potentially a source of power.

He knocked on Stoltz's door at 8:00 A.M. sharp, looking nowhere nearly as dour and dyspeptic as he normally did this time of the morning. He carried a sheaf of computer printouts jutting out from the top of an open diplomatic courier pouch.

Stepanov ignored his host's offer of the visitor's chair and moved to spread the papers across the desk.

"And what have we here, Comrade?" Stoltz asked him jovially.

As was his custom, Stepanov got right to the point. "These are printouts of newspaper articles," he explained. "They were picked up by our clipping service."

The clipping service was, in fact, just that. Somewhere along the line it had dawned on committee leaders that in a so-called free and open society, the richest vein of intelligence was the press. More interesting and potentially useful information appeared in each day's newspapers than could be harvested from a year's worth of clandestine activities. The trick, of course, was to be able to organize and interpret this unmanageable bounty of information. And that was where the computers came in. If they could sift through it all and separate the tiny kernels of grain from the abundance of chaff, the reasoning went, then the expensive and risk-involved efforts—the cloak-and-dagger stuff—could be more efficiently and profitably directed.

Stepanov pushed four articles over toward Stoltz. On the top of each were the name of the publication in which it appeared, the date, the estimated circulation, and the initials of the clipping reader, in case he or she had to be questioned about it later on.

"Individually there is no special significance to any of these stories. In each case the only element that attracted the clipper's attention was the fact that the man in question had served with the Marine Corps, and from their ages at death each could have easily been in Vietnam. Admittedly not much in itself. It was the computer which 'noticed' that there were four of these random deaths conforming to the same military and age profile occurring within a relatively short period of time. All were 'level two demises'—sudden accident rather than illness; victim alone and unwitnessed."

"Hmm, that is suggestive," Stoltz commented.

"That was why the matter was referred to my office—in case we were interested—though the material was still classified as raw data and accompanied by no action recommendation."

"And so you came immediately to your old friend Andrey to help you make sense of this mishmash," Stoltz laughed.

"Not exactly," Stephanov said. "I wouldn't have wasted your time if I did not think there was something there."

"Then presumably you do now, or you would not be here. I know you are not a morning person, Dmitri."

"I believe there might be something," the attaché replied. His naïve eagerness was somewhat refreshing. "Before deciding whether to bring it to the committee's attention, I wanted to find out a little more about these men. And this is what I discovered, none of it deep, but leading circumstantially in a quite interesting direction. Point number one, all the victims had served in Vietnam. Point number two, all were members of the Third Marine Division at the same time. Point number three, all were assigned to the Seventh Marine Amphibious Unit."

Stepanov looked up and waited for a reaction. But Stoltz merely crossed one leg over the other, took off his glasses, and began chewing methodically on the stem.

"I'm sorry to disappoint you, Dmitri. I'm sure it all works together nicely in your own mind. But I fear I am failing to grasp the significance which you seem to attach to this material."

Stepanov appeared undaunted. "I don't think you will if I give you point number four."

"Which is?" Stoltz considered himself an amicable enough sort for a committeeman, but he detested playing games. Stepanov waited for some sign and, not receiving it, hesitated. Stoltz sighed and impatiently motioned for him to continue.

"Remember the Corporal Scourge affair?"

Stoltz thought for a moment. Suddenly the connection came to him. "Yes, of course. Eagle's Talon. The very unit we are talking about, if I'm not mistaken."

"You are not mistaken," Stepanov assured his superior. "Maybe it is only coincidence, but these men were all from Corporal Scourge's unit."

"Maybe it is all coincidence," Stoltz said, "but if not, Comrade, you may have come across something of considerable interest."

4

BETHESDA, MARYLAND

The second round of tests was probably more than Radley Davis had bargained for—upper and lower GI series, gallbladder study, intravenous pyelogram and sigmoidoscopy among them. But Brian wanted to make sure he covered all possible physical bases this time. And with what might have seemed an almost punitive willfulness, he wanted to make sure Rad knew it, too. There's nothing like a barium enema to let an overly insistent patient know how diligently you're on the case.

"I don't suppose he's gonna be riding real tall in the saddle for a while," Gregory Cheever commented when Brian told him what he'd ordered.

"I don't guess he is," Brian replied with a certain perverse satisfaction.

They were sitting in Gregory's office, where Brian had just come for a fresh perspective. He'd gone over all the test results himself and gotten second opinions on some of them. But none of the tests appeared any more conclusive than the first set.

"The upper and lower GIs were a big, fat zip," he explained. "One little diverticulum that everyone agrees has no clinical significance."

"So what else've you got?" Gregory asked, propping his stubby legs up on the corner of his desk.

"The pain on the right side sounded as if it could have been a kidney. He wasn't passing blood, and we didn't find any protein or white cells in his urine, but you never know. So I figured we'd do an IVP on him."

"Let me see what you came up with."

Brian handed him the manila envelope containing the pyelogram films. Gregory planted his feet back on the floor, came from around the side of his desk, and fixed the X rays onto the wall-mounted light box. He stood there studying them in silence. His eyes darted from one film to another, to a third and then back again.

"I got a consult from urology," Brian stated. "They didn't see anything noteworthy."

"That's why we have radiologists, my friend. Because everybody thinks he can read X rays."

"What is it?" Brian said, suddenly alarmed. "Something wrong with his kidney?"

"No, the kidneys are fine. He can piss till the cows come home."

"Then what are you looking at?"

"I'm not sure," Gregory said. He was squinting at the image on the light box. "It's what we would call a corner finding."

"Meaning what?"

"Just what it sounds like. It's not the main subject of any of these films. But look up here in the corner of this tomogram." He took a ballpoint pen from his pocket and traced it along the upper edge of one film plate. He stopped and used it as a pointer.

"Piece of shrapnel," Brian declared. "We already knew he had shrapnel wounds."

"Yeah, but there's something strange about this one. I've never seen anything exactly like this."

"Well, you probably wouldn't have. You've never worked in a combat hospital."

"You mind if we get him back in here? I'd like to get a couple of other views."

"What do you think it is?"

"I don't know. Let me get a few more pictures. There is something very strange about your piece of shrapnel here."

With all he'd been through so far, Rad seemed only too happy to come back for one additional X ray series if it held out the hope of finally "getting to the bottom of his case." He appeared to like Dr. Thorpe's perceptible shift in manner, the same way a child feels vindicated when his mother drags him to the doctor and finds out he really is sick, not just trying to skip school. Brian knew Rad wanted him to believe there was actually something wrong with him after all. Anyway, it put him a step farther away from the VA psychiatrists, and that was worth something in itself.

As soon as the films came out of the processor in the radiology lab, Gregory put them up on the motorized viewer.

"Very interesting."

"I don't see anything," Brian said.

"Damn near incredible. I'm not sure I've ever seen anything exactly like it."

"I still don't see anything at all."

Gregory turned to him and grinned. "That's because you aren't a radiologist and I am. Surgeons think they can do anything, but without us . . ."

"I bow to your superior powers," Brian told him. "Now, what is it?"

Again Gregory held out a pen and pointed, this time to a region near the center of the film. "This shrapnel fragment here, about three-quarters of a centimeter long. It's the same one I picked out on the IVP. I'd say it looks as if it's wedged between the liver and the peritoneum."

"What about it?"

"I think there's something inside it."

"What are you talking about?"

"It's hollow."

"What!"

"Or, to be more precise, there's some sort of tiny hollow chamber inside it."

"You're joking."

"Look for yourself. Right along this axis here."

Brian looked long and hard where Gregory was pointing. He had always figured he could read X rays as well as most surgeons, but in one sense, Gregory was right. In modern medicine radiologists were a breed apart. They were contemporary practitioners of black magic, not much different from the ancient high priests who used to predict the future by reading the entrails of sacrificial animals. The things they claimed to infer from those minute variations of line shading were bizarre, if not downright preposterous. The astounding part was, subsequent surgery or progression of symptoms usually proved they did know just what they were talking about. Radiology was one profession that had a thousand shades of gray, all of them significant.

"Where do you see all this?" Brian pressed him. "And how come no one ever noticed it before? We've taken a zillion films of this guy."

"Because they weren't looking," Gregory said, obviously pleased that he had his friend at a disadvantage. "But to give you a more helpful answer, let's go back to our basic med school theory. Radiology works on the principle that materials of different densities absorb different amounts of radiation, which then therefore register lighter or darker on photographic film."

"I'm with you so far," Brian said.

"Now in this view—the one that shows up on all the other X rays we've got of your man—we see the silhouette of a little chunk of metal, just the way any other piece of shrapnel would show up." He pointed to the next film. "But this was the view I wanted. And this was the one that made me sit up and take notice."

"Why?" Brian asked uneasily.

"All right, try to visualize it this way. If you look at the fragment from the side, as in this first view—call it film number one—there's metal all around the hollow part—front and back—so there's virtually no thickness contrast and virtually no difference in density for the X ray to pick up. But if we can get an end-on shot of the fragment, as in film number two here, we've got the hollow chamber running front to back, so the metal surrounds it instead of covering it, thus creating sharp contrast between the high density of the metal and the low density of the space inside:

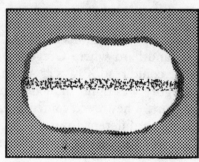

FILM NO. 1

FILM NO. 2

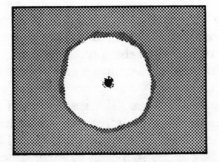

"So what we're seeing—what shows up on film—is the differential of the X rays passing through the hollow chamber and the surrounding metal. On the traditionally oriented pictures there wasn't enough differential to stand out." He stepped over to the final images of the series. "For these oblique shots, I used low kv techniques to enhance the picture, employing the photoelectric effect rather than the Compton effect to get a good differentiation."

Brian ignored the physics and studied the side-by-side images again. "So what's this thing doing in Davis?" he said at last.

"Who the hell knows?" Gregory responded. "But I can tell you one thing: It's definitely man-made. Nothing that's that perfect and regular randomly occurs in nature."

"What other tests can you do to let me know what it is?"

"None, as long as it stays in there."

"So he's got maybe fifteen-odd pieces of shrapnel in him. This is the only one that's . . . hollow?"

"That's the way it looks, Bri."

"And you think that could be causing the **side** pain?"

Gregory shrugged and smiled. "Could be. You know the old radiologist's hedge: 'consistent with . . . suggestive of . . . but can't rule out . . . Recommend clinical correlation and further studies.' "

"Okay, forget all that. What do you think I ought to do?"

Gregory instantly began hobbling around as if his knees were giving out from under him. "A surgeon asking a radiologist what to do? We've got to call Mr. Ripley!"

"Come off it. It's not that big a deal. But you won't tell anyone, will you?" Brian said in a stage whisper.

"Your reputation's safe. Anyway, you know what the main difference is between you and me, Commander Thorpe?" He poked Brian in the chest and grinned. "Other than such obvious and insignificant distinctions as relative physiognomy, of course, the principal difference is that you like to get involved, while I strive to disentangle myself from the fray."

"And how does this answer my original question?" Brian asked with mock impatience.

Gregory held up a palm. "I'm getting to that. You see," he continued, "despite your plaintive plea for advice just now, you do have the classic surgeon's personality, while I have the typical radiologist's. Look at the two of us. Your instinctive response is action, while mine is study. You are invasive, while I am contemplative."

"Which all means?"

"Which means," Gregory said, rapping lightly on the film surface with the tip of his pen, "you're going to go in there and take that sucker out." He clicked the pen closed and put it back in his pocket. "Then we'll both sit down and take a nice long look at it."

Normally he would have had interns and medical students in to watch an operation like this one involving a vital organ. But until he knew what he was dealing with, Brian didn't want to attract undue attention or have to answer any questions. Unless there were unforeseen complications along the way, he didn't expect it to be an extremely complex or risky procedure, so he was able to get by with just an anesthesiologist and Gregory serving as his first assistant. He probably could have gotten through it even a little faster if he'd used a surgical resident instead. But the resident would have been able to see and follow exactly what he was doing. The anesthesiologist, true to form, would look only at his dials and monitors and gauges and could be counted on to forget the whole thing once it was over.

Rad required less explanation than anyone. He was certainly a trial for any clinician trying to make some sense out of his confused and twisted story. But he was a surgeon's perfect patient. Anything *invasive* was *decisive* as far as he was concerned, and the specific details didn't really concern him. In that, Brian reckoned, Rad was a typical marine.

The surgery was fortunately uneventful. As he later described it to Gregory, Brian went in with a number ten blade scalpel through a small midline incision. He dissected through the subcutaneous fat to expose the midline fascia. At that point he could visualize the peritoneum. He opened a longitudinal hole in it about the size of a small fist.

The liver is covered by a membrane known as Glisson's capsule. He pulled it down with his hand and detached the triangular ligament of the organ's left lobe. The shrapnel fragment turned out to be even more accessible than they would have hoped from the X rays. In fact, it was only slightly embedded in the liver, almost adhering to its surface.

"Let me have a True-Cut needle," Brian instructed.

The nurse slapped the large syringelike instrument into his waiting palm. He guided it gently into the exposed liver to take out a biopsy core for pathology. When the nurse looked away, he extracted the metal fragment with his forceps and palmed it to Gregory. Then he biopsied a small piece of tissue in the area surrounding the fragment and gave it to the nurse.

"Send this down to path," he instructed her.

The entire operation took little more than half an hour. When it was finished, Gregory carried the gauze-wrapped fragment with him out of the surgical suite. When they changed back into their uniforms, he gave it to Brian.

Between them Brian and Gregory tried to prioritize the tests they wanted to conduct on the fragment. Initially Brian was all for ripping the particle open. But Gregory pointed out that since they didn't know what, if anything, was inside, they'd better come up with a protocol that would safely work through the more dangerous possibilities.

First, Gregory took it down to the radiation safety department for a Geiger counter test: no detectable radioactivity or radiation leakage. Then he X-rayed it along each of its axes to make sure he duplicated the view that first detected the tiny interior chamber.

"I really can't tell you much more than before," he reported to Brian the next morning in the physicians' locker room. "All I can say for sure is that it has a hollow cylinder and it's filled with some homogenous substance that isn't air. More like the density of water."

"Well, that rules out nerve gas, I guess," Brian said.

"I'd say so."

"And I got back the path report on the liver tissue. Nothing interesting showed up."

"That's a good sign. By the way, how's Davis doing?"

"Fine. He's reveling in all the attention from the nurses." He gave Gregory a grave and studied look and grasped his wrist, hunting with his fingers for the pulse. "But are you sure you're feeling all right?"

"Yeah, sure. Why?"

"Nothing, I guess. It's just that I've never heard a radiologist inquire as to an actual patient's health."

"Cute, Commander. Being around intellectuals must bring out your own deep-seated insecurity."

They stared at each other in silence for several moments, each man already certain what the other was thinking.

"Well . . ." Brian said at last. "Got any plans for tonight?"

"I'm having dinner with Jill. Like to join us?"

"No," Brian said with obvious disappointment. "You have your fun."

"I'll meet you in the pathology lab at eight," Gregory stated. "No, better make it nine. No one else should be there by then."

Brian got off the elevator near the pathology lab a couple of minutes before nine. There was light shining through the small windows in the double steel doors, so someone was still using the lab. He thought about going in and asking them how long it was going to take, but that might seem kind of strange. Maybe they'd have to come back a lot later if they didn't want anyone else around.

Then he began to hear sounds coming through the door. Indistinct at first, they grew into dull thuds as he got closer, like the impact of something soft hitting something much more solid. Then a faint moan.

A raspy gasp. "No! Please. Not again." Then another thud. "I can't take any more." It sounded like Gregory.

Brian burst through the double doors. Gregory, his clothing all askew, was bracing himself against the wall, wheezing and shuddering. His girlfriend, Jill Timberlake, had her hands threaded beneath his armpits and was forcing him into a one-legged crouch. She withdrew, struck another pose, and ordered, "Now bend you knee as far as you can. All right, now grab hold of your foot from behind with your wrist straight, just like I'm doing."

"Have I just interrupted something?" Brian asked.

"In the path lab?" Gregory spluttered. "Don't be kinky."

"We were just doing our exercises," Jill explained.

"She was trying to kill me," Gregory asserted. "Just like you on the racquetball court. Why is everybody ganging up on me lately?"

"We just want you to be fit and healthy," she said sweetly. "You're going to be amazed how much better you'll feel once you've done these exercises."

"You're going to be amazed how many people'll come to my funeral and ask you how I died."

"Stop being a sissy. Look how fluidly and gracefully I do it."

"You can get into these positions with that Barbie doll figure of yours. I can't."

Gregory crawled to a neutral corner. Jill, acknowledging defeat, slipped her sandals back on and, from one of the lab counters, picked up some bulky gray knit thing Brian imagined might be indigenous to South American shepherds. She was a very pretty girl, and tonight she was wearing one of her basic uniforms: a blue Danskin leotard top and tight, straight jeans. Around her head and long blondish hair was a thin, beaded headband of the American Indian variety. Around her neck was a red tie-died scarf of the Eastern Indian variety. And around her waist was a simple rope belt of the unnecessary variety. She would have to be peeled out of her pants.

Jill worked as a civilian in the hospital's data processing department. Among other obvious and not so obvious attributes, she had developed something of a cult following as an amateur computer genius. Anyone who needed interference run with the navy's intimidating machine bureaucracy had to get on Jill's good side. Brian had first required her services when two sets of orders had arrived one day directing him to report simultaneously for "officer development orientation" in Meridian, Mississippi, and Honolulu. Jill volunteered to have the machine crunch one set and earned his eternal devotion by giving him his choice of which set that would be. He still wasn't quite sure what it was she saw in Gregory but was happy for his friend that he'd been able to land such a catch. At the same time he envied Gregory the casual, nonthreatening ease of their relationship, especially after all the ravaged battlefields that had marked his life with Lizzie.

"I have found the ideal woman," Gregory had proclaimed to him not long ago. "A child of the computer age with a 1960s flower child sensibility, an increasingly rare commodity in this Great Age of Perrier."

"That's horseshit, Gregory," Brian had responded. "You just like the way she dresses."

"I do not deny that one whit, Good Sir Knight." Then he went on, for Gregory fancied himself something of a social philosopher. "Is it not indeed ironic that the one fashion vestige to carry over from the 1960s is panty hose? When the women of our generation went to short skirts, I thought this is it. Now they are finally liberated, and things can never be as they were. The women will never again accept being forced to wrap and corset themselves. Who could have predicted that they would come to perceive the symbol of their sexual emancipation as reducing them to mere sex objects?"

Brian knew he could always count on Gregory for fresh and original insights into the world at large.

"Well," Gregory said, bringing Brian's mind back to the issue at hand. He seemed recovered from the ordeal Jill had put him through. "Have you got the goods?"

Brian produced the wad of gauze, unwrapped it, and placed the fragment carefully on a glass slide. He walked over to the microscope and positioned the slide flat on the scope's viewing surface. Then he went to the supply closet and retrieved three sets of paper surgical masks and gowns.

"We don't want to contaminate whatever's in there," he told the other two. "And more important, we don't want it to contaminate us."

The room was calm, quiet at this hour. During the day it continually pulsed with activity as doctors and technicians sat at these counters, analyzing living human tissue, trying to intuit what had gone wrong with it, morbidly searching for evidence of infections and neoplasms. To look at the area now, one could almost imagine the setting to be a high school or college chemistry lab—a place where innocuous formulas from textbooks are mixed together in the name of education.

With Gregory and Jill looking on, Brian peered through the lens, manipulating the fragment with microtweezers while he probed and poked at it with a surgical needle.

"Well, what do you see?" Gregory asked impatiently.

Brian kept examining the object as he spoke. "It's an irregular, pitted surface, not smooth like a shell casing, for example. It's covered with very fine, hairlike metal spikes or projections that look as if they were caused by the initial fragmenting explosion."

"Do you see a way inside?"

"No, not so far. My guess is that the explosion was supposed to break it up and release whatever's inside."

"That makes sense," Gregory said. "Probably a lot of these little chambers in the original bomb or whatever it was."

"I'm going to clamp it with the tips of two hemostats, then use the leverage to bend it back and forth until it gives. Let me just maneuver it into a good position here."

Abruptly Brian's fingers stopped moving. He squinted into the lense more intensely. "Hold on a minute! I've got something here."

"What is it?" Gregory had to restrain himself from crowding Brian away from the microscope.

"There's this tiny—this tiny indentation on one end. And in it, there's a sort of . . . looks as if it might be a plug of some kind."

"What's it made of?"

"I can't tell, except that it isn't metal. But it is wedged in there pretty tight. Practically a hermetic seal."

"Is that like a navy commando who lives all alone in a cave?"

"Very funny. Why don't you make yourself useful? See if you can dig up a twenty-seven gauge needle. There might be one down here for eye dissection."

Gregory rummaged through the drawers and cabinets until he finally found the minutely thin instrument Brian had requested. "I can hardly see this thing," he said, carefully placing it in Brian's hand.

Brian grasped it firmly. With the tip of his tweezers he delicately bent the tip just enough to form a slight hook. He tested its torque with his fingertip.

He picked up the fragment again and braced it within the tweezer tips so it couldn't move. He took a deep breath and held it. Gingerly he pressed the needle down into the microscopic plug, striving to exert the pressure straight downward so the tiny shaft wouldn't snap.

"Okay, it's in." He let out his breath slowly.

He gave the needle a half twist. When he felt slight resistance from the hook at the end, he just as gingerly drew the needle back out. With it came the plug. Brian took his head away from the microscope and held the needle up to his face. The plug was practically invisible to the naked eye.

"Break the needle off from the handle, then seal it in a test tube," he instructed, and handed it to Gregory. "We'll lose the plug if we try to take it off the shaft." Then he went back to the microscope and shook the tweezers to see if anything would come out of the fragment.

"Nothing's coming out. It must be pretty viscous. Have you got another twenty-seven gauge needle? And get me a sterile slide while you're at it."

He inserted the needle into the infinitesimal chamber and worked it around, as if he were foraging for the last bits of peanut butter in a nearly empty jar.

At last he coaxed a drop out onto the sterile slide. Brian and Gregory looked at each other triumphantly. They both hugged Jill.

On the fifth morning following Radley's surgery Brian released him from the hospital. He told him to wait until his postoperative discomfort had fully subsided and then come back and let Brian know if the other symptoms had gone away with it.

The answer to that question, Brian was confident, would come as much from what the fragment turned out to contain as from anything Rad told him. But the ex-marine's main problems, he kept reminding himself, were not primarily physical.

In the cafeteria that afternoon Gregory gave him the less than conclusive news. "Once we ruled out nerve gas, I figured maybe we were dealing with a botulism or some sort of toxin. So I brought a little bit of it over to microbiology and had them plate it out."

"And?"

"And nothing. Petri dish is still clean as a nun's—clean as a whistle. Didn't grow a thing. Then I figured, who knows what? Psychotropic chemical, maybe?" He shrugged. "Your guess is as good as mine. So I ran another bit through the mass spectrometer."

"At least that should tell us what the components are."

"Yeah, it did, all right. We found some hydrogen, some oxygen—your basic."

"That sounds like—"

"I know what it sounds like. So does every junior high school chemistry kid in the world. Basically what you've got, Brian, is water."

"But that doesn't make sense."

"Tell it to the machine."

"So the question is: Could it be something that affects the liver directly, or is it there just by chance?"

"The biopsy shows the liver's clean. The liver function tests said the same thing. And anyway, it's a piece of shrapnel. How do you explode a fragmentation device probably a hundred yards away and aim for a specific organ?"

"I have no idea."

"Well, it was a nice try," Gregory said. "But if there was anything there to begin with, it's long gone by now. I think this is the end of the show."

Not quite, Brian decided, back alone in his office. If the fluid contents of the fragment provided no ready explanations, then perhaps the fragment itself might. The question was where to begin looking.

There were probably artillery specialists who knew something. Maybe some of the marines at Fort Sill, Oklahoma, had seen it before. A lot of them had been in Nam. And there were probably books or manuals he could get from the Military War College. But, then again, he didn't even know where to begin, and they might just as easily turn up nothing. There had to be a more logical idea. He leaned forward with his elbows on the desk surface, meshing his two hands together. And as he casually stared down at the star sapphire on his right ring finger, Brian Thorpe knew what it was.

Hugh Stanway.

Former SEALs, especially those who'd seen a lot of heavy combat, dealt with the experience in different ways. Some simply withdrew. Some purposely or consciously formed no human attachments, and of these, more than a few chose to live far from their native land. A surprising number went into the helping fields like medicine. Some had put their elite SEAL training to what they considered good or profitable use—wherever there was a newly emerging nation wanting to throw off the yoke of imperialism or an old and established one wanting to keep it firmly in place.

And then there was Hugh Stanway, the only SEAL truly to capitalize on his training and lifetime of experience. Stanway was the man the other SEALs always considered first among them. He was the one who had organized and led the raid on November 22, 1970, that had freed forty-eight South Vietnamese prisoners of war from a Vietcong POW camp. Stanway, fourteen other SEALs, and nineteen Vietnamese militiamen broke into the camp, fought a running gun battle with the guards, and finally forced them to flee for their lives. That raid became near legend in special-warfare circles.

For a while Stanway had gone the high-priced mercenary route. He'd been the last white out of Angola before it all hit the fan, and the rumor was that the agency had called on his services more than once for operations too delicate or compromising to handle inhouse. But those were all sidelines, "publicity stunts" he'd called them, even though they were known only to a small cadre that made it its business to keep up on such things. No matter. The word did get out. The Stanway image was fixed in iron. And he never stopped capitalizing on it.

Brian dialed San Francisco information. "Can you give me the number of *Men of Action* magazine, please?"

He put through the call, and when the receptionist came on the line, he said to her, "Let me speak to the top man."

"Would you like the publisher's office, sir?"

"That's right. The boss."

A momentary pause. Then a deep, extremely sexy voice announced, "Mr. Stanway's office, may I help you?" God, this was just like him, Brian thought. And if he knew Hugh, the voice was undoubtedly attached to an amazing pair of breasts and a voluptuous ass—the creation of a man who lives by his gonads.

"Is himself in?" Brian asked.

"May I say who's calling, please?"

"Just tell him it's someone who knows the location of his SEAL tattoo."

The sexy voice was obviously flustered. "Ah, just one moment, sir, I'll see if he's available."

There was a click as Brian was put on hold. Then a rousing, robust version of "The March of the Men of Harlech" came on the line to pass the time. A few seconds later: "Brian Thorpe!" The voice was as robust as the march. "It had to be you. All the others who knew where my SEAL tattoo was are dead! Killed some of them myself. How the fuck have you been?"

"I'm still around, Hugh."

"That's saying something, with all the shit we've been through. You still playing doctor?"

"Yeah. It's not exactly the kind of commitment you just walk away from."

"Great to hear from you! How're you doing, sailor? I heard about you and Lizzie. Sorry."

"Thanks. I guess it just wasn't in the cards."

"Isn't for a lot of us. Just terminated number three myself. Bad choice of words. Anyway, the deal's over."

It was good to talk to Hugh again. The dependable, predictable, self-sacrificing camaraderie from the old days was something Brian would never forget and always miss. There was just nothing to replace it in his life today, only one of the reasons he often felt so lonely. He'd been around medical students; he'd been around residents; he'd been around some of the outstanding physicians in the country. Yet never would he feel as close to any group as he still felt to the men of SEAL Team One.

"So then," Stanway went on, "on to happier thoughts. If you're still playing doctors and nurses, you seen anything good without her pants on lately? In a professional capacity, I mean."

"Not as much as you, I'm sure. In a professional capacity, I mean. Are you still the Hugh Hefner of gun nuts, nationalist zealots, and professional killers?"

"Sex and violence, that's my stock-in-trade," he said proudly. "But we prefer to call our readers serious adventurers."

It had been at least a year or two since Brian had picked up a copy of *Men of Action*. But he was sure it must still contain the same mix of features and reporting that had attracted legions of genuine and make-believe "adventurers" and made Hugh Stanway a multimillionaire in the process. There were the retrospectives about past wars and battles; the updates on new adventure (read "mercenary") opportunities throughout the world; how-to columns on infiltration, hand-to-hand combat, and phony IDs; "consumer" reports on everything from the latest in camping gear to automatic weapons to small surface-to-air missiles; and, of course, the pictorials—not the squeaky-clean mannequins of *Playboy* or the gauzy pseudoart of *Penthouse*, but real-life, amazingly endowed, "we mean business" girls dressed in things like fifty-caliber bandoliers, tiger-stripe camouflage shirts, and nothing else.

But the fact of the matter was that with all this, *Men of Action* was still considered one of the most authoritative sources on conventional combat and special warfare, recent military history, and geopolitics. A lot of the people who read it really were "serious."

"So, Brian, my boy, needless to say, you gravely missed your old buddy Hugh and decided to pick up the phone. But what is the hidden agenda of this call?"

"Actually there is something you can do for me," Brian admitted. "What do you know about North Vietnamese and Vietcong fragmentation devices?"

"Off the top of my head? I know that most of them were Russian-made. The Russkies were their only true-blue friends and steady suppliers during the duration of the conflict. What specifically do you want to know?"

He told Stanway of the strange fragment, keeping the details purposely vague. He described the series of tests which had led him to believe the contents of the tiny capsule were completely inert. And he told him of his theory that it must have been part of a larger device with many such hollow chambers.

"I've never seen or heard of anything like it myself," Stanway said when Brian had finished. "But Vietnam was a strange country, and there was a lot of strange stuff not many people knew about. I'll put some researchers on it and get back to you as soon as I find out something."

"Thanks, Hugh. I knew you were my man."

"Oh, and while I got you, Thorpe, you got to come out here and see me, you hear? Start living the good life. And this isn't just some middle-class, social, go-through-the-motions camel shit either. Just remember, I know where you've got *your* SEAL tattoo, fella!"

"How could I forget?" Images of the Blue Dragon Tattoo Parlor suddenly took center stage in his mind: that dinky little yellow clapboard house across the street from the Thirty-second Street Navy Yard. The two of them must have been drunk out of their minds that night.

"Listen, I've got this house at Big Sur. Kind of a weekend place, six hundred feet above the ocean. You can see thirty-five miles of coastline in either direction. You got to come out. And bring whoever's sharing your life at the moment. Very romantic. I'll meet you there myself and show you what to do if you've forgotten how."

"I appreciate that, Hugh."

"I mean it, Thorpe. I want to see your bright, smiling face. It's been too fucking long. Don't make me kick your ass. I'm serious."

Brian smiled as he said good-bye and hung up the phone. That was one thing about Hugh Stanway that had always been true. If he said he was serious, he meant it.

5

WASHINGTON, D.C.

Since the split Brian had lived in a small two-bedroom apartment on the corner of Connecticut Avenue and Albemarle Street. The redbrick building, though tall by Washington standards at seven floors, had a squat, stolid appearance, having been designed to take full advantage of the small former gasoline station site on which it was built. Along upper Connecticut Avenue, gas stations, old houses, drive-ins, whatever, all had given way to apartment buildings to house the new generation of lawyers, executives, and bureaucrats. The young professionals were marching uptown as inexorably as Sherman to the sea.

Every morning as Brian left for the hospital, he saw them: the men in Brooks Brothers pinstripes and Burberrys trench coats, the women in bow ties, business suits, and running shoes, carrying their office footwear in chic canvas sacks. Commander Thorpe wasn't the only one who went to work in a uniform.

He felt little kinship with the other residents of the building. For one thing, most of them owned their condominium units, while he rented from an owner-investor. For another, most of them headed downtown to the nation's power center each day, while he drove out to suburban Bethesda. But the biggest difference was that most of them were busy seeking "meaningful relationships" to complete and round out their having-it-all existences, while Brian had moved in here still trying to cope with the concussion and aftereffects of a relationship in which he'd probably always invested too much meaning.

The only truly meaningful outcome of that relationship was at this moment in the second bedroom, which had been outfitted especially for her, dressing in front of the mirror, preparing to be picked up by her mother. Brian watched silently from the doorway as she sat on the floor and meticulously buckled her black patent leather shoes, her tongue thrust firmly between her teeth in concentration. That task finished, she picked up her dress from the bed with both outstretched arms.

"Katie, you need any help?" he asked, but he knew what the answer would be. Five-year-olds are the most independent of beings.

"Don't look, Daddy!" she commanded. "I don't have any clothes on."

"It's okay, sugarcane," he said. "I'm a doctor. I'm used to seeing people naked."

"Yes," she lectured him with her finger, "but you're a *surgeon.*" She weighted the word with great significance. "You're only allowed to see them naked from the inside."

Brian's face lit with delight. He strode into the room and snatched her up, squealing, into his arms. He tossed her up toward the ceiling and bounced her down onto the bed. She wriggled away insistently, but he grabbed her by the arm, lifted her undershirt in front, and tickled her bare belly with his tongue. "But I think they taste better on the outside! Especially little girls."

"Daddy!" she cried through her giggles, crossing her arms over her diminutive chest. "You are unbelievably silly for a man of your age!"

"Oh, I am, am I?" he retorted, planting a wet kiss smack in the middle of her forehead. "And you're ridiculously grown up for a woman of your age!" But he knew just where that last remark had come from. How many times had he heard it before, in one form or another?

"This is an unbelievably silly thing for a man of your age to be doing!" Almost the exact words. It was back in early 1969. They were walking along the beach at the North Island Naval Air Station, hunting for sand dollars. Brian had just completed his last semester at San Diego State, and Lizzie had assumed that would mean they would now get married and "settle down." But then Brian had told her of his plans and asked her to wait awhile longer.

"I can't believe you're going back to Vietnam," she practically stammered. "Who's forcing you to go?"

"No one," he said calmy. "I'm going voluntarily."

"You don't even believe in the war anymore."

"I've got more important reasons for going back. Personal reasons."

She forced his eyes right into hers. "And don't you have any personal reasons for staying here?"

"Lizzie, please don't do this to me."

"Come on, Brian! It's what you're doing to yourself . . . to us. You're finished playing war hero now. You're going to become a doctor."

"That's why I have to go back, Lizzie. I'm sorry I can't explain it any better than that."

"But a medic, Brian? Those people have a life expectancy of about ten minutes over there."

"It's not really like that. You've just heard the worst stories."

"Hasn't your country had enough tries at killing you? Can't you let someone else go this time?"

He put his arms around her and tried to pull her close to him, but she tore free from his grasp.

"But will you wait for me?" he asked.

"Wait for what?" she called back to him. "How can I commit my life to a man who's trying to kill himself? If you happen to come back alive, look me up. Then we'll see." She flung the handful of sand dollars she'd collected down at his feet and ran off across the beach.

His daughter's hand pulling on his finger brought him back to the present.

"Okay, finish putting your clothes on now, Katie. We don't want to make Mommy wait."

The child methodically pulled on her yellow cotton top and then stepped into her short blue denim jumper dress. "You can zip me up now," she instructed, turning her back toward him. It was the single aspect of the dressing ritual she would let him help her with. Just like her mother.

Ordinarily Brian would wait with Katie at the front door of the apartment house. Lizzie would drive by and collect her there.

They would be cordial with each other, smile, and exchange pleasant greetings. And then the woman and the child would drive off together, leaving Brian alone for another two weeks. But this morning she had phoned early and asked to come up to his apartment. He had been brooding about what that could mean since the call.

He heard the knocker. As soon as he opened the door for Lizzie, he began trying to read her, to intuit what was up with her. But this was never easy. When together in Katie's presence, they both were always mindful of the psychologist's admonition to show neither hostility, which might upset or frighten the child, nor too much false affection, which might confuse her and raise false expectations for their reconciliation. So they had learned to tone down their overt behavior to something resembling emotional neutrality. And this made any real insight into the other's mood or sensibility virtually impossible.

She did look lovely, though, even better than usual. Her hair was only slightly darker than the natural straw blond it had been when they first met. And there was a lustrous quality to it, to her eyes, her skin, her entire being that seemed to say she was getting on quite passably on her own. Well, it did no good to deny that his feelings about this were mixed. But as traumatic as their parting had been, it had not given him reason to wish her anything but the best.

"Hello, Brian," she said.

"Good to see you, Lizzie."

"Hiiii, Mommy!" Katie screeched.

"Honey, why don't you go play in your room for a few minutes so I can make some arrangements with Daddy?"

She shrugged and ambled off into her bedroom. Brian and Lizzie watched her go. She closed the door emphatically, signifying that she was content not to know what they were discussing but that it went both ways.

Brian turned to his former wife, hoping they could dispense with the ritual and get right to whatever was on her mind. She didn't disappoint him.

"Brian, I've been thinking about this for some time. How would you feel if I went back to my maiden name?"

"Why do you want to do that?" he asked.

"I don't know if I can explain it. For a while, though, I've just felt more like Elizabeth Hackett than Elizabeth Thorpe."

Brian was silent for what seemed to both of them a long time. "Well . . . I guess I can't object to something like that."

"You really don't mind?"

"I really don't."

Lizzie reached out and placed her hands on his shoulders. She pulled him toward her and kissed him. "Thank you. It means a lot to me."

There was another moment of silence as they held each other's gaze. He resisted thinking of her as she had been on the day that photograph in his office had been taken, back as she had been during all the brief interludes of their happiness. It was better to think of her as she was now.

"I guess I'd better get Katie," she said.

After they'd gone, he waited a little while before leaving for work to let the impact of her request sink in. The impact was actually very small, he kept telling himself, of no practical importance and far less significant than just about anything else that had transpired between them since the divorce. It was only that the last vestige of anything shared between them had just vanished. Except for Katie.

Except for Katie.

The phone rang just as he was about to leave. "Commander Thorpe? This is Radley Davis." Just about the last person Brian wanted to hear from at this particular moment. "I called your office, but they said you weren't there yet, so I called you at home." Obviously.

"Well, that's where I am. What can I do for you?"

"Have you looked at today's *Post* yet?"

"I've glanced at it. Why?"

"There's a small article about this place up in Montana. West Deer Creek it's called."

"What about it?"

"The article says they had an outbreak of cattle plague there. People found all these dead cattle lying around. Pretty remote. Had probably been dead like a couple of weeks."

"So?"

"And then they looked around some more and found the rancher who owned them in his house. And he was dead, too. Same thing."

"I'm sorry," Brian said curtly, "but I'm still failing to see why you're telling me all this."

"The rancher's name was Sam Hardesty. He was in our marine unit in Nam."

ATLANTA, GEORGIA

COMMON THINGS OCCUR COMMONLY.
UNCOMMON THINGS DO NOT.
WHEN YOU HEAR HOOFBEATS, DON'T THINK OF ZEBRAS.

It was the guiding principle and informal motto of the Epidemic Intelligence Service, and Diana Keegan had it framed on the wall above her desk. Her boss, Herb Secrest, had given it to her on her first day as a vital lesson in interpretation. When one is primed for the pursuit of strange and exotic diseases, there is always a tendency for the young doctor to overlook the fact that a presentation of influenzalike symptoms is, in all likelihood, influenza.

She had been staring at the sign all morning, not getting any work done, trying to apply the same reasoning principle to the business with Bill. All he'd said was that he was coming to town and would like to see her. Two old friends reminiscing about times past. She'd interpreted the rest. And what made her so sure he wanted to pick up right where they'd left off? She paraded the evidence through her head for the zillionth time. Well, the fact that he'd left his wife, for one. The stuff about the hotel room, for another. And then the old Krug Pinot Chardonnay, for a third. The zebra tracks ran pretty deep.

So she knew what he wanted. Common things occur commonly—remember? But what did *she* want? That was what had been torturing her the entire time since he'd called. She'd gone over it endlessly in her own mind. She'd had excruciatingly involved conversations with Sharon. And here it was Wednesday. He'd be in Atlanta on Friday, expecting her to—expecting her to what? Expecting her to crawl right back into his lap and be his kitten again? The mere thought of that was enough to turn her stomach. But was she then simply going to refuse to see him? Wouldn't that be cutting off her own nose? That was something she was famous for. Again and again she mulled it over in her mind, setting the last moment before lunch as her arbitrary yet incontrovertible deadline for some decisive thought on the subject.

It came, finally, by default. As she had done with other major life choice issues over the years, Diana decided to leave the matter to fate.

She caught Herb Secrest just as he was coming out of his office for lunch.

"May I see you a minute?"

Herb shrugged and, with his outstretched hand, ushered her back into the room. She sat herself in the large, battered walnut visitor's chair and instantly began biting her lower lip. It was something she almost always did when she was nervous. He leaned against the large, battered walnut desk and folded his arms across his chest.

This was where Diana always knew to come for aid and comfort when she had a problem or something on her mind. Herb was the resident father confessor to the entire EIS staff. At the same time she worried that she was becoming too dependent on him, just as she had once been dependent on Bill. She chastised herself for not being more emotionally self-reliant and able to make her own decisions.

She recalled the first time she had been here. It was for her initial interview to work at the centers. Herb had assumed exactly the same pose. In fact, they both had. She distinctly remembered chewing on her lip and worrying about the impression it would make. But she also remembered being completely taken in by the immediate surroundings. Not the standard-issue government furniture—Herb had no interest in what he sat on or worked at—but what was all around it, and in many cases, covering it. Like that of many another CDC professional, the office of the chief of the Special Pathogens Epidemiology Branch was a miniature museum of artifacts he'd collected from remote cultures around the world—among them, tribal masks from Zambia and the Ivory Coast, a Javanese shadow puppet, a Mali rice bowl, a Hopi Indian blanket, a Samoan kava root, and a painted wooden figure of death from southern Mexico. This last one occupied a position of prominence on the top shelf, a place of awe and reverence reserved for one's most respected and powerful enemy. It was both strange and sobering to think that each of these mementos represented a confrontation with some mysterious and terrifying disease. And she'd known at that point she wanted to work here more than anything.

"So what can I do for you?" Herb seemed cool and unruffled,

completely in his element. As much as Diana liked him, there was always an air of being called to the principal's office about these meetings. She couldn't help feeling like an awkward and naughty little girl.

"Have you got anyplace I can go for you?"

"When?"

"Oh . . ." She tried to be casual, but it didn't work. "Today, tomorrow . . . Friday at the latest."

"Why?" He smiled. "You looking to get out of town? I thought you'd made your peace with Atlanta."

"I-I have," she stammered, knowing it wasn't the truth. "But . . ." She looked up to see him sighting autocratically down his nose at her through his tortoiseshell-rim glasses. Why did she feel he was seeing right through her? The principal wasn't going to accept the little girl's excuse. "I just thought I'd kind of like to get back to the field, and if you had any assignments, maybe you'd consider me."

He came around to the working side of his desk and eyed her skeptically. Or was he just toying with her? Was he going to send her outside to play or make her stand in the corner? He sifted through the small jumble of telegrams and Telexes lying in his IMPORTANT! box, then casually glanced up at her.

"How soon could you go?"

"Let me go to the bathroom and then I'm ready." She held up her red official passport for him. Like many EIS officers, Diana had gotten into the habit of carying it in her handbag.

"Spare me the dramatics," Herb told her. "I haven't got anything overseas at the moment. The rest of the world appears to be remarkably healthy on this particular afternoon."

Her shoulders slumped dejectedly, and the corners of her mouth turned down into the beginning of a characteristic pout.

"I do have one thing," he said after he had enjoyed her emotional self-indulgence for a moment.

She perked right up. "Is it far away from Atlanta?"

"Couldn't get much farther."

"As long as it isn't Houston, I'll take it."

"Then you came to the right place, ma'am. You got it."

"What's the case?"

"Apparently an outbreak of some sort of cattle plague. One human fatality: the rancher who owned them. By the time they found him, he'd been stiff a week. Local coroner freaked out, figured he had an 'Andromeda Strain' on his hands, and called us."

"Any other reported outbreaks?"

He shook his head. "Uhh-uhh. What you'll be able to find this long after the body's cooled is beyond me," he said. "I don't expect this to be a big dog and pony show, so don't try to make it into one. But we do have to check it out if a state health department asks us to. And anyway, you did want to get out of town."

"No problem," Diana said as she sprang out of the chair. She leaned far across the desk and pulled Herb toward her for a smothering hug. His expression indicated that he was unprepared for the intensity of her passion. But of course, he would have had no way of knowing that she was also embracing fate—for delivering her, at least temporarily, from her dilemma.

"So where am I going?" she asked cheerily when she had let him loose.

"West Deer Creek, Montana," he answered dryly. "Have fun."

BETHESDA, MARYLAND

So where in hell was Rad Davis? Brian wanted to know. He had insisted on the phone on coming out to Bethesda to talk, and Brian had had to jump through hoops to clear a half hour to see him. Now here it was the middle of the afternoon, and Davis hadn't even bothered calling to say he'd been held up.

He drummed his fingers impatiently on the desk and decided he'd give Davis another five minutes. That was it. If he showed up after that, tough shit. Enough of this foolishness. He had plenty to do for his genuinely sick patients without playing nursemaid to one paranoid loser.

He knew he should have anticipated this from someone so emotionally erratic. The nurse was right. He should have dumped Davis on the VA at the beginning. Instead, he'd played right into his hands. Well, the next time he presumed to show his face in Brian's presence, he'd have him across town so fast it would make his head spin. Let the shrinks over there have him for a while. In the long run, that would probably be the kindest thing anyway.

It was typical of a paranoid neurotic to try to make all these crazy connections. Brian never had quite understood the supposed relationship between Rad's pains and those random deaths from the Seventh Amphib Unit. You could probably find similar statistics from lots of outfits if you wanted to take the time to track them down.

The tiny capsule inside the shrapnel fragment might have been something. But as it turned out, it wasn't. Nothing in it but water. And Hugh Stanway had called back just yesterday to say that his people couldn't find anything on it either. Probably some experimental prototype device, he said, maybe designed to hold nitroglycerin, cyanide, or something.

But one thing was sure: None of it added up to anything. That's what he would have told Davis had he bothered to show up, and that's what Davis would now have to learn for himself. A cattle plague in Montana is just that. There are cattle in Montana, so that's where there's going to be cattle plague. The rancher happened to be from the Seventh. Probably a kook like Davis, too, if he lived all alone like that. But none of that meant you should read anything more than coincidence into it. In medicine you could get into a shitload of trouble reading too much into things.

What was the old expression from med school that summed it up so well? Something about "When you hear hoofbeats, don't think of zebras."

6

Brian had been in the operating room since before dawn. In the middle of the night he had been roused from a dead and dreamless sleep. A multiple-passenger highway trauma required more skilled hands than the on-call surgical resident could muster. Then it had been one of those mornings when they just kept wheeling them through, prepping another squeeze-in between every two scheduled cases. All he could think about was the dull buzz near the base of his skull, and he knew it would be relieved only by his going home and going back to sleep. But he also knew that the chances of getting out early were rapidly diminishing from slim to none.

He was on his way to the cafeteria, trying to sneak in and out before anyone else could collar him, when he passed Gregory at the entrance. He offered a tired peace sign in lieu of a more formal greeting.

Gregory returned it with a salute from a rolled-up newspaper. "Ironic, isn't it?" he said.

"Huh?" Brian was too weary to try and pick up on any of Gregory's normal crypticisms.

"What a goddamned shame. I mean, after getting through Nam and all. And then this."

Brian stopped moving and fixed his concentration on Gregory. "What are you talking about?"

The radiologist held up his newspaper. "Didn't you see the *Post* this morning?"

"No. They called me in to crack a chest in the middle of the fucking night. Haven't been out of the OR since. I don't know what's going on in the world."

"Not the world. Just the city. It's just like *M*A*S*H*," Gregory said sadly. "You know? Fix them up so they can go out and get themselves killed."

He unrolled the paper, folded it back to the second page of the metro section, and handed it to Brian. "Who'd want to hold him up? Probably didn't have ten bucks in his pocket."

"Who? I don't know what you're—" Brian's eyes focused on the small item below the fold. The headlines froze the next sentence in Brian's throat:

EX-MARINE KILLED
IN HOLDUP ATTEMPT

"Guy never did get an even break," Gregory muttered, "did he?"

Brian gripped the paper rigidly, as if it were trying to shake loose from his grasp. He raced through the article.

Radley J. Davis, a former marine staff sergeant and Vietnam veteran who had recently moved to the Washington, D.C., area, was shot and killed outside the residential hotel in which he was staying. While there were no witnesses to the shooting, which occurred early yesterday afternoon, police are citing robbery as the probable motive and state that Davis appears to have attempted to resist his attackers.

Davis, a native of North Carolina, was unemployed at the time of his death. It is not known if he had any friends or relatives in the area, but other residents of the transient hotel told police they believed he had come to Washington to seek medical care. They described him as being polite but shy and uncommunicative. Some said he had been despondent in recent days.

It was as if a land mine had just exploded underneath him and the force waves were shattering his bones from the inside.

"Hey, are you okay?" Gregory asked.

"Can I have this?" Brian asked blankly in return, holding up the paper.

"Sure, but you don't look so good all of a sudden. You want me to go somewhere with you?"

"I'll catch you later," Brian answered stiffly. He made an abrupt detour from the cafeteria entrance. His only idea was to go back upstairs to his office, getting up there as quickly as he could. There he could close the door, and for a little while it would be a refuge against everything—everything but his own thoughts.

There are times in life when the bottom drops out, when the sudden disintegration of one article of faith calls all others into question. And if one is truly honest with himself, it is impossible to go on until that foundation is rebuilt.

He sat rigidly still for a long time, elbows propped up on the desktop, staring straight ahead into shattering silence. All his adult life Brian Thorpe had had other men's lives dependent on his actions. And always there was an accounting for those actions. After every SEAL mission, after every combat medevac, after every surgical procedure, there was always a period of evaluation and self-judgment. It might be something formal—a highly structured debriefing that took in many individuals—or it might simply be a momentary pause to reflect on whether anything he could have done differently would have contributed to a better or more favorable outcome.

And now, no matter how he faced it, no matter what approach he took, there was one simple and unavoidable premise: The mission of the physician is to preserve life, and Radley Davis was dead. Davis had entrusted himself to Brian's care, and he was dead. How had it come to this? What should he—what could he have done differently? Brian hadn't taken Radley's paranoia seriously. If he had, maybe he would have talked to someone about it. Maybe he would have referred him to someone else. Maybe he would have alerted various authorities.

Would it have changed anything?

He retraced every step in his mind, went back over everything Rad had told him and every conclusion he'd drawn from it. It had been a typical PTSD presentation, with exaggerated physical complaints and clearly manifested paranoid delusions. There had been no reason to alter diagnosis anywhere along the line. Brian had been so certain and so smug in his certainty. And now he was haunted by the specter of what he had taken for granted.

Gregory came to check up on him. The last thing Brian wanted at the moment was a baby-sitter, someone to hold the handkerchief up for him to blow into and make sure his thoughts didn't become too black or self-punishing. But the gesture had been well intentioned, so he couldn't send him away. Brian continued to stare silently ahead. With little fuss Gregory sat himself in the same orange plastic chair Davis had recently occupied and said nothing until Brian was ready to talk.

Brian stood and turned toward the window. Gazing out into the middle distance of the Maryland countryside, he began enumerating the facts: four random, unrelated deaths. And now a fifth. A sixth, if you included the rancher in Montana. And why not, since he shared the one crazy thing they all had in common?

"And what about the fragment?" he said, turning back toward Gregory. The zebras were overtaking the horses.

"Has it occurred to you that this still doesn't add up to any proof of anything?" Gregory said. "In fact, you really don't know all that much about it."

But Brian kept coming back to the original point. Somehow he had let Rad Davis down. And now he was dead, possibly because of that. He hadn't really listened to him. Had Radley known something about the other four or about Sam Hardesty that someone would have wanted to kill him for?

"The paper said it was a holdup, Brian."

"And the papers also said the first four were accidents," he snapped back. "But six accidents are no longer accidental."

"You're starting to sound like Davis now."

Brian came back to the desk and stood behind it. His palms pressed down hard on the surface as he leaned forward toward Gregory. "Doesn't it strike you as at least a little bit odd that all six of these men were completely alone when the 'accidents' happened? No witnesses, nothing."

"That doesn't tell you anything for sure."

That was true. He couldn't be sure of anything. But he knew that until he was, the foundation of his own life could not be rebuilt. And if there was even a chance he had caused Rad's death by his own indifference or complacency or obtuseness, then he had to do something. What that would be, he had no idea.

And that in itself, as his friend Gregory Cheever well knew, was not a situation anyone who has ever been a SEAL likes to find himself in.

CHANTILLY, VIRGINIA

The two men were known to each other only as Contact and Background. They met on the observation deck of Dulles International Airport, having approached from opposite sides of the central concourse. Dulles was a convenient rendezvous spot for Background. The airport was one of his embassy's key courier drop points, so he could be there during the late afternoon—when it was most crowded and therefore safest—without arousing the suspicion of his superiors.

A cardinal rule of tradecraft is to do the obvious thing in the obvious situation, so as not to call attention to oneself or give casual observers reason to remember anything out of the ordinary. So Background, plainly not a native, made a point of turning to take in the full expanse of Saarinen's magnificently soaring, up-sweeping glass and concrete terminal behind him and then gazing with awe almost straight up at the huge pagodalike control tower.

Picking up on this cue, Contact waited for the agreed-upon interval before positioning himself near Background at the safety rail. He had been at the airport for several hours already, surveying the entire area to make sure the meeting would be "clean" and that nothing, however seemingly inconsequential, felt wrong to him. Every few minutes he went back and checked the main arrival board in case anyone happened to notice his continued presence in the terminal.

This afternoon's arrangement called for one casual brush-pass before the actual exchange. If either man sensed he was being followed, he would simply keep walking and the meeting would be canceled. But no such precautions turned out to be necessary.

His hands gripping the rail tightly and appearing to wince slightly in reaction to a sudden blast from a jet engine, Contact stared straight ahead toward the runway as he spoke to the man at his side. "What news from our rivals across the sea?"

Background's eyes followed the Concorde, taking off gracefully from the west. "There is reason to believe some of my comrades may have joined you in your special hunt."

Contact was too experienced to react outwardly. "How were they put onto the scent?" he asked calmly.

"Routinely, I understand. The information came up through channels. Then someone was bright enough to recognize it for what it was . . . or might be. Someone with a long memory."

"Do they have the quarry in their sights then?"

"I am not sure they even recognize the quarry they seek as yet." His voice was deep and resonant, with the crisp, clipped accent the Soviets favored in their diplomats. "But let us say this: After years of cooling off, the trail is once again heating up."

BETHESDA, MARYLAND

A plan was forming in Brian's mind. It wasn't complete yet, but working under the adage that doing anything at all is better than doing nothing at all, he was beginning to shape a course of action.

He began, as he had in the old days, by mentally organizing the initial steps and marshaling his resources. He went down to data processing, timing his visit to coincide with Jill's afternoon break. When she came out, he saw she was wearing one of her classic outfits: a pair of terribly chic designer jeans stretched tight as drumskins; above that were two loose, stringlike arrangements amounting to a little less than a vest covering a little more than a halter. It was never boring looking at Jill, Brian thought. Her figure stirred the imagination and at the same time left very little to it.

"Hi there," he said, sidling up next to her and gently taking her arm to lead her in the direction of the cafeteria. "How about letting me buy you some coffee? How about an ice cream cone? Wouldn't a hot fudge sundae be swell?"

She scrutinized him with mock suspicion. "You've got that look in your eyes, Thorpe. I feel a bribe coming on."

He tried to make his eyes look innocent and hurt by her accusation, but he succeeded only in making her giggle at his effort. "Me? How can you say that? I'm just trying to be a nice guy."

"You are a nice guy," she replied, "one of the nicest. But you're much too driven to come down here in the middle of the day just to be friendly."

"Am I that transparent?" He frowned.

She nodded her head emphatically. "Uh-huh," she said, and giggled again. She took his hand into hers and patted it and stroked it, as if silently recognizing and acknowledging his turmoil. Brian found himself deeply moved by the gesture. "Come on," she insisted. "You don't have to play games with me. Buy me an ice cream and tell me what you want."

"I'm going away for the weekend," he explained to Jill when they were seated at a secluded table in the corner of the cafeteria. "I may not be back by Monday, and if I'm not, I want to be covered by annual leave for as long as I'm gone."

"So what's the problem?" she asked. "All you have to do is make a request to your supervisor, in your case the chief of surgery."

"Crowley? He's on such a power trip he'd turn me down just to jerk my chain. Anyway, I think it'd be better if I didn't have to let anyone else in on this until I know more about what's going on."

"I think you just want to go back to playing SEAL." Her tongue trailed playfully along the edge of the top ice cream scoop (rum raisin) as she turned the cone in her hand. It was a smooth passage for about three-quarters of the way around, at which point a protuberance of the rocky road underneath intersected with her nose and chin.

"It's a sensitive thing," he continued. "I'm not sure what's involved yet, so I don't want to send up any red flags that I'm going away suddenly," he said, gently wiping the side of her chin with his napkin. "I want it to look like I have official orders to be away for a few days. And after the way you pulled off that Hawaii business so nicely, I figured you could do it. I figure you can do anything with that computer."

"Not quite." She smiled. "But that was different. You had two sets of legitimate orders. All I did was help the bureaucracy clean up its own mistake. What you're asking for here is to generate data that aren't already in the system."

"And you can't do that?"

"I didn't say that. I can probably do it. The access codes aren't that complicated or hard to find. The question is: Is it important enough that you want to take a chance on that kind of exposure when the whole thing could be handled routinely?"

"It's important enough," Brian answered. "If I don't show up Monday, I want it to look like I'm supposed to be away, but everyone forgot about it. Happens all the time in my department. If you can take care of it for me."

"Is there anything I wouldn't do for you? You have but to ask."

Brian's eyes momentarily lost contact with Jill's and traveled down to her delicate and enticing breasts, barely covered by the double layer of string. He recovered quickly but not, he was certain, before she noticed. He was never sure with Jill whether these little temptations were planned. In any event, he decided to limit his request to what he'd already asked for.

"I'll call you and Gregory Sunday night," he said, "and let you know how long I'll be gone."

Jill nodded her agreement to the plan. He appreciated the fact that she hadn't demanded any more information from him. The first thing he'd been taught as a SEAL was to learn whom you could depend on. And he knew that he could depend on her.

"Oh, and one other thing," he added, dipping a napkin in his water glass and tenderly applying it to the corner of her mouth, "I may have to ask you to do this again for me."

WASHINGTON, D.C.

One task remained before Brian committed himself to his course. It wouldn't give him definitive answers, but it might act as a screening test—the way a blood count or chest X ray can point to the presence of disease without determining the specific nature of the illness.

He had made several calls from his office, and when he left work, he drove directly to the Third District Police Station on Sixteenth and V streets, NW. Detective Lieutenant Alexander Klein was waiting for him. Leaning against the metal cabinet he'd just opened, he unfolded the dark brown manila file jacket and silently skimmed its contents. "DAVIS, RADLEY J.—HOMICIDE," Brian could read lettered on white tape across the top.

After a few minutes Klein looked up. "I took a pretty close look at the case after you called. Seems pretty routine from this end," he stated. "Guy's on the sidewalk all alone in a bad neighborhood, gets rolled by . . . say it's a bunch of young smart-ass toughs. Probably got pissed off and put up a struggle. I see here he was an ex-marine, right?"

"Right," Brian said.

"Yeah, well it figures then that he'd want to defend himself. Worst thing you can do sometimes, I'm afraid. Certainly was here. I hate to say it. We see this kind of thing all the time."

"And you're sure that's what happened?"

"Sure?" Klein replied. "No, I can't be sure. I wasn't there; you weren't there. But from eighteen years of experience I can tell you this crime had some fairly common components, and when we see those components, there generally isn't any reason to suspect anything but common motives. And from the investigative officer's report, from everything I see here in this file, I have to say we think we have a pretty clear idea of what happened. Now you obviously have some personal interest in this case. I appreciate that; we encourage it. And so it probably seems uniquely horrible to you. I appreciate that, too. But I have to tell you that as I said, from our end this is not a highly unusual thing, especially in the part of the city where it happened. There just isn't any evidence of anything else." He snapped the brown folder shut, as if closing the case on any other logical possibilities, before adding, "And evidence, Doctor, is what we go on here."

There was one stop left to make. It was already dusk, and this part of the city was foreign and unfamiliar to him. He found himself in a steady line of traffic plodding slowly down the avenue, continually caught behind drivers deciding to turn left at the last moment without signaling. The halogen anticrime streetlights cast a hazy, surreal glow over the shopfronts passing by, many of them still boarded up going on twenty years after the riots that had lacerated Washington. On nearly every corner groups of men ranging in age from young to old congregated, while screaming and shouting children used the littered sidewalks as their playgrounds.

Brian turned off the avenue and began checking the address he'd written on a prescription blank against the numbers on the tight, neat brick row houses. There was no place to park on either side of the street. He ended up close to three blocks away, squeezing his Volvo behind an enormous pink Cadillac convertible. From the looks of it—the broken windshield, the rims without tires, the shredded top—its surrender to the street had not been a recent one.

He got out of his car and glanced in all directions before starting out. As he walked in this neighborhood, dormant instincts were quickly reawakened. Once again he had come to a strange place where he knew he was not welcome. Once again he was the intruder. His was the only white face in sight, and as he walked, he could sense himself being watched . . . observed, by faces the color of night. The sensation was familiar to him. His mouth went dry. His eyes focused sharply. The surface of his skin was prickly and electric.

He continued with measured stride. Every time another man passed him on the street, he could feel his body grow tense. Every time someone came up behind him, he could feel his shoulders tingle. It had been a long time since he'd felt this much on edge, and he suddenly realized that a part of him welcomed it. A part of him almost wished he'd be accosted so he could test himself against the high standards of his past. It was an instinct that had once made him feel alive, that had made him feel akin to the ancient hunters whose cave paintings of strange and fearsome animals had fascinated him in his youth. But he was no longer young, and he was no longer a hunter. But like a hunter, the worst thing he could do now—on any level—was to overreact.

Lonnelle Jefferson greeted him at the front door and ushered him into what she called the front room. The sofa and chairs were large for the space and overstuffed and covered on all their worn spots with handmade lace. Highly glossed wooden tables held family souvenirs and religious objects. Altogether, Brian was reminded of his grandmother's house back home in Indiana.

Mrs. Jefferson insisted on bringing him coffee even though he assured her he wanted nothing. As he waited for her to return from the kitchen, he studied the photographs that graced the carved mantel. Most prominent among them was a silver-framed image of a young man in a marine uniform, standing in the mud with two others in front of a Quonset hut. Though the picture was tightly cropped, Brian instantly recognized it: the field headquarters of the Seventh Marine Amphibious Unit at Dong Ha. Next to it was another frame. Inside was a ribbon and an enameled pendant bearing the profile of George Washington, the one military medal that actually attests to the fact that the recipient has suffered in the act of earning it—the Purple Heart.

"Did you know my son, Dr. Thorpe?" Mrs. Jefferson asked as she came back into the room, carrying two cups on a silver tray.

"Ah, no, ma'am, I don't believe I did. But we served over there the same time."

"Then I hope you won't mind if I tell you a little something about him."

"No, not at all. I'd like to hear whatever you want to tell me."

The story she told was one of every mother's pride, full of the fear and tearful hesitation over letting a son go off to war and then the joy and exultation upon his safe return. It hadn't been a popular war, she acknowledged, particularly in the neighborhood here, young black men being sent to do the white man's dirty work. But he'd come back with an outstanding service record, and she still had all the letters he'd written from over there, explaining to her why it was important.

"He said it was the most important thing he'd ever done."

Brian could see the happy, faraway look in her eyes fade into the sorrow of the present. With delicate, slightly trembling hands, she replaced her china cup on the silver tray and faced him directly.

"I know what you're probably thinking, Commander Thorpe, especially you being a doctor: black man, no father at home, Vietnam veteran, inner city. Man musta been all hooked in with drugs. But that's not the way it was with Tyrrell; not that way at all. You can ask anyone. It couldn't have happened the way they say it did. Tyrrell just wasn't like that. He was a fine, upstanding man who never gave me a day's trouble in his life. You have to believe me."

He put down his own cup and took her hand in his. His heart went out to her the same as it had to Radley Davis. In this tiny arena, with this audience of one, she was playing the high-stakes game for her son's dignity and her family's good name. She had placed on Brian an obligation he neither could nor wanted to forsake.

As soon as Jill told him about her conversation with Brian, Gregory started calling him. He finally connected late in the evening, when Brian came back home.

"I don't suppose I can talk you out of this," he said after hearing his friend's intentions.

"I'm afraid not," Brian said.

"Then tell me one more time why it has to be done this way. If you're so sure there's something strange and bizarre going on, why can't you just tell someone and let them take care of it?"

"Who?"

"I don't know. The police . . . the FBI . . . the chief of nursing. What's the difference?"

"First of all, I'm *not* so sure," Brian explained. "If this all does turn out to be nothing, I don't want to call a lot of attention to it and get a lot of innocent people involved."

"Okay. Fair enough so far."

"And second, if it turns out to be something, until I know who's behind it, I don't want to call a lot of attention to it and get a lot of innocent people involved."

"I think you're paranoid," Gregory stated.

"That's what I said to Radley Davis."

WEST DEER CREEK, MONTANA

Brian and Diana met on a windswept plain of shimmering tawny grass that reached as far as he could see and made him understand for the first time what the term "Big Sky Country" really meant.

The Hardesty ranch house, where the introduction took place, was in fact little more than a ramshackle board cabin set in the midst of this plain. It stood by itself at the end of a long dirt lane and had been beaten a dull gray by sun and wind and rain. For three directions it was the single thing that challenged the otherwise flat horizon. Only to the west did the craggy sage-colored mountains give any hint that this primeval range did not go on forever. When Brian pulled up in the Jeep Cherokee he had rented in Great Falls, Diana was already there, standing next to another man in the clearing in front of the house and surrounded by large red coolers that made it look as if she had been responsible for bringing all the beer for the fraternity picnic.

"You must be Dr. Thorpe," the man said, slapping his hand against his thigh to clear the sweaty dust before extending it to Brian.

"Yes. Dr. Wilcox?" It had been explained to him on the phone that out here the local physician also doubled as county coroner whenever necessary.

"Call me Elmer, one doctor to another and all. And this is Dr.

Diana Keegan, who's come up from the Centers for Disease Control in Atlanta."

Brian focused on her for the first time. It was clear that she hadn't consciously dressed to be alluring, but the effect was the same as if she had. She was wearing an old khaki bush jacket, rolled up at the sleeves, and matching hiking shorts that accentuated long, trim legs. Her thin cotton blouse was undone several buttons' worth in the heat, and perspiration had made it cling to the evenly tanned skin of her breasts. All in all, she had a terrific figure. It could have been a dancer's body, Brian concluded, but for the enticingly full curve of her chest. And he could already see that she carried herself with an air of confidence that can come only from a lifetime of beauty and success.

She gave him a crisp, formal handshake and a smile that made no promises. He returned it with a simple "Brian Thorpe. Pleased to meet you," and tried unsuccessfully to divert his eyes in a more professional direction.

But shit, he thought. That's all he needed; some cutsey pie government bureaucrat snooping around and looking over his shoulder. For some reason it had never occurred to him there might be someone else poking around into this business. And of course, now that he did stop to think about it, the CDC had a lot more legitimate reason to be here than he did. Well, she was only following orders. She'd take a few samples, file her report, then he hoped get the hell out, go find some nice malaria outbreak somewhere, and leave him alone. Still, this did complicate things; probably meant he'd have to stick around now longer than he'd figured on.

Taking no notice of him, Wilcox spread his arms wide to embrace the entire prairie. "What are the chances three people come together in the middle of Nowhere, Montana, and they're all three doctors?" He seemed quite taken with the idea and his own good luck at being one of them.

Brian tried to direct his attention to the immediate task ahead, how to accomplish it most efficiently now with this new wrinkle. But in spite of everything, he found himself furtively staring at the intruder. He couldn't deny that she was strikingly beautiful.

She wore no makeup, which in itself wasn't unusual in this rustic setting, but her looks didn't suffer at all for not having it. Her face was made up of clean, distinct features that came together in a rare combination of straight and soft: high, prominent cheekbones that highlighted dimples when she smiled; a finely angled jaw tapering along an elegant line to a strong chin. Her nose was slim and somewhat pointy, of the type the English would describe as "patrician." Likewise, her narrow, sensual lips and mouth, which probably tended toward a slight child's pout regardless of her mood and often revealed a tantalizing glimpse of teeth. Rich hair the color of prime English walnut blew softly in the breeze against her neck and spilled down to her shoulders.

Only around her glistening and deep blue eyes could he detect the smallest trace of age or stress, in the form of little webs of lines radiating out from the corners. But rather than detract they gave this exceptionally pretty face a certain worldliness and vulnerability which otherwise it might have lacked.

She exhaled deeply, almost a sigh, blowing a bothersome strand of hair from between her eyes. It appeared to be a characteristic gesture, and he couldn't help being charmed.

"As you know, Sam and his animals had been dead more than a week before anyone knew about it," Wilcox recounted. "Probably wouldn't have known even then except for the fact that Ronnie Baskin down at the service station got in four new tires Sam had ordered. And after a while, when Sam hadn't come by to pick them up and no one in town had heard from him that they could recall, well, Ronnie just decided he'd better go out there and make a special delivery like. So needless to say, when he got out here and saw what he saw, first person he called was me."

"So then what did you do, Dr. Wilcox?" Diana questioned.

"Elmer, remember? Well, I got in my truck and came out straight away."

"And what did you find?"

Wilcox shook his head slowly from side to side. "The cattle were almost all together in one of the close-in fields. He was lying out here, just about where we're standing. It was horrible. I know you two big-city doctors have seen a lot more than I have. But I can tell you both, this was about the worst thing I ever saw: grotesque skin lesions; horrible contortions; visual evidence of central nervous system damage . . . you name it."

Diana asked, "What was your initial diagnosis?"

He shrugged helplessly. "I didn't know. The body had obviously been stiff an awful long time. Meningococcemia seemed a good guess. Possibly rabies; that's as nasty as any of them. Whatever it was, I knew it wasn't something I was set up to handle. So after we got things cleaned up around here, I called the state health department, told them what I'd seen, and suggested they might want to call in the CDC or something." He turned to Diana. "And I guess that's why you're here." Then he turned to Brian, who had said nothing during the entire interchange. "Though I have to admit, I was surprised the navy'd want to send someone, too."

At this Diana's eyes and ears seemed to perk up. "You're with the navy, Dr. Thorpe?"

"Ah, that's right," he replied, hoping she'd leave it at that.

"Commander," Wilcox offered, clearly impressed.

"You're here on ... official business?"

"Umm, you might say that. I'm afraid I can't say any more about it right now."

Brian caught the look in her deep blue eyes. She might not have been aware of it, but he recognized it immediately. He had seen it a hundred times before, especially from women. As soon as he'd got off the plane at Travis Air Force Base. Then again when he'd gone back to finish college at San Diego State. The first time at a civilian party. The first time he'd sat down in class. The first time he'd gone out with a girl since he'd gotten back. That look of fear and superiority and contempt that said, "You're military. You went over there and burned babies. You are forever tainted." It all figured. She had instantly calculated how old he was, what he would have been doing back then. She herself looked about thirty-three or thirty-four—just old enough to have been part of the movement. Just old enough to be fashionably radical. Just old enough for him to resent her beauty and her charm.

"Well, I suppose you'll both want to be getting settled before starting anything serious," Wilcox said. "The actual town of West Deer Creek is about fifteen miles from here. There's only one place to stay, and I'm afraid it isn't exactly the Waldorf-Astoria. But they'll take care of you best as they can. Follow me, and I'll show you where it is."

Diana bent down and hefted up one of the three red coolers. She staggered slightly under its weight and bulk. "I wonder if you both could give me a hand with these monsters." She was breathing heavily. "When you travel for the CDC, you never travel light."

The way she held the cooler, her jaw clenched in determination, Brian could see she would have preferred not asking for help. In fact, she seemed to wear her independence like a badge. He lifted one of the ice chests and looked to her lead where he should go with it.

"I wonder if I could hitch a ride with you," she said. He nodded and began leading her to his Jeep. He wondered how she'd gotten here in the first place.

Apparently there had also been an East Deer Creek once, people seemed to think, but no one was exactly sure. The Roundup Motel occupied a prime spot just on the outskirts of West Deer Creek, which itself seemed not to have changed in anyone's memory. The lodging was a one-story redbrick affair bent around three sides of a dusty gravel parking lot. There wasn't a single nonpickup truck, van, or four-wheel drive in the place. And almost all the vehicles sported gun racks. The desk clerk in the office glanced up from his hunting magazine when Brian and Diana arrived and looked at them strangely, as if to say, "We don't get many of your type out here." They had to convince him they wanted separate rooms.

After giving them time to settle in and change from their traveling clothes, Wilcox met them for dinner at Carson's, where he dissuaded Diana from the chef's salad—which no one to his knowledge had ever actually ordered before—and strongly recommended they both follow his lead in choosing the steak and home fries. "It's that kind of place," he explained. He ordered beer all around without seeking a consensus.

So far Brian and Diana had said little to each other: at the Hardesty place, on the drive into town, when they checked in to the motel, and now here. But it wasn't a void that defined the space between them so much as a distinct and positive tension, as though their two energy fields had chanced to lock in phase and therefore resonate at a higher magnitude of force than either could overcome.

As host Wilcox considered it his role to keep the conversation going. He respected Brian's apparent reticence to explain himself and so made Diana the center of attention. Were it not for Brian's furtiveness, however, it was doubtful the social dynamics would have been appreciably different. Elmer Wilcox was not married, at least at this time, and on his range a pretty young woman came at a much higher premium than did a jaded and taciturn service-man.

"So what exactly do you do for the CDC?" he asked. He turned his body physically toward her and put both forearms on the table, as if he were settling in to sit there and listen as long as she possibly cared to talk.

"I'm with the Epidemic Intelligence Service," she said. "And I work closely with the Special Pathogens Branch, which is why I was sent up here for this case."

"Intelligence service? Sounds kind of like spies, CIA or something, you know?"

"Well"—she laughed pleasantly—"we like to think of ourselves more as disease detectives than as spies, although the service was originally established more along those lines, I have to admit. Our first director, Alexander Langmuir, got Congress to authorize the division as a standing defense against a possible biological warfare attack."

"I didn't realize we worried much about that sort of thing in this country," Wilcox said. "Never happened that I know of."

"There's been more of it than you might realize," Diana replied blithely, but her tone quickly picked up stridency as she went along. "A long tradition, really, and not a very proud one either. It seems Americans have always enjoyed doing it to other Americans. During the Civil War, for instance, the Union Army used to put the corpses of diseased cattle down Confederate wells. And closer to home here, during the fighting on the Great Plains, your ancestors in the cavalry gave the Indians supplies of blankets infected with smallpox. Just one more example of this country's systematic war against its own native population."

Wilcox's facial features suddenly dropped, as if he'd just overheard an adorable little niece utter her first obscenity. "Is that a fact?" he said somberly. Brian knew immediately that she'd stepped into it, not once but twice, branding herself as both an outsider and a liberal. And if you had to pick two topics to watch what you said about in Montana, he would guess they'd be cattle and Indians.

Diana bit her lip in embarrassment when she saw the reaction she had caused. It seemed to be another of her characteristic mannerisms, and Brian had to admit he found it rather endearing. But was she being an innocent or a rebel? Was it a kind of bold, charming naïveté that had led her on with her tale, or was there still some mischievous adolescent satisfaction in thumbing her nose at the establishment?

The conversation had stopped dead with no sign of revival. People from other tables were beginning to stare. When Diana got no response from Wilcox, she looked to Brian, and this time she was asking for help.

He decided to rescue her. "So, is this CDC job a career position?" he asked.

It didn't matter what he'd said. The relief shone in those endearing blue eyes. "No, actually the Epidemic Intelligence Service is a two-year rotation under the auspices of the Public Health Service. I'd done four years in Public Health before my residency, mostly out in California, which was where I went to medical school, so EIS seemd a logical place to go."

She knew she was talking too much. She often did that when she was nervous, most often when she felt on the brink of totally losing it—"decompensating," as Bill had so charmingly put it—as she did right now. *So much for being clever*, she chastised herself. *You're not in college anymore.* Thank goodness for Thorpe's lifeline. And God knew she hadn't given him any reason to help her out so far. It was ironic that the military would end up coming to her defense.

"What did you do your residency in?" he continued.

"Internal medicine," she said, phrasing her words carefully and trying to mask the deep breath she was taking to steady her voice. "I was up in Boston at Mass General. Same place I did my internship."

"I spent a lot of time there when I was in med school," Thorpe said. Still no more than a sentence at a time from him.

"Oh, really? Where was that?"

"Harvard."

That was certainly a surprise. Her first instinct this afternoon had been that he reminded her in many ways of an overage surfer: dark blond hair; blue eyes that looked as if they'd done a lot of squinting at the sun; clean, square features. "And your field?"

"Surgery."

That was maybe not as surprising. He was neither exceptionally tall nor hefty, but trim and well built. She couldn't tell too much else about his body, but the blue work shirt he had on was tight across his chest. His hands were strong and steady. Yes, definitely surgeon's hands. The surfing image disappeared. It was frivolous, and whatever this man was, he was not frivolous. She watched him in repose for several moments. But then he threw her off again by another break in cadence, directing his next question at Wilcox.

"What kind of evidence do you still have?"

The coroner eagerly turned his attention exclusively to Thorpe. Evidently this was to be Diana's punishment for her indiscretion. The girl could no longer be trusted in the company of grown-ups. And subtly, her mysterious and up to now quiet companion had assumed direction of the proceedings.

"We preserved blood and tissue samples from the body," Wilcox said. "They're in my office. You can do what you want with them. And then we saved the carcass of one of the steers—got it in a meat locker we rented. They burned the rest of the herd."

Thorpe turned to Diana. "Can you do anything with what they've got?"

Not much, she would have to admit, but she was grateful he was including her in the discussion. "Well, the tissue's got to be extremely decomposed by now, especially in this weather. And since bacteria grow postmortem, a culture's going to be useless. You'd grow out everything under the sun. We can spin down the blood—I've got the equipment with me—but I wouldn't count on finding anything there either."

"Then what would you suggest, Doctor?" He smiled faintly—midway between teasing and patronizing, she thought.

"I think at this point our best shot may be to go with the cow."

"Steer," Wilcox corrected. And it was then that the waitress set their dinners down in front of them. "Just like what you're eating."

Diana fought with a sudden gagging sensation and didn't know if she'd be able to eat. Thorpe and Wilcox didn't seem to be having any trouble.

There wasn't much talking during dinner. The two men ate quickly, then watched with apparent amusement while she dutifully cleaned her plate. But after they'd finished and coffee was brought, Thorpe leaned back in the carved wooden chair and asked, "What sort of man was Sam Hardesty?"

"Well, sir," Wilcox said, "I don't know exactly how to answer that. He was always pleasant enough when you ran into him, at the store, filling station, places like that. But he never really had much to do with anyone since he moved up here. Never had anybody out to the ranch socially that I know of. Pretty much liked to keep to himself."

"Do you know why that was?"

"I can't say for sure. Folks said that he'd had some bad experiences in the war, that he'd come up here to get away from it. But that's just what folks said. I don't know that he actually sat down and laid it out for anyone. That wouldn't have been like him."

She noticed Thorpe nod seriously, as if he were not surprised to hear any of this. Then he said, "By the way, Elmer, did Mr. Hardesty have any next of kin?"

"None have shown up, though I know the state people are trying to find some." The coroner shook his head sadly. "It must be horrible to die all alone like that."

And it was in response to this comment that Diana thought she noticed the trace of a reaction flicker across Brian Thorpe's face. But it was so fleeting, and he recovered his composure so quickly, that she later decided it must have been her imagination.

What was he doing here?

Why had the navy sent a surgeon out to investigate an isolated outbreak of cattle disease in some backwater town on the edge of the Montana hills? This wasn't even the kind of thing the CDC normally got involved in, so why was the military here?

She sat on the bed in her motel room. It had been hot during the day, but now that the sun had gone down, the air was cold, and there was no heat in the room. She had put on a sweatshirt, which helped warm her body. Now she drew her bare legs up close to her chest and tried to rub the chill off them.

She wasn't ready to go to sleep. She was tired but restless. Bill was in Atlanta by now. She wondered what he was doing and how he'd reacted when he found out she wasn't there. He'd phone, and Sharon would tell him she'd been unexpectedly called out of town on business. An icy wave of loneliness came over her and brought back the chill. She shivered and wriggled under the covers.

She thought of Brian Thorpe in the next room. Just like her, he was alone. But she was sure it didn't bother him as much. He didn't look the type. But what was the type? She couldn't figure him out. He was obviously trying to hide something, or why hadn't he explained why he was here? And he was in the navy. That wasn't exactly the same as being in the army, she supposed. And he was a doctor like her. But not really like her. A person is defined by the life choices he or she makes. And theirs had been very different. Her inbred distrust of all things military went back a long way. He was part of what she'd spent more than half a decade of her formative years protesting and fighting.

She thought about Bill again, and she thought about Jeff Harmon and their years together in the Public Health Service. That had been her choice: to help the oppressed and disenfranchised people here in this country rather than destroy them overseas. Thorpe seemed so different from all the other men she'd known, or known well. They all had tended to be tall and thin, somehow intellectual-looking. And they weren't quiet like him. No, none of them had been quiet. They'd all been very vocal, with terrific senses of humor. As serious as the scene often got back then, that had always been essential to her. But now, as she lay in this unfamiliar bed and mentally reviewed each past friend and lover, traits that had once appealed to her as being clever and charming now seemed brittle and hollow. The word "frivolous" came back into her mind.

She shouldn't think about it anymore. It wasn't accomplishing anything. She was exhausted and overwrought from a long and tiring day, and this was clouding her feelings. Better to conk out and start fresh tomorrow. She turned over on her back with her arms flat at her side and stared straight up at the ceiling.

Why couldn't she get Thorpe out of her head?

Maybe concentrating on her mantra would help her relax. She hoped she remembered it. It had been about ten years since she'd last tried to meditate. Everyone she knew was doing Eastern mysticism. It was something like "Cheyenne," she thought. *No, it can't be that.* The West must already be getting to her. But it had to be close. That's what it was: "Shiam." Shiam . . . shiam . . . shiam. She said it over and over to herself in a dull, rhythmic chant.

And what was he doing here?

This wasn't doing any good. She threw her arms back over her head and twisted her hair around her finger in frustration. She'd be up all night and then do badly all day tomorrow. And she decided she very much did not want to do badly here.

Then suddenly it all came together.

She knew what had killed Sam Hardesty and his cattle, and it wasn't natural causes. And she knew why Brian Thorpe was here. Why hadn't she thought of it before? It made perfect sense. Back in the late 1970s the CDC had been called in to investigate the effects on people who had been involved with secret atomic testing in the Nevada desert in the 1950s. So the government must have resumed secret testing up here in one of the most out-of-the-way places it could find. How could you put anything past the defense establishment? It'd proved its moral vacuousness countless times before. Like the time it infected people at bus stations to see how quickly it could get a bacterium to spread across the country. All it cared about was getting away with it. And it all would have been swell in this case if this reclusive rancher hadn't stumbled into the test area and died of radiation sickness. And that would explain what a military doctor was doing poking around up here.

And that would also explain what *she* was doing here. The military's job was to make sure it was kept quiet, and the centers' job was to see if there was any epidemic potential or public health threat. But why hadn't Herb Secrest briefed her instead of sending her off blindly? He'd seemed so casual about the whole thing. This point really bothered her. She sat up cross-legged in bed and switched on the lamp on the night table.

The CDC works with two types of case definitions—biased and unbiased—depending on what the particular investigation is trying to accomplish. You used a biased definition when you knew approximately what you were looking for—you'd already intentionally "biased" the definition of the case—and went in to locate as many individual examples of the disease as you could. You used an unbiased definition when you'd identified a health threat—people had died or gotten very sick—but you didn't know what was causing it, so you were considering everything as possible etiology. And one medical point of view currently popular at the centers held that the less a trained and open-minded epidemiologist was told in advance about the case, the more unbiased and inclusive he or she would be. So Herb had purposely not told her anything.

That was one explanation.

The other was that Herb didn't want her to know for other reasons—or that he didn't know either. Maybe no one in the entire CDC knew, including the director. The Pentagon had called the centers in to make sure there was no spread but was sending its own people in to make sure they didn't go too far. She pulled the blankets tight around her and shivered again. Just like poor Sam Hardesty, she had maybe stumbled into something incredibly sinister. And maybe she was about to break one of the biggest medical scandals of the decade, maybe of the century . . . unless—

—unless Brian Thorpe could stop her.

She went to sleep with her head pounding. Or maybe, it occurred to her through her haze of pain and fraying nerves, it was simply the hoofbeats of zebras.

8

Diana had spent her childhood taking in stray dogs and cats, tending birds with broken wings, and mending the wounds of rabbits and other small and vulnerable creatures. And she remembered weeping bitterly whenever her efforts failed or her parents made her finally limit the size of her menagerie. But she had never thought much about, or generated much compassion for, anything larger than she could hold in her arms and cuddle. That is, until now.

She and Brian were kneeling next to each other in a dirt clearing—she would have called it a backyard except that it had no fence or readily definable borders—about forty feet behind the building containing the meat lockers. The preserved steer was lying on the ground in front of them. The locker's attendant probably would have preferred that they be even farther off, but this was about all the distance the three of them could drag the carcass. They got to study it or work on it or do whatever it was they wanted with it for one day, they were told, and for not too long after it had thawed out. Then it had to be burned like the others.

Actually a butcher would have been more useful in this procedure than a surgeon, she decided. Neither one of them knew much specifically about the inner workings of cattle. Since Brian mentioned that there'd been a lot of farms near where he'd grown up in Indiana, and since he was obviously the stronger of the two, he got the physical part of the job. Most of the instruments they were using had been obtained from the local hardware store.

But Diana didn't need much formal knowledge of bovine anatomy to know that this animal had suffered greatly before it died. She actually broke into tears when she saw it. Even Brian looked pale.

As Elmer Wilcox had said, it was a horrible sight. There were huge boils and open ulcers covering the hide, which had also just simply split and bled in several places. The steer's eyes were turned way back in its head, and its neck was contorted as if it had flailed about wildly, gasping for breath. The orifices held residues of severe vomiting and diarrhea, while the tongue hung limply out of the mouth, showing evidence of extensive salivation. This might have been what made Elmer think first of rabies. And although there were no obvious bone breaks, the unnatural positioning of the legs indicated to her the possibility of massive neuromuscular invasion. But then most of the symptoms also happened to involve tissues whose cells reproduce the quickest—blood, digestive tract, lymphatic system—the ones most affected by acute radiation sickness.

"What do you think it was?" she asked Brian, testing him.

"I'm not sure." He said it without looking up from the carcass. "But I'll tell you one thing I think. This was an incredibly fast progression of symptoms. Possibly a matter of hours. Certainly no more than a day and a half." Highly possible with radiation sickness, she noted.

Throughout the examination she had been watching Brian for signs—signs that he was looking for something specific or following his own secret agenda. But she could come up with nothing. With eyes more full of curiosity than any particular circumspection, he methodically went about the task of hacking the tormented animal apart. With each new step he paused and glanced over at her to see if she had any new conclusion to draw. She felt as if she were back taking the practicals for the national medical boards.

He slit open the steer's first stomach. As she'd suspected, it was horribly ulcerated. Diana wanted to turn away but didn't want to show him any weaknesses. She stared straight into the festering body cavity and fought to keep from retching.

"Stomach's pretty empty," Brian said, probing around with his blade. "Must have tossed up everything he had in him."

Again Diana felt her stomach muscles contract violently. "I—I guess so," she said. She felt the perspiration beading on her forehead.

She heard the tiny clink of metal against something equally hard. She looked up from the steer and saw that Brian had abruptly stopped what he was doing, as if he'd hit a snag. "What is it?" she asked.

He reached in with his gloved hand and extracted a tiny fragment from the animal's stomach. "A pebble or a piece of rock or something," he said.

"He must have swallowed it while eating grass. Do you think it's important?"

"No." He shook his head. But he held the pebble tightly in his fist. His eyes were somewhere else, deep in thought. Finally he opened his fist as if an inspiration had just taken hold, flipped the pebble a few times, and then tossed it away.

"Is anything wrong?" she asked.

At first he seemed not to hear her, but then he said, "No, nothing," in a way that was hardly convincing. "I was just thinking."

"About what?" She was starting to get that nervous feeling again. He was figuring out some way to get rid of her.

"We've gone as far as we can on this," he said. "We've got to do a post on Hardesty."

"An autopsy?" It took a moment to register. The idea was repulsive to her. It was bad enough on a cow that had been dead for weeks now, but a human being . . . What was he getting at?

"We've got so little to go on it's the only way," he stated.

"But what will it tell us?"

"We won't know until we get in there, will we?"

What was he getting at? she wondered. She was becoming insecure again. What had she missed that he'd picked up on? "Why are you so sure we should be doing this?" she asked.

"Please just trust me," he said.

"Will—will they let us?"

"Maybe. You heard Wilcox. No one has come to claim the body, so it's still there in the morgue. I don't know what condition it's in, but even if it's the same as this animal, we might be able to get something out of it."

"So what are we going to tell Elmer?" she asked.

"Not we." Brian smiled. "You."

"What!" She felt her heart drop down to her belly.

"You have to ask him," he said definitely.

"Why me? You see the way he treats me ever since what I said at dinner."

"But you have an official reason. You can say it's a required part of your investigation."

"What about you? You've got the entire military establishment behind you."

"Not really," he said quietly.

"What are you talking about?"

"Let's just say this is something better handled by you."

There were a lot of things Diana knew she didn't like about herself, but perhaps the one she liked least was the way she felt when she let other people, particularly men, intimidate her. Suddenly she decided she'd had enough of it and it was time to stand up to him. After all, what could he do, short of physically attacking her? And he didn't seem to be the type for that.

She got to her feet while he continued to kneel, and she folded her arms across her chest. She realized she was trying to make herself as large and formidable as possible. "You know where I'm from and what I'm doing here. So suppose you tell me just what it is you're up to, Dr. Thorpe." She held her gaze firmly on him.

He didn't answer right away. "I'm here somewhat informally," he said at last.

"What do you mean?"

"I knew Sam Hardesty. We served together in Vietnam. Nineteen sixty-nine."

So that confirmed one thing about him, she noted. He had been over there. He had taken part in that horrible, immoral war. It made the gulf between them more understandable, more palatable even. "Was Hardesty a doctor, too?" she asked.

"No. Neither of us was. He was a marine, and I was a medic assigned to his unit."

"I'm sorry. I didn't know he was your friend."

"He wasn't. I don't really think I knew him," Brian said cryptically.

But she had started to reevaluate him. Doctors over there were part of the military establishment as far as she and her friends were concerned. They were just as morally accountable as any other officers. Their job was to keep the fighting machine well oiled, patch up the wounded so they could be sent right back into battle. The ones who were too shot up to be of further use were shipped back to the VA warehouses. And that was the doctors' decision, too. But the medics were a different case. They had only one job: to help people who were hurt. They didn't kill anyone; they didn't cause anyone to get killed; they only saved lives—and under the most primitive and dangerous conditions. Many of the medics in Vietnam had been conscientious objectors who had agreed to accept "noncombatant" status because they thought they could do some good. And it was a fact that even though they didn't fight or carry guns, the medics had a far higher casualty rate than just about any of the units they served with. If Brian Thorpe had been a medic, Diana thought, maybe she was wrong about him. Maybe there was more to him than she'd suspected.

"So how am I supposed to get Elmer to agree to the autopsy?" she asked.

"I don't know," he said. "But you seem pretty resourceful. Make nice to him; tell him you're sorry; burst into tears; tell him he's got the potential for an international health threat. I'm sure you'll think of something."

She detected some softening in Brian and was beginning to feel slightly more comfortable with him. "And if I refuse?" she asked playfully, testing him further.

"You're in the Public Health Service, aren't you?" he said.

"That's right."

"That makes you a commissioned officer of the United States."

She nodded emphatically, pleased that he had acknowledged her equal status with him.

"What's your grade?" he asked.

"O-three," she responded proudly.

"That's the equivalent of a lieutenant senior grade in the navy. I'm a commander in the navy," he said with a smile. "That's an 0-five. So I could *order* you to do it."

And she still didn't know what he was doing here.

The morgue for West Deer Creek was actually nothing more than a refrigerated closet and tiny examining room in the back of Elmer Wilcox's medical office. It was seldom needed for more than a few hours at a time—a day or two at most, he told them— and he was anxious to have it cleared out before there was another need for it, preferably one resulting from natural causes. If it hadn't been for that, Diana was fairly sure, he wouldn't have been as agreeable or cooperative about the autopsy.

They had to work at night, when Elmer wasn't using his office. It was just the two of them, formally distanced from each other by surgical masks and gloves. The body of Sam Hardesty lay on the table, seeming almost to fill the small room. The dark, the quiet, the loneliness of this faraway place, the rigid naked corpse in front of them—all suddenly produced in Diana a cold but creepily natural feeling of intimacy with death. *Three bodies, two souls*, she thought.

An autopsy is the ultimate invasion of privacy, the ultimate violation of the integrity of being. The fact that it is often necessary only underscores the fragility of our knowledge and the state of our techniques. When Diana was young, the grandmother of a Jewish friend had explained why the Jews didn't display the deceased in an open coffin at the funeral. "Because he's embarrassed to be dead," the old woman had told her. "You can see him, but he can't see you, and he can't do anything about the way he is now." And while she knew that probably wasn't the official rabbinical interpretation of the custom, it had always stayed with her. When Diana got to medical school, she didn't go to a single anatomy lab that it didn't come into her mind. The class professor, Dr. Hardy, had always insisted on clean white lab coats as a sign of respect to the seriousness of their purpose. And at the end of the term he led the students in a moment of silence for the immortal souls of those who had bequeathed themselves as cadavers in the service of knowledge. "With what we must do here, we cannot always avoid mutilation of the body," Dr. Hardy had said at the first class. "But no physician must ever defile the dignity of death."

She remembered how queasy she had got at the first gross anatomy class, the first time she had to open up a cadaver. Not only she but other kids, too. "This doesn't bother you," she said to Brian.

"It never bothered me," he replied casually.

"No?"

"I'd already seen a lot of gross anatomy firsthand out in the field by the time I got back from Vietnam. I didn't need a textbook to show me where all the vital organs were."

Before they got under way, Diana carefully checked the tag attached to the big toe of Hardesty's left foot to make sure they had the right individual. It was a practical and necessary procedure in a big-city hospital or morgue. Here it was little more than a ritual. But rituals have their value, particularly those that serve to remind the doctor that no matter what he does, in the end his enemy will always be stronger than he, that death will always win out.

In any morgue today a recording system operated by a foot pedal is standard equipment. Since there was no recorder here, Diana agreed to take the notes as Brian spoke. It was just one more unnerving element that brought her back to images of medical school.

"This is Dr. Brian Thorpe. I am performing a postmortem examination on Mr. Samuel Hardesty in West Deer Creek, Montana." He began with the standard opening. It was not only a sign of respect that the protocols be observed but a protection for the examining physician in case anyone had to review the record later on. "We will be employing a modified Virchow technique, examining each organ and system in situ.

"I am entering with a typical Y-shaped incision from both shoulders to directly below the breasts, coming together at the xiphoid process and then extending down in a straight line to the pubis. I will be flapping the skin and subcutaneous tissue to the side and over the head, out of the way of the examination field."

With a Stryker saw he cut through the ribs and then underneath the diaphragm. He removed the breastplate and exposed the heart and thorax.

"Circulatory system looks okay," he reported.

"What about the lungs? Any sign of respiratory failure?"

"I don't think you'd be able to tell that from an autopsy," he said. "But make a note of symptoms secondary to neurologic disease. And from the boils and scabs, I'd say we're also probably dealing with a secondary bacterial infection."

"That's probably postmortem, though," Diana said. She had seen it many times out in the field. Once any organic substance starts decomposing, bacteria grow like crazy. "What about lymphocytic infiltration?"

He probed with the scalpel for several minutes. "I can see pronounced lumps in the armpits along with large abdominal nodes."

He directed his attention down toward the groin. "Inguinal nodes are also enlarged, and the spleen looks congested, too. Yeah, you can put down a marked lymphadenopathy. Also note that I've run across several small bits of shrapnel—"

He stopped talking in the middle of the sentence, as if he'd just gone into a trance. She looked at him. It was several long seconds before he began again.

"—which are prima facie evidence of previous fragmentation wounds." He paused for another several seconds. He had the same expression as when he'd flipped the pebble from the steer's stomach out of his hand.

"I'm going to take a look at the liver now," he told her.

When you see the human body laid open in this manner, it is impossible, even if you are a doctor, to avoid the perception that you possess this same set of viscera within yourself and that it is vulnerable to the same assaults and insults. It is a further unnerving thought to realize that you will one day smell this way. The surgical mask provided only partial relief.

"I couldn't be a pathologist and do this for a living," Diana said.

"I knew one who was affected in only one way," Brian commented.

"What was that?"

"He stopped eating liver. He said that of all the organs it was the one that in death most looked and smelled like what his mother used to make. In fact, he said there was hardly any difference at all."

"Wonderful," she replied. She looked up at Brian and wondered how he could be this dispassionate while examining the rotting insides of a man he had known. Or had he? He still hadn't given her the straight story.

But maybe there were other reasons why he was able to move himself beyond the bounds of squeamishness and sensitivity in ways that she was not. For one thing, he was a surgeon. It was his job to invade the body. But there were further differences between them. Again she remembered that he had also been a medic. As doctors both of them had been taught and conditioned to be comforting and compassionate with their patients. But as a medic Brian had actually known the people he cared for *before* they needed care, before they were injured or sick. He had known his patients first as comrades, while they were still healthy and "equal" with him. *That has to change your perspective*, she decided.

"I can detect clear-cut morphologic changes in the liver," he stated. "It is deep red in color and severely congested. There is evidence of acute hemorrhaging and bile staining. The tissue is soft and flabby and can be folded back on itself with the scalpel without fracture."

He cut into the liver. Its mass adhered to the sides of his knife like chewing gum stuck to the sidewalk. He finally had to spread the tissue with his fingers to separate it fully. For the umpteenth time since she'd gotten to Montana, Diana wanted to throw up. She hadn't even seen pictures like this in textbooks. She couldn't imagine what could do that to a liver.

And that was what made it so frightening. Whatever had infected the cattle and their owner here had taken hold with a speed and viciousness she had never seen before.

It is an inherent characteristic of the profession that epidemiologists tend to worry about things in pairs. This may be because the disease process is one of nature's ways of balancing itself. Diana quickly ran through the relevant pairs in her mind. The most important was always the incubation period and attack rate. In this case, it appeared that the incubation period was short and that all the individuals exposed had developed the symptoms. And since both cattle and a human being were afflicted, the presumption at this point had to be that it was not particularly species-specific. Sensitivity was high, and specificity was low. This was the worst possible pair, the one most difficult to control. Diana felt a cold spasm ripple through her own body as she stared down at the naked one on the table.

Yet in all this there was one reason to be optimistic, she realized. A critical one! This outbreak had occurred at least two weeks ago. No one who had come in contact with Hardesty or the cattle after they were discovered had become sick. Not Ronnie Baskin, not Elmer Wilcox, not the attendant in the meat locker. And so far there were no other reports of similar incidents in the area. When she called in her initial report to Herb in Atlanta, she'd make sure of this.

Near the surface of the liver Brian seemed to run into something. She wasn't quite sure, because her eyes had wandered, but when he withdrew the hand that had been spreading the tissue, it was tightly clenched.

"What's that?" she asked.

"Oh, another shrapnel fragment," he said. "It was in the way of the knife." He continued cutting. It was a tiny piece of steel, not half as large as the nail on her pinkie. And she noticed that instead of just setting the small metal sliver aside or tossing it into the trash can, he casually deposited it in the pocket of his pants.

"Well, it's clear that whatever this disease is, it has a particular tropism to the liver," he stated. There was a chilling kind of objectivity in his voice. But she felt much better about it a moment later, when he wiped his sleeve across his sweat-streaked forehead and said, "I've never seen such a mess in there." Indications of humanity always reassured her.

Painstakingly, methodically, he worked his way through the body. When he finished with the liver, he went back to the Stryker saw and sectioned off a portion of the lower spinal cord. His eyes narrowed, and he moved his head closer into the field. "Even on gross visual examination, we detect massive ganglionic plexus destruction of the larger nerves. We would have to assume, therefore, that the same degree of degradation would be apparent microscopically on the smaller ones. This is consistent with unusual contortions we observed in the steer."

Diana took down his description word for word. Along with everything else, her hand was cramping. But that was probably the least of it. "What else do we have to do?" she asked wearily. She knew she was no longer making any show of hiding the fact that she was rapidly losing it.

"Only one more thing." He smiled indulgently. "You're holding up very well. Now let's take a look at one of the kidneys."

Diana nodded weakly.

Brian said nothing for a while. At this point she was too numbed to worry about following exactly what he was doing.

"This is interesting," he said a few minutes later. It roused her from her semistupor, and she picked up her writing tablet. "I've cut the organ in half and I can see very characteristic necrotizing papillitis."

"You do . . . I mean, you can?" She peered in at the sectioned kidney. Down its center were the six pyramid-shaped projections known as the papilli that drain into the ureter. They were a dark reddish purple in death, almost black. "Diabetes?"

"That's what I think. And to judge from the severity of these lesions, a pretty pronounced case. I'm going to take some kidney slices." He snipped off several small pieces of tissue and laid them out on glass slides. "Can you find me a syringe?" he asked. "I want to see if there's any urine left that we can get out of the bladder." She handed him a syringe. "And do you have a microscope with you in one of those magic red boxes?"

"Uh-huh," she replied. "Not a great one. But it should be okay for most things."

"Good." He turned away from the table so that he was facing her. "Then how'd you like to spend a quiet, intimate evening in your room? Just you and me . . . and a little bit of Sam Hardesty."

9

By the time they finished the postmortem it was well after midnight, and Diana yearned for nothing more than a long, hot shower and a warm, snuggly bed. The muscles in her left hand were twitching from the unaccustomed exercise of rapid verbatim writing, her neck was stiff and sore from the tension of concentrating so hard, and her feet and legs ached from her being on them so long. Surgeons were used to working while standing up for hours on end. Epidemiologists were not.

The easiest thing would have been to tell Brian that she'd see him in the morning and that they could continue their medical exploration then. But he was so caught up in the puzzle and so willing—no, anxious actually—to include her that she knew she'd regret it later on if she gave in to even her basic instincts for rest and comfort.

Also, there was another factor to be considered, she reminded herself—one that was absolutely elemental to the pursuit of scientific research on any level. "You do not go to bed when you are halfway up the mountain" was the way one of her professors had articulated it. Research is a progression from one plateau of discovery to the next. And often what moves you from the one to the next is not so much hard fact as an intersection of so many variables and visceral responses that it is nearly impossible to re-create the same pattern two days in a row. So when you're on to something or think you may be, the practical wisdom has it that you keep following through with it until you reach the summit or discover that your climb has ended at a sheer rock wall.

She sat cross-legged on the bed with her portable centrifuge and testing kit in front of her. He sat at the combination desk-dresser, preparing tissue slides for her microscope. There was a quiet intimacy in the room now, much more cozy and reassuring than the starkly intimate morbidity of the morgue. Maybe it was only because she was physically wiped out and all her normal defenses were down, or perhaps she was really lonelier than she wanted to admit, but she was beginning to feel around Brian a sense of familiarity and ease that she couldn't recall in quite the same way with any other man, particularly after so brief a time. It wasn't that she normally took a long time to let people get close to her, she didn't think. When she was in college, it wasn't exactly a breach of etiquette to jump into bed with a man the night you met him if the "vibes" were right. But that was a different time and place, part of a much larger picture and set of forces. In those days the mere fact that you slept with a man hardly meant you were committed to him, or he to you. She still knew nothing about Brian Thorpe, she kept telling herself, and she felt a stab in her gut every time she thought about the fact that he was in the military. And that made her feelings all the more perplexing.

She wondered what he looked like without any clothes on.

"Let's get it on. How are you coming?"

Coming? "What?" He startled her out of her half dream. "Oh. The blood's not going to tell us anything. Just as I thought, it's too coagulated to spin down. We would have needed a sample drawn right after death. But I think we may have some luck with the urine. Give me about five minutes."

She removed several test strips from her kit. Carefully, so as not to waste any of the fluid, she dipped them into the barrel of the syringe Brian had jabbed into Hardesty's bladder. She held them up to the light. For absolute accuracy she matched them against the kit's color chart. But even without it, there was no mistaking the meaning of the dark, almost blackish green color.

"Well, I think you may be on the right track," she announced. "Four plus for glucose. This guy was spilling sugar all over the place. And I've got a four plus reading for ketones, too." A high ketone level was a definitive sign that the patient was metabolizing fats rather than sugar. She marked the values down on her pad.

"Spin it down," Brian said. "Let's take a look at it under the microscope."

"Sure." She emptied the syringe into the centrifuge, turned it on, and let it spin for seven and a half minutes. Then she picked up the canister, carried it to the bathroom, and poured off the liquid into the sink. She opened a tongue depressor envelope and used the sterile wooden stick to scrape the centrifuge sediment onto a glass slide. She walked over and handed it to Brian.

"No. Go ahead. You do it." He motioned her to the microscope.

She positioned the slide on the specimen plate and adjusted both sets of optics. Fuzzy, double-bordered round shapes came gradually into focus.

"You see any white cells?"

"Plenty," she said. "TNTC." Next to WHITE BLOOD CELLS IN URINE she wrote: TOO NUMEROUS TO COUNT IN HIGH-POWERED FIELD.

"All right, let's take it one more step," Brian said. He grasped her lightly by the shoulders and moved her to the side, then slid himself in front of the microscope. She reflexively took a step backward at his reassertion of control, but he took her by the hand and brought her back to his side. "Pay close attention." He gently chided her. "You're going to learn something." For a moment she was a little girl again, but there was a strange tenderness with him that made it ungracious to protest.

"But what if it isn't what you think it is?" she said mischievously.

"Then you'll learn something else. That's the beauty of science. Everything tells you something."

He peered intently through the microscope lens and then positioned a thin dissecting needle under the objective. "Very interesting."

"What is it?"

"Come over here. Okay, look through the lens. You see that nodular scarring on the glomeruli of the kidneys?"

She nodded her head.

"Those lesions are very characteristic of Kimmelstiel-Wilson disease."

"So we're talking about chronic diabetes."

"Very good. But we're not there yet. Now, one more step and we've got it nailed."

She pulled her head away. He removed the first slide and put in a second. He studied it for more than a minute.

"I suspected it might be this. Okay, you're going to have to look very closely at this one. It's much more subtle. What do you see?"

It was vaguely familiar. She tried to summon up long-ago pictures she'd seen in body atlases. She desperately did not want to get it wrong. "Is that the segment between the proximal and distal convoluted tubules?"

"What do we call it?" he quizzed.

"Henle's loop."

"I can see you've been to medical school." He patted her tenderly on the shoulder. "Now what do you see in there?"

She shrugged in disappointment.

"Don't worry about it. A lot of people would miss this. Unless you're a surgeon or a pathologist, you'd probably never have seen it. The body stores its glucose in the form of its polymer, glycogen. If we see clear vacuoles in the renal tubules as we do here, it's defined as an Armanni-Ebstein lesion."

The name was only a hazy recollection from a med school pathology book.

"And it's a specific sign that the patient died in diabetic coma."

They both were quiet for a time while they considered the implications.

"So do you think this is related?" she asked.

"Could be."

"But none of the other symptoms has anything to do with diabetes or ketoacidosis—the liver, the nerves, the lymph nodes."

"That's true," Brian admitted. "But there's something else to consider. Humans aren't normally highly susceptible to things like cattle plague. But in severe diabetic shock, when the glucose can't get into the cells and the levels rise above one-eighty, the immunologic function of the white cells starts getting impaired. And Hardesty's level was so high that his white cells just crapped out completely."

"Which means he had no immunological defenses. And a disease which normally wouldn't be any problem for the body to fight off could suddenly become fatal."

"You get your gold star back."

"So the way you see it, Mr. Hardesty was just unlucky enough to go into diabetic shock at the same time that his cattle came down with some horrible bacterial infection."

"Coincidence. It's one of the great determining forces in history. Since we can't isolate the bacteria anymore, we'll never know for sure, but that's certainly the most plausible explanation from the evidence we have."

He stood up, signifying that the night's work was through. She waited expectantly, wondering if he'd make the first move and what she'd do about it if he did. It was no longer 1969.

But the only move he made was to the door, leaving her abruptly wondering if in her exhaustion she'd seen things that just weren't there.

"Sleep well," he said, and closed the door behind him.

And so the horses had once again overtaken the zebras.

Whatever it was that had devastated this herd and annihilated its owner, it wasn't radiation sickness. That much was clear. She thought back to her tossings and turnings of the previous night. And when she caught a glimpse of herself in the mirror, she saw that she'd blushed with embarrassment, even though she was alone. "Patty Paranoia" they used to call her back in college. She'd always been the one who thought the SDS meetings had been infiltrated by the FBI. She'd been the one who said that if you were truly committed, it was difficult to trust anyone.

She undressed, brushed her teeth, and settled into the bed. Any bed would have felt exquisitely comfortable by this point. No, it wasn't likely that quiet, mild-mannered Brian Thorpe was trying to cover up any secret experiments for the military.

On the other hand, he still hadn't given her a clue to why he was here.

Early in the morning she called Herb Secrest in Atlanta. It was two hours later there.

She gave him her report. "I saw massive lymphocytic infiltration. There's clear evidence of disease. But I don't think we're going to find anything conclusive this far after the fact. And however long the incubation period was, it's long since passed. I just want to check out one more thing and then—"

"I ran all the preliminary data you sent in through the computer," he said. "The symptoms check out with a known form of cattle plague. But fortunately there are no reports of any remotely similar cases coming in. The state health people have their asses covered, and I don't think there's anything else to worry about. So barring any new developments, I think we're going to classify this as an isolated outbreak, and I'm going to yank you back home. That is, if the coast is clear for you in Atlanta yet."

"What—what are you talking about?" she stammered.

"You don't have to play cutsey with me, Diana. You're a very bright girl. Very bright. You know I think so. But you also happen to be absolutely transparent."

"But—wait a—" she continued.

"Don't worry about it. We love you anyway. You know why you get your way so often?"

"I'm not sure I . . . No, why?"

"Because one way or another you always make it clear exactly what you want."

She opened the door and took a deep breath that filled her lungs. Despite the mild upbraiding from Herb, she felt good this morning, much better than she'd felt for a long time. The air was crisper and cleaner than it ever got in Atlanta and cool enough that she just wanted to revel in it. At least the way she felt today. She wanted to do something physical. The session with Brian last night had reassured her on several levels, about both the containment of the disease and his own intentions. The problem with Bill, while not solved, had at least been put off. Things were "in place."

She spotted Brian about ten minutes later, as he was coming back from breakfast and she was coming out of her room, dressed in a T-shirt and shorts and exercise shoes.

He asked, "Where are you going?"

"I've really been missing my aerobics class since I've been away. I can feel it in every part of my body. So I thought I'd go out for a jog." She bent over with her arms extended straight over her head so that they almost touched the ground. She bounced lightly from the knees and waist. "Want to come along?"

"Sounds like a good idea," he said. "I wish I could motivate myself to go with you."

"The navy doesn't make you stay in shape?" She grasped her outstretched leg in her hands and touched her knee to her forehead.

"Not anymore."

She wondered what that meant.

"How far do you go?" He did seem interested, though. And he was being very friendly. He was also paying close attention to every movement of her body as she went through her stretching exercises. And today that made her feel good.

"I try to do about two and a half or three miles."

"So that's what? About twenty, twenty-five minutes?"

She clasped her hands together behind her knees and pushed her legs backward. When she noticed that his eyes had wandered to the seat of her tightly stretched shorts, she straightened up correctly. "By the time I walk afterward and cool down, make it at least a half hour."

"Which way are you headed?" She pointed up the road. He looked directly into her eyes and squeezed her on the shoulder with what she took to be a hint of fatherly concern. "You be careful then," he warned.

"Don't worry. I'll be fine," she assured him.

"Okay. If you're not back in half an hour, I'll come out looking for you." She watched as he inserted the key into his door and closed it behind him. She resumed her stretching. She had to admit that his attention was flattering, and she was genuinely touched by the concern for her safety. Whatever else he was, he could be very sweet.

He watched through a crack in the curtains as she jogged off down the road. There was a fluid, athletic coordination to her stride and the rhythmic motion of her long, glistening legs. She didn't run like a girl at all, really, except for the charming bounce of her boyishly trim backside. As she disappeared out of sight, he thought it was a shame they hadn't met under different circumstances. Maybe there'd have been a chance . . . No, probably not.

He glanced at the black-faced Rolex diving watch on his wrist. Thirty minutes, she'd said. Twenty, he decided he could count on for sure.

He peered out through the curtains in both directions. There was no one in sight. He picked up the screwdriver he'd taken from the Jeep's tool kit. He went out and closed his door behind him and walked briskly over to hers. He held the doorknob firmly and inserted the tip of the screwdriver into the key slot. It had been awhile since he'd done anything like this. He hoped it still came easily to him.

He jiggled and rotated the tool delicately until he felt the resistance give way inside. A slight, subtle flick of the wrist. He tried the doorknob. There now. It turned easily in his hand. He slipped inside her room and made sure the door was locked behind him. He turned up the Do Not Disturb sign built into the door in case the maid came by to clean.

The first principle of surreptitious entry is to take a moment to memorize the contents and arrangement of the scene. Nothing must be disturbed by accident, especially anything that's obvious or easy to remember if it's out of its normal place.

He surveyed the room methodically. Her crumpled blouse and jeans were draped over the top of the open closet door. Yesterday's socks and underpants lay on the floor by the bed. Clothing of various kinds spilled out from an open duffel arranged haphazardly on the folding luggage stand. From every indication she wasn't much of a housekeeper.

Brian crossed over to the desk on which the microscope rested. From his pockets he extracted the tiny fragment he'd found in Sam Hardesty's liver, then a surgical tweezers and an ultrafine needle probe he'd taken from Elmer Wilcox's office.

The fragment was wrapped in gauze. He unrolled it and laid it on the scope's viewing platform. Holding it with the tweezers, he rotated it obliquely to view its full length. Then he twisted his fingers just enough to turn it on its end, the way the one from Radley Davis had appeared in the X ray Gregory showed him. With the tip of the needle he braced the specimen against shaking from minute tremors in his fingers. He held it so that he could look straight down the end.

Nothing.

He turned the fragment 180 degrees to the other end, steadied it, and looked again.

This time he saw it. A microscopically tiny chamber hollowed out of the center of the steel, as round and regular as the piston cylinder in an engine. Just like the one from Radley Davis's liver. Only this one had no stopper at its end.

It was empty.

There was one more thing to check out before the morning was over. He got into the Jeep and drove the twenty-five minutes out to Hardesty's ranch.

The place was deserted, as he'd hoped and expected it would be. The front door was unlocked. People like Hardesty didn't worry much about unwanted intruders out here.

Brian walked slowly through the house, looking generally at first to see if anything shouted out to him. Then he went into the kitchen and opened the refrigerator door.

He found what he was looking for on the shelf on the refrigerator door: three glass vials arranged in a row. Behind them were three disposable syringes in sealed packages. He picked up the first vial of colorless liquid and read the label:

SHIPLEY PHARMACEUTICALS
INSULIN INJECTIONS USP (REGULAR)
U-100
100 UNITS PER ML.

So Hardesty had known he was a diabetic and was under treatment. Well, at least that took care of one part of the puzzle. No one had mentioned it. Obviously, nobody had bothered looking around the place too closely when they found him. Not surprising, though, when Brian considered that they all must have been afraid they were going to catch whatever it was that had killed the rancher.

There was now another question, though. Hardesty was supposed to be an embittered loner. Had he intentionally taken his own life by purposely not taking his insulin? Or had he perhaps gotten a bad batch of the drug? If that was the case, the manufacturer would have to be notified in case there was any more of it floating around. Brian put all three vials and the unopened syringes in the pocket of his field jacket and left.

When he got back to the Roundup, he lay down on the bed and put through a call to Gregory at Bethesda.

"So when are you coming home? The old place is awfully lonely without you."

"Soon. I'm just about finished up here."

"And how do you like playing cowboy?" the radiologist asked jovially.

"It's not too bad. But it's actually more like 'Spy versus Spy.' I'm not the only one snooping around out here." He told Gregory about Diana and her mandate from the Centers for Disease Control. And then he told about the cattle and the postmortem on Hardesty.

"Diabetic ketoacidosis, huh?"

"No question about it. And that reminds me. Get a pencil." He read off the insulin label and the lot number. "See if Shipley's got any other reports of bad insulin. That'll be your good deed for the day. I'm bringing a sample home with me, and we'll put it in for assay as soon as I get back."

He outlined his theory on the diabetic coma and the cattle disease.

"Sounds good. Anything else interesting come out of the postmortem?"

"I've saved the best for last. When I was ripping apart the cow, I found a pebble stuck in its stomach. I suddenly got to thinking and decided to take a look inside Hardesty."

"And what did you find, pray tell?"

"Another hollow fragment, just like the one we took out of Davis. And in the same part of the liver."

"You're joking!"

"Only this one was empty."

"Does anyone else know about this, Brian?"

"No, just me."

"I thought you said there was a woman from the CDC."

"That's right. But all she knows is that the guy had shrapnel. Finding a piece in the liver's not all that unusual."

"So what do you make of it all?"

"I don't know. But the number of coincidences has just exceeded the laws of probability. It's time to start looking for a pattern."

"You may be right," Gregory said. "We'll talk about it when you get back. Oh, by the by, old man, your old buddy John Winthrop Blagden, *General* John Winthrop Blagden?"

"He wasn't my friend. I met him only twice, I think. He was my commanding officer. But what about him?"

"I found out what he was doing at Bethesda when we saw him."

"What was that?"

"He was here for a complete physical."

"Is there anything wrong with him?"

"No. Strictly routine and procedural. He's about to get a little promotion. I guess Eagle's Talon didn't tar him too badly. He's been tapped to be the next commandant of the Marine Corps. Marine chief of staff."

"No shit."

"No shit. So you've been traveling a pretty fast track with some of your old buddies without even knowing it."

"Sure sounds like it," Brian said. "Well, he certainly deserves it. How many of the big guns these days have even seen combat? That guy's paid his dues."

"Or a lot of other people have paid it for him. Well, no sense getting into that shit on the phone. Anything else I can do for you at this end?"

"No. I'll see you as soon as I can. Just give Jill a big wet kiss for me."

"No problem. Probably would have thought of it myself anyway. But there's one thing you can do for me, Brian."

"What's that?"

"Be careful."

He hung up the phone and lay back on the pillow, staring up at the ceiling. Now that he had finally stopped moving, he realized how incredibly tired he was. A half hour nap would do him a world of good. He remembered what only twenty minutes had done for him after many all-night patrols in the delta.

When he woke up, he'd go touch base with Wilcox, thank him for all his help, and make himself a plane reservation to go home. He could feel the tension draining out of him. In the quiet and stillness of his room he knew it wouldn't take long for the comforting numbness of sleep to overtake him.

The human being develops skills as the need arises. In the jungle, if one is to survive, he develops the ability to *sense* someone ... or something ... around him at times when that entity cannot possibly be seen, heard, smelled, or touched. Brian Thorpe was no longer in the jungle. He was now a doctor. He'd studied the human organism in minute detail, and he still couldn't explain the phenomenon. But from personal experience he knew it to be true.

Long ago Brian Thorpe had developed those skills. And once developed, they are never fully lost.

He sat up and listened. There was no sound.

He planted his feet stealthily on the floor and then stood up and went to the door. He peered through the keyhole. There was no one on the other side.

He looked around the room. The closet door was slightly ajar, and he could see into it from where he was standing. But someone had definitely come in. He tiptoed back over to the bed, bent down, and quickly jerked up the dust ruffle.

No one underneath it.

Only one other possibility, the most obvious one: the bathroom.

He crept up to the bathroom door, extended his foot as far out in front of him as he could, and lightly pushed it open.

The shower curtain was drawn closed. He didn't remember leaving it that way. The maid could have done it when she cleaned, but yesterday she'd kept it just the way he'd left it. Most people are creatures of habit. They don't arbitrarily perform routine tasks two different ways.

He saw a slight flutter at the base of the curtain. The interloper was definitely behind it. He froze and waited to see if there was any further movement. At the same time he ran through the unarmed attack drill in his mind: speed; surprise; accuracy. You get only one chance, so you have to make it good. He took a deep, silent breath, wiggled his fingers and arms for flexibility, and bent his knees slightly.

Then he sprang.

He sailed diagonally across the bathroom, approaching the tub area from the rear. He spread his hands out wide to take in the entire expanse of curtain, thrust forward when he hit, and clinched his arms tightly around the human form behind it. Instantly his hands went for the center of the torso, where his attacker's hands were certain to be, preventing him from moving his weapon into position. He ripped down the curtain from the aluminum rod and clamped his left hand tightly over the intruder's mouth.

Diana Keegan tried to bite through Brian's fingers.

He backed off. "What in hell are you doing here?" he roared.

Her eyes were wide with terror, and there was a scream still stuck in her throat. He took his hand away from her mouth.

"Ah, taking a shower?" She was trembling. She looked as if she'd just been slapped.

"Then you forgot to take your clothes off."

She bit her lower lip, and her deep blue eyes grew imploring. "I guess I—I was eavesdropping."

"Spying."

"I guess so."

"How'd you get in here?"

She pointed to the wall, to the sliding window above the tiled area.

"Didn't your mother ever teach you not to spy on people?"

She sort of half shrugged.

"Didn't she punish you for things like that?"

She sort of half shrugged once more, and Brian loudly muttered something about permissive upbringings.

"Are—are you going to punish me?" she asked winsomely. Her eyes were still wide.

"Yes," he replied calmly. His voice was absolutely dispassionate. "I'm going to have to kill you."

She started to scream. Brian instantly clamped his hand over her mouth again.

"Stop screaming, I'm not going to kill you." He sighed. He took his hand away and raised it menacingly in the air behind her. "But a good paddling might be exactly what you need right about now."

He saw the front teeth go for the lower lip again. He took her sharply by the arm, pulled her over the tub rim, and marched her unceremoniously back into the bedroom. She gave out with a whimper of fear, and her hand went protectively for her backside.

"I'm not going to spank you either," he said. She looked instantly relieved. He glared at her ominously. "At least not yet." She whimpered again, and the look of relief disappeared. He sat her down roughly on the edge of the bed. He paced back and forth in front of her, an interrogator grilling his prisoner. "Now, suppose you tell me what you were doing in here."

She looked squarely up at him looming above her. She had quickly regained some of her spunk once the threats of death and physical retribution had been lifted. "I was trying to find out what *you* were doing here," she said defiantly.

"What are you talking about?"

"Why are you here?"

"I'm the one asking the questions."

"I know. I mean, that's why I sneaked into your room: to try to find out."

"How long have you been snooping around?"

"Not long. You came back just after I got in. I probably could have sneaked back out again, but I thought there'd be a good chance you'd make a call as soon as you came in and—" her face brightened, and she smiled triumphantly—"and that's exactly what you did!"

"What did you find?"

"Well, I found this." She reached into her jeans pocket and fished out the small ball of gauze with the fragment inside. He snatched it from her. She pointed in the direction of the telephone. "And now I know what it's all about."

She had turned the tables on him, the former campus radical SDS bunny beating out the former SEAL. Had he lost his edge or just let down his guard? He had underestimated her, that was sure, and it had been a mistake.

He had to hand it to her. And in spite of everything, he couldn't deny the humor in the situation. She'd basically done the same thing that he'd done to her. So why was her crime greater than his? Well, for one thing, she'd gotten caught. He inwardly laughed at himself. Boy, if that wasn't the old SEAL mentality coming through. And another thing the SEALs taught was that whatever hand you're dealt, that's the one you have to play. So when you have the superior hand, you might as well play it for all it's worth.

But the fact of the matter was that the situation was now altered. She now knew too much for him to let her just go off as if nothing had happened. Yet she remained an unknown quantity, and the SEAL practice and tradition had always been that when it gets dicey, you rely only on people you know you can trust. ("We deal only with the people we deal with.")

He stuck his hands into his back pockets. He stopped pacing, turned, and faced her directly. "So what are we going to do about this?" he asked.

"Well . . ." She was getting bolder but, like a child who realizes she's just avoided a well-deserved beating by the skin of her teeth, still didn't dare move from the spot where he'd sat her. "I guess we're just going to have to start trusting each other, aren't we?" Diana said with a careful smile.

10

Well, Diana, she said to herself, *your curiosity just about got you that time. And are you sure you did it for purely "professional" reasons? You were lucky to get out with your little ass intact. How long is your luck going to hold out?*

Safely back in her own room, she was still shaky from the experience, her heart still fluttering in her chest. But she couldn't deny the sense of excitement and adventure. There was something of a game about it, both frightening and compelling at the same time. Somehow, though she kept telling herself she was a grown-up now, she managed to keep getting herself drawn into situations like this. It's one thing in your teens or early twenties; another in your thirties. But, then again, she'd always lived by the dictum that life can't be much fun if you stop taking chances.

Later, she thought back to college and recalled the 1971 May Day demonstration to shut down the government. There had been mass arrests. The police had just rounded up everybody they could get their hands on and loaded them into paddy wagons. Diana and about twenty-five or thirty other girls were put in a holding cell in the basement of the police station. Everyone had been treating the matter as a lark—a big game—taunting the policemen and chanting peace slogans in unison. No one was worried. They couldn't be held very long, they all reasoned. The dragnet had been so haphazard there was no way the cops were going to make it stick. They hadn't even read them their rights. There was no way the pigs could intimidate or scare them. They all were sophisticated and knew the ins and outs of criminal procedure. Then word filtered down that the captain was fed up and was going to process them all "by the book." Anybody in there might be dangerous, concealing weapons or drugs. Each of the girls was going to be strip-searched.

Suddenly it got very quiet in the holding cell. No one was very bold or smug anymore. Diana had been one of the ringleaders, so she knew she'd be among the first ones taken. They'd make an example of her. She could feel herself losing control, and she was desperately afraid she was about to pee in her pants.

They got the cringing girls into a line. Then, just as they were about to bring them one by one into the Gestapo-looking police matron, word came down that they all were being released without charges. When they got out, all of them bragged about how tough they'd hung the day they got busted by the pigs.

The man sitting across from her now probably wouldn't have been all that sympathetic with her plight that day. She was sure he'd have been on the other side.

Anyway, enough excitement for one morning.

They had gone to the Moose Head Bar in the center of town. It was an authentically rustic-looking place with knotty pine paneling, shotguns on the wall, brass spittoons, and a long, polished wood counter. It looked just like an old-fashioned western saloon. The centerpiece namesake of the establishment, the largest stuffed head she'd ever seen, was mounted on a walnut base just opposite the front door in the middle of the far wall.

"That's grotesque," Diana commented. "How could anyone want to kill something and then keep it and display part of its dead body in public?"

Brian said nothing in response, but when she asked him what he was thinking, he told her about the Vietnamese provincial chief he'd known near Quang Tri who used to cut off the ears of dead Vietcong infiltrators and wear them on a chain around his neck like an amulet. He said it gave him the power to hear his enemies sneaking up on him. And this would have happened just about the time of the May Day protests.

Brian still didn't look too happy about her little prank, but he didn't look as if he were about to kill her either. Anyway, that would have been against the Hippocratic oath.

Once he'd cooled down back in his room, he'd admitted that he had been secretive about his "mission" in Montana. And using what she already knew as leverage, she'd pressed him to open up about the rest of the story. "If you tell me, I'm sure I can help."

"I don't know the full story. But I do know it's not the kind of thing little girls should get involved in."

That really pissed her off, and when Diana was angry, she'd never been shy about showing it. "I'm not a little girl!" she shot back at him. "I'm a doctor, just like you, and I've seen more than my share!"

An amused but respectful smile crossed his face. And that was when she knew she had him. He put up his hands in a gesture of peace and sent her back to her room "to think about it" for a while.

"And do I have to stand in the corner?" she asked defiantly.

"No, just make sure you know what you could be getting into."

She didn't think about it. What she did think about was how a doctor had learned to execute such a stunning surprise attack as he'd sprung on her in the bathroom. His transition had been terrifying. Was he really capable of the kind of violence those actions had held the promise of? She'd known people like that before.

So now they were sitting in a secluded part of the bar, in the shadow of that hideous moose head, and he was telling her the story as he knew it: the man, Davis, coming to see him, and how Brian felt that by not taking him at his word, he had possibly caused or contributed to his death; the series of coincidental deaths of the marines; the two hollow fragments. He didn't try to assign special significance to any of the events, since he admitted he knew of none, but rather laid them out in objective, scientific fashion. While he talked, she rested her chin on the heels of her hands and studied his face. The face was serious, sometimes grim and sad, she decided, but the eyes looked as if they could be happy if only someone had known what to do.

"So what are you going to do now?" she asked him.

"Go back to Washington and try to put it all together."

"Are you going to notify anyone? The police, for instance?"

"What would I tell them? They've already investigated the Davis case and Tyrrell Jefferson, that other one I told you about. Sam Hardesty was clearly just unlucky. There are a lot of strange things going on, but no pattern to them."

"What about the fragments?"

He had obviously been thinking about them, too. "I don't know. It's no coincidence that they both came from the liver. But the first one had absolutely nothing of interest in it, and the second one was open and empty."

"Well, they obviously didn't end up where they did by accident. Someone must have put them there on purpose."

"Good chance. In fact, there's no other logical explanation. And as soon as I get back to Washington, I want to check into it—trace the backgrounds of both men. But why would someone go to all the trouble of planting something like that in them? They don't do anything."

"Since Hardesty's was empty, do you think it had anything to do with the disease outbreak?"

"I thought about that, but I don't see how it could. The evidence for how and why he died is pretty substantial, both the autopsy itself and the microscopic sections: He was definitely in diabetic coma."

"The CDC thinks that's a good explanation, too. I phoned back when I went to my room. They ran a computer check of symptoms and evidence and didn't come up with any other incidents."

"Then you've done your job," Brian said.

"But I want to help you do your job," she stated.

"If I only knew what it was."

The bar was gradually filling up. As the afternoon wore on, men in cowboy hats and hand-tooled boots, worn jeans and checked lumberjack shirts, string ties and silver-trimmed leather vests drifted in and sat together in what were obviously long-established patterns. Conversations centered almost exclusively on the twin sacred rituals of the region: hunting and fishing. Like the subject of politics back where Diana came from, everyone had an opinion, and the disagreements were heated.

Halfway across the room sat a group of people with lumberjack packs by the sides of their chairs. One immensely large man was leaning over the table and pounding on it, railing against the lottery system that assigned moose hunting licenses.

"Seems to me this is supposed to be a free country!" he bellowed to his equally exercised companions. "I got a God-given right to keep and bear arms, and I got a God-given right to use 'em without some pansy-ass bureaucrat telling me you didn't win no pansy-ass lottery." He was at least six feet six, with a full, bushy red beard that obscured most of his face. His gut hung prominently over an immense jade and silver belt buckle, but his arms bulged tightly beneath the sleeves of his red flannel shirt like packaged hams. His expansive chest was just as well muscled, and a curly and tangled thatch of hair spilled out from the three open buttons of his shirt. "North American mountain man—a walking cliché" Diana called him, whispering.

"I know for a true fact that half the time the damn lottery is rigged anyway," he insisted.

"It is not!" his only slightly smaller friend bellowed back at him. "If it wasn't for the lottery, all the moose'd be killed off in a day by all the greedy damn fools like you." The others at the table nodded in sage agreement.

"That's all horse manure!" the lumberjack countered. "There've been moose around here ever since this land was made. And there've been licenses and lotteries for only a few years. So how come the moose didn't die off hundreds of years ago? The goddamned Indians killed a darn sight more of them than we ever could, but they're still around. Unfortunately, so're the Indians!"

"Maybe they should have a lottery for hunting Indians," one of the others suggested, "instead of giving them all those special favors and handouts."

"Custer didn't need no lottery. And he sure took out a healthy number of 'em before they got him." He laughed raucously. "I'll take those odds any day!"

Diana watched them with mounting disgust. "I don't believe these people."

"Indians are a kind of touchy subject up here, I gather," Brian said. "Not with everyone, of course, but you can see how your comment about them might not have gone over really big with Wilcox."

"I know, and I've been paying for it ever since. But I'm not even just talking about that. But these guys are—are just insensitive cretins."

"Don't judge everyone by your own standards. And remember"—he grinned—"they tell you to watch out for the bears this time of year. They're just coming out of hibernation, and they're very hungry. And never corner them, because there's nothing they can do but attack." He indicated the table of lumberjacks.

"I'm sure the same thing could be said for your friends over there."

Suddenly Diana became aware that the conversation at the other table had quieted. They all were looking over in her direction. At the same time she became aware of something else: She was the only woman in the room. When she and Brian had first come in, it had hardly been noticeable since there were so few other people. But now it was painfully obvious. She felt as if she'd somehow wandered into a men's locker room.

By their size and the clamor they were causing, the lumberjacks were the dominant group in the bar. And when they went silent and began to stare, so did everyone else.

The leader broke out into a broad, leering grin. It was one of the scariest looks she'd ever seen. He stood up slowly and ambled over in Brian's and Diana's direction.

Oh, shit, she thought.

He came over to their table and stood looming high above where she and Brian sat. "You know, you're kind of cute," he said to Diana. "Don't believe I've ever had the pleasure of seeing you here before, darlin'." She didn't look up but could feel him staring intensely down at her breasts. "Folks call me Tom. Whata they call you?"

She didn't answer him.

"I don't believe I caught that," he insisted.

"Diana," she said in a low voice.

"You must not be from around this way."

"No, ah, we're visiting."

Brian didn't say anything. He didn't move.

"From where might that be?" the mountain man asked.

"Atlanta."

"Is that a fact? And him, too?"

"Washington, D.C."

"Washington, D.C.! Well, you've certainly both come a long way to be with us. So how about you let us show you a little local hospitality?"

"Ah, thank you, but . . . that's okay."

"Oh, no trouble. I insist." He waved back in the direction of his table. "I'd like to have you come back and say hello to my friends. I'm sure your friend here wouldn't have any objections now, would you?" He glared at Brian, who still said nothing.

"Look, why don't you just leave us alone?" Diana said sharply.

Then she realized the whole bar was focused on her. She had just cornered a bear.

"Leave you alone!" he shouted. "What are you talking about, 'leave you alone'? You people come up here from your big fancy goddamned cities snooping around into our business and you want us to leave you alone? Well, I'm afraid that just ain't the way we do business around here." He grabbed her by the arm. His beefy fingers wrapped easily all the way around it and hurt her. Was Brian too terrified even to utter a protest?

The lumberjack grinned again and pulled her jerkily to her feet. "You be nice to me, and I'll be nice to you. *That's* the way we do business around here, honey."

No one in the bar made a move.

She instinctively put her hand on her skirt, pulling it protectively close to her legs. *Okay, Diana, honey,* she thought. *It's been a big lark up until now. This is where your luck finally runs out.*

"What's your name, sugar?" he demanded as he dragged her away from her chair. "I want to be able to introduce you proper to my friends."

She opened her mouth, but nothing came out. Her throat was paralyzed with fear.

"I think she's playing hard to get!" one of the others called over.

"Yeah, a real cock-teaser," said a third. He wasn't quite as large as his friends. "But I think she picked the wrong stud to pull that kind of shit with when she met up with Tom Bestman!" They all laughed heartily.

Diana looked desperately back to Brian, sitting at the table. His expression was strangely calm and placid. Unless he was just scared shitless.

"Leave her alone," he said quietly.

The lumberjack stopped in his tracks. "Did someone say something?" he asked.

"Yeah, the blond queer from Washington said to leave his broad alone," the smaller sidekick said helpfully.

"That's what I thought he said," said the larger man. "But I still can't believe I heard it. This guy's either braver than I thought or dumber than oyster shit." Without letting go of Diana's arm, he turned and marched back to where Brian was sitting. "Just sit there like a good little boy and we'll give your woman back when we finish with her—if there's anything left."

This prompted a new round of guffaws from the lumberjack table. Diana felt her bowels go to jelly, as if she were about to lose control.

Slowly Brian stood up. "Leave her alone," he said again. The bearded guy towered over him and must have weighed 150 pounds more than Brian.

"And I thought I told you to sit still like a good little boy until we're finished." He put a huge palm on Brian's shoulder and forced him back into his chair. Diana looked on in horror and, through her horror, found herself idly wondering if a small town rape-murder out west would make the papers back home.

"I think he needs a lesson in respect" was shouted from the far table.

"I think you're right," Tom replied. Diana cringed.

It happened before she could register it all.

Brian suddenly pushed back in his chair, extended his leg straight out, and sent his foot crashing into the lumberjack's kneecap. As he reached down to grab it, Brian spun out of the chair, turned, and, from a crouch whipped his leg out to the side, connecting squarely with the larger man's groin. The lumberjack gasped in pain and surprise. His eyes were wild with anger. He lunged for his attacker's neck, but Brian dodged out of the way and landed a combination with his fist into Tom's cheek and the point of his chin. Blood gushed from his mouth.

Diana couldn't believe her eyes.

The other lumberjacks clambered to their feet and rushed over to help. One grabbed Brian's arms from behind while another punched him in the stomach. Brian wheezed. Then he straightened his arms above his head and by suddenly dropping down to his knees was able to slide out of the hold. He elbowed the guy sharply in the midsection and kneed the other one between the legs.

The fourth man had used the delay to climb up onto a chair. He jumped from it onto Brian's back, and the two of them went clattering to the floor. Brian grabbed him around the neck, immobilizing his head, and smashed his fist at short range into his nose. Diana could hear the cartilage collapse.

By this time Tom had recovered his senses. While Brian was still on the ground, he lunged for him. Brian swerved his body rapidly, and Tom hit the deck with a thud that shook the floorboards. The lumberjack grabbed Brian by the ankle and pulled him over to him. Brian managed to whip around enough to kick him in the forehead and break his grip.

As he turned, the other two came at him together. In another moment they were joined by the third. They climbed on top of him and wrestled him to his feet for their leader's retribution. They held him tightly while Tom got into position in front. He punched Brian, first in the face, then over and over again in the belly, punishing him with the full force of his weight.

Diana winced and screamed. The lumberjack leered back at her through his swollen eyes. His battered face was even more threatening now.

"Maybe this'll teach you a little respect," he said, and punched Brian again with a blow that made his eyes bulge.

Brian spit back at him.

"What!" Tom yelled, and went again for Brian's throat.

The force of Tom's lunge was enough to make the men holding Brian loosen their grip to avoid the impact themselves. This was apparently just what Brian had counted on. He ducked as the lumberjack came at him, pivoted, grabbed him firmly around the neck, effortlessly flipped the huge man over his shoulder, and crashed him down onto his back. This then gave him the opportunity to grab two of the others in turn and throw them each against the wall, where they collapsed into a heap. The third one came up from behind, but sensing him, Brian spun around and poked his two outstretched fingers into his eyes. The man grabbed his face in agony and staggered backward.

Tom was outraged. He lumbered back to his feet, rushed at Brian, gripped his shoulder, and squeezed deeply into the muscle. Despite the obvious pain, Brian folded his arm back to keep Tom's hand there, then with the other hand twisted his adversary's wrist downward and halfway around.

Everyone in the room heard the wrist crack.

No one in the bar moved. Tom looked at Brian with a mixture of awe and bewilderment, the blood still flowing from several gashes on his face and chest. The other three were no better off. They looked as if they'd just stepped into the business end of a meat grinder, Diana thought.

Brian took a handkerchief out from his pocket and slowly wiped away the blood from his face. All eyes in the room were on him. He walked over to where Tom was standing and took hold of his forearm. It hung at a painful and unnatural angle. The lumberjack flinched at the touch, but when he saw that Brian wasn't intending to inflict any additional damage, he stood still. Brian pressed two fingers to the underside of Tom's wrist and felt for the pulse. Then he felt along the length of the forearm. "The wrist's broken," he said. "Let's see if we can rig up a splint."

Diana went behind the counter and came back with a long wooden kitchen spoon, the kind used for mixing batter. She laid it gently against Tom's forearm, barely resisting the temptation to hurt him with it. Brian glanced around for something to secure it with. He motioned for Tom to put one foot up on the nearby chair. Then he untied his boot and drew out the lace, which he wrapped several times around the spoon before fastening it.

"I think you ought to see a doctor about that," he said, and walked with Diana in the direction of the door.

"Where'd you learn to do all that?" she asked, taking hold of his arm and making no attempt to keep the admiration from her voice.

The bartender walked over to where Tom, still stunned and silent, was standing. "Didn't you see his star sapphire ring? Anyone who'd been in Nam woulda known he must be a navy SEAL. And you shoulda known better than to mess with him. Everybody knows SEALs are crazy!"

"I'm really sorry I got you into this," she said as they walked back toward the Roundup.

"I don't know that you did," he replied.

"What do you mean by that?"

"Probably nothing," he said. "It's just that with some things you never know."

Back inside the Moose Head, there was one man who'd been drinking alone all afternoon, propping up the end of the bar and ordering one Coors Light after another. He was the only other person there that afternoon whom none of the locals had ever seen before since this was his first time in the place. In fact, this was also his first trip to the state of Montana. Yet unlike Diana, he had cultivated the technique of blending into his surroundings, by both behavior and dress, and therefore had called no special attention to himself. Each time the bartender brought him another bottle, he quickly put his money down on the couner so that the bartender would have no reason to talk to him or direct any special attention his way.

The only way he might have called attention would have been to make his departure immediately after the two easterners had made theirs because once they left, his business at the Moose Head was also at an end.

He might also have called attention, theoretically, by recording the entire incident he had witnessed on film, but that would have been a dangerous and unacceptable breach of tradecraft. As it was, the audiotape from the recorder concealed beneath his vest would be of satisfactory quality, and in the confusion he had managed to snap off five or six telling shots with the Minox LX without being noticed.

He ordered a few more beers in succession and waited a decent interval after the fight had broken up and the apelike lumberjack had been attended to. Then he put down the price of the final beer, left a more than reasonable tip (though not one large enough to call special attention), and headed out of the bar for the pay phone at the local filling station.

There was also a pay phone at the Moose Head which he could have used, but there was no sense taking even the smallest unnecessary chance. And it would have been a very small chance since all he was calling about was to confirm his airplane reservations. The actual report would wait until he got back home.

"Now stay still," Diana ordered as she held Brian firmly by the chin and swabbed disinfectant across the corner of his mouth. He recoiled when she first touched him with the swab but said nothing. "I know it stings," she said sympathetically, "but we have to clean it off."

She was standing and facing him as he sat on the edge of her bed, the standard first-aid kit from her red cooler opened beside him. He wasn't too badly off, considering the pounding he'd taken. Nothing obviously broken. No need for stitches. None of the cuts was very deep, and the bruises all would heal on their own. It was amazing to her he was alive at all.

"You don't think this was . . . related, do you?" she asked.

"What do you mean?"

"Those men. You don't think they were put up to—to hurting you?"

"To hurting me? Maybe, but I doubt it. Possibly to give me a warning. Though I tend to be very dense about that sort of thing, so I'm afraid it didn't do any good. To kill me? No. If these guys had planned to kill me, they could have done it. And a lot cleaner than this, even within the setting of a barroom brawl."

Diana shuddered at the very thought. It wasn't one that seemed to affect him very much, though, one way or the other. He seemed to have a matter-of-fact placidness about death which must have come from seeing so much of it up close, on both the battlefield and the operating table. Since she was an epidemiologist, death to her was mostly an abstraction, a statistic to be included in the CDC's *Morbidity and Mortality Weekly Report*. There were a lot of things about him that were just completely outside her frame of reference.

"Okay, take your shirt off," she instructed.

"Why?"

"To see if you need any attention down there."

He flashed her a wry smile but then stood up and removed the torn and wrinkled shirt. He sat down on the bed again. She moved over next to him and spread her fingers out across the expanse of his chest and midsection, trying to think back to her emergency room rotations and recall the proper technique for palpating for possible subsurface trauma.

The skin had already turned a deep purple where the lumberjack had repeatedly punched him, and he reacted when she pressed in on it. She could have cried thinking of him being held by those others and beaten like that. But his muscles were exceptionally tight and hard. He was in very good shape.

She didn't know exactly when it happened. It didn't matter, really, but gradually, by slow and leisurely stages, the examination became a caress. She pushed his shoulder down until he was lying flat on the bed. Grazing her fingers all along the surface of his skin, she explored, no longer for his well-being but for her own curiosity, the details of his firm and muscular body. Her own body was alive with a deep and urgent physicality, such as she could not recall since those intensely physical days and nights of the antiwar movement—a physicality that penetrated to her core and permeated every cell of her being.

He pulled her down onto him and surrounded her back and shoulders with his arms. Effortlessly he slid down the zipper of her skirt. It fell away to either side, and she quivered from the sudden chill on her naked legs. She wrapped her arms around his neck. He smoothed the back of her walnut hair and kissed her pointy nose. She felt the comforting warmth and moistness between her thighs. He undid her blouse and stripped it from her shoulders. She tugged—at first tentatively, then more insistently—at the clasp and zipper of his pants.

In another moment they had rid each other of the rest of their clothing. Their eyes, then mouths locked with one thought only, and then they took each other in the mounting cataclysm—fulfilling, consuming, crowding all the empty places of their lives with this one great act of nature's faith and trust. She arched her back convulsively, stretching like some great cat, until only her neck and buttocks and heels touched the bed. And the twin cadence of their pulsing unity was as one and absolute.

Afterward they grew instantly quiet and still—each for their own reasons—and lay together totally absorbed, as if time were not moving at all. They had been fantastic together. She could not believe that a man who could fight so savagely could love so tenderly and expressively.

So he was a navy SEAL, she reflected. Or at least had been. One of a group of the most elite, highly trained secret commando killers. Back when she was in college, when the Vietnam tragedy was at its worst, Diana had decided that she could never take a man inside her who had himself taken lives. Did it mitigate in his favor then, she wondered now, that the man in question had subsequently saved many other lives? And more to the point, did it matter that for all her professed pacifism and belief in nonaggression, to watch him rip the shit out of four mountain men had turned her on incredibly? That was the truly honest question.

"Give me someone who is truly honest, and I'll make him into a revolutionary," Che Guevara had said, and she had quoted it often back then.

Learning to be open and to keep yourself alive to new things and new ideas was perhaps the most revolutionary idea of all.

Her fingers moved slowly along his back and stopped at his right shoulder when they felt the skin rise slightly in a long, uneven ripple. She propped her head up to study the painful-looking scar, at least five inches across.

"How did you get it?" she whispered.

"RPD round," he said.

"What's that?"

"A seven point sixty-two millimeter machine-gun bullet. Russian-made machine gun."

"Where did it happen?"

"In the Rung Sat."

"Where?"

"Somewhere in the delta . . . a place you've never heard of . . . back in '66."

She would have been in high school, probably at some dance or party. "Anybody else hurt?"

"I was the only one to make it back."

She lowered her head again and ran her tongue over the taut, whitened flesh of his scars, as if twenty years later she could somehow through her understanding lick away his wounds. She rested her cheek against his neck and held him. Gently she rocked him back and forth, cradling him in her own compassion.

Later, as they both were getting dressed, Diana announced, "I want to come back with you."

"What?"

"Just what I said. I want to come back to Washington with you."

"I don't think that would be a good idea. Not until I find out what's going on."

"I can help you."

He stopped buttoning his shirt and came over to her as she was about to step into her skirt. "You can help me more from Atlanta. I can use your resources there. Go through your computer files, and see if we can come up with a definitive diagnosis for Hardesty's disease."

"I can do that from Washington just as easily. As long as I have the access codes, we can tap into the computer by telephone. And anyway, there are many more important things to be followed up."

"Like what, for instance?"

"The fragments."

He frowned.

"You can't keep it to yourself anymore, Brian. The puzzle belongs to both of us now."

"Yes," he replied sardonically. "I remember. But what are you going to tell them at work?"

"As you said before, I'm resourceful. I'll think of something. I'll say I want my vacation leave. Or better still, I'll come up with some project we should be doing in Washington."

He seemed to mull this over a moment, but finally he said, "No, I can't agree to that. You could be in danger if you're with me."

She crossed her arms over her chest and shook her head once emphatically. "I don't care."

"Look, Diana, you're not in college playing SDS protest time any longer. This isn't any little game we're talking about. You can't go back to your dorm when you get bored."

"I know. But I think I can help. And I want to be with you."

"It's out of the question right now. I can't allow it."

"Then I'll just come back to Washington on my own and hide in your bathroom."

"And this time I really will beat your ass." He patted her there lightly as a warning.

"No, you won't," she answered with confidence, patting him somewhat harder on the same place. "You need me!"

11

It was the first time Diana had been in the city since college. On the ride in from the airport, as the cab crossed the marble span of Memorial Bridge, the Lincoln Memorial, the Washington Monument, and the Capitol dome beckoned in gleaming white against the evening sky. Everything looked in order, just as she had left it more than a dozen years before.

But as they headed up Twenty-third Street past the State Department (scene of a memorable demonstration in the spring of 1970) and crossed Pennsylvania Avenue into the downtown area that was familiar to her, the buildings and surroundings began to take on a noticeably strange and different cast. It was as if the nation's capital were no longer alive or vibrant but had been preserved for her benefit and that of other visitors. All the people on the streets were actors, appropriately costumed, and all the buildings maintained to look as they had between the seventh and eighth decades of the twentieth century. A museum town, like Williamsburg or Old Sturbridge. As soon as possible she had to come back and see these places on foot.

It was after dark when they arrived at Brian's apartment. The building was uptown in a part of the city she'd never had much to do with. Brian unpacked and hunted for a spot for her three red coolers while she wandered.

It was obvious that the apartment had never known the touch of a woman.

The second bedroom had been fixed up for a little girl. From the picture on Brian's nightstand she was absolutely adorable, with his blond hair and beautiful features, which would one day be as strong as his. Her room was all done in yellows and blues, with all the requisite puppy dogs and pandas on the walls and in all the other appropriate locations. Diana went to the closet. She opened it and examined the collection of little-girl dresses hanging there: a lacy purple velvet for wintertime; a gathered white eyelet cotton for the summer. She thought of Brian in the bar in Montana, then tried to imagine him shopping with his daughter and buying her these frocks.

She walked over to the dresser. There were crayon marks on its white Formica surface where the young artist had gone off her paper. Sitting on one side was a clear Sesame Street bank with about thirty-five or forty shiny pennies in it. On the other was a Mr. Potato Head. From the positioning of his anatomical features, one would have concluded he'd been the victim of some cruel genetic accident. There was also a tray of plastic jewelry and different-colored barrettes and a naked Barbie doll, whose own hair could be combed and brushed but in this case was not.

But what dominated the dresser top arrangement was the photograph, a framed picture of a younger Brian. At least it looked as if it must be Brian, standing in a dense jungle setting and dressed in mud-covered green tiger-stripe camouflage utilities. A matching tiger-stripe beret was flopped over his left eye. He was grinning at the camera from a face blackened with camouflage paint, and he carried in his hands a slide-action twelve-gauge shotgun. His chest was crossed with a double sling of cartridge belts, the webbed belt around his waist held a pistol, utility pouches, and several grenades, and there was a long black-handled knife strapped to his calf in a leather sheath. All in all, as she would have said around the time the photo was taken, not the kind of mother you'd want to fuck with.

How times had changed.

Engraved on the edge of the frame was a gold eagle perched on a crossed anchor and trident and clutching a flintlock pistol, which she took to be the SEAL insignia. It was ironically similar to the anchor and winged caduceus of the Public Health Service emblem.

"I'm sorry," Brian said. He'd come up quietly behind her. He was good at that. "For some reason, it happens to be Katie's favorite picture of me. She found it in one of my old lockers, and I haven't been able to get her to part with it."

"Ah, that's okay," Diana replied. The photograph still held her attention. "But I can't believe that's really you."

"It's really me, all right."

"Well, you certainly were a mean-looking son of a bitch, weren't you?"

"That's the image we were trying to cultivate."

"I thought the SEALS were supposed to be mainly swimmers."

"That's part of it."

"Not exactly the Mark Spitz image."

"Mark Spitz never jumped out of a plane into the open sea to mine an enemy harbor."

It was late by now. Diana hurriedly unpacked her duffel and realized she had nothing clean left with her. When she'd packed, she hadn't planned on staying away much longer than the weekend. She'd do her laundry tomorrow, but that didn't take care of tonight.

"Have you got something I can sleep in?" she asked Brian.

"I'm sure I can find something," he said. He rummaged through his closet and came out with an army green T-shirt. "Here," he said, tossing it to her. "This ought to do okay."

She unfolded the shirt and held it up. It was large—his size—and would fit her like a nightie. On the middle of the front in that fuzzy orange lettering was embossed a large "C4." Above it was the translation of the symbols: COMBAT CASUALTY CARE COURSE. Beneath the C4 was written CAMP BULLIS, TEXAS, and the slogan WAR HAS NO WINNERS, ONLY SURVIVORS.

"This place is just full of pleasant little reminders," Diana commented.

"We took that quite seriously," Brian said. "You'd have to be a fool not to."

Brian went into the other room to make a phone call, and Diana went to the bathroom to ready herself for bed.

They got into bed together. She instantly thought back to the previous day's adventure and to the rapturous evening at the Roundup. But tonight it felt different. She was lying next to him, ready to cuddle up close, and his warm, firm body was still the same. But other things were not the same. This was no longer a first meeting on neutral turf. She was suddenly very lonely, and the feeling was all the more painful and acute because it had come over her by surprise. It seemed silly in a way, she thought, but she couldn't get rid of it. Was it that the equality that had always been so important to her was gone? The human equation no longer balanced? She was wrapped in his shirt (God knew what he was doing when he first wore it), sleeping in his bed that smelled only of him and not of her, in a city that had once been hers but no longer was. Nothing here was hers. And she couldn't get over the uncomfortable feeling that the only woman who would ever truly belong in this place was Katie.

She shouldn't have insisted on coming back with him. She always did things like this, and that's what she got for being so impulsive.

She didn't know if Brian could read her thoughts, but he must have sensed that something was troubling her or caught the tears welling at the corners of her eyes because he pulled her over close to him and guided her head down to his chest.

"What can I do?" he whispered.

She wrapped her arms around his neck and said, "Don't leave me," though that wasn't what she was feeling.

"I was calling my friend Gregory Cheever I told you about from Bethesda when I was in the other room," he responded. "He's going to pick up Hardesty's insulin bottle on his way in to work, and his girlfriend Jill's got me cleared, so I don't have to go in till the middle of the afternoon tomorrow. I can spend all the time up till then with you."

She smiled through trickling tears.

"What would you like to do?"

She sat up in his bed, with his T-shirt clinging to her and covering her to the middle of her thighs, and said, "I'd like to show you *my* city!"

Right after breakfast they took the Metro down to Foggy Bottom. The last time she'd been here the subway system was still under construction. While they waited for the train, she thought back to that photo on Katie's dresser. How different a picture of herself at the same age would have been. It would have shown a girl with mini-length skirt and past-the-shoulder-length hair, no bra, a button bearing some radical slogan, and such other articles as her mother would have been certain to disapprove of. That had been *her* uniform.

The train came within a few minutes. It was much cleaner and brigher and friendlier than the ones she was used to in Boston and New York, and unlike Atlanta's sparkling MARTA, it was less of a glorified amusement park ride. But on this particular day she wanted to get off the train and out of the station as quickly as she could. It wasn't part of her Washington.

They went first to the place that most definitely was: the gray reinforced-concrete campus of George Washington University. They walked to the far end on Nineteenth Street, to a huge converted apartment house of colonial red brick.

"This is Thurston Hall," she announced, "the freshman girls' dorm. Universally known as the Zoo for all the obvious reasons. The third floor is where I lived when I first got to college," she explained. *And where I quickly and joyfully surrendered my virginity amid a world gone mad,* she might have added.

"We watched Mark Rudd and Abbie Hoffman speak from this very spot during the November Moratorium. Tom Hayden and the Berrigans were over there behind the quad. GW was the college closest to the White House, so it became a focus for a lot of the movement's activities. Being in Washington, it was the staging area for all the major antiwar demonstrations."

They went inside the lobby and then briefly toured the halls, something that would have been taboo for a man back when she first arrived. But though she had come back here to try to turn her nostalgia into some new reality, what she saw instead was that depressing dirtiness and student squalor that don't bother you until you yourself have outgrown them.

"It's funny the things you remember," she said musingly, not much happier than she'd been.

Brian picked up on this, smiled, and said, "Then let me tell you my favorite dorm story. I'll never forget it. When I was in med school, I was invited to a dorm party over at BU. They had all these hotshot scientists and engineers from MIT over there, and they'd spiked the punch with their own fermented alcohol. So one guy comes in to the party. Everybody knew him as kind of a gork. He's already nearly flat on his ass from swilling beer when he gets there, and he takes a huge swig of this punch. I mean, I'm not exaggerating, the man goes green immediately. He turns in his tracks, rushes out of the party room, and dashes straight down the hall for the closest john. He barrels in, goes straight to the nearest toilet stall, and flings open the door just in time to heave his guts out."

"Oh, my God." Diana grimaced.

"Unfortunately, there's someone else sitting in there, peacefully minding his own business."

"Oh, no!"

"Oh, yes. They put a plaque on that stall. It's a shame they didn't have a photograph to go with it."

They came up Twenty-first Street and stood in the plaza outside the block-long University Center. Classes were out for the spring semester, and the first summer session was just getting under way. The few kids they saw played Frisbee on the well-tended lawn or lounged aimlessly in the sun.

"This campus is a real hotbed of student rest," Brian said dryly.

"I know. It's depressing, isn't it? But it didn't used to be this way. The day after the Kent State killings this whole site was filled with students. You couldn't move, there were so many people," Diana said, remembering. "Then the police started lobbing tear gas at us, and we all ran inside. The university administration tried to force us back out into the streets to get our heads kicked in—they were never exactly sympathetic—but we refused to go. There was an incredible sense of camaraderie then, an incredible solidarity."

"I remember the pictures," Brian retorted. "All these kids in army surplus jackets protesting the military."

"A lot of them came by them honestly," Diana replied. "We had a lot of Vietnam vets in the movement. Terrific people. Guys who'd seen it firsthand and could cut through the lies the government was feeding us."

"I had no problem with any of them. What they said was true, and they'd earned their right to say it. It was the spoiled, privileged upper-middle-class jerks who'd never had to work for anything but knew everything that griped my ass," he stated. "The ones to whom the war was merely an abstraction, something convenient for them to focus their adolescent rage and sexual tension on."

"Oh, you mean people like me?"

"No, that's not what I'm talking about."

"Yes, you are." She said it emphatically but with a smile. "I'm just the kind of people you're talking about. All right, I came from Westchester County instead of the wheatfields of Indiana, and most of us were spoiled and used to having our own way. But we were also serious and dedicated and honestly believed in what we were doing. Our asses, especially the men's, were on the line. The image you have is of a flock of sheep being docilely led by a few wild-eyed, radical, lunatic-fringe people who burn buildings and blow up ROTC offices. But that's not how it was, and if you believe it, that's really a shame. Because if you really believe that there can't be a mass protest movement rising from the passion and outrage of the people themselves, then I don't think you can believe in anything worthwhile. Maybe being spoiled, pampered upper-middle-class allowed us to be motivated by things other than money or completely practical considerations, abstract things like justice. But if we forget about or lose those motivations entirely, what are we left with? I did what I did because *I* believed our cause was right. I still do. I'd do it again. Can you say the same?"

"That's not an easy question," Brian said.

On their way down Pennsylvania Avenue they paused at the gate in front of the White House.

"I remember the first time I saw it," Brian said. "It was on a school bus trip with my junior high school class. We worked and saved up for a whole year. I'd never seen anything so impressive or magnificent in my life."

"I remember the first time I *truly* saw it," Diana said. "The night of November thirteenth, 1969. We began at Arlington Cemetery across the bridge, just when it started to get dark. More than forty thousand of us. I was right behind Dr. Spock. Each of us had a candle in a paper cup to protect it from the wind and a cardboard sign with a name on it—the name of an American GI killed in Vietnam. Mine was Larry Lee Johnson. I still remember. Nobody said anything as we marched; everyone was silent. Then, as each of us got to this spot here, we shouted out the name on our placard into the night. And you can bet President Nixon heard us, wherever he was. It was forty hours later before all the people had passed by and all the names were called. It was one of the most moving things I ever saw. Truly heroic."

She was quiet for a while and held on to the wrought-iron

fence for support. She felt a tear creeping down her cheek, and Brian handed her his handkerchief. But he had the good grace not to dry her face for her or otherwise to touch or help her.

A few moments later she looked up at him and smiled. "Okay, I think we can go back home now."

"I think we have one more stop to make," Brian said, and took her hand.

The Vietnam Veterans Memorial is a wedge of polished black granite the twin 250-foot-long walls of which intersect at a 125-degree angle and cut a deep gash into the soft grassy mall along Constitution Avenue. Its east wall points toward the Washington Monument; its west wall, toward the Lincoln Memorial, both soaring, exalted structures of gleaming white marble which lure the visitor up to them, in marked contrast with the plain black V that leads the visitor down into its depths. Yet it is more emotionally charged than either of the other two, and not merely because of its relationship to our own time and experience.

At the center of the V, at its deepest point below ground level, is carved an explanation of its significance:

IN HONOR OF THE MEN AND WOMEN OF THE ARMED FORCES
OF THE UNITED STATES WHO SERVED IN THE VIETNAM
WAR. THE NAMES OF THOSE WHO GAVE THEIR LIVES
AND OF THOSE WHO REMAIN MISSING ARE INSCRIBED
IN THE ORDER THEY WERE TAKEN FROM US.

Each wall is composed of seventy separate panels covered with chiseled gold lettering—five names to a line, enough lines to list the more than 55,000 who died.

Behind the wall, up on level ground, is a tall flagpole the bronze base of which bears the seals of the five services. And near it is a life-size statue executed in a hyperrealistic style, depicting three representative soldiers of the conflict. All are young and handsome, all are strong, and their faces look toward the two black walls with expressions that are equal parts of resolution and bewilderment.

As Brian and Diana walked down the path of gray granite blocks, they passed an incredible variety of people: tourists in shorts and sandals; pregnant mothers pushing strollers; old people in wheelchairs; workingmen and women in business suits;

soldiers in their uniforms; Scout troops—a cross section of humanity that ranged from the merely curious to the permanently and painfully involved. This last group was obvious by their presence, for they wept openly and made no pretense of disguising their emotions. Since its dedication on Memorial Day of 1982 this place had been their place.

"Each of us remembers different heroes," Brian said to Diana.

Then he walked ahead, to a spot on the wall he seemed to know quite well. Many people here seemed to have similar spots. When she caught up with him again, he was standing right up close. His eyes were almost shut, and his fingertips were tracing over the name GERALD F. MCNEELY.

He stepped back, and Diana said to him, "I guess you know a lot of names up on that wall."

Brian nodded.

"But he was someone special?"

"Yeah, he was someone special."

They continued up the granite path. "I remember the first time I became aware of Vietnam," Diana softly recounted. "It was in the third grade. Mark Mayer had a stamp album. His father was in the Foreign Service and used to bring him stamps from all over the world. He had this big beautiful blue stamp with a golden dragon on it. All the kids admired it. He said it was from a place called Vietnam that none of us had ever heard of. But just the name alone sounded so wonderful and exotic that we all wanted to go. I guess some of us eventually did. It's funny the way these things come up."

On their way out they passed a man about Brian's age. He was sitting on one of the park benches near the directories that list the panel and line location of each of the names. He was dressed in worn combat fatigues and gazed with unshielded contempt at the raucous and undignified tourists for whom this was just one more stop on the Washington tour.

"A lot of people died over there to protect people like you," he declared bitterly as they walked by.

Diana turned in shock, but Brian kept walking straight ahead.

"Did you hear what he said?"

Brian indicated that he had.

"Aren't you going to say anything?" Diana asked him.

"No," he answered. "What for?"

As they headed for the Mall and the Smithsonian Metro station, they shared a panoramic view of the entire memorial site. They could see men and women planting small American flags in the narrow strip of grass in front of particular spots on the wall. They could see others with their hands folded in prayer. And they could see others still, each with white paper and a stone, or gray paper and a piece of charcoal, tracing over one special name. They were different, yet each bore silent testimony to a world of lost joy and lost opportunities: the opportunity to be a son or to have one; the opportunity to be a husband or to have one; the opportunity to be a father or to have one.

Diana shook her head sadly as they left. "What a waste," she said. "What an incredible waste."

"In most ways it definitely was," Brian said. "I'm not sure it was in all ways."

BETHESDA, MARYLAND

There wasn't much for Brian to do at the hospital when he got there in the middle of the afternoon, and he was grateful for that. He was still fatigued from the trip, and the morning's excursion had left him shaken and depressed. The minor procedures on his slate wouldn't be any challenge, but if possible, he preferred not to undertake any major operations when he was feeling this way. Surgery is a totally involving, totally consuming effort under the best of conditions, and when you don't have all your resources to devote to it, well, that's when the mistakes happen.

He hadn't been in his office for more than fifteen minutes or so when Gregory knocked once on the door and then slouched in. He had an uncanny ability to know just where a person was when he wanted to talk.

Brian had been gone for only a couple of days, but he greeted the radiologist as if he'd just come back from a WestPac tour with the fleet. Maybe it was because Gregory was one of the few tangible elements of continuity left in Brian's life, one of the few people or things he knew he could count on.

Gregory ambled over to the orange plastic chair and sat in it sideways, his leg slung over the metal arm. Knowing Gregory wouldn't be offended, Brian went back to his paperwork.

"So the girl from CDC came back with you, huh?"

"Yeah. I couldn't stop her." He continued concentrating on the accumulation of forms and documents on his desk.

"Irresistible charm, I guess."

"I guess."

"How's it working out?"

"I don't know what that means."

"Jill and I are anxious to meet her."

This time Brian looked up. "Let's wait a little while on that one."

Gregory shrugged. "Suit yourself. You know best. So . . . have you made any progress in your little investigation since I talked to you?"

"No. I haven't even had time to think about it yet."

"I picked up that insulin bottle from your place this morning. Thought you'd want to know that the assay came back from the lab just now."

"And?"

"It's one of those old good news-bad news situations, I guess you'd say. Which do you want first?"

"Better give me the good news."

"Okay. The good news is that we don't have to worry about Shipley's having sent out degraded or adulterated insulin. No cause for public panic or concern."

"That is good," Brian said. "Then the bad news must be that Sam Hardesty did want to kill himself," he stated somberly.

"No," said Gregory. "The bad news is that it wasn't insulin at all."

"What?"

"That bottle marked U-one hundred Regular was nothing but sterile water. Brian, somebody went to a lot of trouble to change it on him."

By the time Brian left for the day, his head was reeling. Over and over again he imagined someone stealing into Sam Hardesty's house—just as he had—and replacing his life-giving prescription with a worthless liquid. By the time Hardesty could have noticed anything was wrong, it would have been too late, especially if this had been done to his entire insulin supply.

Brian crossed the pedestrian bridge to the parking garage where he'd left his car. Since it was rush hour, he wanted to avoid Wisconsin Avenue. Instead, he went out the hospital's side entrance, past the Uniformed Services University of the Health Sciences—the military's medical school—and onto Jones Bridge

Road. The light was with him, so he pulled right out into the flow of traffic.

This was a good shortcut back to Connecticut Avenue, Brian had long ago concluded. It avoided almost all the commuter traffic out to the Bethesda suburbs. But the main problem with Jones Bridge Road was that because it was relatively underutilized, people drove on it as if it were an expressway, barreling down the street at fifty or sixty miles per hour.

Today was no exception. Almost as soon as Brian made the turn, a kid in a customized pickup truck with no muffler came whizzing by, weaving insanely between the slower-moving cars. Just as he came alongside, he suddenly cut in front of Brian's Volvo.

Brian slammed on the brakes. Nothing happened. He pumped them furiously. Still nothing. The pedal went all the way down to the floor. He jerked up the hand brake. It slowed him slightly but not enough.

There was no time to do anything else. He saw a spot just up ahead on the right where an expanse of grassy hill led up to the chain-link fence of the golf course behind. He quickly maneuvered into the right-hand lane and swerved the car over the curb, off the road, and into the bank. The Volvo bounced violently, and he cracked his head on the ceiling. A sharp pain stabbed down his neck.

Instantly he sized up his options. If he hit the fence directly at the speed he was going, he'd tear right through it and onto the golf course. There were a lot of people out there, and he'd surely hit some of them. The only chance was to steer straight ahead and glance off the fence from the side, slowing the car down as he did.

He hit the chain fence just about at his right front wheel. He heard the sound of metal ripping. The car dug a trench of several hundred feet as he was thrown from side to side. Thank God he was wearing his shoulder belt.

Finally the car came to a stop. Slowly, carefully he tested the various parts of his body to see that nothing was cut or broken. He'd been extremely lucky. He threw his weight against the door and forced it open. He staggered from the car. People who'd seen the accident and stopped ran over to help him. One was even a doctor from Bethesda.

* * *

Gregory Cheever had just gotten home when the phone rang. It was Brian. "Can you come get me?" he asked.

"Where are you?" Gregory said.

"The Volvo place on River Road. They just towed my car."

"Is everything all right?"

"Sort of. I'll explain when you get here."

"My God!" Gregory exclaimed when he arrived at the dealer and saw Brian and the car. Fortunately the car was in worse shape than Brian was. "What a strange thing for the brakes to give out all at once, and with no warning."

"Stranger than you think," Brian said. "Volvo uses a dual triangular interlocked braking system. That means two completely independent systems. It's one of the reasons I bought the car. If one of the systems fails, the other should still deliver about eighty percent of the braking power. Both systems don't fail at the same time on their own. I mean, it can happen, but it's a one in ten million shot."

"So then . . . ?"

"That's right," Brian said.

Gregory was perplexed. "This doesn't make any sense. It's all main streets between the hosptial and your place, isn't it?"

"Yep."

"If someone had done this to you on purpose, if someone were trying to get rid of you—God, listen to the way I'm talking—he'd know enough to realize that on the route you take home during rush hour, you'd never get up enough speed to get yourself killed. You'd obviously crash without your brakes and probably get yourself banged up pretty bad, but not bad enough to kill you, especially in a Volvo."

"You're right."

"So, I hate to even say it, but if someone wanted you out of the way, why didn't he just try shooting you or something? Or at least wait to futz with your car till he knew you'd be out on the highway, driving at high speed?"

"I asked myself the same question. But a shooting makes noise, and it's pretty obvious, particularly if you're going to shoot a doctor. You'll have the police out in droves. And I said the same thing to myself about the brakes. Between the hospital and my place no brake failure is likely to cause a fatal accident. But look at this."

He brought Gregory around to the front of the car, had him

kneel, and pointed up behind the rubber-coated bumper. There was a little box wrapped in tape with wires coming out of it that was attached to the inner metal lining. "This is pretty slick."

"What is it?"

"That's a blasting cap. Don't worry, I've already defused it. And this is a container of Composition C-three. Not the kind of thing you just happen to have lying around the house. It's a highly effective plastic explosive that catches fire easily. We used to use it a lot back in Nam for underwater demolition work."

"What sets it off? A timer?"

"It can, but not in this case. Look closely over here. A tiny plunger attached to the blasting cap whose head rests directly against the inside of the bumper. Now the Volvo has a bumper sensitive to a three-mile-per-hour impact. So if I'd even *touched* another car or a barricade or anything with the bumper, it would have been 'Kiss me good-bye.' "

He stood up, and they walked around to the side of the vehicle. "Oh, and I also found this in the back seat." He pointed to a practically empty liter bottle of Cutty Sark. "I'm sure it was put here for the benefit of the police. If they found pieces in the vicinity, it would help explain the accident since there wouldn't be enough of the car or of me left for a meaningful investigation."

12

"Someone's just tried to kill you!" Diana exclaimed. "Why aren't you upset?"

"I am upset," Brian quietly assured her.

"Then why aren't you showing it? Why aren't you even a little bit hysterical?"

"What good would that do? It wouldn't change the fact. Someone would still be trying to kill me, and I'd be out of control." That was simply the reality. It seemed self-evident to him. And if it didn't to her, there was nothing he could do about it. If you didn't understand on your own, it was not the kind of thing someone could easily explain. He stood up, walked across the room, and stared out the window so as not to have to provide any elaboration.

"Sometimes I really don't understand what makes you tick," Diana called after him, punching her fist into the pillow on the sofa back to show her exasperation.

They sat in the living room of Brian's apartment. The reflection of traffic intersecting the halo of streetlights on Connecticut Avenue moved gray shadows across the ceiling. Gregory and Jill were there with them. Diana had spent the afternoon writing her EPI-2, her field report on the Montana case. She was wearing a pair of cutoff jeans and Brian's C-4 T-shirt since she'd been in the middle of doing laundry when they all showed up. Brian introduced her quickly to his friends. Under the particular circumstances a long, involved greeting didn't seem to be called for. And after that no one had said anything for a while.

"What about going to some authority?" Diana finally suggested.

"The Montgomery County police interviewed me after the accident," Brian replied. "I've reported everything that would be helpful to the insurance company. It'll put an investigator on the case. If either one of them comes up with anything, fine. But I don't think they will."

"Probably not," Diana said. "You haven't given them anything to go on."

He turned back to her. "Nothing I tell them is going to help them protect me. And any additional information I give out only increases my exposure."

"Then go tell someone else who can do more," she said challengingly.

"Who else should I go to?"

"I don't know. But someone's trying to kill you!"

"We've already established that," said Brian. The strain of fatigue was plain in his voice.

But she clearly wasn't letting the issue drop. "Brian, someone's got to be able to help. All you told the police was about the accident itself. Did you say anything about the other people who died or the fragments or anything else that's happened?"

"No," he replied testily.

"Why not? Why do you insist on playing secret agent?"

He came back over to the sofa and sat sideways, facing her. He put one hand on her shoulder to direct her attention to him. "Look, Diana, I'm not trying to avoid this, and I'm not making a game of it. But there's something you've got to understand. Whoever's done this isn't just a common criminal who'd break into your house or snatch your purse. He or they are pretty sophisticated. They know exactly what they're doing. They're expert at covering their tracks. And they've obviously got good sources of intelligence. The local police aren't set up for this kind of thing. They don't have the manpower, the resources, or the experience." He paused. She stared straight at him. She didn't offer any rebuttal, but the set of her jaw and the unwavering depth of her clear blue eyes stated that she wasn't backing down either.

"I know what I'm talking about," he said.

"Aren't you at least going to report the fake insulin business? That was a clear-cut crime—a murder—that someone should know about. And it probably affects us directly."

"Report it to who? The West Deer Creek sheriff? What good is that going to do?"

"What about the FBI?"

"You can't just call up the FBI and invite them to come over and investigate. There's no motive, no suspects. There's no evidence of anything within their jurisdiction."

Up until this point the two visitors had been merely spectators, but now Gregory sat forward and inched closer to the front of his chair. "I understand what you're saying, Brian," he said, "but Diana's right. You can't just sit back and do nothing."

"I never said I was going to do nothing," Brian replied.

"I mean, they failed this time," Gegory continued. "But whoever it is, won't they try to get you again?"

"Could be," Brian said, not able to keep the slight trace of hostility out of his voice. "But if they're professionals, as they obviously are, they'll realize that they've blown one well-planned chance. The greatest risk for professionals is exposure. So the odds are they won't come right back and try again. At least not right away."

"For some reason, I'm not taking much comfort from those odds," Gregory said.

"Neither am I," Brian said. "But one thing *is* for sure. If they know who I am and what I've been doing, they know who I've been associating with and can surmise that I've been talking. So we have to assume that anyone close to me is no safer than I am."

Gregory blanched. Maybe it was the excitement and confusion of the past few hours, but he hadn't thought in those terms up till now. It was unnerving to think that for the first time in his secure and complacent life he might be in real physical danger. It was unnerving to be drawn this far out of his element, to be sucked into a web of uncertainty and violence. And it was unnerving to sense that Brian was being drawn deeper into his own element, one that had merely been dormant but never completely gone.

"So what do you think we ought to do?" he asked.

"I'm not sure," Brian replied. "But we've got to do it fast."

He divided his gaze among the three of them. They, in turn, looked to each other for answers or suggestions.

"All right," he said. "What have we got to work with so far? And where do we begin?"

Everyone was quiet. Diana bit her lip, and Gregory played with his thumbs. Finally Jill began tentatively. "I'm used to working with computers. And computers figure everything out using very simple logic. No matter how complex the problem is, a computer program reduces it to a series of yes-no propositions. It may come up with a string of a thousand or more of them, but everything is still broken down into extremely basic components."

"I think Jill's on to something," said Diana.

"What do you mean?" Brian asked.

She moved herself onto the arm of the sofa to speak more easily to the other three. Brian could see that it was one of the instinctive physical moves she had cultivated to assert her control quickly over a situation. "I don't deal with computers except tangentially," she explained, "but in my field we approach poblems in a lot of the same ways. The first thing we do when we investigate a case is try to come up with a descriptive epidemiology: who has been affected in terms of age, sex, occupation, physical condition, socioeconomic level; proximity to the source; preexisting conditions. . . . I could reel off a whole long list for you. Then we figure out which of these descriptive characteristics are most commonly and most severely associated with the condition."

Brian touched Diana on the wrist. "So what you're saying is?"

"Very simple," she said, turning her body to him. "We have a number of deaths that we know about, none, apparently, from natural causes. They seem random, yet from what's happened, it's reasonable at this point to assume they might be in some way related. And they also might be related to the attempt made on you. So we begin by compiling the descriptive data about each of the subjects and move out from there. It may not work. It may not get us anywhere, but it's all we've got to go on now. And even if it ends in a blind alley, that'll tell us something, too."

"What sort of descriptive data are you talking about?" asked Gregory.

Diana counted off on her fingers. "Well, we know, for instance, that they're all men, all approximately the same age, and all were marines in Vietnam at the same time."

"And in the same unit," added Brian.

"Right," she said. "And that's a good place to begin because we're able to define a general target population. But in epidemiological terms, that only scratches the surface. The questions get increasingly subtle and sublime. What did each of these men do while he was in the marines? Did any or all of them have contact with the same individual or group? Did they all get along, or did they dislike each other? Maybe most important, have they had contact with each other since they've been back, particularly in the time leading up to their deaths?"

"And how do we find all this out?" Gregory inquired.

"Some of it will be in written records," Diana answered. "When we need this kind of information for an EIS investigation, the first thing we do is figure out what kinds of written records exist. If we're dealing with an outbreak at a school, for instance, there are usually pretty complete health records on each student. The military is particularly good on this, because it keeps personnel files on every recruit. Most of the work we did on the effects of the A-bomb testing in the 1950s was based on personnel files. So a lot of what we need will be in files, if we can just get access to them."

"I'll do the best I can on that part," Jill said.

"Then from there it's just a question of following up every possible lead." Diana eased herself down off the arm of the sofa and back to her place next to Brian.

"And how do we go about that?" Gregory asked. A high-energy level had never been one of his strong suits, and he was growing noticeably tired just thinking about the implications.

"Well," said Diana, "the emblem of the Epidemic Intelligence Service is a sole with a round hole near the toe, which symbolizes 'shoe leather epidemiology.' We just get out there and pound the pavement."

Gregory's yawn was too overwhelming to stifle. While he was totally absorbed with it, Jill poked him playfully in his soft, rounded gut. But he reacted—predictably—with a squeal of protest, as if any slight assault would do him irreparable harm.

"You're such a sissy," Jill said.

"Yeah, and I'm still alive, and I take great personal pride in that accomplishment. Can't anyone let me be a coward in peace? If you survive the elementary school playground, sissies are left alone. It's the heroes like Commander Thorpe over here that the baddies are out for. What people like me have to watch out for is when we happen to stray accidentally into the line of fire."

"They might make a hero out of you yet." Jill grinned.

"What would be the appropriate thing for me to say right now: 'Over my dead body!'? Don't worry, that's what I'm thinking." He watched Brian's broadening smile. He was used to this type of reaction. People like Gregory had to get used to it. "You don't have to be so smug, Commander," he called out. "You know I'm not going to abandon you in your hour of need"—he shot a glance over to Jill—"much as I'd like to."

It was then that Jill hit him full force with the sofa pillow and said threateningly, "We're doubling your aerobic workouts as of tomorrow! It's high time we got you in shape."

"If one thing doesn't kill me, another will," Gregory said glumly.

"That's the spirit!" Brian declared, leaning over and slapping him firmly on the shoulder.

"Would you like to hit me, too?" Gregory said to Diana. "Why should you be the only one left out?"

She laughed but didn't take him up on the offer. "Thanks, but I'm still a pacifist," she stated.

"A hard-core pacifist," Brian said. "She'll kill for her principles." Diana stuck her tongue out at him. "Okay, we're even. So now where should we go from here?" he asked her.

She sat still for a moment with her arms folded across her chest. "The first thing we do is list everything we know about each of the dead marines. If we were talking about a potentially huge group like those we deal with at CDC, we'd have to set up a computer program. But for six people, we can do it mechanically. Then we compare the lists and see if we notice any significant overlaps."

"Then what?" Brian prodded.

"Then comes the shoe leather part," she answered. "We have to find and talk to anyone we can who's been close to any of them or can tell us anything about them. If we do it right, this is usually the most telling step."

"That sounds great," Gregory said. "But these guys were spread all over the country. You're talking about an enormous amount of shoe leather, not to mention the fact that we've all got jobs and places we have to be. And you're not even in yours at the moment. Pretty soon you'll use up your leave and they're going to start missing you. So how can we even pull this off?"

Diana was not used to letting mundane details stand in her

way. "Well, Sam Hardesty didn't have any family or anyone close to him. We know that. And Brian and I have checked out the physical details pretty carefully. There's not much more we can accomplish there, so we can write that one off for the time being. Brian had extensive dealings with Radley Davis and has routine access to all his medical records, so getting at other stuff in his file shouldn't be a problem. Tyrrell Jefferson lived in Washington, and Brian has already done some looking into that case. So that leaves only three others. If we can just get at them somehow, then I think we can—"

Gregory stood up, as if to make himself seem more assertive for what he wanted to say. Diana stopped talking. "Brian," he said, "if you pursue this on your own like this, you're not only risking your life but risking your career as well. You're laying it all on the line. Military medicine's been under fire for a long time. I don't have to tell you that. People have been playing fast and loose. A lot of heads are rolling; some of them deserving, some not. You know I'm not the kind of guy who generally sheds a tear about that or even gives a shit as long as it doesn't affect me personally. But I do care about you. And if there's even a hint that a navy surgeon's been snooping around where he shouldn't be or bending the rules, it's going to be one heavy-duty scene." Gregory's face had turned red. He wiped the sweat from the side of his neck.

Brian seemed to smile, a gesture of appreciation for his friend's concern. "I think you're right," he said. "So the trick is, as my friend can tell you from recent personal experience"—he turned to Diana, and his smile grew broader—"the trick is, not to get caught."

Diana flushed with embarrassment as she thought of herself standing inside the bathtub at the Roundup and furtively listening to his telephone conversation with Gregory. "I'm taking lessons from the master," she commented.

"But the fact remains," Gregory said, "what you're talking about we can't do by ourselves. This isn't one of your elite SEAL missions in Vietnam. Whatever we decide to do, we're going to need help."

"And who can we call on, if not the police or some other authorities?" Jill asked.

"Who do we know who'd be willing to help us that we know we can trust?" said Diana.

It was a question Brian Thorpe had thought about far more deeply than most people. And through his experience he had come to the realization that there was only one consideration that mattered in formulating the answer, one test that meant anything at all and rendered all others insignificant, one simple, single sanction that applied equally to anyone: Could you trust that person with your life?

In his own adult existence Brian had only come across one group of people he knew he could absolutely depend on.

He stood up, removed his wallet from his back pocket, and hunted for the slip of paper on which he'd written down the unlisted home telephone number of one member of that group.

SAN FRANCISCO, CALIFORNIA

Hugh Stanway—Big Stan or Standup Stanway to his special friends and enemies—was tall and broad and barrel-chested. He had dark, nearly colorless eyes and the kind of thick, square jaw our ancestors must have needed for cracking bone. His hair was steel gray, midway between curly and wavy, and was cropped close on the side and somewhat longer on the top and back, giving it the distinct look of a lion's mane. Like everything else about Hugh Stanway, this was not an accidental effect.

The *Men of Action* editorial offices occupied several floors high up in one of the modern steel towers of the Embarcadero Center. Stanway's private sanctum was a large, glass-walled corner suite that overlooked the entire bay, and he had his desk positioned to take full advantage of the view. In his mind it was without a doubt the most magnificent urban vista in the United States, if not in the world. And he never ceased exulting in the fact that he had been able to achieve it, doing what came naturally, without ever compromising his principles or beliefs. Directly in front of his window he could look out at the Oakland Bay Bridge, intersected by the twin squared expanses of Treasure Island, the landfill island built for the 1932 world's fair and subsequently taken over by the navy. Stanway had been assigned there briefly before going to Basic Underwater Demolition School. To the left of his view was Alcatraz, the grimy rock prison set defiantly in the midst of the beautiful natural cove. Behind it in the distance lay the lush green Oakland-Berkeley hills. And from the far edge of the window he could just about see back to his house along the ridge of rooflines of Pacific Heights, where he commanded another equally dominating view, this one of the Palace of Fine Arts, the sailboat-flecked marina, and the Golden Gate.

Every morning at 0830 hours Stanway met with his executive assistant, Cassandra Melville, for the daily "situation briefing." He thought of Cassie as his "girl Friday," and he had called her that without apology for a long time before finally settling on the more professional designation. Stanway liked women who were sufficiently independent and self-assured not to need to be "liberated." Besides, she was young and tough and absolutely gorgeous. He'd used her about a year ago in a pictorial on wild boar hunting in Central Africa. And her image—in a black headband and revealingly ripped woodland pattern khakis, striking a defiant, hip-jutting pose and sporting a Uzi automatic on her shoulder—adorned the current *Men of Action* "recruitment" poster. In his business women with merely those attributes were easy to come by. But Cassie was far more than the free-lance adventurer's pinup girl. She had proved to Stanway that she was as smart as she was tough and pretty. And the former SEAL liked his people—men and women—to be able to prove themselves.

Stanway sat behind the massive oak plank desk. It had been made from the decking board of an eighteenth-century British man o' war. On the wall in back of him was a large aerial photograph of Harlech Castle in Wales, perched solidly on its craggy promontory high above Cardigan Bay, where in 1294 a garrison of thirty-seven men held off the massed armies of Edward I. Next to the picture was an equally prominent poster bearing a stark white death's-head in a U.S. Special Forces beret. Under it was the slogan "Mess with the best, die with the rest."

Cassie sat opposite him in one of the steel-frame lounge chairs upholstered in tiger-stripe camouflage canvas. All the chairs in the suite were covered with it. She had on a tight gray-green jumpsuit of ripstop cotton that hugged her seductive curves as if it had been made for her. It had been.

"Okay, what have we got today?" Stanway asked her.

She studied the clipboard balanced on the knee of her crossed legs and checked off the top item. "The story on the political instability in Africa has come in."

"How is it?"

"Good. A real action piece. Thinks there's going to be several possible revolutions coming up before too long." She idly drew several boxes around the heading on the sheet. "There's a copy in the in box on your desk. It's slugged 'African Trouble Spots.' We were thinking of using that for the headline, too."

"No," said Stanway with a smile. "Let's get more consumer-oriented. Call it something like 'New Employment Opportunities Abroad.' Okay, what's next?"

Cassie looked down at her list again. "We've got an investigative report on the MIAs. Do Congress and the DOD know more than they're letting on? Is avoiding political embarrassment considered more important than coming through for the people who came through for the country?"

"Good. Let me see it as soon as you can. I want to write an editorial to go along with it. Let's stick our bayonets up some of those bureaucratic asses and see if there's enough left inside them even to yell."

"Fine. There's nothing else that can't wait," Cassie reported.

"All right. I've got something, then," Stanway said. "Take down these names: Anthony 'Sonny' Lofton, San Bernardino, California; Maxwell Craig, Wilkes-Barre, Pennsylvania; Christopher Schuyler, Little Compton, Rhode Island."

She wrote the names at the speed Stanway dictated. "I've got them," she said.

"You might as well add to your list: Tyrrell Leon Jefferson, Washington, D.C."

"Who are they?" Cassie asked.

"They're all former marines with the Seventh Marine Amphibious Assault Unit out of Dong Ha in 1969. They were one of the last marine regiments to be pulled out of Vietnam. I want a background done on each one of them: what they'd been doing, who they'd been talking with, whether they'd seen each other, that kind of thing. The basic recon-one stuff."

"Is it all right if we talk to them personally or let them know what we're up to?"

"It's all right, but you can't do it," Stanway replied. "They're all dead. But whoever you talk to, there's no problem with telling them you're from *Men of Action*. In fact, it would be best that way. Say it's for a story on war heroes or something. I'll give you whatever information I have on these guys today."

Cassie stood up and took one step toward the door. That was another thing Stanway liked about her. As he put it, she always "hit the deck running."

"In the meantime, I'll get hold of a stringer from each of those cities and tell him to wait for a preliminary briefing on the assignment," she said, continuing toward the door.

Stanway put up his hand. "I don't want you to do that," he told her. Cassie stopped and took a step back toward the desk. "I want you to use our own staff people," the publisher said. "I'm talking about guys like Klavan, if he's in town. The best ones we've got."

She clutched the clipboard with both hands and pulled it close to her breasts. "That means at least three people, pulling them off what they're doing, paying for plane fares, putting them up in hotels and paying per diems—all on an open-ended assignment. Hugh, that's going to cost a fortune."

"I don't care. Do it anyway."

"Is there even a story in it?"

"Maybe, maybe not. I don't know yet. But a friend asked me to do it. And I can't let him down."

Cassie nodded and made for the door. She knew that "friend" was not a term Hugh Stanway threw around lightly. And this being so, she knew better than to press the matter any further.

MOSCOW, USSR

The black Volga sedan with official number plates pulled up to the guard station in front of 2 Dzerzhinsky Square. Alone in the back seat was Andrey Stoltz, trying to look nonchalant while the driver handed over his credentials and orders. He had worked in this building for years at the beginning of his career and had reported back countless times since then. But there was something about the place which never failed to intimidate, regardless of the subject matter of his meeting or whether he'd been called back to be commended or to offer excuses. Perhaps it was those rooms along a single corridor in the subbasement, rooms he had never seen but the uses of which were vividly described in rumor and threat. Perhaps it was simply the routine stress of having to account to higher-ups for policy decisions. Or perhaps it was nothing more than the weight of history pressing down upon the bricks.

The building was an ornate Renaissance-style edifice executed in a surprisingly placid shade of yellow-beige—that is, from the second story up. The two lowest levels were of the more familiar coal gray granite, lest the overall effect prove too warm or inviting. Stoltz glanced across the road to the resolute statue of Feliks Dzerzhinsky, the aristocratic Pole who had seen the light, joined the Bolsheviks, and become the first head of the Soviet secret police. The statue was positioned with its back to the building, as if the rest of the country required its constant scrutiny far more than the powerful, dependable machine the man had set into motion.

The meeting was to be chaired by Anatoly Nikolayev, deputy chief of Directorate S, First Chief Directorate and therefore Stoltz's immediate superior. Directorate S was responsible for all committee clandestine operatives throughout the world.

Inside the meeting room Stoltz was greeted by familiar faces. He didn't know all of them personally, but there was none he had not at least seen in photographs. His instincts had been correct then. The powers that be did consider this a fruitful avenue of endeavor.

"I believe you know Aleksander Kuznetsov of Service I and Boris Polyakovsky of Directorate T," Nikolayev said as he ushered Stoltz to his assigned place at the table. Stoltz wasn't surprised to see someone from Directorate T at the meeting. After all, this matter could be said to fall under the general heading of science and technology. The fact was the scientific gnomes had their noses into almost everything these days.

"And we've also asked Dr. Yury Mironenko of the Zagorsk Scientific Research Institute to join us. I'm sure his view and perspective will prove invaluable to our discussion."

Stoltz extended his hand to the scientist, who shook it formally and without comment. The two men stood near the doorway, blankly staring at each other.

Nikolayev quickly called the group to order to cut short the potentially awkward moment. That was the trouble with scientists. They were beyond the bounds of traditional discipline or even traditional manners, for that matter.

"Let us review the information thus far," he began. "Comrade Stoltz will be leaving to return to Washington this evening, and I do not want to have to detain him any longer than is absolutely necessary. At the same time I very much wanted him here since without his close attention to detail, this episode might very well have slipped between our fingers."

Stoltz acknowledged the congratulatory nods bobbing around the worn oaken table.

"We have two significant pieces of intelligence to work with," Nikolayev went on. "First, we have now made sufficient observation to conclude that Commander Brian Thorpe of the United States Naval Command, Bethesda, has become involved in the case. We have not as yet been able to determine who assigned him, but there is reason to believe that his service with the Marine Corps has given him what might be called a special expertise. Whether he realizes this or not is also as yet to be determined. But as a medical doctor as well he could be considered the perfect candidate. Recently he was sent to the state of Montana to investigate the incident there."

A series of photographs taken of Commander Thorpe, obviously with a long telephoto lens, appeared on a screen at the end of the room. Stoltz thought the images projected on the screen were wonderfully bright and sharp, considering that the room lights had not been turned off. In some of the pictures Thorpe was seen with an attractive woman with long dark hair. Stoltz noticed Dr. Mironenko concentrating heavily on the girl's long, sleek legs and tight-fitting khaki shorts. There was something about American women that the Russian girls, even the prettier ones, couldn't quite duplicate. Stoltz sometimes comforted himself by chalking it up to the decadence of Western civilization. But in his more honest moments he knew it ran a lot deeper than that. To state it simply—and sadly, he decided—the Russians had little flair. Everything . . . everything was heavy and serious. Much as Stoltz loved his homeland, he couldn't deny that he was happiest when he was away from it.

When he had clicked through the series of photographs, Nikolayev continued his commentary. "It is further not clear whether he is reporting through traditional command channels or whether he is on special assignment and reporting on a need-to-know basis. There is some evidence of interagency cooperation here, as he is currently in the company of a Dr. Diana Campbell Keegan of the National Centers for Disease Control in Atlanta, who was also sent to Montana to look into the disease outbreak there. This might be nothing more than a routine investigation from their perspective however because we have determined that there was a request from the Montana state department of health. Regardless, Commander Thorpe seems to be moving closer to his objective."

Aleksander Kuznetsov removed his tortoise-rim glasses, whipped his crumpled handkerchief out of the breast pocket of his dour tweed suit, and began cleaning the lenses. It was the signal that he was prepared to make a pronouncement. Everyone looked in his direction.

"If my aging memory does not fail me, Comrades, there was some discussion earlier in the course of this enterprise as to whether perhaps Commander Thorpe, or anyone else who strays too close to the fact, might be physically enjoined from further inquiry. Yet as far as I know, nothing has ever materialized in that direction."

Leave it to Kuznetsov to bring that up, Stoltz thought. *That was always the way with the old guard. When in doubt, purge them. Sort it all out later when the dust settles.*

"That is not entirely the case, Aleksander." Nikolayev answered him, straining for tact. "Yet suffice it to say that there are two important considerations in this regard. The first is the workability of such a scheme without tipping our own hand to the other side. And second, there is the question of whether he might not lead us in the direction we wish to pursue—that is, to fill in the critical gaps in our own knowledge which would finally permit us to exploit this interesting turn of events to the fullest possible advantage."

"I say the risks are too great!" Kuznetsov declared. He looked as if he were about to stand up from the table and leave the room.

"Yet surely the benefits are even greater," Boris Polyakovsky asserted.

"In any event," Nikolayev stated with authority, "termination efforts against Commander Thorpe have not proved possible up till now, which, pragmatically speaking, makes the second perspective all the more attractive from an operational point of view. And this, in turn, leads me to the second significant piece of information. Thorpe has enlisted the services of Hugh Stanway, his former comrade in the navy SEALs, who is the publisher of *Men of Action* magazine. If you check the background dossiers provided to each of you, you will note that Stanway is a professional adventurer who has been repeatedly involved both personally as a contract operative and as a recruiter. Among his frequent employers has been the Central Intelligence Agency. So I think you can grasp the implications." He gathered the papers in front of him into a stack and rapped them into alignment.

Stoltz settled back in his chair. Soon they would be getting into his field of expertise.

"Now, before we engage in any further discussion of these issues," Nikolayev said, "perhaps we should hear from Dr. Mironenko for or the practical considerations."

13

"So what happened was he actually showed up here at the door. Didn't call or anything, just showed up with a big bunch of roses in his hand. I guess he wanted to surprise you. Well, the surprise was definitely on him when I said that you were in West Deer Creek, Montana!" A huge grin spread across Sharon Mowbray's face. It was a satisfied, almost vindictive smile that seemed to raise the incident from the specific to the universal and proclaim, "You can score one for our side!"

"What did he say?" asked Diana.

"He didn't say anything. At least not for a while. Like the whole thing hadn't registered. He just sort of stood there with his mouth looking like it was about to drop open. Finally, I said, 'You must be Bill,' and then he sort of nodded. He hadn't even bothered to tell me his name."

"That doesn't surprise me. He assumes the whole world knows who he is . . . and cares."

"Well, we kept him guessing."

And one more time he's managed to keep me guessing, Diana thought. *Was I too afraid of myself and the power he might still hold over me that I had to run away from him? Was I so afraid that I wasn't even willing to see if anything was still there? There was no question but that if I'd given him the right signals when he got here . . . Or was I just simply afraid of moving backward? It was still probably a shabby thing for you to do,* she told herself. *You're all the time saying that even if you can't always avoid hurting people, you should never trifle with them. That's what Bill did to you, and you swore you'd never do it back to him or anyone else.*

"I suppose I really should feel guilty," she said.

"I suppose you really should," Sharon replied, and they both looked straight at each other, barely suppressing the giggles of conspiracy in behalf of their sex.

"I'm sorry I put you in such an awkward position," Diana said, growing more serious again and shifting her guilt into a more manageable direction. "I had no idea he'd just come on over like that. But that's the way he's always been. Always wants to control the situation totally, keep the other person slightly off-balance. So maybe I've just paid him back for a little of the crap he dished out to me all those years."

"Men really can be shits," Sharon commented.

They were spread out in the living room, Sharon still in her work clothes, Diana in the same cutoff blue jeans she'd brought on the trip, as well as Brian's T-shirt. By now the jeans were so broken in and comfortable they had taken on her every contour from her waist to the tops of her thighs. They had become her second skin. Sharon was sprawled on the green, lumpily stuffed sofa, and Diana was sitting on the floor with her back resting against the matching lumpy chair. Both women were subdued and relaxed, sipping their third wine coolers of the evening.

Diana had just gotten back into town that afternoon. In fact, her appearance at the apartment had been as much of a surprise to Sharon as Bill Eschenberger's had been. She hadn't wanted to come back to Atlanta at all just then, didn't really feel ready or up for it. But both logic and reality had dictated the return. Sometimes you can avoid logic. Diana knew she was often good at that. Reality is more difficult to get around.

There was nothing more Diana could do by remaining in Washington. She and Brian both had to admit to that. More to the point, as Brian explained to her, she added to his danger. As long as she stayed with him, she could be perceived by whoever was after him as his confidante, a conspirator, or simply a member of his "team." She compromised his ability to act quickly and flexibly if the need arose. By her going back to Atlanta, there would be no evidence to anyone observing them that there was anything between them or that he considered her presence or information necessary or valuable. What he was probably trying to tell her was that he was trying to remove *her* from the threat of danger. But he knew he couldn't come right out and say it because for herself, she never would have left.

"But when can I see you again?" she had asked him as he dropped her off at National Airport. She had decided ahead of time that she wasn't going to cry in his presence, and she didn't.

"I'm not sure," he had responded. "We're going to have to let things cool off for a while."

Cool off. She hadn't had the heart to ask him how he meant that. But however he did, the enforced separation for who knew how long could have but the one effect. They'd been together only a little while. There wasn't enough there yet to build on to sustain any prolonged period apart. It was like the people she knew who'd gotten married just before starting medical school. In every case she could think of, there hadn't been enough established yet between them to carry them through the stresses and the loneliness and the mutual anger and frustration that kind of experience imposes. All the marriages had broken up. Every one of them. She had been lucky. Or at least at the time she had thought so. The relationship with Bill had come at a much better time for her. Of course, that one hadn't been exactly the same anyway. It wasn't like one partner's going through the experience and the other one's having to live it vicariously and take all the abuse. They'd both gone through medical school and had a tremendous amount to share. In its way it was every bit as intense and emotionally charged as the movement days had been.

"He really was good-looking," Sharon was saying. "From the way you were talking about him—up on him one minute, down the next—I didn't know what to expect. For a couple of seconds back then when he was standing at the door, I thought: *Well, Diana doesn't seem to want him or she'd be here herself. He's here for the weekend by himself, and he's separated from his wife, so what's the harm?* But then I thought: *No, that really is bad news. If Diana didn't want to be here because of him, there must be a pretty good reason for it.* So then I thought . . ."

Diana's mind drifted away while Sharon was talking. She and Bill had had a tremendous amount to share, and maybe that had been all that had kept it going. But he was now well-off, professionally secure, and she knew that at least at one time she had loved him. Was there any point in asking for more than that?

On the other hand, she and Brian had nothing to share, unless you consider this mess with his car's being sabotaged and all the dead marines. Yet no matter what she thought about Bill, trying to recall all the good times and the tingling, exhilarating way his well-cared-for body used to make her feel, it was Brian and the image of Brian's combat-scarred body that she couldn't clear from her mind.

It was strange because they were so different. Or actually, it was rather that they were so similar in such different ways—it was that confusing. In bed last night they'd gotten to musing over things, talking about the war that represented such a gulf between them, that at the same time represented the experience they had most vitally in common. To tell the truth, as she thought back on it, the conversation had become almost an argument at times. Voices had been raised, and she had experienced that old rush of adrenaline coursing through her system as they both felt the growing need to explain, to justify their past thoughts and actions. That was something they'd probably never escape, either one of them. He'd told her about some of his combat experiences. And some of the things had been beyond any description she'd ever heard, beyond any of the horror stories either side had put out. How anyone could go through that and come away sane was incredible. Yet at the end of it all, in a moment of what must have been extraordinary candor for him, he'd admitted to her, "With all that, I'd be lying if I said it wasn't the most thrilling experience I've ever had."

And then, when she went on to tell him about what she was doing back home in the antiwar movement at the same time, she found herself saying, "I've never felt as fully alive as I did then."

She'd been caught up in the life force back then. Even years later it had never embarrassed her to remember that the best sex she'd ever had had been right after a peace march in Central Park in New York. Her partner had been one of the national SDS organizers, and he'd gone to bed with her, flushed with the success of the march and the impact it had had. It wasn't just that they'd performed exceptionally well together—as they had. It was that they were so full of their cause and the larger issues and the possibility that ordinary people like them could make something big and important happen that the physical act just seemed to be part of a much larger and all-embracing field of energy which the two of them had done nothing more than tap into.

Yes, Diana recalled wistfully, that evening in the East Village had been the best lovemaking of her life. Until the afternoon in Montana, that is. And now she didn't know if she'd ever see him again or, if she did, whether any of the fire could still be there. Circumstances had brought them together, and now circumstances had pulled them back apart. Once again, she mused, she found herself caught up in the swirl of events.

All she could do for the time being was go about her business. Tomorrow, when she went into work, she'd busy herself cleaning up her EPI-2 report on the trip and following up the specific symptomatology on the computer to see if anything else kicked out. She doubted it would—Herb had already had a preliminary check run—but it would give her something to do and just might possibly shed some light on the case. Anyway, the business with Bill had sort of been resolved, and she would start getting back to a normal routine. That was what she most needed now.

The most important thing was to try to get her mind off Brian. Why should that be so difficult? she asked herself. She'd always been independent enough in the past. And what was really so special about him? It was a mental game similar to the one she'd played before when she wanted to convince herself to swallow the bad-tasting medicine. All right, he could be high-handed, trying to tell her what to do. He was still in the military and reacted to everything with that mind-set. She'd practically had to blackmail him into trusting her since she wasn't one of his precious SEALs. And when he caught her snooping in his motel room, there was a time when she thought he was actually going to beat her. Aside from that, he had proved he was dangerous to be around since someone was trying to kill him. So what was the problem? Why should someone like that be so difficult to walk away from?

Yes, Diana. Why? And don't say it's just physical, because that's never been enough of a pull for you if all the other pieces weren't there. You've always been able to take that part of it for what it was and walk away from it when it was done with. That's one type of enslavement that your generation, and your sex in particular, did manage to throw off. And the mere fact that you'd been spending your nights alone for longer than you'd have liked just prior to your escapade in Montana doesn't mean you're a different person from the one you always were. You can't play games forever.

Diana's adventures with the military. Who would have thought? Isn't it strange what we become, often in spite of ourselves?

She tried to clear her mind by thinking of another man she'd known who'd also been in Vietnam. Actually, he hadn't been a military man when she'd known him. He'd been a boy her own age in her high school homeroom in Westchester. He was a terrifically nice boy, not overly intellectual, a kind of jock. Probably wouldn't have gone on to college under any circumstances. He was outgoing and popular, especially for his sense of humor when the math and science and language teachers gave him a hard time for never coming to class prepared. But he was suffused with a patriotism and sense of himself that she had never seen before. All he wanted to do was join the Marines after graduation. Serve his country, he said. Brian might even have known him. He would have been over there around the same time. He talked about going all the time, what boot camp would be like and how he was already mentally preparing himself for the challenge. He was anxious to be judged and anxious not to be found wanting. She lost touch with him after graduation, the way she had with most of the kids.

He'd been over in Vietnam for two weeks, she'd heard later. Just two weeks. He'd been out on patrol with his unit. There'd been no shooting or anything. He'd stepped on a land mine, and that had been that. Nothing more to the story. The first thing Diana thought of when she heard was that someone her age whom she'd known and did things with could actually be dead. It made life into a perversion. It didn't make any sense. It wasn't even as if he'd had cancer or been hit by a car crossing the street or anything like that. Someone her age—a teenager—had been killed in a war! At his funeral, which Diana had come home from college for, his coffin had been open. His face looked amazingly intact and lifelike, considering what they said had happened to him. But there was something about the way his two hands and arms were lying there attached to his body that gave her the creepiest feeling she'd ever had. It just wasn't—it just wasn't natural the way they were stuck back on. The mortician had done the best job he could, but he hadn't gotten it right. Later on, after she'd had anatomy and orthopedics, Diana could have explained specifically what the anomaly was. But at the time all she knew was that it was just plain wrong, like everything else about that horrible war—that war that was swallowing up people like her friend in that yawning pit of Southeast Asia. That was when she made her own personal commitment.

"You're crying," Sharon noticed. "I've said something to upset you."

"No, you haven't," Diana replied, compelling herself by force of will to stop sniffling.

"I shouldn't be talking about Bill like this. I know how important he's been to you."

"No, that's okay, really," Diana said, wiping away what she was determined would be the final tear. "I was thinking about something else."

WASHINGTON, D.C.

It was a week during which every car running a yellow light was bearing straight down on him, every tray dropped in the cafeteria was a gunshot, every wastebasket moved by the cleaning crew a booby trap. Every little sound around him was amplified until it reverberated in his ear like an artillery blast, and each corner he turned held out the threat of ambush. It was like being in the jungle again, having to live constantly at the top of his senses. Only things had been different back then. He had been a lot younger, and everyone else around him had been forced to live the same way so that they all had been looking out for each other. Also, they'd known who the enemy was and what they had to watch for. But this was different. And he couldn't take it indefinitely.

It hadn't stopped with his physical safety either. If people thought he might know something they didn't want him to, they might try to discredit him before silencing him. Three times now during the week he'd sent units of drugs from the operating room out for assay. In one case, the label on a bottle of lidocaine looked slightly askew. In another, he could have sworn the sterile seal on a unit of succinycholine had been tampered with. In each case, it'd come back from the lab completely clean.

Brian was alone in his apartment. He didn't read or watch television or listen to music. It had been his weekend to take Katie, and the emptiness of not having her was as great inside him as it was in the air around him, like a diver who has reached perfect negative buoyancy. But as much as he ached to have her with him, he knew he couldn't risk it. He had called Lizzie and told her he might have been exposed to something at the hospital this past week, so it would probably be best if she kept the child. At first he'd debated whether he should tell her the truth. But from what he knew of Lizzie, that would have been as good as having her take Katie away from him forever. And he couldn't honestly say he would have blamed her for it either.

What a life, he thought, *in which the way you protect people close to you is by keeping them far away.* And that was when he began thinking about Diana, whom he'd also sent away for her own good.

Actually he'd been thinking about her all along, he realized. But as was the case with many of the things that were most important to him, he had the capacity to suppress the thought as long as it "made sense" to do so. Images of her ran through his mind, forcing everything else out of the way. To be perfectly honest, he had more than thought about her. He had longed for her, pined for her, craved to take hold of her and draw her close to him.

She was so unusual, so different from all the others. She was such a strange, unpredictable combination of spunk and independence and vulnerability. And it came across in everything she was, everything she did, but particularly in her lovemaking. She was by turns almost sentimentally tender and then wildly aggressive, as if sometimes wanting to use her body to soothe the wounds of the world and sometimes wanting to use it to open up new ones, sometimes wanting to caress and sometimes wanting to hurt and, whether she knew it or not, making it very plain that that was what she wanted in return. And of all the female bodies he'd had the opportunity to see in his time—and a doctor gets to see more than his share—how many could he perfectly and easily recall in all its nuances as he could this one—clothed and unclothed, prim and exquisitely in place, sweaty and disheveled, dressed sharply for work or in T-shirt and aging jeans? None ever. Not even Lizzie's, he had to admit, not even during the too brief but soaring heights of their ecstatic bliss together.

No, he'd never known a woman like Diana before. Not that it was a perfect mesh. Far from it. And no matter what happened, it probably never could be. But that was probably what made it exciting and invigorating and made the chemistry work between them. With Lizzie, he realized, he'd always been looking for the formula for perfect love and harmony, the magic answer that was finally going to make it right between them. Anything that jarred the fragile domestic equilibrium in any way represented a material threat to the marriage. And when it dawned on them at last that they'd never find their ideal peace, there turned out to be no fallback position or safe harbor for them. There turned out to be nowhere to grow but apart.

But this one was different. Neither he nor Diana, it seemed, felt the need to minimize the gulfs between them. In fact, they both were constitutionally incapable of it. On the plane back from Montana, then during their tour of downtown Washington, then again in the intimate solitude of their shared bed, they continued fighting the more than two decades-old war between themselves.

He had talked to her about duty and heroism, and she had countered by talking about responsibility. He had talked about patriotism, and she had talked about blind waste. He had lectured her about what they had been trying to do over there, and she had defied him to point out one thing that had been accomplished for all those young and precious lives. None of the threats had come true, none of what Johnson and Nixon and their henchmen had deluded the gullible American public with. Even though we lost, had all those dominoes fallen? Not a one, except maybe Cambodia, which would have been all right on its own if Nixon and Kissinger hadn't brought the war straight to its doorstep. He hadn't disagreed with her there, and she had gone on to describe her own and her friends' commitment, but then he had reminded her of the unalterable facts of recent history after the end of the American presence.

"When push came to shove," he had said chidingly, "how really dedicated were you and all your counterculture rad-lib friends? How committed were you to your cause? After the U.S. pullout from Southeast Asia and the end of the draft, what did you all have to say about Pol Pot and the Khmer Rouge and the boat people and all the slaughter? Where were all the mass demonstrations and peace marches and protests against the North Vietnamese aggressors? Where were all the speeches and the taking to the streets? Where were all your high-minded moral leaders? I don't remember hearing much of anything. The history books will one day refer to it as the Great Cop-Out. Once your own sanctimonious asses were no longer on the line, this great generational vision of peace and national liberation evaporated like the bubbles in your Perrier water into BMWs and designer running shoes and Harvard M.B.A.'s."

They both were naked in his bed at the time, the sheet pulled down to the foot and spilling over onto the floor. It was perhaps significant that they chose to wage their most sensitive and cutting battles when they were most exposed and vulnerable.

She sat straight up and looked at him, her hands resting casually and without self-consciousness in front of the perfect dark triangle of her pubis. "I didn't cop out," she retorted, "any more than you did. Maybe I wasn't marching anymore, and maybe I wasn't as concerned with affecting national policy. But there are different ways of showing your commitment."

She swiveled around, tucked her legs under her, and rested her weight on one hand. "I used to do volunteer work in the GW hospital emergency room while I was in college. One night, when I was there, they brought in a kid with severe abdominal pains. No more than five or six. All doubled over, distended belly—the works. Thought at first it was acute appendicitis or maybe worse. Turns out his mother didn't have anything for him to eat or drink in the house and didn't even know how long it had been. He was just hungry, but they were so used to that it didn't occur to her that was her kid's trouble. This was a time we were spending thirty billion dollars a year burning peasant villages halfway around the world! Thirty billion dollars a year, and this little boy was starving to death not three miles from the White House. I cried all night. That's when I decided there were other kinds of commitment, and that one incident is probably why I went into the Public Health Service after med school. And let me tell you, dealing with migrant workers' kids who've got open, festering sores and no chance for medical care and with third world mothers who don't even have the wherewithal to keep their children from dying of chronic diarrhea is a more effective form of liberation than a lot of things I can think of!"

That was what he loved about her: the deep, genuine sensitivity and caring that made her bleed—albeit selectively—for the entire world. The way she stood up for herself and always let you know it. The courage to do things because she wanted to without worrying about the consequences. The impulsiveness and assurance with which she approached everything she did. And the endearing, overstated self-righteousness that never quite completely believed in its own pretensions.

He wished with all his heart he had her here next to him.

The phone rang once. Less than a complete ring, really, as he snatched the receiver off its cradle like a bobcat pouncing on a prairie dog. His heart was pounding. No question, it all was getting to him. He held the phone away from his ear momentarily and forced himself to calm down.

"Hello?"

"Brian—it's Stanway. How are you? You hanging in there okay?" The voice was comforting—firm, deep, and steady.

"Sure, Hugh. But I hate it."

"Of course you do. Only dumb son of a bitch kids like we used to be like it. And even back then I don't think we liked it quite as much as we pretended to at the time."

"I'm glad you called," Brian said. "It's good to be able to talk to someone."

"Well, let me tell you what I've got here, son." Stanway naturally took control.

"Any possibilities?" Brian asked. A strange sense of calm settled over him. It was as if Stanway were once again right here next to him, just as in the old days.

"Could be. I want you to know, I put my best people to work on this for you, Bri; people you can trust to do the job, just like us. We did satellite charts on each one, the way the CIA does. We started with each subject, then looked up the people around him, then the people around each of them. We went three levels out. That's usually enough to find out whatever's there to be found, and it cuts out a lot of unnecessary busywork."

"Sounds good."

"So let me give you the rundown one at a time. As you probably suspected, there's no hard evidence. Almost never is in this kind of thing. All we've got are a number of suggestions."

Brian picked up the notepad next to the telephone. "Go ahead, Hugh," he said.

"Right. First, this guy Christopher Schuyler. An accident at sea doesn't give you much to go on. Weather and water conditions around there are unpredictable. Technically speaking, anything could have happened. I've had several experts look at the Coast Guard report, and they see no red flags in it. On the other hand, from all reports, this Schuyler was an excellent, experienced sailor. You know, Princeton, high-society dude, the works. Forget women—all those guys jerk off dreaming about winning the America's Cup. When they talk about a wet dream, they're talking about smooth sailing on Narragansett Bay. But people who knew him and sailed with him say there wouldn't have been many situations out there he couldn't have handled. He had a radio on board. He never tried to use it. We just can't be sure on this one. I'd have to call it a wash.

"Let's go on to your friend Tyrrell Jefferson in D.C. What his mother told you was apparently true. As far as we could tell, he wasn't the kind of guy who'd ever take his own life. For one thing, he was a very religious Baptist. I don't know what happened to him. There weren't any witnesses. But nothing at all in his background points to suicide.

"Now here's where it gets a mite touchier. Maxwell Craig—the great white hunter. We really did a job on this one. Very complete. Do you know that no witnesses to the incident were ever found?"

"I wasn't aware one way or the other," Brian commented.

"I don't know if you've ever been deer hunting up in Pennsylvania, but those woods are crawling with gunners. It's real strange that no one saw anything. What's even stranger is that the hunter who shot him was never seen or heard from. In nearly every hunting accident the guy who's done it generally surfaces pretty quickly, is scared shitless, and goes straight to the authorities. Remember, if you think you've hit something, you don't walk away from it. You go get it. If you then look down at your feet and see it's a person rather than a deer . . . Well, you get my drift. That didn't happen in this case. That in itself makes me suspicious."

"Yeah, but as you say, Hugh, it's still not conclusive."

"Right. But here's the kicker, Bri. Through our own contacts, we managed to obtain the bullet that was removed from Craig's body."

"How'd you manage that?"

"Let's just say we managed. In this business you meet a lot of people in that line of work. People owe each other favors. Now I owe. Anyway, we took the bullet back to our own people and ran ballistics tests. Brian, it was a one-sixty-five-grain match bullet, and it didn't come from a Remington or a Colt or anything you'd expect to find out in the woods there. It was fired from a Steyr-Mannlicher SSG-PII."

"I didn't know you could identify a weapon without having it to match up with the bullet."

"There are ways, my friend, if you know what you're doing and have the right people doing it for you. It's not easy and costs some bucks. Most of the local departments and agencies don't even know about it, but we've done it from time to time."

"I'm impressed," Brian stated. "At any rate, I don't know the rifle you're talking about."

"The SSG-PII is a NATO-standard detachable scope system with a twenty-six-inch barrel. It's a pretty specialized piece of equipment, one of the best police sniper rifles made. SWAT teams use it all over the country. Not the kind of thing you'd bring along to take out your favorite neighborhood deer. Strictly for people."

"Well, this certainly puts it all in some perspective," said Brian.

"There's more," Stanway said. "Anthony Lofton. We checked out the California highway patrol report on the accident. You know, suspicious tire skids, positioning of other cars, things like that. Nothing shows up. Also, no evidence of tampering to the vehicle itself. We've got very good sources with the highway patrol. We can trust them. And his blood alcohol level was way above the legal limit. He was definitely intoxicated."

"So Lofton doesn't give us anything to go on."

"I didn't say that. There is one interesting development. According to his wife, not too long before the accident, he'd started complaining of abdominal and side pains. He'd gone to his regular doctor, who didn't find anything.

"Lofton was a salesman for a machine tools company. He traveled up and down the coast a lot. So the next time he was here in the Bay Area, he stopped in down the peninsula at Palo Alto to see a Dr. Calvin Chandler Harley at Stanford Medical Center."

"Cal Harley," Brian intoned.

"I thought the name might ring a bell. He was a surgeon with the Third Marine Division while you were there on your medic tour."

"That's right. He operated out of the medical battalion headquarters at Phu Bai," Brian recalled. "I can't tell you how many times I came in and out of there. I even scrubbed with him a few times during the heavy action when they were short of nurses. The guy was one first-rate surgeon. Kind of cold and abrupt personally, but at what he did, he was the best there was. There's something about combat surgeons, even after they go back into civilian life. They have a certain kind of confidence that just doesn't allow for any hesitation or doubt. A lot of wounded grunts wouldn't be walking about today if not for him. And I'll tell you something else: If I ever needed a serious operation, he'd be the man I'd want doing it."

"If I ever needed one, you'd be the man I'd want doing it," Stanway said.

"I appreciate the vote of confidence, but I'm not in Harley's league. Very few people are."

"Well, it must be a pretty fancy league because he's out at Stanford now and apparently has a big-time following there. The leading light of the department, by all accounts."

"That's what I heard."

"And apparently the late Mr. Lofton held the same view of him you did. Because when he didn't get any satisfaction from his own doc, he said Harley was the only one he trusted. Lofton's wife said he'd been wounded over in Nam and Harley had been the one who put him back together."

"Did Harley treat him when he went to Stanford?"

"Yes. He performed a procedure called a laparotomy."

"That's just a general term for an operation through the abdominal wall, usually exploratory," Brian explained. "I wonder what he came up with."

"I'm not sure. Lofton spent a long weekend recuperating in the Stanford Hospital and then went home. We didn't contact Harley directly, but we can if you want us to."

Brian thought for a moment. "No, better not. Let me take it from here."

"Whatever you say, buddy. You know best." There would be no further discussion on this point. Among this elite camaraderie of men who had worked so closely together and entrusted their lives to each other, there was neither false modesty nor pride. Each person had the unqualified faith of all the others. Each person was relied on to do what he did best for the team and expected to know what that was. Second-guessing was a bourgeois nicety that in their business they could ill afford.

"Hugh, I don't know how to thank you for what you've done," Brian stated simply. He had never been very good at this, but it was important to him to get it said, and said straight out. His meaning would be clear enough.

"Don't worry about it," Stanway replied. "You just remember one thing, and you remember it good: The pledge we took back then was a pledge for life, and none of us treats those things lightly. We're still a team. Always will be. Whatever you're in, I'm in there with you. I'll drop everything if you need me, whenever and wherever. And if it turns out we need some of the others, I assure you they'll be there, too. Too many men died for that trust ever to go back on it now."

Brian knew better than to try to thank Stanway again. You don't thank people for being themselves. "I'll remember that, Hugh. And I'll talk to you soon."

"See that you do, cowboy," said Stanway, and hung up the phone.

And for the first time that evening Brian was not unhappy being alone.

ATLANTA, GEORGIA

Of all the objects and mementos that cluttered Diana's small and cramped office, it was the pair of empty Watney's ale bottles she most cherished. They stood together on the sill of the window that overlooked the Emory campus, sandwiched between a watering can that was hardly ever used and three small potted plants that weren't doing very well as a direct result.

The Watney's bottles held meaning to her for two reasons. The first was that they represented part of the Alexander Langmuir Prize, named for the founder of the Epidemic Intelligence Service and awarded to the EIS officer who writes the best medical journal article in the course of a year. The second reason had to do with the circuitous path of symbolism which led to the form that the prize—an entire case of Watney's—had taken.

Watney's is the brand of ale served at a pub on Broad Street in London which stands today on the site of a pump that belonged to the Southwark and Vauxhall Water Company. It was to this pump in 1854 that an obscure anesthetist named John Snow, through meticulous medical detective work, traced the source of the great cholera epidemic that was decimating the capital city. This astounding feat was accomplished in spite of the fact that the *Vibrio cholerae* bacterium was not isolated under the microscope until 1884. The pub is named for Dr. Snow, who became the patron saint of epidemiology, and has become a place of pilgrimage for CDC personnel visiting the British Isles.

Diana had always been taken with the story and inspired by the notion that it was possible to start from whatever limited or sketchy information you were given and, through dogged determination and methodical reasoning, come up with the solution to a challenging and important problem.

And that was what Brian was asking of her now.

"Can anyone hear you?" he asked.

She didn't think anyone would bother but told him to hold on, got up, and closed her office door just to be sure. She came back to her chair, tucked one foot under her, and let the other dangle idly inches above the floor. She cradled the telephone receiver comfortably against the side of her face.

"My first thought was to go see Dr. Harley myself," Brian explained. "But then I got to thinking, no matter what I say, one military surgeon questioning another former military surgeon about a patient who was a marine has got to seem like a challenge to him. He could call the chief of surgery here and start asking questions."

Diana listened to his logic and then said, "There's something else going on here, Brian. What is it?"

"I don't know what you mean," he replied edgily.

"Okay, fine. Now, tell me the real reason you don't want to see Harley yourself."

"That is the real reason." Then a silence. "But there is another thing," he said. "How shall I say this? I know you're not going to understand. But back when we were working on the same team, he was already a prominent surgeon. I was only a medic. I wasn't even an officer yet. It might be awkward for me to approach him now as an equal."

"I had a feeling it was something like that," Diana said. "You are such a military animal. And we think the British are the only ones with a class system."

"With your CDC credentials, you could come up with a legitimate-sounding reason for interviewing him. And if you told him that there was possibly a public health matter at stake, he'd be all the more likely to be candid about his relationship with Lofton."

"Don't worry. I'll be happy to sacrifice my honor to keep yours pure," she rejoined.

"Is that how I came across?" He sounded hurt.

"I'm only teasing you," she told him. But she didn't want to tease too hard. She realized how difficult it must have been for Brian to ask her for anything, especially something like this. When they were in Montana, arguing about whether she would go back to Washington with him, she had convinced him by saying she could help him. But he had never taken her up on it. She wasn't one of the sacred band of brothers. She hadn't been through the same rites of passage. She'd never be able to.

Now he was opening the door to her, however slightly. And whatever it took, she was determined not to give him the chance to close it again.

"Not to worry, I'll take care of it," she said. And the silence on the other end told her Brian was still not fully convinced he'd done the right thing by her.

She knew exactly what he must be thinking: Was he compromising her safety by asking her to do this? Was he possibly making her jeopardize her professional position, just as she'd joked? His own safety was of little concern to him, she knew, but there were other questions that would have been constantly on his mind. Was the blood debt he felt to Radley Davis equal to the risk of danger to her, to the others? And what even gave him the right to weigh those two values against each other? Knowing Brian as she thought she did, she was sure that all these things must be plaguing him now.

"You're consumed by your own sense of responsibility," Jill Timberlake had said to him that night they'd all been together. She seemed quite a perceptive woman to Diana. "You thought you had to win the war single-handedly. You think you can, and have to, save every one of your patients. And deep down you actually think you're capable of saving the world. That's quite laudable in its way, Brian. It also happens to be extremely egotistical. It also happens to be totally impractical."

Diana decided it was best not to push it by getting all sentimental on him. Besides, that had never been her nature. "I'll get on it right away and call you as soon as I've got anything," she said.

"Okay," Brian replied. "I'll talk to you." She could tell he wasn't comfortable leaving it at that. But sometimes that is the way it has to be.

She hung up and immediately began considering the functional elements of the plan. Saying yes to Brian's request was one thing—in the final analysis she almost always acted on impulse—but figuring out how to accomplish it was another. And while his world view may not have been practical according to Jill, the procedures that came out of it would have to be if they were to have any chance for success.

There was the matter of transportation out to California and back. As an EIS officer Diana often had to travel on the spur of the moment without waiting for orders or tickets to be ground through the bureaucratic mill. She had therefore been issued a GTR (government transportation requests) book, good on any airline for any destination in the world. The question was did she dare use them. These were what the GAO auditors, who came from time to time to scare CDC into running a tighter administrative ship, referred to as "accountable documents."

Then there was an even larger problem. How was she going to account for her absence? Was Herb going to chew her up when he found out? There had to be a way, she prodded herself.

Well, one thing she had going for her was that Stanford had been her med school and Harley had already been affiliated with the hospital by the time she got there. All the EIS people were expected to do independent research, so she could say she was going out to Stanford for consultation. However, as much as the independent research was encouraged, it was never a high budgetary priority.

Of course, there was always the possibility of coming right out and telling Herb the truth and asking him to approve the trip. And there was the equal possibility that he would say no. Since she was determined to go anyway, that would mean directly disobeying him, and that would be worse. Well, the research gambit would be the one she'd have to go with and just hope for the best. And if she were going that far, she reasoned, she might as well go all the way and use her GTRs to get there.

She felt like a child who, in deciding whether to risk a foray to the forbidden cookie jar, tries to weigh the benefits of getting away with it against the severity of the punishment if she gets caught. But in her specific case it was merely a calculation, like figuring out miles per gallon on a road trip, something that you want to know but that won't stop you from proceeding regardless of the determination. Ever since she'd been a very litle girl, Diana had always followed her own lead and instincts. She had always gone ahead and done what she'd decided upon without regard to the possibility of punishment or other consequences. It was, she admitted in her more reflective moments, both her strength and her weakness.

Besides, in this case there really wasn't any choice.

14

PALO ALTO, CALIFORNIA

It was good to be back at Stanford. It was good to be back among all those romantically Romanesque buildings with their red-tile Spanish roofs and golden beige sandstone walls and gracefully arched colonnades. The campus was bright with spring. Flowers of all descriptions were everywhere she looked, in the courtyards and along the miles of walkways. She passed by the stately arches of Memorial Hall, where the tall, swaying palms and Chinese magnolias were coming back to life. And down by the old mausoleum, where the Stanford family lies buried under the eternal protection of the two stone sphinxes, even the cactus garden was in full bloom. Stanford was like no place else she'd ever spent time, a made-up land. And inside its expansive boundaries, Diana felt once again secure and protected.

Even the conflicts there took on a genteel, not completely for-real aura. Across Serra Street she saw the austere, no-nonsense lines of Hoover Tower rising against the blue California sky. It housed the self-importantly named Hoover Institution on War, Revolution, and Peace, an endowed conservative think tank the philosophy of which was always at odds with that of the liberal student body. But even the protests and the marches here, and the time they'd all joined hands and completely ringed the tower, were storybook peaceful compared with what she'd been through back East.

Calvin Chandler Harley had agreed to meet her at noon in his office in the Stanford Medical Center, on the northwest side of the campus. She had purposely told him very little about the reason for her visit, other than that she was conducting an investigation for the CDC and that he might have some knowledge or information that could be useful.

"I appreciate your taking the time to see me on such short notice," Diana said. "I know how busy you are."

"Not at all," the surgeon said. "I'm always happy to help when I can, especially a Stanford alumna. Did I ever have you on a rotation, Dr. Keegan?"

"No, I'm afraid I missed out. The luck of the draw. But I always wished I could scrub with you. Everyone did. And I certainly knew you by reputation."

Harley shot her a humorously reproving glance. "I've heard about my reputation around medical students. I know they call me the Iron Chancellor."

"Oh, no. That's not what I meant." But she did not protest the point too strenuously as she realized he rather relished the nickname. For her own part, thinking back on all the other things she'd been called in medical school and how she had so often felt she'd never reach this state of grace, Diana was relishing simply being referred to as Doctor by someone of the stature of Calvin Harley. She let the feeling play in her mind for a moment before going on.

"We're doing a longitudinal follow-up study of post traumatic stress disorder in Vietnam veterans," she informed him. Harley had a spacious, stylishly appointed office with a separate reception area, which was where he had conducted her for the interview. He sat facing into the room on a leather-covered wing chair that he said was good for his back. He gave her the expensive-looking couch, from which she could see the stately main entrance to the campus, lined by royal palms on either side of the road. Between Palm Drive and the Medical Center, Diana had a good view of the Anatomy Building, the place where her sensibilities as a physician had first been shaped.

"We're doing two things in this study," she continued. "We're generally comparing the psychological profile of our sample group to a same-age control group of nonveterans. Then we're also focusing in on specific individuals who were injured or suffered particular trauma in combat to see whether we can correlate battle wounds to subsequent psychological distress." She'd rehearsed the explanation many times before she arrived until she was satisfied with her ease and nonchalance in delivering it.

Harley nodded silently as she spoke, apparently anticipating the payoff to her request to see him. He was a fairly small man, immaculately dressed but beginning to show his age, with thinning gray hair and heavy owllike glasses. But his physical stature in no way diminished his commanding presence. There was an air of confidence and intensity about him that Diana recognized immediately as the mark of a first-rate surgeon. In the makeshift mobile hospitals Brian had described in Vietnam or the huge ultramodern operating facilities of Stanford, she could see that Calvin Chandler Harley was a man very much in charge.

"One of the subjects assigned to me was Anthony Lofton," she explained. "According to his service record, he was injured in combat and then operated on by you. His wife told me that he was experiencing considerable pain and discomfort and came in to see you—"

"His wife?" Harley said. He arched his heavy eyebrows.

"That's right. He was married. No children."

"Yes, I know he was married. I'm just a little confused by why you would mention this information as coming from his wife rather than him personally. Unless there's some secret here that—"

Suddenly she realized. There would be no reason he would know anything beyond the time he last saw Lofton. She felt like a policeman who has to break the news of shooting to the unsuspecting next of kin. "I'm—I'm sorry," she stammered. "Mr. Lofton is now deceased."

Harley's brow instantly creased, and the color drained from his face. "What! When? How did this happen?"

"Not long after you treated him here. An automobile accident on the San Bernardino Freeway in Los Angeles. He was alone in the car at the time. The police record states he was intoxicated and that probably caused the accident."

Diana wasn't sure, but she thought she perceived Harley loosen up slightly as he learned that the death had been caused by an accident rather than any possible medical problem, nothing he could have affected. That was only natural, she supposed. A surgeon's greatest single asset is his ego. If that is damaged, all his other skills become meaningless. She wanted to make sure he knew she wasn't accusing him of anything and wanted to figure out some way to let him know she wasn't there to second-guess any of his treatment decisions. But she concluded that it would be insulting even to raise the matter with him.

"I'm—I'm sorry to have to be the one to tell you this," she said. "I know it's never easy to lose a patient, especially one you've known this many years."

"Sometimes it's less easy than others," Harley said reflectively. "We bring all the vast resources of modern medicine to bear in diagnosing and treating a patient, we achieve results that would have been considered science fiction back when I was in medical school, and then something totally unexpected, totally out of our control, and having nothing to do with the original problem intervenes to cancel out what we've done." He shifted his gaze up to the ceiling. "Well, what is it they say? 'Physicians never cure anyone. They merely postpone the inevitable.'"

He looked back down after a time, signifying he was ready to continue. It was as if nothing had happened. He had by then totally recovered his composure and regained full control. Diana was not surprised by his resilience. No effective surgeon will let control lapse for long.

"Since the matter is now, ah, somewhat academic because of what's happened, do you mind if I ask you about the specific procedure you used with Mr. Lofton?"

"Anything you like," Harley answered. By his very ease and friendliness, Diana became conscious of taking up his time.

"My understanding is that he presented to you with intermittent but severe right-side abdominal pain."

Harley buzzed his intercom and requested Anthony Lofton's chart. Within three minutes, his secretary had laid it on the desk in front of him. He opened it, studied it a moment, then said, "That's right, abdominal pain."

"How was he behaving when he came in?" she inquired. "Was he calm? Agitated? Did anything strike you that seemed unusual?"

"Not particularly, as I remember. He was in pain, and that

usually affects a person's behavior. But keep in mind, Mr. Lofton was a former marine. He was used to tolerating a fair amount of discomfort without whimpering or whining."

Diana couldn't tell if this was a subtle gibe at her or her sex, but she decided she'd better let it pass and press on. "But there was no disorientation or paranoia or anything like that? He didn't seem to be suffering from any stress disorder that you could detect."

"Absolutely not," Harley replied. "I would have noticed that. No, under the circumstances, I would say he was quite rational and pleasant. I wish all my patients comported themselves in such a manner. We had a good conversation, and I became reacquainted with his case. I operated on hundreds, if not thousands, of young men over in Vietnam. So needless to say, I did not remember him specifically. But as I reviewed the record, I realized it was a rather routine one that we could proceed with in a routine fashion."

"And then what did you do?"

"Let me see ..." He looked back down at the forms on his desktop. "Yes, right. We did a series of X ray tomograms, and from these we decided that it had something to do with his shrapnel injuries in Vietnam."

Diana felt her pulse quicken and worked hard not to show it.

"Either fragments that had worked themselves into bad positions or adhesions from the original surgery."

"And so you ..."

"We did a right-side laparotomy. Turns out it was the shrapnel itself." At this Harley smiled, one doctor to another. "At least I was glad it wasn't adhesions—nothing I was responsible for. I hate to operate to clean up the 'loose ends' of a previous operation. Anyway"—he sighed—"we took out three good-size chunks of metal, and as far as I knew, that took care of it for him. Recovery was quick and uneventful."

Diana asked, "You say you operated on the right side. From what part of the body did these metal chunks come?"

"Well, let's see what it says here. All right. One from the liver, near the surface. One from the hepatic flexure of the colon. And one just at the base of the stomach, in the vicinity of the pyloric sphincter."

"Was there—was there anything at all ... unusual about the shrapnel fragments you removed?"

"How exactly do you mean?"

"I don't know," she said, trying again to be casual. "It's just that when you mentioned the fragments, it got me to thinking that we've had a couple of reports in this study of peculiar varieties of shrapnel, odd shapes and the like. I was wondering if anything particular about it struck you."

"I saw a lot of shrapnel during my two years in Vietnam," Harley stated. "And I can tell you it comes in all shapes and sizes, so I can't say that one piece would stand out over another to me. Anything that was large or near an artery or threatening to provoke hemorrhaging, we always took out right away. The rest stayed in unless or until it started causing problems, which is apparently what happened with Mr. Lofton here."

"No, this didn't have to do with size or shape so much as, I guess you'd call it structure."

"I'm afraid you'll have to be a little less oblique," Harley said.

Diana thought for a moment. "The shrapnel pieces you removed from Mr. Lofton, did you examine them closely?"

"Reasonably so, I should think."

"And did any of them look as if they'd been worked on?"

"Worked on?"

"Altered in some way that made them different from ordinary random fragments. Did any of them look as if they'd been hollowed out or appear to be closed on one end with a tiny stopper?"

"No, I don't think so," Harley said, disquieted. "You've found others like this?"

"Ah, those are only the reports I've received," she said offhandedly. "We haven't been able to correlate them with anything, so it probably has nothing to do with the scope or subject of our study."

"I'm sure I would have studied Mr. Lofton's shrapnel in the operating room, and I certainly didn't notice anything there. I would have remembered that. Of course, on the other hand, whatever you're describing is not the type of thing one would be looking for. And unlike a piece of biopsied tissue, a metal fragment wouldn't routinely be sent down to pathology. So to answer your question, I couldn't absolutely rule out the possibility, but I would consider it highly unlikely."

"Do you still have the fragments somewhere, by any chance?"

"No. I'm sure I threw them away right then and there, just as I would have back in Vietnam. Sorry."

"Please don't be," she said imploringly. "I'm sure it's nothing. I was just grasping for straws, hoping I could get some things to come together. And what you have told me has been extremely helpful." She closed her spiral notebook and put it back in the bag by her feet. "You've been very kind to talk to me, and I hope you'll allow me to call on you again if necessary."

"By all means," he said. "Whatever I can do to help, please let me know."

Diana rose to her feet. "Thank you again," she said, presenting her hand far out in front of her.

Harley took it and asked, "Will you be staying out here with us long?"

"I wish I could," she responded. "I didn't realize how much I missed the place until I came back. But I really do have to get back to work, so I've got to catch a flight to Atlanta this afternoon."

"Too bad," the surgeon said. "I really think that Stanford is at its most delightful in the spring."

"I couldn't agree with you more," Diana said.

"Perhaps it's something in the air," said Harley. He then took a moment to regard Diana, standing there straight and tall before him. "Or perhaps it is merely all the lovely young ladies like yourself who seemed to blossom this time of year."

Diana blushed politely, more because she knew it was expected of her than from any reason of her own. "That's very sweet," she said. "I wish it were only true as well."

"I'm sorry you can't stay with us longer," Harley stated.

"I am, too," Diana replied. "But with any luck I'll find a reason to be back here before too long." He was still holding her hand in his. She casually drew it back. "Dr. Harley, it's been a real honor and pleasure." In that, if not the reason for her visit, she was being totally honest. Any surgeon Brian would look up to with such awe must have something very, very special. She was glad to have had the opportunity to come in contact with him, however briefly or tangentially.

And then she turned, left his office, took the elevator down to the lobby, and walked out onto Campus Drive and into the dreamworld that Stanford was for her.

Calvin Chandler Harley watched in silence and waited until Diana Keegan disappeared down the corridor. Then he walked casually over to the window and waited until she emerged into view on Campus Drive, passing by the Anatomy Building. He watched her from behind for several minutes. When she was finally out of sight on the other side of the Frost Amphitheater, he left the window and went back over to his desk. He reached for the telephone, then stopped. He walked over to the door and made certain no one was lurking in the hall outside. He went back to the desk, sat down, pressed the last button on the telephone console, waited for the tone, then punched in the code which had been given to no one else. There were two rings, then the short beep announcing that the scrambler was in operation.

"Yes?" came the voice at the other end.

"We're in trouble," Calvin Chandler Harley quietly announced.

CHICAGO, ILLINOIS

By the time she'd booked her flight, there were no nonstops available in either direction, and Diana had had to take a routing through O'Hare. That airport was always such a mess to travel through, and today was no exception. Not only that, but her flight had come in at what had to be the farthest gate there was. It was practically in Waukegan. Now, as she walked down the endless crowded concourse to her connecting plane, a minor epiphany occurred to her. She did not want to go home.

At least she was making progress if she could consider Atlanta as home, she decided. But Stanford was still very much with her. She would have liked to have stayed there as long as she could, and the prospect of going back and facing her apartment and then Herb and even Sharon filled her with the kind of free-floating anxiety she thought she'd pretty much conquered in the past couple of years. Nothing said she *had* to get on that plane.

Well, she'd already raided the cookie jar. Might as well get what was coming for taking two cookies as one. It didn't take her long to make the decision. She wondered if it was a sign of any kind of moral decay that these decisions were seeming easier and easier.

She walked over to the first airline counter she saw—she didn't even focus on which company it was—and asked to see the current universal flight schedule. She found the flight she was looking for, then asked if she could exchange her ticket. The man behind the counter suggested she might want to deal with the airline whose flight it was, but Diana pleaded that she was in a hurry and blinked her large eyes rapidly, as if she were about to cry. She hated doing things that way; it was so antifeminist. But it happened to be highly effective with men, and it was never a good idea to dispense arbitrarily with any of the weapons in your arsenal.

Once she had the new ticket in hand, she felt a strange sense of liberation, of delivery actually. She walked over to the bank of telephones, stepped into the booth, picked up the receiver, and dialed in her credit card number. God, she hoped he'd be home. If no one answered, would she still get on the plane and ... She had to make a decision fast.

Please let him answer. I'll be good from now on if you do.

"Hello?" she heard Brian say after the second ring. Thank God.

"Hello, yourself," she replied with flooding relief. Then, snuggling as best she could into the phone booth to avoid the din of the concourse and feel as close to him as she could, she said, "I've got the report from Palo Alto. How'd you like me to deliver it in person?"

ATLANTA, GEORGIA

Sharon Mowbray walked back to her office triumphant and ready to take all comers. It was a marked contrast with the wretched figure that had trudged timidly and fearfully out of that same office less than ninety minutes before. It had been unfair to spring the annual evaluation on her with only a half hour to prepare, and she had been sure she was going to blow it and send her promising legal career plummeting off the twenty-eighth floor of the Trust Company Tower. There was too much on the line for the partners not to give her the chance to psyche herself up. And that, of course, was why they had done it. Always keep the underlings off-balance. Always make them jump for it.

But it had gone splendidly, better than she possibly could have hoped. There were three senior partners and four junior partners sitting across the inlaid walnut conference room table from her. No one said anything for a long time. She sat there trying to look natural and poised, conscious of keeping her knees together, and all she could think of were the deodorant commercials on TV. "Never let them see you sweat." They took forever glancing at the hidden contents of the personnel folder in front of them. And when, in what seemed years later, they finally told her that it all looked pretty good, she thought her racing heart was going to pound clear out of her chest.

"Definitely on track," one of them had said. She couldn't even remember at this point which one it was. But when he said "track," she knew he was referring to partnership track, the ultimate carrot at the end of a very long stick.

"So just keep your nose clean, keep doing your excellent good work, and we should have more to say to you next year at this time." Then they'd gone around the table one by one and shaken her hand and offered nice little words of encouragement.

That had been all. No qualifications, no admonitions to clean up this or that part of her act. They *had* recognized her abilities and her efforts. All those nights and weekends and anonymous staff work had not gone unnoticed. They saw what she could do and they appreciated it. She was "definitely on track."

And that called for a celebration. Well, maybe that wasn't quite practical on such short notice, but something at least a little bit special. She deserved a break after all this time. She'd worked like hell. She'd earned it.

Suddenly she knew what she'd do. She'd break the legal drudge pattern. Just for one night. She wouldn't work late. The stroke of six she'd be out of there like a lightning bolt. Diana would be home tonight. She missed Diana, missed her a great deal, she realized, now that she stopped to think about it. She hardly ever saw her anymore, and this made her sad. Tonight it would be different, though. Tonight she'd make a point of being there when Diana got home from the airport. Diana would be tired, but with the good news today, Sharon was sure she'd be willing to go out and have a few drinks and celebrate.

Except for those times when Diana didn't come home at all— and there hadn't been very many of them lately—Sharon couldn't remember the last time she'd gotten home before her. But tonight she would. And wouldn't Diana be surprised?

ALEXANDRIA, VIRGINIA

She didn't spot him until he came right up behind her and put his hand on her shoulder, but that didn't really surprise her because he was good at not being seen when he didn't want to be. And airports were always a good place to lose yourself in the crowd.

"My own personal commando," Diana said teasingly.

"Could have had you there," Brian said playfully, and gave her a light kiss on the lips. Diana thought it a good sign he could joke about this.

"Yeah. You also could have made me jump through the ceiling when you touched me like that," she answered chidingly, "not to mention screaming across the room."

"I didn't think you would," he replied, taking her duffel from her and guiding her toward the exit. "You're too tough."

"Thanks," she said dryly. She latched onto his arm and nuzzled her cheek tenderly against his shoulder. She also thought he might be angry that she'd come back to Washington on a whim like this. It had been impossible to tell from the phone conversation. But now that they were together, he seemed as glad to see her as she was to see him. It hardly mattered that she hadn't thought beyond tonight and the fact that tomorrow morning she'd have to think up some powerfully good excuse for not being in Atlanta. Herb was going to cream her. Well, no sense thinking about that until she absolutely had to, preferably tonight in bed with the lights out.

National Airport was particularly busy. "I'm surprised to see you inside," she commented. "I was going to wait by the curb since I didn't think you'd be able to find a parking space."

"I didn't drive," he explained. "I took the Metro."

"Didn't you get a rental car till your Volvo's fixed?"

"I did. But I decided to take the subway anyhow. It's easier to tell if you're being followed."

"Oh," she said quietly, and didn't say anything else until they were on the platform at Metro Center waiting to change trains for the Red Line.

"Were you able to get all the information I asked for?" she inquired. She had quickly picked up his habit of glancing around to see if anyone seemed particularly attentive to the conversation. And she'd gotten nearly as quick at sizing up the possibilities, noticing if anyone looked suspicious. That was a new talent she wasn't sure she was all that happy with.

"I think I've got it all," he said. "I told Jill what you thought we needed after you called, and she was going to try to figure out a way to pull as much of it as she could out of the computer. She said the way the files are arranged, we'd probably have to wade through a lot of garbage we didn't need before coming up with anything useful. She and Gregory are coming over tonight after dinner to get started."

"So my timing in coming here was actually pretty good," Diana said as the train pulled into the station.

"Yes, I'd say your timing was pretty good indeed," he replied, and leaned over and kissed her again, unconcerned about who might be watching.

ATLANTA, GEORGIA

It felt strange being alone in the apartment, at least while it was still light out. It had been so long since she'd spent an evening by herself like this Sharon hardly knew what to do with herself. First, she decided to luxuriate in the bath, after pouring in two and half vials of the green bubble and moisturizing gel Diana had brought back from that hotel in Lisbon. Then, before getting dressed in fresh clothes, she put on her bathrobe and sat cross-legged on her bed to do her nails. She didn't use her normal polish. Instead, she tried on a color she'd been wanting to experiment with, knowing that if she didn't like it, for once she had plenty of time to take it off and start over again. Tomorrow morning she would be back to the grind, back to being a serious high-pressure lawyer. For tonight she was determined first to pamper herself completely, then to enjoy herself completely with Diana as soon as her roommate got home. Just the two of them on the town; two independent girls making their own fun. They'd be completely independent, and the rest of the world could kiss off if they didn't like it. And with that "who needs them?" attitude, maybe they'd even get lucky and find two men with similar needs and desires.

The nail color was fine. It turned out much better than she'd thought it would and nicely complemented her complexion. Some days just everything works out for you no matter what you do. This was obviously her day. She'd have to remember this shade next time she went to the drugstore.

She took off her robe, hung it on the hook on the bathroom door, and went over to the closet to select leisurely the appropriate attire for the evening. After shifting back and forth in her mind for at least ten minutes, she finally settled on the blue chiffon blouse and matching skirt. Yes, that was definitely the right choice. It was easy, comfortable, and alluring, without being too obviously come-on. It was the kind of outfit in which she could make herself into whatever she wanted to be, depending on the situation. Diana seemed to be able to do that regardless of what she was wearing, regardless of anything really. She couldn't possibly envy her, though. Diana had always been too sweet and caring for her to do that. But Sharon just wasn't like her and so had to be more careful and calculating in the way she handled herself.

Diana should be home anytime now, she thought. Actually she would have thought she'd have been here already.

The doorbell rang. That was funny. People were supposed to have to use the intercom from downstairs. She wondered how anyone had got through without buzzing from the front door. Unless it was a neighbor who was already inside the building. But who would be calling on her this time of night?

She looked through the peephole in the door. There wasn't anyone there. It probably was a neighbor, just letting her know he was dropping off some mail that had ended up in the wrong box. That happened a lot lately. Postage rates kept going up, and it seemed that the mail delivery got sloppier and sloppier.

She opened the door.

Instantly two hands grabbed at her face and neck and pushed her back inside the apartment. The door slammed behind her. She jerked her head around. The man was wearing a ski mask and tight rubber surgical gloves, and there was another man behind him, and he was wearing a ski mask and surgical gloves, too. They both looked like the police artist sketches of bank robbery suspects shown on television. Her insides froze. She was beyond terror.

"What do you want?" she gasped, although she knew there weren't many possibilities.

Neither man said anything. This made her all the more panic-stricken. She was being held in a tight hammerlock around her neck. He was choking her so hard that she could hardly breathe. She felt her Adam's apple squeezed into the crook of his elbow.

The other man hustled down the hall in the direction of the bedrooms. The one who had been holding her threw her to the living room floor and jumped on top, cupping her mouth with his hand. He grabbed her chiffon blouse by the collar and ripped it down. She could feel the hot breath through his woolen mask on her bare chest. She thought she was going to be sick. From one of the bedrooms—she couldn't be sure which one—she heard the crash of drawers being smashed against walls and hitting the floor. *Oh God*, she cried to herself, *how could this all be happening to me? Please don't let them kill me. Please don't let me die!*

She thrashed from side to side, trying to heave her attacker off. He pinioned her with his knees so that she couldn't move at all. He took his hand away from her mouth and used it to grasp both her wrists together and stretch them above her head. She opened her mouth to scream, but he slapped her hard across the face, stifling any sound she would have made. With his free hand he forced her skirt up above her waist and hooked his foot around her ankle to spread her legs apart.

Again she tried to scream, and again he slapped her with the full force of his leverage.

He had his thumb inside the waistband of her underpants. She could feel his fingers grazing the bare skin of her belly. But then the other man came back into the living room, and he stopped. The other man was carrying something in one hand. Sharon couldn't tell what it was.

"Did we find what we were looking for?" the one on top of her asked him.

"No," the other man replied.

"Shit."

Then he took something out of his pocket, put his gloved hand tightly over her nose and mouth, and the world went black.

WASHINGTON, D.C.

The computer printouts—heaps of wide, dull green, fan-folded, perforated pages, compressed into tight little stacks which made their contents seem even more formidable and daunting—were spread across the dining table. Jill had been running queries on the computer all afternoon, trying to come up with "back-door" entries into files that were supposedly classified secret. She had arranged telephone hookups with computerized navy data bases all across the country, and this was what she had come up with. The greatest single source had been the computer data base at Camp Pendleton, the home of the Third Marine Division.

"It wasn't as hard as you might think getting in," Jill said. "Remember, even though personnel files are classified, a whole lot of individuals have to have access to them. They have to, so people can be paid, processed, reassigned, evaluated, discharged, et cetera, et cetera, et cetera. So if you know what you're doing, you can get in. The bigger problem is figuring out what to ask for, so you don't get overwhelmed with material." She indicated the small mountain of paper on the table. "Even so, we've got our work cut out for us."

"But at least you've got one more set of hands and eyes," Diana commented.

"And it looks like we're going to need them," Brian said.

They had spent the first half hour hearing and digesting Diana's report from Stanford. Now they prepared to correlate it with what Jill called the raw data.

"Where do we begin?" Gregory asked.

"Well, let's begin with what we know," Jill said. "We know that all the subjects were enlisted-grade marines serving with the Third Division. They all were serving in the same part of Vietnam during the same period in 1969, which happens to be the same time that Brian was over there with the Third Division as a medical corpsman. Further, they all were assigned to Colonel Blagden's Seventh Amphibious Unit. Now, Brian, where would you like to go from here?"

Brian thought for a moment. The old rules were coming back to him. In any type of group effort always have the team members working in parallel. "Let's all try to be doing the same thing at the same time. Why don't we each take a couple of these printouts and look for the same answers simultaneously?"

"Good idea," Jill said. "Let me just show you all how to read these things. It isn't difficult, but you've got to get the hang of it."

They gathered around Jill, and she instructed them in the finer points of reading computer files as set up and organized by the United States Navy. Diana already had experience with computers in her work and so picked up on the particulars quickly. Brian listened and observed patiently, nodding when he was ready to go on to the next step. Gregory squinted at the page in front of him and twisted his pudgy face into an expression of hopeless befuddlement until Jill, in desperation, began resorting to baby talk. He came around quickly after that. Jill handed around the files, keeping two for herself.

"Now," said Brian, "we know there's something here. Let's see what we can come up with."

The room was silent for many minutes, the only sound being

the occasional scratching of pen or pencil on yellow legal pads. Most of the information would be useless or meaningless. They all knew that, yet they also knew they would not be able to tell that until they had gone through the effort.

"Look at this," Diana said. She held up her printout. "I've got a note of a combat injury for Christopher Schuyler the same day as the one we know about for Anthony Lofton."

"What kind of injury?" Gregory asked.

"It doesn't say," she replied. "But he got a Purple Heart for it. That's how I found it, through this citation that went along with it."

"I wonder if it was a fragmentation wound," Brian said. "Look up the date."

She scanned the printout until she came up with what she was looking for, then compared it to the notes she'd taken on Sonny Lofton's file at Stanford. "The same date as Lofton." Her voice betrayed the trace of a quaver.

A hushed silence fell over the room, different from the silence of only a few minutes before. They all four looked tentatively at each other. Then Brian, who was studying Tyrrell Jefferson's file, and Jill, who had Maxie Craig's, looked reflexively back down at their printouts.

"I've got an entry here," Brian said. "Jefferson also has a Purple Heart. I should have remembered that," he stated solemnly. "I saw it at his mother's house."

"Craig's got one, too," said Jill. She leaned over to the printout she had positioned next to his on the table. "So does Christopher Schuyler. And the dates match up perfectly."

And again they looked up, and their eyes met in silence.

It was one of those moments when the last vestiges of coincidence give way to the first solid outlines of pattern. Up until such a moment it is still possible to dismiss each individual occurrence, the way one might optimistically ignore individual bodily symptoms until they resolve themselves into an unavoidable pattern of disease. Up until then there is always a chance, and that chance can be enough to sustain one. But at a certain point the weight of evidence becomes just slightly too heavy to turn away from, and the false security of ignorance fades harshly away. Six marines from the Third Division. Six injuries at the same time. And more than fifteen years later six deaths. Somehow the first two facts had to relate to the third. And only by relating them, one to the other, did Brian think they might have a chance. Only a chance, but those were the best odds being offered, and so those were the ones you took.

How serious had each of the wounds been? he wanted to know. And were they all from shrapnel? As soon as he got to the office, he would put a trace on their medical records and see if he could find out.

Once the four of them knew what they were looking for, the corroborating information was readily available in the personnel files. Each man showed a medical leave entry for surgery at the base hospital at Phu Bai. But when they went back to look at the service records themselves, they found none of the men showed discharge or reassignment after the procedure. In fact, each man apparently returned to combat shortly after the surgery, indicating that at the time the fragmentation wounds were not considered too serious.

"Does that make sense?" Jill inquired.

"Sure," Brian answered. "It could. It all depends on where it gets you. Most of these pieces are very tiny and don't penetrate in a vital spot. There are a lot of men still walking around today carrying a load of World War Two shrapnel."

As another point the group noted that all the marines they were studying had been decorated for bravery in combat in addition to their Purple Hearts.

The inquiry continued. Had Calvin Chandler Harley performed all the operations?

The file didn't contain that information. With luck they could get it from the individual medical files. But if he had—and Brian said there was a good chance of it—he must have been an iron man. This had been a period of intense action for the marines near the demilitarized zone. Fighting had been almost constant, and combat casualties were high.

"Also," Diana said heatedly, "maybe that explains why each of these men was returned to battle so soon after his injury in what I can only think of as a total perversion of logic and medical ethics. It's so typical of everything about that perverse, disgusting war. Nobody gave a flying fuck about those men. That much was obvious. Any sensible, humane system would have immediately sent them home . . . to avoid permanent psychological damage, if nothing else."

"You weren't there," Brian answered her coolly. "You can't judge."

She started to say something but then stopped and pursed her lips, indicating that she had decided not to pursue it. This was neither the time nor the place.

"Then there's the liver finding," Brian went on. "I took a closed fragment capsule from Radley Davis's liver and an open one from Sam Hardesty's up in Montana. That placement is certainly more than coincidence."

"And even though Calvin Harley doesn't think the fragments he removed from Anthony Lofton at Stanford were hollow, he did remove one from the liver," Diana added. "Is there anything about liver involvement in any of the other records?"

"No," Jill replied, scanning once more to be sure.

"There wouldn't be," Brian affirmed. "If you got any specific medical note at all, it would only be on the pieces taken out, not the ones left in. But that probably wouldn't be in a personnel file anyway, unless it was part of some merit citation. And the way it was back then I wouldn't expect to see any detailed postsurgical notes when we get into the medical files."

"Could we get X rays?" Diana asked.

"Theoretically, yes," Gregory said. "They're supposed to be kept in each soldier's medical file at the hospital at which they were taken. But you're talking about a war situation. It would be tough to lay your hands on them this many years later."

Diana thought about it, then said, "We may not need them."

"What do you mean?" Brian asked.

"Even if every X ray shows a fragment in the liver, that doesn't prove anything. At least not in a way we can use."

"So what do we want to do?"

"Well, to go back to the epidemiology model, now that we've come up with our case profile, after Brian gets hold of the medical records, the next step would be to identify, interview, and take specimens from a control group that also fitted our case definition."

"I'm not sure I'm following," Jill said.

"In the case of an unknown disease that attacked, say, middle-aged men with respiratory difficulties, once we'd identified and studied the ones who came down with it and come up with that case definition, then we'd go out and assemble a control group of other middle-aged men with respiratory difficulties who didn't come down with the disease. Then, by comparing the two groups, we'd try to narrow down what it was that distinguished the first group from the second."

Gregory rubbed what there was of his chin. "So how does that translate into what we're doing?"

Diana was still thinking it through as she spoke. "We have a certain profile here that all the victims fit into. Right?"

"Right."

"Okay. Then, the way I see it, we should be going one step further now in identifying other subjects who fit the case definition: members of this amphibious unit of this Third Marine group who also served at the same time and who were wounded by shrapnel. Then we have to go out and find them and see how this control group compares to our profile of known victims."

"And find out if any of the others have strange capsules in them?" Gregory inquired.

"Exactly."

"But that first one we looked at didn't do anything," he said. "It was just water. And the second one was opened up."

"Yes, but what was its relation, if any, to the cattle plague? We've got to see if we find any more of these capsules in our control group."

"And if we do?"

"As Sherlock Holmes said, and they quote it to us all the time down at CDC, 'It is a capital mistake to theorize before one has data.' But now at least we know which way to turn."

"Sounds like a good idea," Brian said. He turned to Jill. "Can it be done?"

"Just about anything can be done," she said. "The question is can it be done manageably when you've got so much data to cull from." Then she put her hand reassuringly on the back of his hand. "But we'll see what we can do."

She and Gregory got up to leave. "First thing in the morning," she told Brian.

"That reminds me," Diana said. "First thing in the morning I've got to call in sick to my office. I'm supposed to be there. Brian, don't let me forget."

He stood up with Jill and Gregory and walked them over toward the front hall. When he had kissed her, clapped him on the shoulder, and then closed the door behind them, he turned around to find Diana standing just in front of him.

She put her arms around his neck and guided herself in close to his body, until she could feel the rhythmic expansion of his chest heavy against her breasts. She pulled her arms tight around him. "So, are you glad I'm here?" she asked.

"What do you think?" he said.

He nudged her chin with his hand so that her huge, brimming eyes faced him directly. She had looked at him like that before. It was a look that would melt iron. "Of course I am," he said.

"You're not angry?"

"No. Why should I be?"

She shrugged, but not enough to break his grasp. "I don't know. But you've got this thing about having your 'orders' obeyed."

"And you've got this thing about not obeying orders." He laughed, holding her tighter.

"That's because at heart you're still a soldier and I'm still a revolutionary. I guess neither one of us can escape our nature."

"You must be tired," he said.

"I am." She gave him a kittenish smile. "But not too tired."

"Then how would you react if I were to 'order' you into the bedroom?"

"I think I might be inclined to obey that particular order," she stated, and then took his hand to lead the way.

Seemingly within seconds they both were undressed, entwined in each other's arms and deepest feelings, once again filling each of the other's empty spaces, beginning the steady rise to the summit of their mutual passion.

The telephone by the bed rang.

"Oh, shit," Brian said.

"Let it go," she pleaded.

"I can't. What if it's an emergency from the hospital?"

Diana sighed and rolled over next to him on her back. She pulled up one tawny leg and then the other in an effort to stretch the tension of unfulfilled lovemaking from her body. Brian ran one hand gently along her hip and thigh.

"Hello," he said into the receiver.

A sobbing, grief-stricken voice filled the line. "Is—is Diana there?"

Diana saw his face turn suddenly grim. She sat up on her elbows and asked with her eyes what was going on. He handed her the phone.

"Yes?"

"Diana?" The sobbing continued just as strong. "Diana, it's Sharon."

"Sharon! What's wrong? Where are you?"

"I'm—I'm at home. I ... When you didn't come back, I thought maybe you were there."

"Sharon, what happened? Are you all right?" Diana rose to her knees on the bed, her body straight, still naked. She shifted the phone from ear to ear.

"I guess ... I don't know. They attacked me. Tried to rape me."

"Who did?" Diana demanded. She motioned for Brian to get on the extension in the living room.

"Two men. They just broke in. I thought they were going to kill me."

"Okay, tell me exactly what happened." Diana struggled to maintain some semblance of calm in her voice.

Sharon told her the story, beginning back with her superior evaluation that afternoon, through coming home and waiting for Diana, up to the ringing of the doorbell and the beginning of the living nightmare. Diana listened as patiently as she could, prodding when Sharon broke down completely, sifting out whatever wasn't immediately relevant, trying to contain the terror that gripped her.

"Did you call the police?"

"Uh-huh."

"Did they take care of you? What did they do?"

"They came and looked around and took pictures and stuff, and then they took me to the hospital and examined me."

"Were you ... Sharon, were you ... raped?"

"No. No, I wasn't. I thought I was going to be before they killed me." Diana could feel her roommate shuddering on the other end of the phone. "One of the men had me down on the floor with my dress up and he was—he was about to do it until—"

"Until what, Sharon?"

"Until the other one came in from the bedrooms and he was carrying something from there. And then he showed it to the one who was on top of me. They both stared at me. It seemed like a long time, and I thought they were going to kill me right there.

But then the one on me put a cloth or a handkerchief or something over my face, and I passed out."

"What was it that he showed him?"

"I couldn't see it at the time. I didn't notice until I woke up and they were gone and it was on the floor beside me. The glass was broken," she said sadly. "I'm sorry, Diana." She began weeping openly again.

"The glass was broken on what?" Diana asked firmly.

"That picture from your dresser," Sharon responded tearfully. "The really cute one at the beach. The picture of you."

UPPERVILLE, VIRGINIA

The man known as Contact to some was called Michael Swansea by those with whom he shared a more traditional relationship. The house he occupied was also rather traditional, a columned colonial mansion set on eighty acres in the midst of Virginia's most exclusive hunt country. But those invited to the meeting today were unable to take advantage of the cool, comfortable veranda that extended the entire length of the house in back or admire the authentic period furnishings in the expansive drawing room at the front. They had assembled in the small brick structure behind the lake that had once served as the estate's smokehouse. The fact that it was hardly large enough to accommodate five men comfortably was not an issue. Since the renovation the tiny locked house was nothing more than the protective covering for a spiral metal staircase that led to the underground room below.

The men at the meeting also had names, of course, but they weren't necessary in this context. For the sake of clarity and precision, colors had been assigned. Two of them—Red and Green—were still bleary-eyed from all their recent traveling. They'd only had time to change their clothes and briefly freshen up in the facility built into the barn. Their knitted ski masks were still in their briefcases.

"Well, it was almost a model operation," Swansea began, wasting no time on welcome or pleasantries. "We did everything right, everything by the book. We made it look like a routine rape-robbery. We even had a third man who didn't match your descriptions 'seen' by the neighbors prowling around the complex. Only one thing went wrong. It was the wrong girl."

"There was no way to predict that," the first man—Red—

commented. "All the intelligence was sound. Our information said that Dr. Keegan would be returning home that evening, and the roommate almost always works late at her law office. She should have certainly been home by then, and she should have been home alone."

"I'm not criticizing you," Swansea said. "We'll review the entire mission in due course, as we always do. But for right now we have to deal with the realities. Reality number one, Dr. Keegan should have been home by the time we got there. God knows why she wasn't. Reality number two, we expected the Centers for Disease Control to become involved with the incident in Montana. That would be routine. But is it merely coincidence that they are now engaged in a study of post traumatic stress in veterans? And is it merely a coincidence that Dr. Keegan, who investigated the Montana outbreak, was assigned to it? And is it a further mere coincidence that she chose to interview Dr. Harley at Stanford? These, gentlemen, are the issues we have to deal with at the moment." He removed his glasses and drummed them lightly on the tabletop.

"How serious is it that we didn't get the girl last night?" one of the others asked. His designation was Blue, and he was considered among the more practical-minded in the group.

"That's what we've got to determine," Swansea said. "Quite clearly Red's and Green's mission was to intercept her before she had a chance to report in the following morning. They didn't accomplish that. Potentially now—" He stopped himself. "Now I won't say 'unmanageable,' because no situation is ever unmanageable, but potentially this particular situation could have become infinitely more difficult with her report.

"But it didn't," Swansea continued, and at this point he stood up for emphasis. "Why? Because our intercept of CDC project listings, completed just this afternoon, contains no such post traumatic stress project."

"How reliable is our intelligence?" Purple asked.

"Very," Swansea replied.

"So then Keegan is free-lancing?"

There was a discreet silence around the table as the implications of this conclusion sunk in.

"That's the way it's beginning to look," the chief stated.

"Which gives us one more new, unknown factor to have to work with," Purple said.

"I'm afraid that's what we have to assume," Swansea said, and he did nothing to hide his displeasure. "And now we've missed our chance with her."

Blue put up his hand. "How much do we think she knows?"

"Potentially as much as Thorpe."

"And how much is that?"

"We're not sure. But in a way it doesn't matter. To the extent he's already involved, he can cause us extreme problems."

"So are we going to try another operation on him?"

Swansea sat back down again. He leaned well into the over-stuffed leather chair and came as close to slouching back as he ever did. "There's been some difference of opinion on that matter from the policy makers above us. There seems to be logic on both sides. And for the time being we'll just have to be flexible."

He was about to go on to the next point when he saw the pained expression on Green's face. "What's the problem?" he asked.

"I was just thinking," Green said. "Under the circumstances, when we found out we had the wrong girl last night, do you think we should have gone ahead with the rape-murder?"

All the others waited for their leader's response.

"Absolutely not," Swansea declared. "Under the unfortunate and unforeseeable circumstances, you did the right thing. Once we start killing people unnecessarily, we're no better than our enemies."

15

WASHINGTON, D.C.

Sending Diana back to Atlanta was now out of the question, Brian had quickly decided. The threat was no longer theoretical, no longer an extension by implication of the attempt made on him. Had she gone straight back home as she had originally planned and not come to Washington instead, she would now be dead. It was that simple. And all through that night the fact had preyed on both of them.

Diana's first instincts, once morning had come and the initial shock had worn off, were to get back home as soon as she could. She was on the phone to the airlines before going to bed. Brian wasn't surprised, and he admired her for it. She wanted to get back to be with Sharon. Sharon needed her now, Diana said. It was because of her that this horrible thing had happened. She was responsible for what had been done to Sharon, for this attack, this hideous violation. And the most frightening thing of all was that it was not a random attack. It had been planned and premeditated, although Sharon was still the innocent victim. But wasn't Diana also an innocent victim? they both reasoned. After all, she had done nothing to provoke this violence. Innocent, yes, but not uninvolved. And there was one thing Diana had learned from life and her years of commitment to various causes. There is always a price to be paid for involvement.

Brian couldn't blame her for the way she felt and what she wanted to do, but he couldn't let her go either. Forbidding Diana anything she'd set her mind to was essentially impossible, Brian knew, unless one was prepared to strap her down physically. But after a long go-around that lasted for most of what was left of the night, he had managed to convince her that the best thing for the time being was for neither of the women to be staying at the apartment. From Sharon's description it was acutely clear that the intruders wanted one thing, or rather one person, and they were willing to go to the most extreme lengths to get what they wanted. The important thing was for Diana to stay out of sight and for Sharon to stay out of the way.

So Diana spent much of the next morning on the telephone to Atlanta. She had a long, emotionally draining conversation with Sharon at her office, convincing her that with all she'd been through, she should move out for a while. Wasn't there someone at work she could room with, just for a week or so, just until she pulled herself back together?

"But why?" Sharon wanted to know. "Do you think they'll be back?"

"I can't say," Diana replied. "We don't know anything about these people. But why should we take the chance?"

"Diana, is there something you're not telling me?" Sharon challenged her.

"No!" Diana said hastily. Then more softly: "No, not really. I don't know any more than you do."

"Then when are you coming back?"

"I'm—I'm not sure." It was the logical question, but she illogically wished that Sharon hadn't asked it. "I wish I could come back right away and be with you. That's all I really want. But—but something's come up with work, and I have to be away longer than I expected." She hated herself for lying, but in a way, she thought to comfort herself, it wasn't really or completely a lie.

"Does it have to do with that trip to Montana?" Sharon asked.

"Yes, that's right," Diana said, and felt slightly better that she was edging slightly nearer to the truth. "You just promise me you'll stay somewhere else safe for a little while."

"I promise," Sharon said glumly.

"And call me back here as soon as you know where it'll be. And I promise I'll call you every night till I come back."

"Okay, Diana. Bye."

Diana hung up the phone with a sad and empty feeling in her stomach. But as Brian had said, there really wasn't any other way for her right now. At least Sharon would be all right if she stayed away. The two men might very well come back to the apartment, but it would be Diana, not Sharon, they would be looking for. As long as Sharon stayed away from Diana, she would be safe. And that was another reason for keeping out of Atlanta.

The second call was even more difficult and involved an even bigger lie. It was getting to be a way of life all of a sudden. Diana had been forced to lie so much lately that when she looked in the mirror, she almost expected to see her nose start growing.

She needed something that would give her an excuse to be not only away from her desk but also out of town. The first thing that came to her was the "sick mother" explanation. But as she began putting together the details in her mind, she soon despaired of making it work. It was such an obvious cliché she didn't think she could deliver it straight, even over the telephone. Furthermore, Herb probably wouldn't buy it anyway. He was too smart for that. And her credibility with him wasn't exactly at the highest plateau at the moment.

Instead, she decided to be sick herself. That made much more sense. She'd caught some kind of flu bug out in California, and it had really decked her. You couldn't argue with that one. And she'd get sympathy for it besides. So instead of coming straight back to Atlanta, she'd flown on to New York so her mother could take care of her until she felt better.

"So how was California?" Herb asked a few minutes into the conversation. She was both surprised and pleased by his show of interest.

"Terrific," she said, trying to balance enthusiasm with an aura of brave fluey weakness. "It was really nice to be back after all this time."

"Stanford, wasn't it? Palo Alto?"

"Yep. My old stomping grounds."

"How long did you manage to spend? It was only for a couple of days, wasn't it?"

"That's right," Diana said. "No more than that."

"You caught a flu bug out there and it's already decked you? Huh. My, my. As an expert on infectious disease doesn't it strike you a little odd that the virus would incubate that quickly?"

Oh, shit, Diana thought. "Ah, yeah, I guess so," she said.

"That must be it. I guess maybe I picked it up back in Atlanta then. I guess you don't think it about it rationally when you're the patient."

"I guess not," Herb said. "It's funny, but I haven't heard about anyone else getting flu or anything like it around here in the past couple of weeks. And you live just a couple of blocks from the centers, don't you?"

"Right."

"Many people have it in your apartment complex?"

"Ah, not that I know of, Herb."

"Well . . ." There was a long pause. "I guess you got unlucky. But you just rest up, take it easy, and get yourself back in shape as quick as you can. We already miss you around here. You know that."

Diana relaxed finally as she sensed this softening of his attitude. Herb really was no problem once you had figured out what worked with him. He really was a terrific guy to work for. She liked him an awful lot. "Thanks, Herb. That's just exactly what I'll do."

"I'm sure with your mother's tender loving care and chicken soup, you'll recover and be back to us in no time."

"Thanks. I do feel much better being at home when I'm not feeling good."

"I understand," Herb said tenderly. "Well, you take care of yourself. Tell you what, why don't you give me the phone number at your mother's house in case I have to get in touch with you? That's Westchester County. Area code nine-one-four, right?"

"Ah, right." Son of a bitch. Now she had to call her mother and have her cover for her. Precisely what she didn't want.

"Oh, and Diana—one other thing." Herb took another one of his dramatic pauses. "What exactly were you doing in California?"

She had practically bitten through her lower lip before she realized she was doing it.

The misdirected attack on Sharon had raised the stakes to a fevered level. They had also made the time factor all the more critical. Things do not stand still once they reach this stage. As Brian saw it, there was no telling when and where another attempt on one or both of them would be made. And then, since it was likely they were under some form of surveillance, there was also the possibility of additional danger to Gregory and Jill. They had to institute the next step of their investigation as quickly as humanly manageable.

The next two days were protracted, endless and interminable for Diana as she and Brian waited for the responses to come back from his "official" inquiries. He went to work in the morning, pursuing his normal routine, leaving her all alone during the day. He had unequivocally forbidden her to leave the apartment under any circumstances, to answer the door in his absence, or to pick up the telephone without his ring–hang up–ring calling code. There was absolutely nothing for her to do while he was at the hospital. She hadn't brought any work with her, and she found it impossible to get into any books. The numbing boredom quickly closed in on her. So for the first morning she paced around the apartment, exploring it deliberately, square foot by square foot. She looked in all the closets, studied the details of dressers, shelves, and countertops, and even peeked in drawers, hoping for some additional insight into this man she had become so enigmatically drawn to. It wasn't too long into the day that she found herself sprawled on the sofa, half dressed and in a stupor of lassitude, losing herself in the earthshakingly mindless problems of soap opera characters whose complex and bizarre lives she was coming to too late to follow. And that was how she remained for most of the afternoon. The ritual was repeated the following day.

And every once in a while it again dawned on her that someone had tried to kill her. Willfully. Violently. And apparently dispassionately. Why she didn't know. But she did know that Brian was right. Until they did know why, neither one of them would be safe. And then she would go back to the soap operas.

It was a state of semireality that could be broken only by the intrusion of the terrifying new reality of threat and danger. And the sooner she faced it, she decided, the less crazed and jumpy she'd feel.

It was the evening of the third day that Brian came home with what they'd been waiting for.

"I had to put a rush request on it," he explained. "I didn't want to, because that's the kind of thing that can flag it for whoever's paying attention. But I figured we didn't have the time to just let the bureaucracy take its course."

He held up copies of the medical reports on the dead marines, traced back from the hospital facilities connected to each of their last billets. Some of the records still contained X ray reports; some, only the physicians' notes that had gone along with them. But for Brian's and Diana's purposes, that was sufficient. This information would lead them on the next step of the journey or send them back to the starting point. Either way, it was movement. And after the several days of this forced, tense inactivity any possibility of movement was seen by Diana as a deliverance.

They settled onto the sofa in the living room together. Brian hadn't bothered changing out of his uniform. Diana crossed her legs under her and faced him solemnly.

"This is what I found out," he reported. "And it's not too different from what we suspected." He had the copies of the records themselves in his hands, but he was reading from notes he'd made late that afternoon on a prescription pad. The important findings were easily contained on the one small square of paper. "All the wounds were from shrapnel," he said. "And from the X rays it's pretty certain that wherever else they had fragments, each man had one in the liver, none of which, interestingly enough, was surgically removed at the combat hospital."

"Isn't that a little unusual?" Diana asked.

"Maybe yes, maybe no," Brian stated. "Although the liver is highly vascular, as long as the fragment isn't in a particularly sensitive spot, it's often more dangerous to try to take it out than to leave it in there. That's true even in civilian accidents. If it's pressing on an artery or if there's danger of hemorrhage, that's another story. But according to the notes in each of these cases, apparently it wasn't a problem."

Diana was still suspicious. This many years later everything about that war still made her uneasy. There had been so many lies and so many misstatements for so long that even now she couldn't bring herself to believe anything related to it, including its contemporary medical literature. "Remember, Brian, the notes would have been written under combat casuality conditions," she said. "How do we know we can trust their accuracy ... or even the competence of the guy who wrote them."

"We can trust both," Brian told her. "Because that's another interesting thing I found out from the reports that came in today. All the initial surgery at the Phu Bai battalion hospital was done by the same man. Not just Sonny Lofton but all of them were operated on by Calvin Chandler Harley."

"He's certainly turning out to be a key player in all this," Diana commented. "Any other notable coincidences?"

"If you want to call them that." His voice had suddenly grown curiously distant. But it came back to her with the next sentence, and he fixed her directly in his gaze. "Every one of the men fought at Eagle's Talon."

Eagle's Talon. Where had she heard that before? She couldn't remember much about it or why she found it so disquieting. Just a name from a long-ago newspaper story or television broadcast, like so many others. But a name that instantly chilled her to the core. Long Dinh ... Khe Sanh ... Parrot's Beak ... Eagle's Talon. And she could tell from the grim expression on Brian's white face that her own reaction was not inappropriate. The two words had become a gulf between him and the rest of the world.

"What happened at Eagle's Talon?" she asked. Her voice was quiet, almost hushed.

Brian took a long time before saying anything. He looked as if he were in physical discomfort. He hunched over with his forearms resting on his legs and his hands between his knees. He looked for all the world like a picture she'd seen of a football player sitting dejectedly on the bench, taken out of the game in the last quarter when all hope had already been lost. Once again her heart melted for him. She wanted to edge up close to him and put her arms around his hunched shoulders, to have her body touch his and share with him the hurt of his remembrance. Instead, she pulled herself farther away, almost to the end of the sofa, offering the distance he would need to tell the story cleanly and without emotional indignity.

"Eagle's Talon was a marine engagement," he said somberly, "one of the last important ones of the war before they were pulled out in '69 and '70. It's a little crescent-shaped valley in the highlands toward the western end of the demilitarized zone. That's how it got its name. From the air the cleared land is supposed to look something like an eagle's claw. There was nothing there of any value, no important villages, landing strips, anything like that. But it happened to be in direct line with one of the major staging areas of the Ho Chi Minh Trail into Laos and Cambodia. As you remember, we tried to shut down the trail and its supply line into the South throughout the war. It never really worked.

"One day—this was late in '69, and they were already planning the major troop withdrawals—an intelligence report came in from marine recon saying that a large concentration of Vietcong and North Vietnamese regulars would be assembling in the valley for a massed troop movement toward the South. Maybe it was into Da Nang itself, I don't remember exactly what they thought. Anyway, if it happened, that could have been the beginning of the invasion of South Vietnam by the North Vietnamese Army that had been predicted for a long time. Apparently all the signs were right."

"So what happened there?" Diana gently prodded.

"This was still a period of heavy engagement up around the DMZ. The main marine deployments from the Third Division had their hands full, and there wasn't time to move in any of the army units, which would have had to come from even farther south. Besides, there was no time to plan a major assault, and the location made Eagle's Talon a logistical nightmare. So that's when they decided to send in Colonel Blagden's Seventh Amphibious Unit to confront the North Vietnamese and hold the position until the main units of the Third Division could be concentrated in the area. Blagden's group was going to insert into the surrounding hills and wait to ambush the enemy troops when they showed up. It was a job only the marines could have done. And pulled off properly, it could definitely mean a speedup to the end of the war."

"And did they do it?" she asked.

He shook his head bitterly. "Not exactly. When the Seventh arrived early in the morning, there were no North Vietnamese regulars to be seen; there were none anywhere in the area. But a detachment of Vietcong was already there, heavily armed, waiting. I don't know how they slipped past marine recon, but they did." He stopped again and thrust his hands deep into his pockets, extending his feet straight out in front of him on the floor. "It was a slaughter," he said. "No contest."

"And how do you know so much about it?" Diana asked, afraid to hear his answer.

"I was a navy medical corpsman with the Third Division, assigned to the Seventh Amphibious Unit. I was there at Eagle's Talon. I was the only medic to come out of it alive."

16

They were living out of time. A pattern of obscure and indecipherable events had taken over from regular existence to determine a new discipline and order to their lives. It was not only Diana's days, spent in aimless and dreary haunting of the small apartment, that seemed so unnatural. Brian's normal routine of surgery and consultation and attending to all the mundane details of military and medical bureaucracy also took on the qualities of the unreal. Both pursuits became suddenly forced and artificial and very, very tenuous, as if the ordinary activities of their lives no longer mattered, as if the hidden agenda that had commenced in the deaths of six marines held the key to their true destinies.

Lizzie called once and put Katie on the phone. The little girl asked tenderly, and with real concern, how her daddy was feeling. It took Brian a moment to recall what he'd offered Lizzie as his reason for not seeing the child, but he recovered in time to tell his sugarplum that he was feeling much, much better and that he hoped to see her "as soon as soon could possibly be."

Katie seemed satisfied with this good-faith effort and did not press him for specifics. She seldom did, much less so than most young children of his acquaintance. She took things as they came. It was almost as if her little head had somehow already grasped that this was a capricious and indefinite world we live in, that performance was never certain, and that the most that could be reasonably asked of another human being was good intentions. It made him cry to think of her carrying around the burden of this insight so long before her time.

The thought of having Katie removed from him for so long, of not being able to see her and hold her and cuddle her in his arms became, of the moment, intolerable to him. He could not stand to be deprived of her any longer, and it spurred him on all the more to figure out how to extricate himself from his dilemma, to find the clue that would offer redemption.

Diana heard only Brian's side of the conversation, which was by far the less verbal and animated. But it required little imagination to know what was going through his mind. She could see it plainly on his face.

She began to tiptoe out of the room as he hung up the telephone, intending to leave him for a time to the intimacy of his private torment. But without a word he pulled her by the fingertips over to where he was seated, and in a moment she found herself sitting awkwardly on his lap. She didn't at first know how to respond. In all their times together, in all the times now that they had held each other and played with each other and loved each other, she had never done that before, and the feeling was strange. He kissed her hair and stroked it with one hand. The other he rested affectionately on her thigh.

Diana felt her skin grow tense and her throat tighten. This was something she hadn't faced, and she didn't know quite what to do about it. With his background of training and experience Brian didn't succumb to pressure the way normal (or less disciplined) people did. But that didn't mean he didn't feel it. And here now this was tangible evidence that the strain was getting to him, too.

She stood up abruptly. Brian's hand fell to the sofa. She would try to be as much to him as she could. But one thing she could not be was the surrogate for his five-year-old child. She turned toward him and stood directly in front of him. Then she guided him to his feet and led him by the hand into the bedroom to remind him of what she could be instead.

When it was over, they did not lie together long. After a few minutes Diana propped herself on one elbow and announced with enthusiasm that was only half forced, "Time to get on with things!" She knew the only thing that was going to do them any good, and there was no sense waiting.

"And what things did you have in mind?" Brian asked, looking at the clock on the nightstand.

"We have a tremendous amount of work to do," she replied. She got out of bed and stepped into her panties, which had been lying on the floor. Then she went over and picked up the pile of Brian's clothes from the chair where he'd left them and handed him the bundle. "Here. Put these on," she instructed while she searched for her bra and T-shirt. She found them on the floor on the other side of the bed.

"What kind of work?" he asked. "Where are we going?"

"Call Jill. See if she'll meet us at the hospital."

"Now?"

"Now's the best time. There won't be a lot of other people around to ask questions."

Jill sleepily agreed to meet them at the hospital, accepting the promise that she'd get a full explanation when they all arrived. Diana explained her plan to Brian on the drive over.

With the new data Brian had gotten hold of, they now had what amounted to a detailed case definition: Third Marine Division, Dong Ha, 1969, Seventh Amphibious Unit, fought at Eagle's Talon, wounded by shrapnel, had a fragment lodged in the liver, operated on by Calvin Chandler Harley at Phu Bai.

"Now," Diana announced, "we have to put together our control group."

And by that she meant a group of men who could be described by the same set of characteristics—with one exception: They were still alive.

"It's going to be a kind of drag coming up with this stuff," Jill said when they all were together. "Because the computer files weren't set up for it, there's no way we can program in this list of criteria and have it spit out a list of names. We're going to have to begin with the entire division and work our way through, point by point, till we've gotten through every point on your list."

The hospital's data processing department was gray and cold because computers are always gray and cold, and at night there is no human warmth there to offset them. Seeing them like this, Diana couldn't fathom how anyone could be moved to imbue the machines with human characteristics. But Jill was like a zookeeper, lovingly consumed with her animals. And when Diana observed the care and delicacy with which the young woman applied her fingers to the keyboard and the keen interest with which she eyed the screen, she found herself hoping that the computer properly appreciated all of Jill's attentions and indulgence.

Diana and Brian stood behind her and watched as Jill typed in the queries one by one. The first produced a list on the phosphorescent screen of all the men from the Third Division who'd also served in the Seventh Amphibious Unit. Jill typed in the print command, and the printer next to her whirred to life. When it was finished, she tore the paper off at the base and handed it to Brian.

"Save that," she said. "When we finally get all the information we need, the last step we have to do by hand."

From that they narrowed it down to another list of those who had taken part in Eagle's Talon, and another of those who'd been wounded in action that month. There was no computerized list of Dr. Harley's patients or of Phu Bai's patient manifest. Brian would have to request them in writing and hope for the best, unless Hugh Stanway's people could get their hands on them. After that he would have to match up and then request another set of individual medical records to see if the men under consideration had actually had shrapnel wounds to their livers.

And so Diana was condemned to an additional sentence of house arrest in Brian's apartment, of sleeping late and watching daytime television, of gazing out the window and looking at all the people who had someplace to go, of staring at the clock and waiting for her man to return home. Even as much as she cared for Brian, with the self-image she'd so carefully nurtured for so long, this last was the most unbearable part of all.

"I'm going to go out of my head crazy if I have to sit here another day," Diana announced to Brian in the morning. He was getting ready to leave for the hospital. She hadn't even bothered getting dressed.

Brian turned and shook his index finger at her, as if reproving a wayward child. "Don't you dare leave this apartment until I get back," he said.

"What about you?" she protested. "You're in just as much danger as I am."

"It's not the same," he said.

"You just don't think I can take care of myself the way you can. But you're wrong. And I can prove it!" She climbed out of bed and padded over to face him directly.

Brian started to respond but then pursed his lips with exasperation. "Just don't do anything foolish or you're going to be in big trouble."

"Oh, so you're threatening me again!"

He took a step toward her and put his arms around her. "I'm just trying to keep you safe," he said.

She wriggled out of his grasp and showed him a little-girl pout.

"Look, I know it's been hard for you," he said. "But we'll have something to go on soon, maybe even today. And anyway, we're only following your plan." He kissed her on the forehead, then on the lips, then went to the front door. "Now be a good girl and stay right here till I get back."

That was the worst thing he could have said, Diana decided. She, like too many women, had spent too much time conforming to other people's ideas of what a "good girl" was. But when she thought back on it, what she'd gotten the most satisfaction from over the years were all the times she'd decided to be a "bad girl"—when she'd joined the antiwar movement, when she'd discovered sex, when she'd pursued an M.D. instead of an MRS., when she'd decided to tend to the migrant workers of California instead of the socially correct of the Upper East Side.

She stewed about it through a morning's worth of soap operas. She continued stewing as she went meticulously through the newspapers, concentrating on stories she never would have bothered with had she not been so bored, her fingers growing progressively blacker from the ink. And she was still stewing when she went into the kitchen to fix herself the last grilled cheese sandwich she ever hoped to eat. How many had it been now since she'd started this vigil? She'd completely lost count.

The cheese tasted like rubber and the bread like cardboard, dry, indistinct, and nearly impossible to swallow. Not surprisingly, it was all that was left in the apartment since neither of them had been to the food store. In the last couple of days she'd finished the orange juice, the milk, the beer, and the soda. She was now reduced to polishing off Katie's Hawaiian Punch. This was no way for a grown, intelligent woman to live. She got angry with herself just thinking about putting up with it. Who was Brian Thorpe to regulate her life and tell her where she could and could not go?

That did it. Whenever she let other people control her, she always hated herself for it. It was time to take control back, even if it only meant going out to the food store to restock the kitchen. She almost hoped Brian would call while she was out. No, then he would worry and race home and yell at her, and it would be a whole hassle. But that didn't matter. The important thing was she'd decided to go, and no one was going to stop her. As soon as she went out the glass front doors of the building and hit the sidewalk, Diana felt as if she'd been freed from prison. It was the first time she'd been out alone since she returned to Washington, she realized. The weather was beautiful, one of those rare, pollution-free days when you just want to take a deep breath and fill your lungs with the air. *Definitely a favorable sign*, she thought. *I was meant to get out of the house today.*

She quickly surveyed the scene on Connecticut Avenue, the same one she'd been viewing enviously through the apartment window for so many days. Everything seemed fine. There was absolutely nothing to worry about. So then, with a lilt in her walk and her handbag swinging briskly on her shoulder, Diana proceeded triumphantly down the block toward the Safeway.

"Yep, that's her," said Green as he peered through the binoculars from his vantage point in the apartment building diagonally across the intersection. They'd been occupying the top-floor flat for several days now.

"If she was here, we knew she had to come up for air eventually," said Orange. "And now at least we know where she is." He took the field glasses from Green and held them up to his own eyes for confirmation. Green picked up his notebook and entered the time and specific location of the sighting.

"It's the weather," he continued. "I've never seen it fail in this city. It brings out all the pretty girls. It's like they've been hibernating or something all winter."

Orange picked up the Steyr-Mannlicher SSG-PII that had been leaning against the wall, coiled the leather strap tightly around his forearm, and brought the weapon up to his shoulder. He sighted down the scope until he picked up the young woman walking down the west side of Connecticut Avenue toward the supermarket. He flexed his right index finger several times and then laid it with utmost delicacy on the rifle's trigger. "I've got her now," he said. "Clear, straight shot."

"Be careful," said Green. "You pick her off by herself and you immediately send him underground, not to mention putting the entire Centers for Disease Control on alert."

Orange continued watching through the rifle sight. "Yeah, and even if we got them both in the sight together, we still wouldn't get a clearance to take them out."

"Probably not," Green confirmed. "I think the boss wants them to tip their hand first before we terminate them."

"I don't know why we're even wasting our time here," Orange said.

"Keep your finger in practice," Green replied, "because you never know."

The three men had registered at the hotel under the sponsorship of the Ukrainian Chess Federation. One of them had made it very clear he wanted a room high up in the building with a northern exposure. "In the morning I don't want the sun in my eyes," he had explained to the desk clerk. His companion did like the sun in his eyes in the morning and so requested a room facing east, overlooking Connecticut Avenue. And the third visitor liked the idea of being able to watch all the Americans going to work in the morning, so he wanted a room looking downtown on the south side of the building. The desk clerk cheerfully took this all in, asked no questions, and was happy to comply.

Beween them now they had all vantage points covered. And as soon as they carried their bags to their respective rooms and set up their practice chessboards for the benefit of the chambermaid or bellhop, they assembled their matching tripod-mounted Zeiss telescopic sights and began scanning the areas outside their windows.

The sights were equipped with double prism objectives so that they could be fitted not only with standard eyepieces but also with specially modified thirty-five-millimeter cameras. The committee analysts were thorough. A written report was seldom sufficient documentation.

It was the man with the north-facing room who found what they were looking for. He called his two associates in, positioned his sight, and had each look through it. "There they are," he said. "Top floor of that apartment block. Three windows in. They've probably been set up there for several days."

"You could figure they'd come here looking when they lost track of the girl in Atlanta," one of the associates said, staring through the sight. The skin on his forehead was tightly knit.

"One of them's got a high-powered rifle. Do you think he's prepared to use it?"

"I noticed that right off. I would hope they wouldn't be so precipitous," the first one said. "But one never knows exactly what their objectives are."

"Keep watching and pay close attention," said the third member of the team. "I don't want them out of our sight. There are too many variables all the way 'round now, and we don't know who knows what. That is always the most difficult phase." Then he picked up the phone, dialed in the scrambler code, and rang up the Soviet Embassy to file his report.

At the food store they'd asked her if she wanted her groceries in the traditional brown bag or one of those white plastic sacks they all were offering lately. Diana took more than a normal amount of time to respond. After the last several days even this insignificant choice seemed a welcome opportunity to assert her free will. The point was nobody was going to tell her what to do. She didn't have to answer to anybody, she resolutely decided as she walked up the street and turned off the sidewalk to the red-brick apartment building. And she didn't care what anybody thought.

She ran into Brian on the elevator and almost wet her pants.

He had gotten on at the garage level and was standing there in the cab when she came on at the lobby, merrily swinging her plastic grocery sack. He was carrying a manila file folder in one hand. "Where have you been?" he shouted.

She felt her knees turning to jelly. "I, uh, um, ah," she held the white sack out timidly in front of her. "We, uh, needed some things in the kitchen," she stammered, biting her lower lip in the usual way, as if she knew she'd been caught being a bad girl and was now going to get it.

He raised his hand up toward her. Was it for emphasis or was he going to hit her? "I thought I told you not to go out!" His voice was still raised threateningly.

And that was when the righteous indignation took over and transformed her cowering, guilty, little-girl posture into an attitude of proud defiance. She suddenly remembered herself and the frustration of the past week poured out of her. "What do you mean, you told me!" She exploded. "Where do you get off telling me anything? I'm not your child. You can't spank me for crossing the street without permission. And this isn't the navy or the marines either. You can't order me around and then throw me in the brig if I disobey."

"If I ordered you around, it was for your own good," Brian said tersely. "I have some experience with orders. I know why they're given. And I know that disobeying them can get people killed."

"In your war more people got killed obeying them," Diana declared hotly.

"Don't start that with me again," he warned. "I'm not going to fight the war over again with you. But your roommate almost got herself killed—totally innocently. And if it had been you instead, you would have been. You don't know who's after us, or why. You don't know who's out there."

Diana held out her arms, as if to demonstrate that her body was still intact. "Well, I went out and I came back and nothing happened to me and it felt great. So quite clearly no one was lurking out there to get me!"

Brian seemed unmoved. He could be infuriating, Diana knew. Didn't he ever let up? There had to be a chink somewhere in that military armor. She dropped her voice seductively. "Anyway," she intoned, sidling up next to him, "I know you're angry that I didn't listen to you. But aren't you glad that nothing happened, that it turned out I was right?"

"I'm glad you're all right," he replied, and seemed maybe to be softening a bit. "But that doesn't mean you're forgiven."

"I'm not asking to be forgiven," she shot back at him as the elevator door opened on their floor.

Inside the apartment they retired to neutral corners until they felt they'd punished each other sufficiently, and then the armistice was declared. But in the meantime, the uneasy truce gave Diana the opportunity to reflect on how quickly and easily the gulfs can surface. Behind a closed door she sat on the bed in Katie's room, more than casually aware that she was creasing the shiny pink spread. Diana knew that she was taking this whole thing too seriously and that one of them should make some overt gesture of conciliation before too much time went by.

She didn't want there to be this gulf between them, but she didn't want to let herself be bullied or dominated either, even by someone she loved. No, especially by someone she loved. To love someone is one thing. To surrender yourself to him is something else. And why was this something women always had to face, and never men? She thought back to college, to her SDS days. It had been no different then, even though everything else in the world had been different then. They all were fighting for equality, the perfect ideal. Yet that was always something on the outside. On the inside it never quite worked out that way. How often had various men—lovers and friends and casual comrades—sidestepped charges of sexism and chauvinism by hiding behind the immediate needs of the movement? There was always the movement to think about—"we can't ever lose sight of our mission"—and Diana and the others were expected to suppress their personal aspirations for dignity and status and instead be good little soldiers of the revolution. Everyone has a role to play. Obey orders. Maintain party discipline. The sorting out would come later, and that's when amends would be made. In a revolution there is no room for hurt feelings. And now the revolution was over and done with, just like the war that spawned it. But certain vestiges remained, and in many ways those promised amends had never been made. She was still in the army, and the only things that had changed were the commanding officer and the nature of the enemy. There was still the mission to think about, and that was reason enough to suppress her own feelings yet again. She was still expected to be the good little soldier. And that, she supposed, was why she could not bring herself to leave the scampering puppy dog and jumping cow sanctum of Katie's room and make up to him. Let Brian be the one this time. He wasn't as burdened by history. He had less at stake.

It wasn't long before she heard a knock on the door. Before she had a chance to respond, Brian opened it and appeared in the doorway. He asked, "Are you ready to talk?"

"Yes," Diana answered solemnly. "What do you have to say?"

He held up the manila folder he'd been carrying in the elevator. "I think I have the information you wanted." He opened the file and showed her a single page printout. There were handwritten notes in the margin.

Jill's search had yielded nine names, nine men who conformed neatly, category by category, to the profile Diana had established, with the exception of the fact that they were not dead. Only two, however, could be readily located. Roger Moreland was an insurance executive—and by all accounts a successful one—living in New York City. Tim Dantley was the other name.

"No one seems to know what he does," Brian reported. "But he's supposed to be in the area here, so we might as well start with him." He paused and folded his arms across his chest. "Now, what is it you want to do with them?"

So now it was Diana calling the shots and Brian, apparently willingly, following them. She locked the epidemiological model firmly in her mind. She wanted to make sure she sounded authoritative and completely in control when she spoke. "Well, the first thing we have to do is interview each of them—extensively. See if anything in their experience leads us to understand what the connection is. And then we have to go one step further."

"What do you mean?"

"We've got to look inside them. Or at least inside one of them," Diana explained.

"What are you talking about?" Brian pressed her.

"Of all the factors we've come up with, what's the strangest single thing?" she quizzed him.

Brian thought for a moment. "It'd have to be the hollow capsules in the livers."

"Right," she said. "Now it can't be just coincidence that Radley Davis and Sam Hardesty both had them. And there's reason to believe the others might have, too, since all of them presented with a shrapnel fragment near the surface of the liver. So now we've got our control group identified. If one of them also happens to have this same sort of capsule, I think we can reasonably conclude that they all did."

"So we do the same sort of X ray tomograms that made it show up in Davis," Brian said.

"Right."

"And then?"

Diana stared back hard at him. "And if the films show the same thing, we go in and take it out."

"Are you serious?"

"There's no other way. At least one of these two. It's our only possibility of finding out what those capsules were intended to do."

"In Davis it didn't do anything, except give him pain after about fifteen years."

"Who knows what it would have done if you'd left it in?" she said.

"And in Hardesty it didn't do anything at all as far as we know."

"As far as we know," Diana repeated. "That's the key. And as far as we know isn't very far. That's why we have to get more complete information. We're still walking around this thing blind. These two people you've come up with are our best hope." She paused, placed her hands in her pockets, and leaned casually against the wall. When he said nothing, she added, "Unless, of course, you have a better idea."

"No," Brian admitted. "I don't."

For what was left of the day Diana seemed quiet, distant. Brian's periodic attempts to engage her in conversation or involve her in the planning or execution of dinner quickly sank of their own weight. She was noncommittal when he asked if she wanted to watch television, listen to music, or sit around and read, and when he asked for alernatives, she was strangely and uncharacteristically silent. And later on, earlier than they normally went to bed, she broke out of her reticence long enough to announce that she wouldn't be spending the night with him.

"It's nothing against you, Brian," Diana explained, and here she took his hand in hers. It was the first time she had touched him that evening. "I'm not angry or upset. But the way I've been feeling, I think I'll sleep in Katie's room tonight if it's all right with you."

"Ah, yeah," Brian said, "if that's what you want." But in the center of his belly he felt a stab of what he could only describe as sorrow, deep and abiding and profound. "Whatever I've done to you, I'm sorry for it," he told her.

"You haven't done anything," Diana replied. She was making an effort to be reassuring. "I just have to be alone. It's just for this one night. Please don't make me talk about it anymore." With parted lips she kissed him lightly on the mouth, then quickly retired to the bedroom and closed the door.

Brian lay on his own bed for a long time, thinking. Whatever was upsetting Diana, it obviously had something to do with what happened when he saw her on the elevator, but he didn't claim to have a fix on exactly what it was. She was so complex and unpredictable, so bound up in things he couldn't relate to or understand. Maybe it was just the tension of the past several days, having to stay all alone in the apartment all day long. He wished it were that simple, but knew it wasn't.

He was sorry he'd chastised her so severely in the elevator, but at least he was secure in the knowledge that it was totally out of love. He was only trying to protect her. It was the same as if he'd had to punish Katie for doing something that could have hurt her.

And maybe that was the problem. And maybe that was why Diana was now in Katie's room, cut off from him, sleeping in Katie's bed instead of his.

Was he being oversensitive, he wondered, or was she? She should be more mature about it. There was no getting around the fact that this was serious business they were facing. So she didn't like taking orders and feeling as if she were being treated like a child. Well, Brian thought, whatever else he'd done, for his entire adult life he'd been a soldier. And soldiers take orders all the time. Real men, soldiers were, and by the very nature of their business they were always taking orders, so why couldn't she without feeling as if she'd given up something precious of herself? But how do you get these real men to follow those orders and follow them unquestioningly, even at the risk of their own lives? Maybe, and this thought made him shiver, maybe it was only by treating them like children.

In any event, beginning tomorrow, they would be following her scenario, so she could give the orders for a while and see how she liked it. He couldn't quite fathom her action plan, wrapped up as it was in all that epidemiological protocol. But as she'd so sharply pointed out, he didn't have any better ideas, and he'd already said that whatever they did, they had to do it quickly. He'd gotten the information she wanted, and now they were ready to begin.

Diana was right about one thing, he acknowledged. They were walking around this blind. And that was what made them vulnerable. And the more he thought about it, the more Brian realized that her plan might have a potential result far different from the one that she had explained but that he was still vague about. Diana's plan involved getting them both out into the open, raising their profiles, seeking people out, meeting them, taking chances. Whoever was watching, whoever was tracking them was bound to take notice, was bound to follow along. The new plan of attack would force their hand.

Yes, Diana's plan was the only possible one at the moment,

though not necessarily for the reasons she supposed. But this was something he could never share with her. That horrible afternoon in the Rung Sat swamps came back to him, that day when he had left McNeely in the midst of the small clearing as a lure for the VC, unconscious and mutilated from Brian's own knife. As he had had to do so many years before, Brian found himself once again rigging a trap for the unseen enemy with live bait.

With the thought of that clearly focused in his mind, he bounded out of bed in his shorts, padded across the hall to Katie's room, quietly twisted the knob, and opened the door. And there in silence he stood for a long time watching Diana sleep.

17

SYLVESTER, WEST VIRGINIA

All they had to go on was a post office box, but the town was
small and the postmaster was likely to know everyone in his
district. If he didn't, Brian reasoned, the police chief likely
would.

The town of Sylvester was just across the Maryland state line,
where the Potomac River is narrow and the water clean and good
for fishing. It took about an hour and a half to get there by car
from Washington, and to Brian the area bore about as much relationship to the frenetic, self-important capital city as the rural
hamlets of central Vietnam had. The town reminded Diana of
some of the places she'd been assigned to in the Public Health
Service. "It's hard to tell the difference between 'quaint' and
'poor' until you've been somewhere for a while and gotten your
feet dirty there," she commented.

The post office was a single-story house built of clapboards that
had long ago weathered to dull gray. It made Diana think of Sam
Hardesty's cabin back in Montana, which she would forever associate with meeting Brian. When the two of them walked in, there
were no customers, and the room was empty except for the man
behind the counter, who seemed genuinely pleased to have some
company. It was so different from most of the city post offices,

where the lines were endless and she was made to feel as if she were inconveniencing the clerks by even being there.

"We're looking for a man called Tim Dantley," Brian said.

"You'd be among the first then," the man said amiably.

"How's that?" said Brian. "He doesn't get many visitors?"

The man shook his head. "Nor mail either."

"Could you tell us where he lives?" Diana asked.

"I could," the man asserted. "Assuming you mean to do him no harm or serve him with any bills he wouldn't be in a position to handle. Not that you don't have the right to do that, mind you, if that's your business. It's just that it wouldn't be neighborly to give you any more information than I'm officially required to if that were to be the case."

"I assure you we wouldn't be doing that," Diana said, and consciously softened her face into a smile. Like most beautiful women, she had the ability to calculate and predict the effect of each of her expressions and mannerisms on the casual observer, particularly the casual male observer.

But the postmaster seemed to be sizing up his visitors according to a set of standards that had nothing to do with Diana's winning smile or Brian's resolute bearing, or the code of U.S. postal regulations either, for that matter. When he appeared satisfied that they had passed his personal test of integrity, he said, "You go down this road that you came on, see, until you get to the second Y. There won't be any sign or anything, but you take it to the right. Drive all the way down the hill as far as the tire grooves'll take you, then get out of your car and follow the gully the rest of the way until you see Dantley's place. I expect he'll be there or close by, at any rate."

"And I guess if we get that far, we can't miss it from there," Diana wanted to confirm.

The postmaster started to shake his head in the affirmative, then stopped to reconsider, as if suddenly remembering that this was a city girl he was dealing with who would have endless capacity for getting herself lost and confused out here. "I don't think you'll have any trouble," he said with his own smile to close the discussion. "If you do, come back and I'll give you more detailed directions."

They found the turnoff without any trouble. They drove down the muddy twin automobile tracks as far as they could, just as the postmaster had directed them, then set off the rest of the way down the hill on foot. Knowing they'd be out in the country, Diana had wanted to wear jeans and sneakers but didn't think they'd convey the proper professional image necessary to pull off her plan. So she had dressed up. As it turned out, though, the intended image was partially nullified before they got to Dantley's house. On the way down the slope she snagged her skirt on a dead branch and then stumbled and ran her stocking on a thorn that made her leg bleed.

"So much for image," she muttered, and tried to pull her skirt around so the rip wouldn't show. She cupped her hand into the gully to collect enough water to wash off the blood and then proceeded down the hill with her jaw set in determination. Brian laughed to himself but was careful not to let her see.

The house at the end of the wooded trail was built of the same weather-beaten boards as those at the post office but was so small and in such a state of disrepair that Diana immediately felt sorry for its occupant. From her days with the Public Health Service she was already inferring what his life was like. She walked up the broken steps, smoothed her skirt and hair one more time, then knocked loudly on the door.

The man who answered it was not large—no taller than she was—dressed in shabby clothes of no particular style, and he had one of the worst skin allergies she'd ever seen on an adult. His face and hands were mottled with deep, festering red sores that made her want to scratch herself and then immediately wash off. She caught herself before he could register that she was staring. Either that, or he was used to it and it no longer affected him. She felt foolish having concerned herself with how her ripped skirt and torn stocking would look.

"Mr. Dantley?" The man nodded. "I'm Dr. Diana Keegan from the National Centers for Disease Control. And this is Dr. Brian Thorpe." As soon as Brian extended his hand, she realized that she had not, and it made her more self-conscious. Dantley seemed to sense this and, instead of taking Brian's hand, raised his own in a kind of a casual wave.

Diana found his behavior perplexing, not the well-timed face-saving wave, for which she was grateful, but his general attitude and demeanor. There was something very strange. He seemed hardly surprised by the visit, as if it had been inevitable that she and Brian would find him like this.

"Do you know why we're here?" she asked.

"Of course," Dantley replied. They were the first words he had spoken to them.

"How do you know?" asked Brian.

"She said Centers for Disease Control. They're the ones who got the project after the Veterans Administration blew it. So it's about the study, right?"

"The study?" Diana repeated.

"The Agent Orange study," Dantley said. Then he turned to Brian. "Unless you're a psychiatrist. But then why would you bother coming all the way out here?"

"And why would you be expecting a psychiatrist?" Brian asked.

"Because I tried to kill myself," he replied with a deadness of emotion that Diana found chilling.

"Ah, is it all right if we come in, Mr. Dantley?" she asked.

"Sure," he responded flatly. Diana felt it was like grand rounds in a teaching hospital when you surround the patient's bed with twelve interns and medical students and then say, "Can we ask you a few questions, Mrs. Smith?" What else is the patient going to say?

The cabin was furnished sparsely, and not with the simple, rustic pieces that would have seemed appropriate in such a setting. It was obvious most of the furniture had come from junk piles, and rural junk piles at that. A few of the better pieces looked like what people give to Goodwill to be repaired and resold. Only here no such refurbishment had taken place. Dantley steered them to a sofa that was losing its stuffing, the only upholstered or padded furniture in the room. Then he pulled over one of two straight-backed chairs from the kitchen table. He moved stiffly, hesitating momentarily before turning his body in certain ways. Once he had arranged the chair, he sat facing them, waiting for one of them to say something.

Diana had planned to use the same ruse she'd employed with Dr. Harley, letting her CDC credentials cover for her. But unexpectedly now Dantley had given her a wider opening than she'd anticipated, and she decided it was wisest to pursue it from his angle.

"You knew we were here because of the Agent Orange study," Diana said.

"That's right," Dantley said.

"Because you feel you are suffering from the effects of the agent?"

Dantley brought his hand up close to his face and indicated his cheek. "It's rather obvious, isn't it?"

"How do you mean?" Diana asked.

"You're a doctor. When have you ever seen as bad a skin case as this before? No, wait a minute, that's stupid. Of course you have. On all the other guys exposed to Agent Orange. We're not naïve anymore, none of us. The government can't put anything over on us. We know what the symptoms are. Does this look like some punk teenager's skin rash to you? Because that's what they're trying to put over. 'Similar to teenage acne.' And that was the only side effect they found. That's what the VA said. That was so ridiculous even the Congress couldn't buy it. And that's when they handed it over to the CDC. But you know that already or you wouldn't be here."

Diana hadn't actually had anything to do with the study Dantley was talking about. In fact, it hadn't even been a EIS project. But it didn't take any special sensitivity or direct hands-on experience to know that he was talking about one of the twin chemical curses of the Vietnam War. Long after the passions of the moment had died down and the political issues had been forgotten, two names were destined to continue conjuring up images of death and incredible, mindless destruction: napalm and Agent Orange. The one, a jellied gasoline mixture dropped from airplanes to burn "enemy" villages and flesh of their inhabitants, the other, a laboratory-produced spray meant to rob the enemy of the protective cover of leaves and shrubs. The one deadly to its unwitting targets; the other deadly to its unsuspecting handlers. The case histories that had already come out on Agent Orange were legion: neurological problems and memory loss, violent rages and kidney and bladder failure, rare and chronologically unusual cancers, and children with grotesque and nearly unimaginable birth defects. So far, she understood, the government and the Veterans Administration were calling all these findings "anecdotal"—no proof that they were directly traceable to exposure. Stealing a quick glance at Brian, Diana knew what was going through his mind. He had been there. He knew what it was like. The corners of his eyes were already moist.

"And have you experienced any other symptoms?" she asked.

"Pain, stiffness in the joints," Dantley said. "Sometimes it hurts just to get out of bed in the morning. That's not normal for a guy my age no matter what anybody tells you."

"Anything else?"

"Not so far. But I'm waiting."

"Waiting?" Brian said.

"It's only a matter of time," Dantley said. "Once you're exposed, ain't nothing you can do about it. And the DMZ, up where I was, was one of the most heavily defoliated areas of the country."

He rubbed his hands together, as if he could somehow erase the scaly red blotches from his wrists and fingers if he rubbed hard enough.

"It was just another chemical in a big tin drum. Agent Red, Agent Purple, Agent Pink. This one had a wide orange stripe around it. What did we know back then? Did we know its active ingredient was dioxin? Did we even know what dioxin was? That it was the most toxic substance made by man? And now they tell us they can't tell whether it affected any of us? Five million acres sprayed with twelve point eight million gallons of Agent Orange when *one drop* of dioxin can kill a thousand people! And they don't know whether it's affected us. I've had buddies who hardly touched a drop of liquor in their lives and they die of liver cancer in their thirties. I've seen their wives giving birth to babies without arms and brains and assholes. I'm not just talking one in a million. I'm talking about over and over again, sometimes two or three times in the same family! Babies born without goddamned brains! And the government doesn't know if it had any harmful effects."

He continued wringing his hands. "We trusted them, and look what they did to us." He raised his eyes to meet Brian's and Diana's. "This is the thanks we get. We laid our asses on the line, and then we came back home and they treated us like shit."

He wasn't railing at them, Diana could tell. It was just that they were the ones who had come to listen, so they were the ones expected to carry the message back to the ones with power. With all her heart, Diana wished she could throw off the charade of officialdom and objectivity, to break down and tell him she agreed with him completely, that he and his loyal comrades had most assuredly been shafted and that it had all turned out just as she and her comrades had said it would. But she couldn't do that. There was a bigger picture to keep in focus. She hated herself for having to think like that. But she did it anyway.

"I know it's only a matter of time for me," Dantley said, and looked away.

"Tim," Brian said soothingly. It was only one word. Maybe it was the way he said it, Diana thought. Normally, she'd noticed, he observed the military potocol of addressing people by their last names until invited to use the first. But Diana could tell he felt a special kinship with Dantley and wanted to break through the artificial barriers, one soldier to another. It was interesting that he hadn't mentioned anything about his own service with the marines. But Brian was like that. She remembered the guy they'd seen at the Vietnam Veterans Memorial.

"Tim, you said something before about trying to kill yourself. What was that all about?"

Dantley shrugged. "I guess the VA psychiatrists would have said I was despondent." He looked up again, and this time he almost laughed. "How many times have you heard that one before?"

"Tell me about it," Brian gently instructed him.

Dantley glanced over to Diana before speaking, as if trying to decide if this was something she could be allowed to hear. Once again she felt she was struggling to remain inside an order whose only membership qualification was male experience.

He began haltingly, with the air of someone who has told his story time and again and wants to see if it is going to meet with any greater acceptance this time before he commits his full energy to the telling. "I was out of a job for a long time. I got little things here and there, but nothing steady, nothing I could feel good about. So I decided to take things into my own hands. In the marines I'd been an infantry squad leader and mortarman. I was even at Eagle's Talon. Ever hear of that?"

Brian nodded.

"But what can you do with that kind of training back in the World. What good is it? So I thought, why not the police? Same kind of thing, working with people and all. I applied to the force in Detroit." Then he stopped for a moment, as if his attentive listeners could infer the rest. "I would have liked that—police work. I was doing okay there, went through training real good. But then during my probationary period they told me I was being terminated because of—what did they call it now?—my 'history of depression and emotional instability.' Let me go, just like that. And then, after I was out on the street again with no job and no place to go, I tried to get my veteran's pension reinstated. All I kept getting back was letters saying be patient and we're looking into it and all that crap. And in the meantime, I got no money and no job and nothing."

"So that's when you decided to do it?" Brian asked.

"I waited a long time," Dantley responded in a voice that sought understanding. "I wrote letters; I demonstrated; I talked to reporters. Nothing seemed to work, and nobody gave a damn." He sat up straight in his chair to be able to fill his lungs with a full draft of breath. "And that's when I decided to do it," he said.

"How?" Diana inquired.

"Colt automatic. I'm used to guns, feel comfortable around them."

"This was in Detroit?" she asked.

"No. Washington. Early one morning, just before dawn at the Vietnam Veterans Memorial."

The memorial. Those black walls cast a magic spell, Diana thought. This generation of warriors' holiest of holies. Its stark, pure image kept coming up again and again, never far from the consciousness of any veteran. It was something the veterans couldn't let go of. They were forever being drawn back to it, it seemed, just as they were forever being drawn back into the remote and bloody past it solemnized.

Diana had to know, had to figure it out for herself. "Why—why did you go there to—to do it?"

Dantley gave her a curious smile, almost beatific. It seemed to come from somewhere else. "I wasn't afraid of dying. I'm still not. But the thought of dying alone is . . . it terrifies me. This was the one place I never felt alone."

Diana looked over to Brian, and his eyes were tightly closed. His lips were pressed tightly together, as if in pain, and his head was nodding slightly. And finally she understood about those black walls. The memorial was the one place where the war survivors knew they'd be fully accepted, the one place where they knew that what they'd done had lasting value and meaning.

"I decided to take things into my own hands," Dantley said for the second time during the visit. "But the police stopped me. There's a group of veterans who keep a vigil by the memorial all the time. One of those guys must have called them.

"Were you really that alone?" Diana asked.

Dantley nodded. "I was married once. After I got back from Nam."

"What happened?"

"Didn't work out. We loved each other fine, that wasn't the problem. But then she wanted to have kids. I did, too, in spite of the fact that I knew my nerves weren't what they used to be. But then, when my buddies started having these kids with . . . Well, I told you about them. I knew I had as much of a chance as them. We just couldn't do it. And . . ." He took another long breath. "It just wasn't the same after that. Just couldn't get it back together."

Dantley stood up, as though he could no longer sit still for his memories. He hooked his thumbs behind his massive brass belt buckle and paced with some difficulty of movement in back of his chair. "And what was it all for?" he said. "What did we all die for over there—to prove to the world how big Lyndon Johnson's cock was?" He shook his head and looked directly at Brian, who by now had reopened his eyes. "Hardly seems worth it, does it?"

Brian waited for a suitable time to pass, then asked, "How has it been going for you since then . . . since that morning?"

"You can see for yourself," Dantley said, indicating with his hand the room behind him. "I get by, I guess. I'm seeing some other guys every once in a while, guys in my position . . . who feel the same way I have. I'm doing the best I can."

Diana shifted uneasily in her seat. "Mr. Dantley, according to our records, you were wounded in action—"

"Three times," Dantley said with grim-faced pride.

"One of those times by shrapnel?" she asked.

"That's right."

"Do you have, or have you been having, any problems from your shrapnel wounds—any particular pain, for instance?"

Dantley stood behind the chair and leaned heavily on its back. "Pains?" he said. "I have pains everywhere. But I don't know if they're from shrapnel. I don't think so. I know what they're from, and no one can do anything about them."

She wanted to do something, anything, to help lift the enormous weight of this man's burden. But really, if he was right about the Agent Orange exposure, there was almost nothing she could do. Only the vast, complacent bureaucracy that had so far turned its face from him was capable of doing anything meaningful for him. Finally she settled for rising and turning around and reaching out to put her hand on his, resting on the back of the rickety chair. "I know how you must feel," she said. "I really do."

"Do you?" he said, and turned himself to face her. "Do you really? You're good-looking, with a fancy government job, and I'll bet you've got a house and a nice husband or boyfriend, too." Diana withdrew her hand and cast her eyes downward. "That's okay," he went on. "I think that's great. I really do. And I don't resent you for it. Not one bit. I just think it makes it a little difficult for you to 'really know how I must feel' is all."

Diana resumed her seat on the sofa, and as he talked, Dantley came around so that he was standing in front of her. "For example, these wounds you mentioned—the shrapnel and the other stuff? Would you be surprised to know I don't resent the North Vietnamese gooks or the VC for giving them to me either? What do you say?" Dantley's eyes drilled into her, forcing a response.

Diana swallowed hard and said, "Yeah, I guess that would surprise me. If it were me, I'd certainly resent them."

Dantley dismissed the answer with a shaky wave of his hand. "They were only doing their job, just like I was. It was what our own government did to us, what they did to us and then wouldn't own up to—that's what I resent."

It was clear to all three of them that the interview was over. Without saying anything, Diana and Brian made their way the short distance to the door. Dantley followed behind them. "You aren't a psychiatrist, are you?" he said to Brian.

"No," Brian replied.

"Because, do you know, before Vietnam, I could never remember whether I dreamed in color after I'd woken up. I didn't think so, but I was never sure, and it kind of bothered me not knowing. But after I was in-country a couple of weeks, I was sure I did. Not only color but smell. I would wake up in the middle of the night in horror from the stench of burning meat. Burning human flesh was what it was. But I was always safe in my bunk when it happened. It was all just part of the dreams."

When Brian and Diana were standing in the open doorway, she turned to Dantley and offered her hand—more in a professional manner this time. "When we get back, I'm going to do everything I can to make the people in charge aware of all that we've talked about," she said. But she knew that those people were already aware of it and had already chosen to do as little as they could get away with.

Dantley preempted her. "That's fine, but don't worry about it. I've seen how much they're going to do." Then his eyes narrowed, and all the features on his blistered and pockmarked face sharpened in a way that Diana was sure she'd remember forever. "But someday, somehow, I'll get back at them. I'll get back at all of them. I'll figure out a way."

As Dantley closed the door behind them, Diana turned to Brian. "I'm sorry. But sitting in there, I just couldn't go through with it. I just couldn't do it to him. I'd feel we were no better than all the others who've been screwing him around, and I couldn't have lived with myself."

"I understand," said Brian, and they began walking up the muddy hill together in silence.

"I'm sorry," Diana repeated as they neared the spot where the tire tracks began and the car was parked. "But I just couldn't use him that way."

"It's okay," Brian said. "I understand."

She stopped where she was and turned to face him. "So what do we do now?" she asked.

"We have to use the other guy instead," he answered.

When they reached the car, Diana thought for the first time about the trip home. She started to turn back down the hill to ask Tim Dantley if she could use his bathroom. Then from her high vantage point she saw the narrow wooden shed out back behind his cabin and decided she'd try to hold out till they got back to town.

18

Since his marriage ended and he began living alone, Brian had resisted the idea of a telephone answering machine. It was preten-
tious and artificial and trendy, he thought, and there weren't
many people in his life he cared enough about to mind missing
their calls. Besides, he never could get the recorded message to
sound right. Whenever the hospital needed to be in contact with
him, he carried a beeper, so he saw no point in giving the rest of
the world any special access.

The one person who wouldn't accept this was Lizzie. And she
was the one person in a position to make him do what she wanted,
by holding out the only thing he truly cared about, the one coer-
cion that was always effective—Katie. "I can't make arrangements with you and I can't feel secure about leaving Katie here if
I don't know I can get in touch with you," she had argued. And
though he suspected that her reasons for insisting on the contact
had more to do with the rapid appeasement of her own demands
and requirements than any special concern for her daughter,
Brian didn't want to chance making an issue of it. He believed,
deep down, that character was a comprehensive term and everything mattered, that everything a person did, said, or had was in
some way a reflection of character and attitude. And agreeing to
be tied down to the machine constituted a violation of his. But he

also knew that even though everything mattered, only a few things were worth going to the wall over. So far Lizzie had been good about Katie, and he would do whatever he could to keep it that way. So he went out and bought the answering machine, and when he remembered, he even turned it on.

He had remembered to turn it on before the trip to West Virginia, and when they got back, the machine's counter indicated that there had been a call while they were out. He ran the tape back to the beginning, pressed the Forward button, and listened.

"Thorpe, this is Stanway. Call me."

Brian called him back at his office on his private line. A woman who identified herself as Stanway's assistant said he was at his house at Big Sur and gave him the number.

"What's happening, boy?" Stanway bellowed into the phone. "I hadn't heard from you. I was starting to get worried."

"Doesn't sound like your style, Hugh," said Brian. "I didn't think you worried about anything."

"I worry about everything," Stanway replied. "It's the secret of my success. So bring me up-to-date."

Brian filled him in. He laid out his theories and enumerated his fears. Stanway listened without interrupting. "So what are you going to do now?" he asked.

"Hope for the best," Brian said. "The plan's still pretty vague."

"Sounds like you're going out in the field without proper recon," Stanway observed.

"I'm not thrilled about it," Brian answered. "But it's not something we can work out ahead of time. I think it's one of those things we're going to have to size up when we get there."

"And you're bringing the girl along with you?"

"Yes," said Brian. "It's her plan."

There was quiet on the line. Then Stanway said, "All right, Thorpe. Let's talk serious for a moment here. You're getting yourself into some potentially heavy action, and you're involving a woman with you. If you're right, the other side are pros, whoever they happen to be."

"I understand," Brian said, and looked at Diana as he talked. She was sitting on the floor with her legs tucked under her, and at the moment she looked all innocence and light.

"You're a good man," Stanway continued. "One of the best. I'd trust you anywhere. But this isn't your line of work any longer.

You've been fighting a different kind of war the last few years. I'm sure all the instincts are still there, but it's been a long time. You're out of training. And that's when the percentages start going against you. That's when it starts to get risky."

"I understand, Hugh."

"Fine, you understand. But don't try to be a hero. The minute you think you're in over your handsome blond head—and I mean, the minute, Thorpe—that's when you call me. Don't stand on ceremony; don't stand on nothing. Just call. I can always be contacted at the first number you dialed, and I'll be right out."

"I'm glad to know that."

"Right out. In my own private jet. Do you hear what I'm saying?"

"I do, Hugh. Really."

"All right then. But keep the communication up. Let me hear from you one way or another."

Brian promised he would and hung up.

"Why is this Hugh so interested and concerned for your well-being?" asked Diana, who had been in the room listening to the conversation.

"It's difficult to explain," said Brian, and it was obvious to her that it was uncomfortable for him to talk about. "Let's just say we had to entrust our lives to each other. That means you're always watching out for the other guy . . . on every level. I guess you stay in the habit."

The male bonding sacrament again, Diana thought. The inside circle, forever closed off to her. Its effects were never far from the surface. It was a permanent part of Brian's psyche. And whenever he was under stress, it was the first thing he was going to rely on, she realized, so she'd better get used to it. If she could get him to rely on her as well, then that was as much as she had any right to hope for. But as far as displacing it . . . that was never going to happen.

That night she came back to Brian's bed. But she was still too bound up by conflicting passions to give herself fully over to him. They lay separately, side by side, and after a long time she finally fell asleep thinking about how much she wanted him.

The next morning Gregory picked them up before work to take them to Union Station. He brought with him the X rays he'd requested from Roger Moreland's file. He had traced them down to the naval hospital at the Camp Pendleton Marine Base, Moreland's last posting in the service.

Gregory held one of the films up to the window. The early-morning sun had the same effect as a light box. "This is part of an abdominal series done shortly after Moreland got back stateside. I asked them to send the preop films, too, of course. But I got back a note saying they weren't in the file. At first I thought everything must have gotten lost in the shuffle when Vietnam fell and it must have been a bitch getting any records back. But then I thought: *Didn't the marines pull out long before the fall of Saigon?* Wasn't it several years before?"

"That's right," Brian confirmed. "The last of the land-based guys were out in 1970, less than a year after I was there."

"Right," Gregory said. "So you would have thought that as each man was processed back home, all his records would have come with him in an orderly fashion. I mean, the whole fucking military moves on bureaucracy. I've seen records all the way back from World War One. Now don't you think it's kind of interesting that we can't locate the preop films of any of our little group of marines? Not a single one of them."

"When I asked Dr. Harley, he didn't seem to know anything about it," Diana said. "He said there wasn't any reason why they shouldn't be there."

"Well, he would, wouldn't he?" said Gregory. He pointed to a spot on the lower right of the X ray plate. "But this is the important thing for you right now." Brian and Diana closed in around him. "On this film we see an array of shrapnel fragments in a basically circular pattern starting at the lower groin and going up as high as the pectorals. This is what you'd expect to find as a result of a ground-mounted fragmentation device exploding, let's say, about fifteen yards from the victim."

"Makes sense," Brian said.

"But there's one fragment that stands out a little bit—not much, nothing you'd really notice unless you'd studied it hard. But it is slightly out of the pattern. This one right here in the liver." He held his pen right up next to the spot. "Look at it closely, Brian. That's the one you've got to get for us."

"So what are we going to do?" Diana asked Brian. They were on the New York Metroliner, somewhere between Baltimore and

Wilmington. They'd taken the first seat in the car for maximum privacy.

"I don't know," Brian said, then added dryly, "this is supposed to be your plan."

"I came up with the general idea," she said. "You're the one who's supposed to figure out how to implement it. You're the commando."

"No longer, as Hugh Stanway never tires of reminding me."

"But seriously, Brian, we can't just go up to this guy and say, 'Excuse us, but you may have something in your gut that's highly interesting. Would you mind if we open you up and take a look around?'"

"We may not have a choice if that's what we think we need."

She drew her body back in the seat to look at him more squarely. "Are you serious?"

"This guy isn't a down-and-out like Dantley or Rad Davis or a recluse like Sam Hardesty. He's a very successful businessman, an insurance executive, makes a hell of a lot of money. More like the 'typical' Vietnam vet in my opinion. In fact, he's a certified hero. Spent time in a North Vietnamese POW camp after Eagle's Talon. So he's paid his dues. And he's obviously extremely intelligent. Maybe we should just take a chance and level with him."

"Is that how you've been handling it so far?" Diana asked. "Leveling with him?"

"Not exactly," Brian said.

"How'd you arrange for us to see him?"

"I called and said we'd like to come in and talk about insurance."

"We?"

"My wife and I. Now that we were expecting a new arrival, we had to start thinking about these things."

"I see," she said, summoning up her best reproving glower. "Is that to make it easier to get us into a hotel room together?"

"We won't be going to a hotel," Brian replied.

An immediate look of disappointment came over Diana's face. All along she had been thinking that was to be the expedition's bonus. After being cooped up for so long, she was looking forward to a night or two in a fancy New York hotel to bring her natural romanticism back up to the surface. "We're not?" She pouted. "Then why did we bring clothes and overnight stuff with us?"

"We are staying overnight, just not in the city," Brian explained. "I called Moreland and told him that he'd been highly recommended by a friend and that I'd be in New York and would like to come in and see him. He said that his wife was away somewhere and he was going out to his house at Sag Harbor for a long weekend. As soon as I heard that, I knew he must be doing well. So we got to talking a little, and when I told him I had served with the Third Marines while he was there and that I'd been at Eagle's Talon, he invited me and my 'wife' to come out to the house with him, talk over old times and such. And I figure this way we'll have him alone for a couple of days. We'll have time to build up a trust relationship with him, find out what he knows and what he can tell us. The longer we get to talk to him, the more chance something will emerge that could be useful, something we may not even be thinking of yet. And then maybe, if things go well, we really can level and tell him what we want."

"I don't know," Diana said.

"Look, it's the best chance we've got," Brian replied. He nudged her on her shoulder closest to him. "Don't you think it'll be kind of fun spending the weekend out among the rich people? See what things would have been like if we both hadn't been so damn dedicated. We'll have a room to ourselves in a fancy house, wake up with the sun coming up over the trees. . . . It's not exactly the Plaza, but . . ."

He is trying to put the pieces back together, Diana thought, *even with everything else that's going on.* And there was that element about him she could never deny. She felt the comforting moist warmth between her thighs. "Now I see why you brought me along," she said. "And I don't think it was for my mind."

She noticed him looking down at her skirt, the way it outlined her legs and draped down between them. "I'm going to get coffee," she declared. "Do you want anything?"

"Do you think that's a good idea?" Brian asked as she climbed over him.

She stopped right above him, bracing herself on the armrest against the train's sway, the curve of her hip close to his face. And when he put one of his hands on her backside to help steady her, she didn't say anything or try to take it away. "This is the Metroliner, not the Orient Express. No one's going to grab me from the snack bar. It's only the next car up."

"No, I mean, about the coffee," he said, and patted her belly as she continued by him. "Do you think you should be drinking coffee now that you're . . . you know."

"Very funny, Thorpe," she snapped back. "See when you next get any from me, sun coming up over the trees or not!" She slapped him lightly on the cheek and turned up the aisle toward the next car. At least they were joking about it now, she thought.

LANGLEY, VIRGINIA

Michael Swansea didn't like to brief operatives in his office. He didn't like to have them there at all. In fact, he preferred being completely out of the agency compound for the meetings. He prided himself on keeping his own people "pure," and there was too much opportunity for "cross-fertilization" with other sections and individuals unless he consciously kept them at arm's length. It wasn't merely a matter of personal operating style either. Ever since he'd been with the agency—and in one guise or another that went back to the mid 1960s—Swansea had operated as a loner— an agent whose assignments involved such sensitivity that no one else had to or could be permitted to know about them. They were best officially "forgotten," so that even the director had deniability.

That was the whole point of Covert Action. Even Swansea's use of color codes instead of proper names for his operatives meant that their true identities were known only to him and not even to each other. The idea was that they became nondescript to the point of invisibility. It took a special personality to spend an entire career outside the comforts and safeguards of the traditional intelligence bureaucracy. And over the years, from Southeast Asia to Central America to the Middle East, Michael Swansea had repeatedly proved himself to be that special personality. It was in the peculiar nature of the work that virtually no one would ever know this.

Among his few peers Swansea was certainly considered an imaginative man. But his track record had little to do with this occasionally counterproductive trait. One of the key reasons for his success was his obsessive pursuit of control and maniacal unwillingness to deviate from standards or procedures. "Whenever possible," he was fond of saying, "limit the variables to one. If that isn't possible, then two at the maximum. If there are more than that, it probably won't work."

But something had come up, and it had come up quickly. And unless he reacted immediately, regardless of the number of variables, the situation promised to get completely out of control. That was the one intolerable. There had been no time to get everyone together at the safe house, so he had reluctantly summoned them to Langley, to his inner office, deep within the high-security vault area.

It was a large, functional room, sparsely furnished and betraying no specific taste or point of view. That was the way the man known to most simply as Contact preferred it. He stood behind his desk with his hands balled up into fists in his jacket pockets. "As you know," Swansea began, "we've been lying low on Subject Moreland because of his relatively high profile in the business and social communities as well as the danger of a pattern beginning to emerge from too many seemingly random deaths. But we've just learned that Commander Thorpe is at this very moment on his way to New York by train to see him. We can only surmise what the results of this meeting would be, but as you might suspect, I am not at all sanguine about the possibilities."

He leaned back against the edge of the desk, as if now that he had gotten the unpleasantness off his chest, the meeting could become somewhat more relaxed. In a professional setting this was as relaxed as Swansea ever was. And by design, no one in the room had ever seen him in any other context.

Yellow glanced at his watch. "So presumably Moreland is already in his office. It's going to be tough to get a man up there and then out again without being detected. Maybe we could leave a change of clothing in a janitor's closet on the floor, though we don't have much time to check it out."

"Wouldn't it make more sense to try to take him out on the street when he goes out for lunch?" Blue suggested. "We could count on a crowd, and with a silenced Beretta . . ."

"I wonder if we have time to stage a suicide," Purple speculated. "At least then there are no suspects to worry about."

"Even if we could, we haven't done enough research for a proper note and story," Green pointed out. "There's no assurance we could get it to hang together."

Swansea listened to the discussion for several minutes, not wanting to cut it off lest he stifle some inspiration or piece of originality that had not occurred to him. He had learned that the greatest danger in this line of work was to ignore the obvious. Yet in the wilderness of mirrors the obvious could be the very thing one thought of last.

The telephone on his desk buzzed. The room grew quiet. Swansea punched the last button on the console and lifted the receiver to his ear. He listened wordlessly for more than a minute. "I see," he said finally. "Is this line secure enough for you to hang on? Good." He pressed the hold button and turned back to the assembled group.

"That was Amber, calling from Manhattan. Moreland is not in his office today. He's at his weekend home in Sag Harbor, Long Island. Moreover, his wife and two children are out of town, so he is expected to be alone. Since the weekend plans were made in advance, according to his secretary, it is Amber's belief that Thorpe and Dr. Keegan are going out to Sag Harbor as houseguests."

A small degree of tension drained from the room. The group had been collectively prepared for a virtually impossible situation. Any deviation which lessened the degree of difficulty in any way was bound to promote relief.

"I'm putting Amber on the speaker," Swansea said, and pressed another button on the console.

"He must have a car out there, doesn't he?" Yellow asked.

"He does," the static-charged voice said. "The secretary specifically said he was driving out."

"How complicated would it be to rig it up?"

"Not complicated at all," Swansea stated. "But there are two problems. Problem number one, we can't be sure he'll use the car before Thorpe and Keegan arrive. Problem number two, even if he does, or even if his guests arrive and conveniently go out and take a ride with him, an automobile explosion is something that very definitely calls attention to itself. It is not the kind of thing that is greeted with indifference. No, whatever the solution, it must be the kind of job that looks random, that attaches no particular significance to itself beyond its own unfortunate details, just like the Radley Davis exercise."

"We could stage a kidnapping," said Green. "That would take him out of the picture for a few days, a few weeks if we had to. We could make sure the ransom demands are impossible to meet, then his body could turn up in a car trunk somewhere. Since he's a businessman with a lot of money floating around, there wouldn't necessarily be any connection made."

"Too many details," the chief declared. "Anyway, it's too cruel, too hard on the wife and family. It's like torturing to death an animal that you merely need for food."

Purple raised his finger for recognition. "What about the surprised burglar scenario?"

"That's the one I have been most strongly considering," said Swansea. "It seems to dovetail most cleanly with the circumstances as they've been presented to us." He began ticking off points with the fingers of one hand. "First, it's a wealthy neighborhood. Second, the house is known to be unoccupied on weekdays, so a burglar would have reason to feel secure in being left alone. Third, the area is reasonably secluded, making for an efficient getaway. Fourth, the area is low in crime, so there are no elaborate police facilities. All in all, gentlemen, this seems to be the best possibility on such short notice. You're the closest to it, Amber. How do you feel?"

"Sounds like a winner," said the metallic voice.

"Does it matter that Thorpe and Keegan will most likely be the ones to discover the body?" Blue asked.

"I'd prefer to avoid that," Swansea said. "But it shouldn't make too much difference in itself."

"Well, why not wait a little while longer and take out Thorpe and Keegan at the same time?"

"I considered that, but we can't risk it. The problem of the pattern again. Even if all three appear to have come in and surprised the burglar, we can't take a chance that investigators would draw connections among the three of them. The first thing they'll ask is what Thorpe and Keegan were doing there. As soon as they learn that Thorpe and Moreland were in Southeast Asia together and that Keegan is with an important government agency, things could begin to unravel for us."

With his fingers behind his back at waist level, he pushed himself off from the edge of the desk and paced around the small group until he was directly behind them. Heads turned in unison to follow him. It was a frequent trick of Swansea's, designed to reassure himself that he had full and undivided attention at all times.

"Though we've understandably wavered back and forth on the appropriate disposition of those two, it does now look as if termination will be the only safe and effective outcome. But clearly now is not the time. At this point it is more important to eliminate the quarry than the hunters. We will get them soon enough, though, at the next convenient opportunity."

Swansea returned to the front of the room.

"So who's going to do the job?" Yellow asked.

For a split second the leader looked almost wistful. "I think you'll all have to agree it would have been right up Magenta's alley," he said, "were he still with us." He paused a moment, apparently to show his respect, then grew instantly businesslike again. "But in a way it's probably just as well he is not. This exercise is by its very nature too hasty. It benefits from none of the normal safeguards or intricacies of planning. Besides, there is the logistical problem. We could certainly get Amber to Sag Harbor before Thorpe. But I don't like the exposure. So unless anyone has any objections, I'm going to have him farm this one out to a free-lancer. Strictly need-to-know, complete deniability on this end. As far as the man will know, he's got a contract from the New York–New Jersey mob. He doesn't know who we are, so whatever happens, he can't trace it back to us."

The color-coded operatives nodded their approval.

"I'll get on it right away," Amber promised.

"Oh, needless to say, though, you know who to go to."

"Affirmative."

"And the usual method of payment."

"Right."

Swansea signed off with Amber. Then he resumed his place behind his desk, the sign that the meeting was over. "Please maintain your minute-by-minute availabilities," he called to the team members as they stood up with their briefing books to leave the room. "The situation remains extremely fluid, and it is difficult to say when the next action will have to be taken."

When the operatives were gone, Swansea leaned back in his chair and allowed himself one of his rare moments of reflection. Despite his naturally introspective nature, he purposely kept these musings brief and widely spaced. Too much contemplation could make one indecisive, incapable of definitive action.

He thought back several months to the meeting with Background. It was a rendezvous at the German restaurant in Georgetown, and it had confirmed Swansea's worst fears and set the wheels in motion. At a secluded booth in the rear Background had whispered to him, "Ratsbane is alive."

"What do you mean?"

"Just what I said," Background replied in his thick Slavic accent. A trace of annoyance had crept into his voice. Like Swansea, he was not a man to mince words.

"The Russians know?"

"They've always known. At least, they've always suspected, based on what was given to them. But now they think they're getting closer to the proof. And when they do, they're going to expose it to the world."

Then Swansea cast his mind back farther, almost two decades farther, back to the inception of Ratsbane. The program had started out with such bright potential, he recalled. A strategic tour de force. The simple, elegant solution to a losing, intractable mess. But now, long after it had been dismissed and forgotten by the few who even knew of its existence to begin with, Ratsbane was threatening to swallow up the best and the brightest this country had to defend it.

Just like that morass of a war for which they'd all be so much fish bait.

SAG HARBOR, NEW YORK

From Pennsylvania Station they had taken the Long Island Railroad to Jamaica, where they changed to the South Shore line for the train to Bridgehampton. On the train Brian was quiet, almost sullen, Diana thought, staring straight ahead, wearing his withdrawn-into-himself mask.

"Have you thought any more about how you're going to bring up the subject of the fragment?" she asked.

"No," he replied.

That remained the stalemate point, the one thing they had to get through before they could even begin figuring out what to do next. An image had come into her mind and refused to leave. She pictured them both racing through a jungle, furiously chased by a horde of savages up to an imposing river gorge, hundreds of feet deep. They didn't know what was on the other side of the gorge; they knew only that they had to jump across it. Once they did, there would be other perils, just as terrifying. But they couldn't even think about them until they somehow got across the gorge.

She gazed out the window at the placid Long Island landscape passing quickly by her view. But it all seemed like a hazy illusion, just put there to distract her from reality, the way the Russians had once set up fake idyllic peasant villages along Catherine the Great's carriage route. The contented suburban souls going about their business behind the façades of their pleasant tract houses were all a fake. The jungle in Diana's head was the only reality.

She could sense the stakes getting higher by the day. A pounding, pulsing relentlessness unlike anything she'd ever known before had taken over their lives, and it was being fed by the scent of blood. Or maybe what she was calling relentlessness was actually nothing more complex than inevitablility: that of her life racing toward its ultimate encounter, whatever it turned out to be. She tried to trace back the steps by which her existence had turned so completely upside down. Was it that chance trip to Montana, itself occasioned by Bill Eschenberger's call out of the blue? Or was there something deeper and all-encompassing operating here? Could this all have been avoided, or like so many other stages of her life, had she been merely swept up by events . . . and by her own destiny? The questions continued to hammer at her. And if it all was destiny working itself out—like the war and civil rights and women's equality—was there anything she, or Brian, or anyone could do about it?

Knowledge, information—that was their only possible salvation. "And ye shall know the truth, and the truth shall make you free."

If they lived long enough.

The phrase caught midway in her brain. For the first time, it suddenly dawned on her, she was genuinely fearful for her life. She supposed she should now break out into a cold sweat and reach over and tightly squeeze Brian's hand. But she didn't. Instead, she realized, she was approaching the prospect with a strange and rather chilling objectivity. And maybe that was the most unnerving observation of all.

Why wasn't she shakier? she wondered. It must be that practical considerations kept getting in the way. She should be grateful for that, she told herself. She was finally beginning to understand how men like Brian could be so cool and detached in combat, when their lives were constantly in danger. Focus on the practical and immediate. That was the only way.

One way or another she was certain that Roger Moreland held the key puzzle piece, in either his mind or his body, or both.

Well, one of them had better come up with an idea pretty quick. *Time to show some initiative, young lady.*

She reached over and locked her arm through Brian's, pulling him back from wherever he'd taken himself and forcing his attention to her. Her eyes were wide and alive. She ran her tongue tantalizingly across her upper lip and then just as enticingly licked off the glistening trail of moisture it had left. "Maybe I'll seduce him," Diana said brightly.

Brian suddenly seemed to perk up, and his eyes came alive. "That may be fun for you," he commented, setting out the bait. "But then what?"

"All right, sailor boy. You come up with something better,"she responded, her hard-won bouncy coolness undimmed.

From the Bridgehampton station it was an easy cab ride to Sag Harbor. Along the way the taxi driver kept up a running commentary on his principal patrons, the slick city people who had taken over the Hamptons as their playground of choice.

"To tell you the truth, I don't understand what they see in this place," he said confidingly, once he had assured himself that he was speaking to outsiders who could not communicate his heresy back to the regulars. "It's full of rich people from Manhattan who spend hours in bumper-to-bumper traffic to get out here every weekend or sweat the train, like you both just did, and when they get here, they wait in long lines at expensive restaurants, where they all see the same people they saw during the week, and do you know why they all say they come?" He didn't wait for an answer. "To get away from it all! Whattaya think of that, huh?"

They turned from the Sag Harbor Turnpike onto Main Street and from there onto the half-paved lane whose houses were sufficiently large, well spaced, and secluded to make house numbers unnecessary. Just as they made the turn, a car coming in the opposite direction sped toward them, kicking up dust. Diana's breath jerked from her chest; she was sure they were going to crash. Brian instinctively grabbed her by the shoulders and held her back. The driver cut the wheel hard and swerved to avoid the car. The two vehicles passed with a margin of inches.

"Son of a bitch!" the driver muttered. "These people think they own the fucking world, just because they've got a little money. We ought to put up a fence and keep them all out!"

Diana finally caught her breath. If this was supposed to be a peaceful, restful community where highly stressed New Yorkers could get away from it all, she'd seen no evidence of it so far. That man could have killed them.

"Nice place your friend's got," the driver commented. They pulled up in front of an imposing but comfortable and inviting Cape Cod style house, separated from its closest neighbor by a mature and well-tended hedgerow. And as soon as she opened the car door, Diana could smell the crisp salt air. She understood why people from the city would put up with all the nonsense to spend weekends and free time out here.

They got out of the cab, and Brian paid the driver. Even at its slow speed the cab kicked up dust and small stones, just as the speeding car had done. Brian and Diana looked at the house, then at each other. "Well, I guess we are moving up in the world," he said, and Diana began thinking now of lying in bed early in the morning with the sun coming up over the trees.

Brian rang the doorbell, and they stood on the front porch waiting. He rang again and then knocked. "Maybe he's not here yet." He looked around the property. "But there's a car in the driveway. Think he's trying to tell us something?"

"Try the door," Diana suggested. "This isn't like the city. People probably leave their doors unlocked out here."

Brian tried the doorknob. It turned easily in his hand.

He opened the door, and they both stepped cautiously inside. "Anybody home?" Diana called out.

They looked up at the carved oak balcony that ran along the entire length of the entrance hall. They saw no one.

They looked down at the polished oak floor and saw a man about Brian's age lying in a pool of blood.

"Oh, Jesus," Diana gasped.

Brian quickly crouched down and cradled the man's head in his hands. He put his fingers over the nose and lips. They came away covered with bloody spittle. Brian ripped the man's shirt open, leaned over, and pressed his ear to the chest. Then he shoved his fingers deep into the man's neck.

"Found it," he hissed to Diana. "Weak pulse, still alive."

"What is it?"

Brian ripped the shirt buttons the rest of the way down. "Gunshot, I think."

Diana's eyes darted around the room. "Where's the phone? I'll call for help." She ran to the first door, then stopped. "I don't even know where we are or what to tell the ambulance."

"Go see if you can find a neighbor," Brian ordered. "Hurry."

Diana ran from the house. Brian worked feverishly over the unconscious body, trying to stem the bleeding.

She came back within minutes. A middle-aged man with thinning gray hair and a paunch was with her. "Oh, God," he said.

"Brian, this is—"

"Phil Rosenfield. Just tell me what you want me to do."

Brian didn't look up. "We've got to get him to a hospital. No time to wait for an ambulance."

"My car's right outside. We'll go to Southampton."

"How far?"

"Twenty—fifteen minutes if we speed."

"Okay, let's go. You take his legs. I'll get him under the arms. Diana, put your hands on the back of his head. Don't let it fall back; he's already shocky."

Rosenfield had a fairly large car, an Oldsmobile or something. Brian was in the back with Moreland, whom they had angled to stretch out as far as possible. Diana was in the front passenger seat, crouched on her knees, leaning over into the back for whatever help she could give.

And Rosenfield drove like a demon.

"The pulse is getting weaker, and I'm getting bulging veins in the neck," Brian told Diana. "Breathing is shallow. I'm not getting any movement in the right chest." Brian's eyes darted around. "You don't have a first-aid kit in the car, do you?"

"No, sorry." Rosenfield's voice was trembling.

"What about a knife, anything like that?"

"I'm sorry," the neighbor stammered.

"How about a knitting needle."

"I—I don't think so. My wife doesn't—"

"I need a long, thin tube that's hollow inside." Brian's voice was raised and urgent.

"I'm—I'm sorry. I don't have anything like that," Rosenfield replied desperately.

Brian was silent for a moment. Diana could sense the movement behind his eyes. "Have you got a tire gauge then?"

"I think so. Glove compartment."

Diana turned around and fished through the storage bin. "Here it is." She handed it back to Brian. He grasped it firmly and twisted the head until it broke apart. He pulled the calibrated slide out from the middle.

"What are you going to do?"

"He's got a tension pneumothorax," Brian explained tersely. "Air is filling in the space around the lung and compressing all the structures on the right side so he can't breathe. If I don't relieve it, he's going to suffocate. We should use a number fourteen hollow needle, but we can't wait." He held the broken tire gauge up to his lips and blew through it to make sure the passage was clear.

"That doesn't look very sanitary," Diana said.

"That's the least of his problems," said Brian. "Good sanitation doesn't much matter to a corpse."

Rosenfield shuddered and clenched his fingers around the steering wheel.

Brian felt along Moreland's upper rib cage to the second intercostal space, high on the right side. He spread his hand out across the chest to hold him rigid. Diana turned her head away and, to be sure, squeezed her eyes shut. Brian pursed his lips, stared down intently at his target, raised the tire gauge up above his shoulder, and brought it down hard, puncturing Moreland's chest between the ribs.

The instrument broke through with a dull, ripping sound. There was a rush of air from the opening Brian had punched, and a fresh rivulet of blood instantly leaked from the jagged wound. Diana forced a peek. The silver tire gauge stuck through the skin like some bizarre prosthesis. She had to swallow back the bile that burned at her throat as she regarded the makeshift valve with perverse fascination. Moreland's body became less rigid. Brian felt the neck for the carotid artery and pressed. He put his face right up next to Moreland's mouth until he felt breath.

"Pulse and breathing are stronger," he reported. "We've got a chance!" Then he grasped the hand of the unconscious patient, bent over and patted him roughly on the cheek, and urged, "Just hang in there, buddy. Don't leave me now!"

And at that moment Diana had the eerie feeling that her companion was back in Vietnam, once more the medic ministering to a dying marine. The time since then had not existed. The facts that this was Long Island, that they were in an Oldsmobile and not a Huey, that Brian was now a doctor and Moreland an insurance executive all were merely details.

SOUTHAMPTON, NEW YORK

The emergency room team swarmed around the prostrate body as Brian explained what had happened and what he had done to try to stabilize him. Within seconds they had shoved a tube down Moreland's throat, inserted three large-bore IVs and a chest tube. Diana and Phil Rosenfield stood by, looking on with horrified attention.

The resident looked incredulously at the tire gauge. He pulled it out and put in another tube in its place.

The nurse monitoring blood pressure shouted, "He's hypotensive—fifty palpable. He's bottoming out."

The resident dissected down into the chest wall and a fountain of bright blood spurted out.

"Blood pressure's improving," the nurse reported.

"Pericardial tamponade," Brian said. "His heart can't pump with all the blood that's filled in around it."

The resident looked up at him with a mixture of annoyance and disbelief. "Is that a fact? Suppose you just leave this to me and we'll take care of your friend good and proper."

"Then stop screwing around and do a pericardiocentesis! He's going to die if you don't!"

The resident looked down and muttered something inaudible. "Syringe!" he demanded. The nurse slapped a large needle into his hand. The resident inserted it into Moreland's naked chest. He drew back on the plunger, and it came out full of the blood that had filled in between the heart and its surrounding sac. He filled two more syringes.

The improvement in Moreland was dramatic. The nurse reported all the vital signs on the way up. The resident looked over his shoulder at Brian. "That's what it was all right. You must be a doctor."

"Good guess," said Brian.

"We've called the attending surgeon," the resident told him with suddenly increased respect. "He's in the building and should be down any minute. The OR's all set." He stepped away from the table to leave Moreland momentarily to the rest of the swarm.

"How does it look?" Brian asked.

"Touch and go," the resident said. "But I'll say this. He was damn lucky you happened to come along."

"I'm not so sure about that," Brian muttered.

The resident looked at him quizzically but then shrugged his shoulders and let the matter drop.

The attending surgeon's name was Bryce Chambers. He was white-haired and distinguished-looking in his surgical greens and clearly nearing the end of his career. And when he saw Roger Moreland lying on the table being prepped for the operating room, the color drained from his face.

"It's been a long time since I've had to do a trauma," he announced, shaking his head.

"Are you saying you're not qualified to perform this surgery?" Rosenfield asked, bearing down on him.

"Well, I'll do my best," he said. "But you have to understand that—" His hands were beginning to tremble. He seemed almost befuddled. In spite of the tension in the air and Moreland's life on the line, Diana found it within herself to feel sorry for the old surgeon.

"I'll do it," Brian said.

The resident's eyes flashed. "Out of the question. You're not credentialed here. It violates every principle of hospital practice. We don't know that—"

"We don't know anything except that your man here can't do it by himself," Rosenfield broke in. He held up his hand toward Brian. "This man has extensive experience in trauma surgery, and so far he's saved your patient's life."

"But he doesn't have privileges," the resident said. "We can't just let anyone in here. The insurance ... The legal implications of this are—"

"I'm a lawyer," Rosenfield said. "And I'll tell you what the legal implications are if this man dies because of your incompetence. I'll see that you're socked with a lawsuit that'll close this place down tight. I don't give a shit whose toes are getting stepped on. Now let's stop fucking around and get him into that operating room!"

The resident looked around helplessly, as if seeking out higher authority. Chambers worked his jaw up and down several times before he could get a sound to emerge from his mouth. Finally he said in a voice that bordered on pleading, "Doctor—I don't know what your name is—if you could 'assist' me with this procedure, I'd be most appreciative."

"My name's Thorpe," Brian said. "And this is Diana Keegan.

She's a doctor, too, and I want her in there with us." Diana's eyes went wide with surprise.

"Whatever you say," Chambers replied. "You both scrub and I'll meet you in the OR."

"Right," Brian said, and motioned Diana over to him. Then he turned to the surgical nurse, who had shifted her attention from Chambers to him, as if command had just been transferred. "How's the hematocrit?"

"Dropped down to twenty."

"Okay," Brian said. "I want him typed and crossed and in the OR by the time I get there. And tell your blood bank I want ten units on hold and three units of fresh frozen plasma. Where's the scrub room?"

The nurse pointed. Brian took Diana by the arm and led her along with him. He saw Phil Rosenfield standing by the emergency room door. Brian stopped. "Thanks for your intervention back there," he said.

"Thanks for yours," Rosenfield replied. "That man is my neighbor and one of my best friends. But don't thank me so fast," he added with a wry smile, "because if you lose him, he might also become my client."

"Why do you want me in there?" Diana asked when they were alone in the scrub room.

"You're the only one I can trust," Brian said, pulling off his shirt.

"But I haven't scrubbed on any surgery since med school. I don't think I remember anything from it."

"You're the only one I can trust," Brian repeated firmly. "I need you in there."

Diana had just removed her dress and peeled off her panty hose. She held out the baggy overalls of the green scrub suit, about to step into them. She stopped halfway through the motion and let her hands drop in front of her. Her eyes were bright with the sudden realization. "I just figured out what you're talking about," she said.

"Clever girl," said Brian.

"But I still don't know if I can do it." Her voice quavered. "I haven't done anything like it before."

"Look, you helped with the autopsy back in Montana, didn't you?"

"Yes, but that was different. That was—"

"Well, this is practically the same thing," he remarked. "The only difference is that the patient is still alive."

"Right," Diana said dryly.

"And the object of the game is to keep him that way."

"Brian, I can't believe this is happening," Diana whispered on their way down the corridor of the surgical suite. "This is all crazy. It's surrealistic."

"Just keep smiling behind that mask, baby," he whispered back. "And pretend you do it every day."

In the operating room Brian worked quickly. Time is the enemy of trauma victims, and the longer they are subjected to the further trauma of surgery, the greater the jeopardy. And since Brian knew he had to save a few minutes for "himself" at the end, he knew he couldn't afford to waste a second of Roger Moreland's life.

In fact, Moreland's wounds were as close to combat trauma as anything Brian had seen in civilian life. A shotgun can do horrifying damage, and at close range it is as devastating as a fragmentation bomb. Brian opened up a large midline incision to explore the extent of damage. The first priority was the lungs and thoracic vasculature. Then he stanched the bleeding of the mesenteric artery, repaired the ravaged spleen, stitched up holes in the large bowel, and cauterized the entrance wounds that perforated the diaphragm. All the while Bryce Chambers stood behind him, closely observing the procedure so that as surgeon of record, he could recapitulate each step in his postoperative report.

Brian glanced over at the anesthesiologist.

"Stable so far," he stated, meeting Brian's look.

Then this would be the time.

Brian resected the muscle and connective tissue around the liver. He was grateful that it appeared free of damage. He caught Diana's eye, and she nodded back to him. As she subtly maneuvered herself into position next to him, he palpated the liver with his fingers until he felt a hard spot.

"I'm now repairing a perforation across the surface of the liver," he explained for Chambers's benefit, while Diana's position blocked Brian's hands from the view of the others around the table.

Diana felt every inch of her body running with nervous sweat.

Her underwear was sticking to her skin, making her even more self-conscious of her movements. She was glad the surgical gown covered her completely.

She watched carefully as Brian's scalpel sliced into the liver, just as it had done in the autopsy in Montana. And her heart skipped and left a hollow ringing in her chest as he pulled the firm reddish tissue aside and uncovered the tiny metal fragment.

She forced a peripheral glance at the scrub nurse and anesthesiologist to make sure their fields of view were still blocked by her body. She listened as Brian maintained a running commentary on how he was repairing the nonexistent injury to the organ. She was astonished he could keep his story straight and coherent while performing an equally delicate procedure that had nothing to do with it. It was an amazing bit of illusion, unlike anything she'd ever seen or imagined before. The stakes were incredible, she acknowledged to herself, greater even than the patient's life. Because if there were any slipup, if Brian needed Chambers's assistance, or if Moreland died and there were an autopsy—and there unquestionably would be in a homicide case—or if there were any reason to open him up and go back in in the near future, they'd see what Brian had done. It would be the end of his career. Worse. He'd probably be arrested and charged, and she along with him. She bit her lower lip until she thought she could taste blood in her mouth.

Just keep smiling behind that mask, baby, she told herself.

With tiny motions of the scalpel blade Brian had sheared the fragment free. With his index finger and thumb pinched together, he pried it loose and transferred it to the inside of his fist.

"I've got a tear in my glove," he announced, and moved away from the table. "Diana, come over here and help me."

"I'll do it," the scrub nurse declared.

"No, stay with the patient," Brian replied. "If anything happens, Diana won't know what to do and you will."

Diana took one last glance into the surgical field before stepping away and saw that Brian had covered his work with a large sponge clamped into place with hemostats.

At the back of the room Diana peeled off Brian's latex glove. It went inside out as it came off, securing the fragment safely inside. She looked around quickly, then stowed it furtively in the back pocket of her scrub suit, underneath the sterile gown. *Act natural*, she kept warning herself. *Don't give yourself away.*

From her other pocket she removed a used bloodstained glove that they had retrieved from the waste bin in the scrub room. Now she turned and made a show of depositing it in the operating room's receptacle. She fitted a new glove on Brian's upraised hand, and together they returned to the table.

On the way back he gave her a wink.

Moreland's condition remained critical, and the next several days would tell, the attending physicians said, but there was no question in anyone's mind that without Brian's intervention he would have been dead. Bryce Chambers went over the details of the operation with Brian to make sure he had them down correctly, and the resident who'd tried to block him conceded that it was one of the finest examples of trauma surgery he'd seen. The nurses had put their bloody clothing through the hospital laundry while they were in the operating room. The panty hose Diana had been wearing had gotten torn in the car and now she bought a new pair in the gift shop.

The Suffolk County police were cooperative and understanding and, keeping in mind what Brian and Diana had been through, tried to inconvenience them as little as possible. Everyone professed admiration for what they had just done. Detective Lieutenant Jerry Cooper ushered them into the surgical waiting lounge and took their statements. They stuck to the details they had agreed on during the train ride, except the part about being married and having a baby on the way. That was too easy to check and would arouse suspicions. Cooper asked for a phone number where they both could be reached. Brian gave his number in Washington, then excused himself to go phone Jill and have her report him on sick leave.

"Now let's get the hell out of here before someone catches up with us," he whispered to Diana when the policemen had left.

Phil Rosenfield offered to drive them wherever they wanted to go, which turned out to be La Guardia Airport. "There's no way I can ever thank you enough," he attested, and seemed to miss totally Brian's expression of discomfort as he said it.

"I don't want to put you out," Brian said. "Just call us a cab if you wouldn't mind."

They went back and forth for awhile about it, but Brian finally won out under the condition that he would allow Rosenfield to pay.

They said good-bye to the attorney in the main lobby, where they had gone to wait for the taxi. It was a long, emotional parting, the kind reserved for people who have been through something together that forever binds them to each other. Rosenfield strode out the door with the promise that he would always keep in touch and would certainly keep them informed of Moreland's condition. Then they settled back into a couch upholstered in bright yellow vinyl, the type of material designed more for its ease of cleanup than for any comfort or particular aesthetic appeal.

That was when the tears finally broke loose—a torrent of raspy, choking sobs that left Diana wheezing for breath and racked with the violent heaving of stomach and ribs. She cried because there was finally the luxury of time for it, and she wept for herself and Brian and all the people whose lives they had had the misfortune to touch. And she wept for the ominous future, for their future, which was somehow tied to the tragic past in ways she could not begin to fathom.

Brian cradled her face against his shoulder. He tenderly kissed her head and smoothed down her matted hair as if he were comforting a child who had just suffered her first loss. But he did not try to stop her sobbing or to dry her wet cheeks and glistening eyes, reddened from the sting of her salty tears.

Other people in the room looked on from a discreet distance but displayed no discomfort at the scene. In a hospital lobby open expressions of extreme joy or grief are not uncommon or out of place.

For Diana, the tears were neither an indulgence nor a play for sympathy but an exercise in self-preservation, something she knew she needed in order to continue getting through what could not be avoided. She knew her own limits, and she knew how long the therapy could be allowed to go on. So by the time the taxi pulled up at the front door for them, she was fine.

19

ATLANTA, GEORGIA

The headquarters of the National Centers for Disease Control sprawl along Clifton Road, just on the edge of the Emory University campus. They are housed in a large cluster of fifties modern concrete and redbrick buildings which, appropriately enough, very much resemble a hospital. There is a little garden in front, no more than a triangular patch of green plantings amid the cement of the front walk, really. And in that garden on a marble pedestal stands a bust of Hygeia, the Greek goddess of health.

Diana had always been drawn to the sculpture, ever since she'd noticed it on her first interview here. And she liked the fact that it was placed prominently near the main entrance of this institution dedicated to the most scientific and technologically sophisticated pursuit of healing. The marble bust, to her, was an acknowledgment that medicine was also inspired by some far deeper and more mythic source, one that resonated through the very essence of the term "healing *arts.*"

She and Brian arrived late in the day. They walked respectfully up to the statue, where Diana stopped for a few moments of silent contemplation, her hands clasped in front of her. And then they strode purposefully through the impersonal and rather lifeless elevator lobby, at a time when most of the staff had already left the building. Just like before, the main thing was to act natural, she had decided, as if nothing were wrong and she'd never been away. If anyone noticed her and asked where she'd been, she'd say she'd had the flu but she'd been back for several days now. And funny they hadn't run into each other lately, wasn't it?

They went up to the fourth floor, to stow their overnight bags in Diana's office. In her absence the plants on the windowsill had gone from dying to dead. It was depressing to think that they might have been the only ones here that had missed her while she was away.

She could see that Brian was edgy. "Let's get this thing into a lab," he said.

"Not just any lab," she said, her voice rising on a note of triumph. "That's why we're here."

They took the elevator down to the basement level. No one else got on during the short ride, and Diana took that to be a good sign. The more the staff thinned out, the less likelihood they'd be questioned or disturbed. They got out and walked down long cinder-block corridors, past warning signs in several languages that repeated every few yards.

In one sense the Centers for Disease Control are a citadel of modern science, and that was how Diana regarded them. All the battalions the forces of disease have mustered against humankind are interned here, held under armed guard, stored in refrigerated cabinets behind bolted metal doors. The 1918 swine flu, the 1952 poliomyelitis, the 1976 Legionnaire's disease—all are represented and kept alive to share their secrets. Since 1980 the fearsome scourge of smallpox has been eliminated, after centuries of devastation. Today it lives only two places on the planet: the World Health Organization in Geneva and the Centers for Disease Control. The battle is waged to the death, but prisoners must always be taken.

They reached the end of the hall. There was one gray metal door. On the wall beside it was a sign which read:

WORK ON ALL SPECIMENS WHICH MAY BE
OF CLASS IV POTENTIAL MUST BE CARRIED
OUT IN MAXIMUM CONTAINMENT LAB ONLY!

"What's a Class Four specimen?" Brian asked.

"It's a designation primarily applied to viruses," Diana explained. "Viruses with no vaccine . . . and no known cure in humans."

"I see," Brian replied soberly. "And that's why we're going to this maximum containment place?"

"In this outfit we take no chances," Diana responded. "We're both soldiers, you know. The only difference is that my enemy is more deadly than yours."

She opened the door, and they went through. It led to a hallway and another door. Next to this second door was a slot in the wall, and above it was another sign: ADMISSION TO MAXIMUM CONTAINMENT LAB BY KEY CARD ONLY.

Diana opened her purse and rummaged around. The card she came out with looked to Brian much like a credit card. It was plastic, with a magnetic stripe. The only difference was that instead of her signature or a photograph, it carried a thumbprint. She inserted it halfway into the slot. There was a whirring sound and something like the clicking of gears; then the solid door slid to the side, allowing them entry.

"We're not in the main building anymore," she told him. "We're out back in a modular outer building constructed over a completely independent inner core. This place is totally separated in every way. If there's a hurricane, the outer shell protects it. If there's an earthquake, the inner core is suspended on a floating foundation. It's quite extraordinary, really."

She led him to a small room designated PERSONNEL CHANGE AREA. "Leave your clothes on this side of the air lock, inside the locker. This isn't like an operating room. Here you have to get really clean. I'll see you after we both shower," she said.

"Is that really necessary for what we're doing?"

"Probably not. But we've brought it this far, so we're not taking any chances. And if you play the game, you have to play by the rules. Scrub down good. You'll find a white lab suit in the cabinet as you come out."

"Then can I at least shower with you?"

"No, you can't! Now behave yourself and try not to embarrass me."

You enter the Maximum Containment Lab by stages, gradually leaving the outside world and being absorbed into an artificially created one, designed—if necessary—to enclose death and hold it inside.

Brian and Diana emerged from their respective showers into the air lock chamber, a room that kept the inside atmosphere separated from the outside and contamination-free. Brian and Diana both were dressed in shimmering, stiff-legged phosphorescent uniforms that had the look of some science-fiction movie whose vision of the future was particularly bleak and impersonal.

"Isn't this a little overly dramatic?" Brian asked.

"Folks here don't seem to think so," Diana answered.

The Maximum Containment Laboratory, she related to him, had been established in 1969 in response to a terrifying incident at Yale. A sample of the deadly Lassa fever virus brought back from Africa for study somehow got out. It killed a research technician and nearly killed the director of the project. The only reason he survived was that he was able to get transfusions from a nurse who had had the disease. It was a lucky break. It was also lucky that many more people didn't succumb. The scientific community realized at that point that microbiological and genetic research had reached a level of sophistication where the potential for destruction—massive, uncontrollable destruction—was too great to ignore.

So a separate, isolated, and thoroughly planned facility was designed and set up in a corner of the parking lot behind the CDC's main building. Based on the army's secret biological weapons research installation at Fort Detrick, Maryland, the Maximum Containment Lab leaves nothing to chance. It has sealed floors through which nothing can seep, pipes and wiring outside and independent of the walls, specially treated sewage tanks not connected to the municipal system, and filtered negative air pressure ventilation throughout. In the unlikely event of a leak anywhere in the facility, the greater air pressure outside the lab would keep every potentially deadly molecule inside. Nothing could be allowed to violate the integrity of the lab.

So far, Diana stated with careful pride, the safety record of the Maximum Containment Lab had been perfect. But that was a statistic no one at CDC took for granted.

She ushered Brian into the animal lab room. "They've got everything here from rats and white mice up to human-size primates."

She walked over to the sterile glass-walled cages and selected a small brownish gray rabbit. She picked up the furry bundle with rubber-gloved hands and cradled it lovingly in her arms. "What's your name, bunny?" she purred, while she carried it over to the counter-high laminar flow work station. Like the animal cages, it was completely encased in glass. And along its side, four holes gave access to clear, flexible hand and arm gloves. They looked like tentacles sticking out from the walls of a fish tank and allowed the researcher to reach into the case almost up to the shoulders.

The Maximum Containment Lab was designed so that dangerous or questionable materials could be moved from one work station to the next—from microscopy to centrifuge to incubation to culture plating—without being removed from behind their protective glass barrier. All one needed to do was to move down to the next set of tentacle gloves.

Diana unfastened the door at the end of the cabinet and placed the rabbit inside. It scurried around the perimeters once and then huddled in the corner, shaking with fright.

"Now don't be afraid," she said soothingly. She fitted one arm through the glove hole and petted the rabbit reassuringly. The animal quieted instantly. Brian marveled at her touch. He could imagine she must have had the same effect with children.

From the pocket of her lab suit she removed a plastic bag fastened with a tie band. In it was the metal fragment Brian had removed from Roger Moreland's liver. Inside the other end of the work station, separated by a movable partition, was a microscope and a full set of instruments. Through a fiber optic lens system, the scope's objective came through the glass wall and could be adjusted to a comfortable height and angle.

Diana placed the fragment on the microscope's viewing surface. "It's all yours," she said.

Slowly, and awkwardly at first since he wasn't used to working with a glass barrier between himself and his subject, Brian repeated the procedure he had performed at Bethesda on the fragment from Radley Davis's body. Peering through the lens objective, he used tweezers to angle the metal sliver into place on its side, where he could see that it had the same type of microscopic stopper at one end. With a fine-grade needle, he gingerly hooked into the stopper. Holding his breath to steady his hands, he withdrew the needle and left the tiny inner chamber open and exposed.

Diana tried to peer over his shoulder and, when that didn't work, asked, "Can you see if there's anything inside?"

"Looks like the same stuff that was in the Davis capsule," he said. "Just a little drop of some clear fluid."

With the tweezers he lifted the fragment again and placed it in the center of a Pyrex Petri dish at the base of the microscope.

Diana glanced over at him. "Doesn't look like much, does it?"

"Sure doesn't," Brian said. "So if this turns out to be a dud, then what?"

Diana remained silent, focused on the experiment in front of her.

"All right," said Brian. "It's the same thing again. I can tell by looking at it. Let's pack up and go home."

"One rule of epidemiology," she said cautioningly. 'You can't tell anything just by looking at it."

Diana removed the lock on the Plexiglas partition that separated the two halves of the work space. She slid it out from its grooves and laid it in its specially designed container to keep it from scratching. The control animal was now exposed to the test specimen.

Diana observed the rabbit for a moment. It showed no ill effects. In fact, it hardly noticed. She dropped her shoulders and expelled a long column of breath. "Well, that takes care of the big hit," she said.

"What do you mean?"

"It's not a poison gas or any sort of toxin," she stated. "That's what I really thought it might be and was mostly afraid of. The lethal potential for something like that is tremendous. But if it had been, the effects would have shown almost immediately. The bunny would have been belly up by now."

Brian relaxed slightly for the first time since she had told him of the lab's history.

By this point the rabbit seemed totally accustomed to its new environment. It displayed no fear as it waddled across the floor of the cabinet. It sniffed at the dish as if to see if its friends had been thoughtful enough to leave anything there for it to eat. It looked up trustingly at Diana through wide pink eyes, its nose twitching with curiosity.

"Sorry, furball," she said, though the animal could not hear her through the thick glass. "You're going to have to wait a little while for dinner. Can't do anything to compromise the experiment. But if you're good, I'll bring you back the biggest carrot I can find at Kroger."

With that the rabbit settled back down; out of contentment or boredom, it was impossible to tell.

Brian and Diana looked at each other. "Well, I guess that's it for a while." She sighed.

"You seem disappointed."

She looked as if she'd just been caught at some social indiscretion. "No," she quickly told him, "I'm relieved."

"You should be."

Still, there was a corner of her that wished it all had have turned out a little differently here. Brian had the excitement of the operating room and, before that, the battlefield. This lab—with its futuristic suits and sterile air—was her own touch of drama. Or at least it could have been had they found something more compelling than a half drop of inert clear fluid. She silently apologized to the bunny for the admission she had just made to herself, the confession that she would have been willing to see this innocent little creature dead for her own intellectual satisfaction and glory. It was totally out of keeping with everything she believed in. *God's going to punish me for this*, she said to herself. *He's going to bring me back as a lab animal.*

And they still had no idea what the purpose of those capsules was or how they had been incorporated into fragmentation bombs. There had to be a connection to everything that had happened. So far these tests hadn't offered a clue.

She looked down through the glass at the rabbit. It was working its diminutive jaws back and forth as though it wished it had something to chew on. "As soon as this is finished, we'll let you out and feed you," she said.

She suddenly felt her own stomach rumble in sympathy. "I'm starved. Let's go get a pizza or something. We can bring it back to my place. That should give the fluid in the capsule time to interact with the air. Then we'll come back, spin it down, and put it through qualitative analysis. If there's anything there at all, we'll find it," she stated. She said it more for her own benefit than his, her voice possessed of an edge of determination as rigid as forged steel.

Returning to the apartment was like going back for her fifteenth high school reunion. There was a certain recognition and air of familiarity about the place, but it was filtered through so many recesses of time that it no longer had any relationship to her life. Indeed, so much had changed since she had left that the person who had lived here seemed another incarnation.

Sharon had moved out. How could she have stayed in this place where she'd been so horribly violated? Diana had received a call the next day from her roommate saying that she'd found somewhere else. It was only the first of two calls she'd received from Atlanta that day. The other was from the local police, asking her every conceivable question and asking her to speculate on who might have wanted to do this to her. Any recent fights? Any bad experiences with boyfriends? One of them ever beat you up or anything like that? Drug use—you or anyone you know? As a physician, aren't you licensed to prescribe controlled substances? Do you ever keep any around the apartment? She was sure they'd combed the place looking for anything that might have tied her into the attack. And she had to promise that as soon as she got back to Atlanta, she'd come in and go through another round in person. One more little chore to add to her list.

Diana quickly surveyed the apartment. With Sharon gone, half the living room furniture had gone with her. Gray dust balls looking like miniature tumbleweeds dotted the carpet around the indentations made by chair legs. No doubt all the coffee mugs would be gone from the kitchen, too. They were also Sharon's.

Diana and Brian set down their bags. They washed up and ate the pizza before it cooled off too much. They'd hardly had anything all day, and Diana's stomach continued to grumble, but neither one had much of an appetite. The pizza grew cold. The ice melted in the sodas they'd selected for their caffeine contents. They sat silently across from each other at the small butcher-block table which was still too big for the kitchen's breakfast alcove. She knew what was on both their minds, but it was left to Brian, finally, to bring it out for discussion.

"Look, maybe we're barking up the wrong tree, trying to pin everything on this fragment," he said. "Maybe we should forget about trying to figure out whatever they are. When you think about it, there was no reason to suspect that this one would have anything different inside it from the other one."

Diana had gone through this line of reasoning with herself already. In fact, she'd been torturing herself with it. So she had pushed the sequence of logic one notch farther. "There has to be something to them," she protested. "It's what every one of the marines has in common. As you said yourself, once you have a certain number of coincidences, they're no longer coincidences. It has to be the key."

"But there's been nothing inside the fragment," Brian said. "It just seems to be water."

"Maybe so. But they're all about the same size, they all have perfectly machined centers almost microscopically small, they're all found in the victim's liver, and both the dead marines we know about *and* the guy from our control group had one. That's not by chance. What's more, anyone who's got one of these fragments or knows anything about them doesn't seem to have a very long life expectancy these days."

"Including the two of us if we don't get smart pretty soon," he replied. "There isn't a whole lot of time. So where do we go from here?"

It came as a challenge, almost an affront, the slap across the face with a glove that prefaces a duel. Perhaps he didn't mean it that way. Perhaps it was nothing but a simple inquiry. But with all that she'd been through, with all that they'd both been through, it set her teeth on edge, like chewing on raw tin foil.

She had blown it. That's what she could sense he was telling her. She had had a theory, and he had trusted her. He'd given her the ball to run with, and she'd punted. And it was going to cost them, cost them heavily.

She stared across the table at him, blinking back the tears of frustration and exhaustion. She had already cried once today and was determined not to do it again. That would have been the easy way out, in some ways the most comfortable—collapse in a blubbering heap and leave Brian, if he would, to pick up the pieces. The other possibility was to curl up in a little ball and crawl into the corner until it all went away.

No. She wouldn't. It had beeen a long, trying, horror-filled day, and it was taking its toll on both of them. She was trying desperately to fight off the numbness and the fatigue. For with the numbness, she could already feel, came a sense of resignation, of ceasing to care, and, ultimately, of capitulation. First would be the crawling into the corner and then the lying down and giving in and allowing herself to be overwhelmed, just for the momentary relief it would bring.

She stood up from the table. "I'm going into the other room to change," she announced calmly. "Then we can go back to the lab and finish up." There was always a chance fresh clothes and some cold water on the face would make her feel better. She couldn't feel any worse.

Brian said nothing as she left him at the table and walked into her bedroom. It was the first time she had been there, Diana realized, since leaving on her trip out to Stanford. She'd run off rather hastily that day, she recalled, and left her room a shambles. As usual, she had been late for the plane.

But now the room was neat as a pin. The bed was made. Everything had been put away in its proper place. Sharon was such an angel to do that for her before she moved out. She imagined the scene as it must have been when Sharon cleaned up, playing surrogate mother for her. She smiled as she thought of Sharon clucking to herself about what a slob Diana was and how she'd better mend her ways if she were ever going to hope to keep a man. Dear, sweet, compulsive Sharon.

She went over to her dresser for a new blouse and fresh underwear. On the top surface she noticed something amiss. A crack in one of the picture frames—the one of her at the beach that she liked so much. Sharon must have dropped it as she was cleaning and straightening.

Then she remembered. Oh, God. That had been the picture that had saved Sharon's life, the one that made them realize she wasn't Diana. Her belly turned to ice. She felt violated, standing here in her own room. Suddenly a different image of Sharon cleaning up the room came into her mind. It was an image of her cleaning, scrubbing, straightening, sobbing all the while, as if she could somehow expunge the intruders from her memory by erasing all traces of their presence in the room. But the cracked glass of the picture frame was just one reminder that demons are not so easily banished.

Diana realized she couldn't stay here any more than Sharon could. Not after what had happened. It was as if the apartment were controlled by someone else now, some sinister force she'd never even seen. Even thinking about it was too frightening. Without Brian here, she couldn't have even spent the night. Tomorrow afternoon, after she'd finally gotten some sleep, she'd go over to the Emory housing office and see if she could find another place. That was the way she'd found this one; that was how she'd met up with Sharon. Maybe Sharon would even be willing to room with her again in her new place. But that might be too much to ask. Her associations with the attack probably had as much to do with Diana herself as they did with this apartment. She couldn't really blame Sharon if she didn't even want to see her anymore. That was the worst of it for Diana. Sharon was the only real friend she had in Atlanta, and being able to see her would definitely be good right around now. Also, she owed Sharon something for all she'd had to go through, and somehow, if by no other means than her presence, Diana felt a need to start paying her back.

Unless, of course, it was the absence of her presence that Sharon would consider the proper payment.

Diana was so tired now, so completely strung out from the tension, that she found she had to concentrate physically on the mundane task of changing her clothes. She rummaged through the drawer and opted for a cotton turtleneck that allowed her to go without a bra—one less distraction.

She looked down to pull on her jeans, and when she looked up, Brian was standing in the doorway. She hadn't expected that. He came over to her, and before she could get her pants buttoned, he had drawn her close to him with his arms locked round her waist. Who was this, she wondered, who had broken out of his shell in an attempt to break into hers? Was he being Brian, the tender, sensitive healer, come to salve the wounds and give her hope for the future? Or was this Brian, the elite SEAL shock trooper, trained to quick, decisive action and conditioned to getting what he went after? And in her current state of need, which of these two prototypes did she reckon would do her the most good?

She followed the downward angle of his gaze, and when she realized her nipples were standing prominent and erect through the soft tight cotton of her shirt, she had her answer.

He raised the fabric up above her breasts to get at them and touch them in the flesh. She remained stationary, her legs parted, playing passive and submissive for once to his marauding advance, her fingers interlocked and flexing behind her back. "Is this your solution to everything?" she asked dryly, her voice and spirits having momentarily regained their form.

"Not everything," he replied. "But some things."

He pulled her tighter to erase all distance between them. His hands traveled up to her head and held it rigidly in his grasp. She yielded her mouth to him, then her tongue, then her whole body, as if by yielding she could elicit some deep down, vital, unrehearsed response and thereby prove to herself she was still fully alive. His thumbs hooked inside her panties and brought them down to her thighs. She felt him, already rigid and hard, rubbing against the soft fleece of her triangle. His aggressively exploring fingers found her wet with excitement. She must let her body respond with total abandon, she told herself, without consulting her mind, without thinking about it, without considering the possibilities. She must let herself succumb to the feeling of exquisite, exhilarating vulnerability, to a fear that compelled her to go on.

He took her farther than she had ever been, farther than she had ever thought possible. He kept her going until there was nowhere farther to go, until she had given up everything inside her, until she had given up all there was to give, until there was nothing left but the fullness of their coming together and absolutely, fearlessly being themselves.

Because never, Diana knew, never is a person more fully alive than when the entire being is on the line and the entire future is in the balance and the outcome is exceedingly, acutely, overwhelmingly uncertain.

"I just thought of something," Diana said as they walked back down Houston Mill Road toward the centers. It was nearing dawn, and the forest-lined residential road was quiet and deserted. "I wasn't thinking about it before, but it may be the prime time of the month for me. I'm not taking the pill or anything." She flashed him a look of exaggerated suffering. "Hadn't been getting it regular enough to worry about. I'm not sure of the timing; I've lost count with all that's been going on." She turned her head to him. "How do you feel about that?"

Brian turned his head to meet hers. "I guess we'll put ourselves in the hands of fate." He half smiled. "We're practically there anyway."

"Yeah, I guess we are," she replied. Outwardly he didn't seem angry about it. He didn't even seem nervous. And in her time she'd become sufficiently adept at the game to have seen through it if he was. It hadn't been intentional on her part, she was sure, not even subconsciously. But it gave her a warm and reassuring feeling, knowing that on this level, too, he was willing to cast his lot with her, whatever that involved. Or was it just that he had been through so much in his life that he knew better than to protest that which was already a matter of fact? Well, whatever it was, she'd worry about it later. They had enough to worry about now without it.

Brian took her hand and interlocked his fingers with hers. "I guess we ought to keep the rabbit around for a while then, huh?"

She grinned back at him, two conspirators against the rest of the world. "I guess so."

They hadn't walked more than a few steps farther when she stopped again. "Oh, gee. I was supposed to bring back a carrot for our friend. That poor little rabbit. He's going to be starving. Well, we'll just have to find something in the animal lab for him."

"You know something? You happen to be a very good person," Brian stated, following the pronouncement with a quick cuddle and a kiss.

"You think so?" Diana responded, privately wondering whether it was really true and, if it was, how much it counted for in the scheme of things.

When they got back to the lab, the rabbit was dead.

Its agonized-looking little body was twisted into hysterical contortions. Its tawny fur was slick and matted from the blood and pus that had oozed through the cracked skin. Its tiny pink tongue, glazed with vomit, hung limply out of its mouth. Diana realized she had never seen a rabbit's tongue before.

But what most haunted her were the eyes: eyes still open, stretched wide with terror; eyes into which she read the accusation of betrayal, of having purposely subjected their guileless owner to this gruesome death. It was incomprehensible to her that this much torment and suffering could be contained in such a tiny creature. And it followed directly in her mind that were it not for the double thickness of industrial glass, she and Brian would have suffered the same wrenching agonies.

Diana thought immediately of the steer in Montana. The presentation was nearly identical.

"Oh, shit," she said out loud, and her voice was quavering.

"The outbreak at Sam Hardesty's ranch," Brian solemnly articulated. "It wasn't cattle plague after all. It was something from the capsule."

"Had to be," she grimly said. She paced slowly, trying to contain her fear. "Let me think about this for a minute. I want to reason it out"—she continued pacing—"because what occurs to me off the top of my head isn't good."

Brian remained silent, giving her the time and distance she needed. She kept circling the glassed-in work station. And as she did, her eyes kept darting back to the miserable rabbit as if she were a little girl trying to get up the courage to look into an open coffin.

Finally she stopped. She put her hands together in front of her mouth in a praying position and talked through them. "The rabbit didn't die from a poison gas or toxin. That much is clear. If it had, the reaction would have been nearly instantaneous. It's not radiation sickness, although the symptoms are similar; the Geiger counter would have picked that up. And it doesn't behave like bacteria, which would be the next most logical possibility. Most of what we deal with here involves bacteria, one way or another. And I don't know of a single bacterium in the world that reacts so decisively within a matter of hours. The serious ones generally take weeks to present, at least days."

"So it's too slow for toxin and too fast for bacteria. That means . . ."

"Yes," Diana said. Her voice was still shaking. "Only one logical possibility. We'll culture out the secretions to be sure. But I think I already know. I was trying to tell myself it wasn't, but it is. It has to be a virus."

Virus, she repeated to herself. The tiniest, simplest, most primitive of organisms, and the strangest. Too small to be seen under anything but an electron microscope. Not alive like bacteria, but not inert either; occupying that hazy netherworld between life and nonlife. Unable to survive on its own, yet remarkably proficient in invading living cells, taking them over, and altering them to its own mysterious purposes, forcing the cell to manufacture new, exact replicas of it, even though this might mean the extinction of the cell itself.

Viruses. Many are insignificant, self-limiting, and cause only a few days' inconvenience, so benign that the term itself holds no fear or great unpleasantness to the health-paranoid general public. "I haven't felt great this morning. Must have picked up a virus or something." And if the body can withstand the virus, it develops antibodies to it which automatically immunize against a second onslaught of the identical intruder. Yet those who know—physicians, epidemiologists, health care professionals—shudder when a new virus is uncovered. Perhaps it will be only another form of the common cold. Or perhaps it will be a deadly strain of flu, another cancer, or something new, unexpected, and every bit as horrifying. Like AIDS. And the professionals realize something else that has slipped by a public lulled into cozy security by a generation of antibiotics and "wonder drugs." Unlike bacteria, a virus which does not limit itself can be vanquished in only two ways: through the introduction of a vaccine made up of the virus's own genetic components or through the death of the host organism. And though some vaccines—smallpox among them—have proved highly successful, many others, including the common cold, have eluded scientists for generations.

"I guess for some reason I refused to let myself think that it might be a virus," Diana said. "I guess I couldn't face it."

"How long will it take to culture?" Brian asked.

"A couple of weeks probably. Viruses don't grow out overnight like bacteria."

"Well, we obviously can't wait that long."

"No, we can't," Diana said. "We're going to have to alert the people here right away. I'll write up a memo now and file a full lab report after I've had some sleep."

"You can't do that," Brian said.

"What?" Diana looked stunned.

"Not yet."

"I don't think you understand."

"I understand what will happen if this is made public," Brian declared firmly.

Diana sighed patiently and looked at him. "Let me tell you a little story."

Brian snapped back at her, "I don't need to hear a story."

"Please listen."

Brian sullenly folded his arms across his chest and shifted his weight to one leg, indicating that this had better not take too long.

"When Legionnaires' disease first broke out in Philadelphia," Diana told him, "do you know why the people at the CDC were so terrified?"

"Because people were dying."

"Of course. But that wasn't the specific reason."

"Then tell me."

"It was because of what it appeared was causing them to die. They had all these people in one place presenting with severe, incurable pneumonia and the rest of a constellation that looked remarkably like the 1918 swine flu—the swine flu *virus* that had killed *twenty million* around the world one winter. Virtually no one in the country carried any antibody immunity to it anymore. There was no vaccine to fight it. No one had even thought of doing it. And producing one that was effective, let alone getting it out in sufficient quantities, would take at least a year. So the guy who came up from the CDC figured that if it was swine flu and it had already broken out, the country was finished. That simple."

"I understand," Brian said. "But we still don't know who we're dealing with with this thing."

"But we now know *what* we're dealing with!" Diana replied. "And it ain't good. The incubation period is ... How long were we away—six hours maybe? Allowing for the much smaller body size of the rabbit, that still represents an incredibly short, a terrifyingly short incubation period. As far as we know, the attack rate is a hundred percent, and so is the mortality rate. The method of transmission could be anything—airborne, fluid, who knows? And the constellation of symptoms makes swine flu look like a cough and a runny nose. Brian, there are thousands, possibly millions of lives at stake."

"Yes, and what worries me is that they may be in even greater danger if we let this information out."

"Why?" Diana demanded.

"We don't know where the virus came from, who put it there. We don't know why or how desperate they are. The one thing we do know, or can assume, is that it's been in those capsules a long time, ever since Eagle's Talon. But if we suddenly let on what we've found and gear up the entire Centers for Disease Control, there's no telling what's going to happen or what the people responsible for the capsules are going to do. Then it's not just us in danger, Diana. It's everyone."

"So what are you saying?"

"The virus is horrible; I don't deny that. How could I? I've never seen anything remotely like it. But so far it's contained. There's no evidence of its existing anywhere outside these capsules. But if we get the CDC involved and there's a mass alert, then we've tipped our hand. We become sitting ducks. The people responsible for those capsules could get suddenly desperate and release it. Before we do anything that might make that happen, we have to find out more about them."

Diana brought her fists to her hips, squared her shoulders, and faced him. "So you're suggesting a cover-up? I guess that would be the standard military response, wouldn't it?"

For a split second she saw violence flash through his eyes, and she was so certain he would hit her that she braced for the impact.

The narrow-minded brute, she thought in the instant. *That's what you get and what you deserve for getting mixed up with people like that, and why didn't you call this quits long ago before it came to this?* But when the blow failed to come, she realized that just as Brian's instinct to attack had been honed to a fine point, his ability to control that instinct must have become equally acute. She thought back to Montana when he'd caught her hiding in the shower. And though she thought he would, he hadn't struck her then either. That was just one of the many differences between Brian and Bill Eschenberger, who had. It suddenly dawned on her that she had been tarring Brian with a brush long ago dipped for others.

"What do you propose we do?" she inquired, trying to control the edge of her voice as Brian had controlled his temper.

"One thing doesn't change," he replied. "We still need to know more. What this does is give us one more clue, one more piece of evidence. And more than that, it gives us a direction."

"How do you mean?"

"Now we know that those shrapnel capsules *did* something."

"All of them?"

"That would be the logical assumption."

"What about that first one—the one you took out of Radley Davis?"

"I don't know," Brian said. "But there has to be an explanation, something that's in keeping with everything else we've found. Something that explains not only that and the cattle plague but also the 'random' deaths of the other marines and the attack on Roger Moreland and the rigging of my car and everything else."

"That's a pretty tall order, Commander."

"We'll figure it out," Brian told her, and, when he saw skepticism in her face, added, "We have to."

Diana walked over to the secretarial unit beside the ultracentrifuge. Workers could bring nothing in from outside, and so a full range of clerical supplies, all carefully sterilized, was maintained inside the maximum containment lab. She opened the cabinet and found a laminated slate and grease pencil. Everything was carefully compartmentalized and marked to discourage rummaging. She put her name and department number on the slate and underneath wrote in large letters the standard DO NOT DISTURB! The slate was designed to slide into a metal mounting on the side of the work station. According to the protocols of the lab, that was all she needed to do to protect the integrity of her experiment.

She decided to take one more crack at Brian. "Look," she said with empathy, "I can understand that you're squeamish about a full-scale pathogen alert. So how about if I just tell my boss, Herb Secrest? Just let him know what's going on."

"No," said Brian emphatically. "There's too much at risk. Until we have a better handle on what's going on, we can't take a chance on anyone we can't be sure of."

"You're not saying that Herb is one of 'them,' I hope," she said incredulously.

"No, I'm not saying that. I'm just saying that I don't know him at all and you don't know him well enough to predict how he'll react or what he'll do once he has this information."

"I think I know him pretty well," Diana said. "You don't have a corner on insight into human nature."

"I know how long you've been here, and I know what the operating relationship is. You don't know him well enough to take a chance on him in this situation." Brian stated his case emphatically, as if wanting to close the discussion.

That damn SEAL mentality again, Diana thought. *Only trust the people who've bonded themselves to you with their blood.* And wasn't she fortunate that he'd made an exception in her case? Well, he didn't have any damn choice now, did he?

She could force the issue, she knew clearly; take the initiative upon herself. All she had to do was tell Herb on her own. But she knew just as clearly that she wouldn't do it. Somehow the cult had gotten to her, too. For some strange reason, more than anything else, she knew she wanted to be worthy of Brian's trust.

"So you're not willing to rely on anyone in a position of authority on this?" she asked.

"I didn't say that. There's no way around it."

"But one of *your* people."

Brian hesitated for a moment. "In a manner of speaking."

"All right." She capitulated. "We'll do it your way. But whatever we do, we've got to hurry. If the disease breaks out now, *it* wins. We don't have much going for us. And the thing we've got the least of is time."

They finally made it back to Diana's apartment after dawn. By that point Diana had completely expended her reserves of energy and had sufficient resources remaining only to take off her clothes and drag herself into bed.

She drifted off to sleep amid images of friendly, prancing animals, a reverie that rekindled latent images of her own prepubescent childhood. But this time the rumination took on a sinister twist. The principal players turned out to be a cow and a rabbit. And there was even a distinction between the two. Because when the dream began, the cow was already dead and decaying, the flies buzzing around its head, whereas the bunny was very much alive until she blithely proceeded to torture it to death.

20

Diana tried to get up several times before she finally made it. She staggered from her bed over to the CDC shortly before lunchtime, stopping first at the Maximum Containment Lab to see if there was any progress on her experiment. During the several minutes it took to undress in the decontamination unit there, shower, and suit up, she worked on steeling herself for the experience of facing the dead, contorted rabbit, still lying in its own vomit and excreta. She should have disposed of the corpse last night, she knew. As unpleasant as that would have been, at least it would have been done with. Then she could have come in today and just concentrated on the culture dishes and the capsule itself. Maybe she was punishing herself for what she'd done, for secretly wanting the rabbit to be dead; making herself return to the scene of the crime.

Her mind kept turning over the case definition she had worked out. The virus had a universal attack rate, a remarkably short incubation period, and a particular tropism for the digestive tract, liver, and kidneys. But its overall effects were so devastating that its initial targets within the body hardly mattered. They were more an issue of medical curiosity than an indication of possible avenues of treatment. If, in fact, it was a virus—and it bore every indication of being one—then the only possible defense was a vaccine. And if it happened to get out into the general population before one were available, the results would be nothing short of apocalyptic.

She was terrified by the possibilities, terrified by the commitment she'd made to Brian to sit on the evidence, and terrified that that commitment left her bearing the full weight of responsibility for one of the potentially greatest threats to public health this country had ever seen. Whatever it was, how many people at CDC alone were better qualified to deal with it than she was? Career professionals, internationally known experts. She wanted nothing more than to turn it over to the heavy hitters, sit back, and let someone else worry about it. But there were other ramifications, she had to remind herself. *It's not just the virus. It's what's ... and who's behind it.* And here she was, a lowly second-year EIS officer willfully entered into a conspiracy of silence. *You'd better come up with something from that fragment, Diana dear, or your life in medicine is about to come to a screeching halt.*

When she reached the glassed-in work station, her experiment was gone.

The rabbit was no longer there; the Petri dishes were missing; there was no sign of the shrapnel fragment. The laminated slate with her name written on it had been removed.

Her first instinct was fear. Someone had to be on to them. That was the only possible explanation. But that didn't make sense, at least not inside the Maximum Containment Lab. The sensation smoothly transformed into anger. Something had to be done right away. She quickly reversed the lab entry process, stripping off her lab suit, showering again, and putting her own clothes back on. She moved as rapidly as she could through the air lock and stormed up to her own office on the fourth floor.

When she got there, she briskly went through her mailbox and surveyed all the messages and correspondence that had accumulated since her absence. Nothing that couldn't wait, she decided. Except for one, that is: a note to see Herb Secrest as soon as she got in. The note was dated this morning.

Well, fine. That was the first thing she'd want to do anyway. He probably wanted to bring her up-to-date on what she'd missed, let her know what her next assignment was. But she'd give him an earful before he did. She didn't know who was responsible for this business in the lab, but she'd damn well make sure Herb took care of it and kicked ass clear across the room.

The more she stewed about it, the more outraged she became. Forget even about common courtesy. This violated the most basic principles of science. The Centers for Disease Control were one of the leading forums of open and unbiased scientific inquiry. It had been set up that way on purpose because the founders were perceptive enough to understand that bureaucracies don't do well with immediate and sudden threats. And they'd worked hard to create the kind of institution that could. Here the individual was every bit as important as the team. Every officer was encouraged to follow his or her own leads and instincts to see where they went. That was where scientific and medical breakthroughs came from. Nobody had a right to mess with someone else's work.

She charged down the cinder-block hallway, past the division secretary, and into Herb's office without waiting to be announced. He looked up calmly from the stack of papers in front of him, elbows on the desk, his two hands gripping a pencil by both ends. He caught her off guard as he half smiled and said pleasantly, "Welcome back, Diana. How are you feeling?"

"Ah, fine, Herb," she replied impatiently.

"You look a little tired."

"I—I guess I am."

"Especially around the eyes. I would have thought you'd have gotten more rest while you were out. Wasn't that why you went home to your mother? That's the only thing you can really do for most of these flu viruses. But I don't have to tell you that." He let out a self-deprecating laugh. "This is your field."

She didn't have the patience for these games this morning, however well meaning her boss was trying to be. "Do you know about this business in the Maximum Containment Lab?" she demanded.

"I certainly do." His sense of calm hadn't broken.

"Then I hope you're prepared to ream out someone's rear end over it."

"I certainly am," he told her with equal equanimity. "Yours."

It took her a moment to realize her mouth had dropped open. "What did you say?"

"That's right, Diana. I'm suspending you. Starting right now, you're relieved of all your duties until further notice. Leave your ID and key card with Flo on your way out."

"But—but why?" She began biting her lower lip.

"Well, we can start at the beginning if you like."

"Do you know who threw out my experiment?" She wanted to sound tough. When she was put on the spot, it had always been one of her techniques to shift the offensive.

"No one threw it out," Herb stated. "Since we didn't know what it was, I had the Maximum Containment Lab technician put on a pressure suit and move it to the lockup area, where you can't get at it."

"You—you have no right—" she stammered.

Herb rose to face her, glaring. "No, Diana. *You* have no right. You should know you had no business using the Maximum Containment Lab without specific authorization. It's not only an abuse of your key card privilege, but you weren't even supposed to be in the building. You were on sick leave. And a rather questionable sick leave, I might add."

She was close to tears, tears of livid outrage mixed equally with badly injured pride. He was right, but he was wrong. She couldn't give in. "But still, why did you do that?" she protested. "You could have let it go through. You know you can trust me. My work's always been first-rate."

"It always has been," Herb said. "Until recently. Diana, I don't know what you're trying to pull here, following your own agenda, but you've got some highly questionable substance that's killed a control animal—which you also took without authorization, by the way—and you're treating it like your private chemistry set. I got that stuff out of your reach to protect your little ass, not to mention mine. If the centers director found out one of my people was using Class Four facilities for her own purposes, we'd all get our heads handed to us."

"So you're suspending me for that, without even hearing my explanation?" She was instantly sorry she'd said that and wondered if it showed.

"I expect you to give me your explanation," Herb replied coolly. "We're going to culture out all of the animal's fluids and follow all the protocols, and it would certainly help if we had some idea of what we were looking for."

"I don't know yet," she lied.

"How did you come by this substance?"

She considered her promise to Brian. "I—I can't say."

"I find that quite incredible coming from you. At the very least it violates the trust and responsibility placed in you here."

"I'm sorry." Diana shrugged, then began to plead. "But there is a good reason. I'll tell you what it is as soon as I can, and once I do, I'm sure you'll see it my way." She wasn't nearly so sure as she wanted to believe.

"Does it have anything to do with that trip to Montana?"

"Not really." That was stretching it but at least technically accurate.

Herb eyed her skeptically. "I'm not sure I believe that," he muttered. "Why didn't you just come to me in the first place?"

"I'm afraid I can't explain that right now either."

"And I'm afraid I can't tolerate that kind of response."

"Then that's why you're suspending me," she said bitterly.

"Diana, anyone else here would have *fired* you outright. I still might, once I've had time to think about it. Where do you want to start? Insubordination? Dereliction of duty? Withholding critical information? It's not just for what you did last night, and you know it. There's something going on with you lately, Diana, and I don't know what it is. But it's been going on ever since you got back from Montana; maybe even before. I sent you there because it was obvious you wanted to get out of town for the weekend. Okay, fine. You're entitled. You've always done a good job for me in the field. I didn't say anything when you took an unauthorized trip to California, even though you went without saying anything to me and it's coming out of my budget. And I even looked the other way when you suddenly 'took sick' on the way back. Then you come sauntering in here in the middle of the damn morning with your cute little nose all out of joint because someone's messed with your toys. I've always covered for you in the past because I like you tremendously and have just as tremendous a respect for your ability. Everyone here does. But this time you've gone too far. I don't know where you stand anymore, and I don't know whether I can trust your judgment anymore. And that's why I'm suspending you, Dr. Keegan."

He hardly ever called her that. It was the adult equivalent of when her mother used to call her "Miss Keegan," an appellation always delivered in a stern tone of voice and solely reserved for times of correction. *Don't you know what I've been through!* she would have liked to yell at him. *While you think I've been screwing around and playing frivolous games with my love life, I've been hunted and threatened and seen people shot and run for my damn life. Why can't you just trust me a little bit, Herbert? Trust your own first instincts about me. I'm still the bright young girl you hired.*

Diana shifted her weight uneasily and dug her hands into the back pockets of her skirt. "So I have to go stand in the corner until I decide I'm ready to come out and be good?"

"Until I decide," Herb replied. "And the way you're handling this, I don't feel a change of heart coming on anytime in the near future. You'll be lucky if you're not brought up on charges." He leaned slightly forward over his desk and looked straight at her. "I want you to think of this suspension as more than just a punishment, Diana. You've got to do some serious thinking about your career and your commitment. I want you to think of this as another chance because I don't want to see a promising future like yours go down the drain."

She waited for him to finish, let a few beats go by, and then asked sullenly, "Am I dismissed?"

"Yes, Diana, you're dismissed," Herb responded. He sat down behind the desk. "But I hope you'll go home and think about what I've said."

She turned and strode out of the room, trying mightily to keep her injured and outraged feelings under control. When she was almost to the door, she decided the effort was not only futile but pointless. She stopped and turned back to her boss, who was still watching her. The corners of her mouth were quivering. "I'm sorry, Herb," she managed to get out before beginning to cry. And then she turned again and walked as swiftly as she could, without saying anything, all the way back to her office.

Diana went forlornly through her desk, looking for anything she might like to have at home with her. There wasn't much. She thought back to the only other analogous situation in her life: the time she was suspended from college for participating in a building takeover. That suspension hadn't lasted long; she'd been reinstated on appeal within a few days. But she remembered how afraid she'd been to tell her parents and what their reaction would be.

The news would spread through Briarcliff Manor like wildfire. Her mother would perceive it as a life-threatening disgrace, and there was an excellent chance that when she found out, she would ground Diana for the rest of her natural life. Her father would likely do a lot worse.

Preparing for the unavoidable call home, Diana had weighed several possible defenses. But the one that had played the smoothest in her mind had been the appeal to integrity. Her mother and father had always taught her to stand up for what she believed in, ever since she'd been a little girl. And that was what she would tell them. This would be a good test of whether they really meant it.

At least this time around she didn't have to answer to anyone. Except herself.

Was this a matter of integrity? She tried to reason it out, summoning up the inner righteousness of Joan of Arc going to the stake. She could always go above Herb's head, straight to the director. That was one of the great things about the CDC. Because of the nature of the work, because of the immediate, pressing nature of disease, it was built into the system that any EIS officer or any other public health official could go right to the director, without wasting time going through normal channels.

But how would that look in this case? She would be perceived as going to him just to grind her own ax over being suspended. And to be honest, the director wouldn't likely be overly sympathetic to the experiment's being taken away from her since she was in there without authorization to begin with. Nothing is taken so seriously at the CDC as Class IV substances. People who are perceived to abuse them don't get a whole lot of consideration. So if she even got as far as making her case for being in there, he'd ask her what the experiment was all about. And since she wouldn't want to go against Brian, she wouldn't be able to tell him. No. All in all, it wasn't a viable option.

And there weren't a whole lot of viable options left.

ALEXANDRIA, VIRGINIA

Unlike many other professionals of his acquaintance, Michael Swansea liked meeting at airports. It seemed to him the perfect backdrop for his line of work. There were always large crowds to melt into, most people were totally wrapped up in their own concerns, and since tension was high anyway with everyone dashing to make a flight, he never worried as much about his operatives looking out of place.

Not that he had to worry about Amber anyway. The man had the ability that is either innate or else completely unlearnable to blend perfectly into his surroundings. It was the same gift that Swansea himself had used to such advantage in his career.

Swansea met his asset at the New York shuttle gate at National Airport. Sure enough, Amber emerged into the long concourse looking indistinguishable from the hundred other business types to whom the shuttle has become a lifeline. Swansea, of course, had spent the previous hour casing the entire route they would be traveling together back to the car so that if there were a single face anywhere in the crowd that had been there previously, he would recognize it.

The two men shook hands and exchanged small talk, as if they were moderately friendly business associates returning from a week of professional travel. They conducted the meeting as they walked. Swansea firmly believed this to be the safest practice.

"So what have we come up with?" he asked.

"Nothing, I'm afraid," Amber replied. "I've checked the obituary pages of every newspaper in Long Island and Manhattan. No mention of Moreland's untimely passing. We have to assume an incomplete job."

"Police reports?"

"Yes. There is a file of a shooting, which dovetails with the details of our contract. But it's listed as an attempted homicide, and there's no ultimate disposition. So far I haven't been able to get into the file itself to see if there were any witnesses or vehicular reports. We're working on it, though. There's a good chance, of course, that Thorpe and Keegan would have been the first ones on the scene and discovered the body—I mean, the victim, as it probably turns out."

"And of course, we can't forget that they're both doctors."

"Yes, but without any equipment at the scene," Amber said. "Unprepared for an emergency."

"Not true, I'm afraid. We must always keep in mind that Thorpe was a SEAL. Everything he does is conditioned by that fact. By his very nature, he is never unprepared for an emergency. He's trained to be resourceful. Remember the incident in Vietnam from his file where he performed the amputation under enemy fire with a Ka-bar knife?"

"I didn't have to read it," Amber commented. "I already knew it. That story has made the rounds for years. It's famous inside the Special Forces community. When you mention the name of Thorpe, that's what everyone remembers."

"I assume you contacted all area hospitals and emergency facilities," Swansea continued.

"I did," Amber said, "using the standard distraught relative scenario."

"That's the one I would have chosen under the circumstances."

"But Moreland's not registered at any of them."

"Strange."

"From Sag Harbor the most likely facility would be the Southampton Hospital. But they've got no listing of his being there or ever having been."

"And presumably he's not at home, either at Sag Harbor or in the city."

"Definitely not."

"And Thorpe and Keegan?"

"Gone."

"Well, that was to be expected. But they'll surface again in time," Swansea said with confidence. "I have no doubt about that. And when they do, we will be prepared."

By this time they had reached the car. "In the absence of obituaries or other confirming evidence, we have to assume the termination attempt was—shall we say?—incomplete," the chief stated.

"I'd have to agree," said Amber.

"But a wounded man in critical condition does not simply disappear in my experience."

"Certainly not without help," Amber said.

ATLANTA, GEORGIA

Diana returned directly home, marching up the hill on Houston Mill Road with defiantly exaggerated strides, wounded and confused and hostile to the world. She was still steaming when she plopped down wearily onto the living room sofa and told Brian her tale of woe.

"And what about the fragment?" he asked urgently.

"They've taken it away from me."

"I don't understand."

She told him what had happened, emphasizing how she'd probably just blown her entire career by stonewalling her boss.

She studied his face for reaction. He wasn't saying anything, he wasn't overtly accusing her, but in some ways that made it even worse. She had blown it again. He had let her carry the ball again, and this time she'd actually lost it, let it disappear from under her nose. Now they had nothing concrete to go on, and somebody else had the evidence.

"I guess we'd better lay it all on the line to them now," she said. "We really will have to let the CDC authorities in on what we know."

"Just the opposite," Brian said. "All the more reason not to."

"But we don't have any idea what we're dealing with and, without the fragment, no way of finding out."

"And no way of finding out for sure why they've taken it away from you," he said.

"I told you what happened," said Diana.

"You told me what they told you. Doesn't it seem a little odd to you that your work efficiently disappears from the highest security lab the very morning after you put it there and you're not even consulted about it?"

"It's *because* it's the highest security lab." She tried to explain. "And they *tried* to consult me on it. But because of what you made me promise, I couldn't tell them anything. I can't really blame Herb for what he did to me."

"That's neither here nor there," Brian said.

"You're just making this more difficult for everyone!"

"We don't know who's behind this," he said.

There was no point pursuing it, she decided. After what had happened, there was no way she could convince Brian that the removal of the experiment wasn't part of some large, monsterlike plot, its tentacles stretching into the heart of the public health establishment. "I'm sorry, Brian," she finally said. "There was nothing else I could do, and from their standpoint, it's totally logical to handle it this way."

She tried to prepare herself for the berating she knew she was going to get. Her teeth scraped the surface of her lower lip.

"Were you suspended with or without pay?" he asked almost casually.

"I'm not sure," she answered. The question had taken her by surprise. "I didn't think to ask."

Brian smiled. "There's a sure sign of someone who's grown up having everything handed to her—never worrying about where the next dollar is coming from."

"Oh, will you come off it!" she replied, but it was a relief that with the serious setback they faced, he was content merely to pick at her a little while. That was a lot easier to withstand. "Do you know how long I've been taking that rap?" she asked rhetorically. "It's what they said about the entire antiwar movement just because we were committed to something other than lining our pockets. The whole world is kicking me. You want to join in?"

Brian put up his hands in a backing off gesture. "Not me," he said. "Remember what they told us in Montana: Never come up on a wild animal that's wounded or hungry."

"And what's that supposed to mean?" she said, raising one of the cushions in front of her as a sign of self-protection. "Anyway, I'm being punished, so I guess that means I'm not getting paid, if that makes you any happier."

"Of course, it doesn't make me any happier," Brian said. "But the suspension does make one thing a little easier for us."

Diana lowered the cushion. "What do you mean?"

Brian grew serious again. "Someone is still looking for us. You can be sure of it, especially after Sag Harbor. The first place he's going to look is Washington." He took a pause, giving her time to reason out what he would say next. "This is the second."

"So what you're saying is—"

"We've got to get out of here."

"To where?"

"That's a good question."

"I was hoping you had a good answer."

"Your faith is touching. But at this point our first mission is to survive."

There was the SEAL talking again. She gave him a wry smile, trying not to dwell on the implication of what he was saying. Okay. She'd blown this round whether it was her fault or not. It was up to her to make up for it. She tucked her knees up under her on the sofa, bouncing slightly on her heels to get comfortable. It was one of the signs Brian had come to recognize in her whenever she was becoming excited or intrigued. "We don't have the evidence anymore, so we have to figure it out on our own," she announced. "And we've got to do something right away." Brian looked at her with an expression that said he was waiting to be told something he didn't already know. "What do we know so far?" she asked.

"We've been through this before," he protested.

"I know," she said, dismissing his complaint with a wave of her hand. "But time is running out. So let's just net it out for once. Lay it all on the table. Now, why is someone after us?"

"Presumably, because of what we know, or could find out, about some of the men I served with in Nam."

"And what have we found out?"

"Okay," Brian said, humoring her. "Here goes. All those affected were marines with the Third Division, Seventh Amphib Unit, stationed at Dong Ha in 1969."

"Good." Diana prodded him. "Go on."

"All were wounded by shrapnel . . ."

"Keep going."

"All had fragments lodged near the surface of their livers, and we assume that each of those fragments contains a hollow capsule."

"You're doing fine."

"At least two of the capsules contained a deadly and highly infectious virus. And we would assume that they all did if it weren't for the fact that Radley Davis's capsule didn't do anything."

"Yes, but that may be a red herring," Diana said.

"Four of the marines died under mysterious circumstances," Brian continued. "Two more were clearly attacked. One was a diabetic who went into coma after having his insulin secretly taken away. He's the one who caused the 'cattle plague.' And, to come back to the beginning, all of them fought at Eagle's Talon."

"All right now," Diana stated, extending her hand out and grabbing hold of Brian's knee. "The key piece of information has to be: How did those hollow capsules get inside those men?"

"They were in shrapnel fragments," Brian replied.

"Yes, but all shrapnel is is just random bits of exploding metal, isn't it?"

"That's right."

"I mean, you don't explode a bomb or a hand grenade or anything and have it break up into even, predictable pieces of metal, do you?"

"No," Brian replied.

"So even if you had a big chunk of metal with a bunch of little hollow chambers inside, you couldn't predict how it was going to break up so that the chambers would remain intact with just a little covering of metal around them."

"That would seem unlikely."

"And then on top of that, what would be the chance that all these guys at one battle could be wounded by these random bits of metal which all just conveniently happened to have hollow chambers after exploding and all embedded in the same parts of their livers?"

"Pretty farfetched," said Brian.

She folded her arms across her chest in triumph. "So even though the little bits of metal *look* like shrapnel fragments, they haven't behaved like them. Then what are the other possibilities?"

They looked at each other for several seconds. "Somebody put them in there," Brian said at last.

"That's incredible," Diana said in a hushed voice. "I just can't believe it."

"Think about it," he said, and now he was leading her.

Several minutes went by. There was absolute stillness in the room. Finally Diana spoke up. "It's the only possible explanation. Now the question is who."

"Someone who wanted to wipe out a lot of people in a big hurry," said Brian.

"Like an enemy population, for example?"

"That's generally the idea behind germ warfare." He stopped. Germ warfare. The term itself made him inwardly cringe. Images of soldiers doubled over and gasping for breath in the trenches of World War I imposed themselves on his consciousness. Of all the horrible outgrowths of war in the twentieth century, this was perhaps the most horrible. Of all the crimes against human decency perpetrated in the name of national honor, this was the only one that all the nations of the world had jointly agreed must stop. The history of the twentieth century is a history of war and destruction, but this was one type of destruction so heinous that no one was prepared to let it continue.

"So the North Vietnamese implant these capsules of deadly virus in the livers of American marines," Diana went on. "First of all, where does this virus come from?"

"The Russians would be my guess. The North Vietnamese wouldn't have had the technology. And the Russians were their one consistent ally throughout the war."

"And why the liver?"

"Well, it's not too hard to get to," Brian replied. "And it's highly vascular."

"So what?"

"It's the bloodstream that carries the virus throughout the body," he reminded her.

"Good point. But the virus is encased in a capsule. How does it even get to the blood supply?"

Brian sat back and thought about it for a time. "I don't know," he said. "It must have something to do with the little stopper."

"And all that's been put out of our reach in the Maximum Containment Lab," Diana said sadly.

"That's true," said Brian. But then he smiled. "But some of us took precautions. When Gregory and I examined the Radley Davis fragment at the path lab in Bethesda, I had him save the stopper. It was stuck on the end of a surgical needle, and I had him put it in a test tube for safekeeping. I'll call him."

"Good for you," Diana said. "I am impressed. Now, back to this business about the North Vietnamese. I can't believe they would really do such a thing."

"No, I guess you couldn't, could you?" said Brian. "Kindly old Uncle Ho wouldn't let his children do anything that wasn't clean and honorable and upstanding, even to preserve the mother country. They weren't like the running dog American baby killers, were they?"

"Okay, we don't have to fight the war again ourselves," she said pleadingly. "Let's call a temporary truce. So then, if we assume the North Vietnamese did do this, how could they get to these marines to implant the capsules and make them look like shrapnel fragments?"

"Somebody had to operate on them."

"You said Roger Moreland was a POW who escaped. Maybe they took captured soldiers, operated on them, implanted the capsules, then 'let' them escape and come back to infect their own people."

"No, that doesn't pan out. Not all these marines were POWs," Brian said. "I think maybe Maxie Craig was, but none of the others." He put his hand out to her. "And there's something else," he said. "I've opened up three of these guys now, and I've seen X rays on some of the rest. They definitely had shrapnel, classic fragmentation wounds. And I can assure you, no one spent time sewing in each little piece. It's impossible."

Diana nodded and let this sink in. "That doesn't add up," she commented. "You're saying they all were definitely wounded by shrapnel, but the fragment with the hollow center had to be implanted, as in 'surgically implanted.' "

"That is what I'm saying."

"So did they do these implants and then explode shrapnel around them?"

"I sincerely doubt it," Brian said. "More likely the marines each had shrapnel wounds already and were surgically given one more. Same principle as hiding a book on the bookshelf. It's the one place it won't stand out."

"But why this particular group of men?" Diana questioned. "What was so special about them. What else did they all have in common?"

"Eagle's Talon," Brian grimly replied.

"Then whatever was done to them, whatever happened, happened at Eagle's Talon."

"Yes," he said, and from his eyes Diana could tell that Brian was once again back there, once again part of the horror that the name still conjured. "Just a second!" His finger shot up. "No! Not at all! That was the one part that didn't make sense. Until now."

"What are you talking about?"

"They all were wounded by shrapnel, and all fought at Eagle's Talon," Brian stated.

"That's right. We've established that from the medical and service records."

"But think about the dates," Brian said insistently. "We compiled that information very carefully from the printouts Jill got us. Those men all fought at Eagle's Talon but were wounded *before!*"

Diana wrinkled her nose in contemplation. "I don't think I understand."

"I'm not sure I do either," Brian said. "But it's almost as if—as if this all were done in *preparation* for Eagle's Talon."

They settled back onto opposite ends of the sofa, staring at each other and trying to reason out what they had just detailed. An uneasy feeling was settling over Diana, a sensation no doubt related to, but at the same time wholly separate from, the paranoia that had gripped her ever since that late-night phone call from Sharon. "There's only one person I know of who had access to all the marines before Eagle's Talon," she said.

"I was thinking the same thing," said Brian. "The old professor."

"Calvin Chandler Harley."

SOUTHAMPTON, NEW YORK

The most obvious time for the mission would have been at night, when the hospital was less crowded and there would have been fewer people to see them come and go. But hospitals rarely discharge patients in the evening, so it was finally decided that they would call less attention to themselves by staging the exercise during normal daylight hours.

The two men dressed as policemen preceded the two dressed as doctors down the corridor to the nursing station. They had come up in the elevator together, the two doctors displaying on their faces a look of stressful concern. The policemen looked rather bored, as if this were far from the most interesting of assignments. They showed their orders to the chief floor nurse, and one of the doctors gave her a copy of the discharge order. The gurney they had requested from hospital transportation had already been delivered to the ward. The doctor made assurances that the fact that they were moving the patient to a city hospital in no way reflected on the excellent care he had been receiving here. Rather, it was to make him closer to his home and business, as soon as he was ready to resume any sort of activities.

Moreland was in a private room at the end of the ward. He was still unconscious. Just to make sure he remained so during the transfer, one of his new doctors had given him an injection, duly registered on his chart, to help him weather the trip to the new hospital more comfortably. When the nurse offered assistance in transferring him from the bed to the gurney, his attending physicians thanked her but said they thought they could manage fine on their own. If they did need help, the two accompanying policemen could certainly provide it.

Moreland was wheeled down the corridor, down the elevator, and out to the ambulance dock without incident. The mission leader, Goncharov, had wisely figured that no one would stop to question physicians accompanied by policemen. He himself had chosen to be one of the policemen in case any disputes arose. Not only was his English flawless, but his ability with accents allowed him to adopt that pronounced Brooklyn dialect the people out here seemed to expect from their law officers and public servants.

"It isn't like back home," he reflected when they were outside on the dock and away from other hospital personnel. "Back home the last person to whom you would volunteer information would be a policeman. In this country they will tell everything they know to a man in a uniform without even being asked. It's touching how trusting Americans can be."

"Or else it speaks to the ineffectiveness of their law enforcement agencies if no one is afraid of them," said Panov, dressed in a doctor's white lab coat. "Certainly their crime rate here would tend to support that idea."

"Were it not for the friendly neighbor, it would have been a great deal more difficult to locate the subject," said Testrake. He was attired as the second policeman.

"I know," Goncharov said. "It would not immediately have occured to me that Mr. Moreland should be placed in the hospital incognito. Though in thinking about it, I can say that it was a good idea as he had already been the victim of a criminal attack. He is lucky to be alive," the leader added. "If my guess is correct as to who perpetrated this, they do not often make mistakes. Anyway, I am glad we could locate him before any further harm befell him."

"Thanks then to the friendly lawyer." Testrake laughed. "And we were always taught that all lawyers were supposed to be bloodsuckers and vultures. Another American myth shot to hell!" All four men chuckled at this.

They carefully transferred Moreland from the gurney to the collapsible stretcher inside the ambulance. Panov wheeled the gurney back inside the building and thanked a hospital attendant there for its use. He came back outside as Goncharov was starting the engine of the ambulance and the other two were arranging themselves inside.

"You know, it really is quite amazing, Comrade," he said, taking his place next to Goncharov in the front seat.

"What's that, Comrade?"

"One week we were in Washington and we were international chess masters. The next we are in New York as policemen and doctors."

"That is true," the leader replied.

"So the propaganda from the West is true. In America you can be anything you want. America truly is the land of opportunity!"

21

PALO ALTO, CALIFORNIA

Calvin Chandler Harley's house had been designed by Frank Lloyd Wright in the mid-1930s for a young Stanford professor and his family. It lay on the edge of campus, on land still owned by the university. In typically Wrightian style, the house was constructed primarily of local materials: California redwood and wire-cut San Jose brick. And like many of the master's greatest designs, it can be seen metaphorically to complete the gentle hillside it clings to, its several levels adjusting harmoniously to the undulating contours of the slope. The back of the house, which gives out onto the hillside terrace that runs its entire length, is a nearly continuous expanse of lead-framed glass, testimony to a safer and more trusting time.

The inside of the house was equally arresting, with the use of the natural materials being carried through for interior walls and spaces. All the furniture was designed by Wright himself. Diana had known about the house while she'd been at Stanford and had been by the outside many times. But she'd never known who lived there or been invited in. Now she gazed wide-eyed around the spacious entryway and living room. There was an incredible harmony about the place. Everything seemed to be perfectly ordered and proportioned, as if in totality it could not possibly be imagined any other way. She was so awestruck, in fact, that she kept having to prod herself to remember the circumstances of their visit.

"I can't believe we've broken into someone's house," she whispered to Brian.

"Why not?" he whispered back. "You were pretty bold about hiding in my shower in the motel in Montana."

"That was different."

"And back in college you used to occupy buildings illegally all the time, from what I understand."

"Yes. But it wasn't the same."

"No, I guess not," Brian said. "Because there it was all a communal game. Unlike here, where if you get caught, you go to jail."

She crossed her arms defiantly. "You keep thinking it was all such a lark. You're not the only one with experience. I'll bet I've been in jail more times than you have."

Brian grinned back at her. "I should hope so. Anyway, you wanted to come along, so stop grousing."

He moved slowly and observantly through the dining room and back into the entryway. Diana tagged close behind, sometimes touching the back of his waist, not wanting to be separated from him. Of all the places to break in, she thought, a registered architectural landmark. She was fascinated to note that one basic design motif—the hexagon, or honeycomb shape—had been used to unify the entire house. Wright had been obsessive, it seemed, using it everywhere, from the dimensions of rooms to the placement of the hearth to the shapes of the beds. She wondered what it would be like to live in such a place, where the personality of someone else had left such an indelible stamp. But every time her mind began to wander, the eerie gleam cast by the moonlight through the glass wall brought her back to reality and made her feel that the entire San Jose peninsula must be staring in at her.

Room by room, she watched as Brian methodically surveyed every length of wall space, moving pictures aside to see if there was anything behind any of them, feeling every seam in the wood to see if it revealed a hidden panel. She had looked on with a strange thrill as he had used a jeweler's screwdriver to jimmy the lock on the terrace door. Now he was going around the house like a burglar casing the joint. Her heart was thumping in her throat. She couldn't understand how he could be so calm.

"How do we know Harley won't come in on us?" she demanded.

"Good recon," said Brian crisply.

"But what if someone catches us here?"

"Then we'll just have to deal with it," he said without turning or looking away from his work.

She felt the nervous tension continuing to rise within her. "What if I have to go to the bathroom?"

"Then you'll go," he replied, his voice dripping with indulgence she knew she would ultimately pay for. "Only try to clean up after yourself if you do." He continued running his hand along the wall surface. "By the way, you always manage to think of that at the strangest times."

"Girls are different from boys," she snapped.

This time he did turn around. "So I've noticed."

He padded stealthily into the master bedroom, one step at a time, as if leading a patrol through the jungle. Diana had never focused on it before—except, perhaps, during sex—but there was something utterly graceful about the way he moved, a calculated economy to each action or gesture. It only raised her level of excitation.

They had been at this for fifteen minutes or so and had come up with nothing. Diana wondered how Brian could be so confident of finding something when they didn't even know what they were looking for. Well, as long as they didn't get caught . . .

There was a small dressing area between the master bedroom and the bath. Brian opened the doors of the redwood built-ins, pushing Harley's suits and shirts to the side. He stopped for a moment, and Diana knew he had found what he wanted. She came up behind him and saw the gray metal combination safe, its front flat against the rear wall of the closet.

"That's ingenious," Diana whispered.

"No, it isn't," said Brian. "Those other places I looked first would have been ingenious. This is just where you'd expect to find a safe."

"How are you going to open it?" she asked. "You're not going to blow it, are you?"

"Don't be gauche," he replied. "Remember, the idea is not to let anyone know we've been here, rather than bring the entire Palo Alto Police Department down on our necks."

"But how—" She watched quietly as Brian brought his ear right up next to the tumbler. He twisted the dial back and forth several times and wrapped on the metal surface area around it with his knuckles. He then pressed his ear to the safe front and held his breath. Diana followed suit and held hers. Brian closed his eyes in concentration. After what seemed to her a long time he began twisting the dial again, three or four times back and forth. He opened his eyes, pulled his head away, and gave the dial one final turn. Diana heard a distinct click. He pulled on the gray door. It glided open without effort.

"That's amazing," she gasped. "Where did you learn to do that?" As if she couldn't figure it out on her own. He was definitely a man with a very unusual combination of talents.

Brian shrugged. "It's just a question of getting the hang of it. Like driving a stick shift."

"Uh-huh."

Brian brought out the contents of the safe. Mostly there was Mrs. Harley's jewelry.

"Nice stuff," Diana commented. "The practice must be doing well."

There were several routine papers—deeds for property; inventories of personal effects; insurance policies. They revealed little about the man, less still about his activities at any given point in time. Brian looked carefully through each box and envelope, making sure it held no hidden treasure. When he was satisfied that they had combed through the contents of the safe, he replaced them, carefully making sure they were back in their original positions.

"So what do we do now?" Diana questioned.

"Go into the study," Brian answered. "See if there's anything interesting in his desk or files."

But there wasn't. Twenty-five minutes of meticulous searching, sifting, and scrutinizing revealed nothing more provocative than the fact that Harley had been named outstanding clinical professor by the senior medical students three years in a row and that he had recently written a letter on behalf of the department of surgery protesting what he felt to be exorbitant rates for malpractice insurance for surgeons. From every indication Calvin Chandler Harley lived his life very much out in the open. Everything was right up front. Not so different from what you'd expect from any big-time surgeon, Diana thought.

The mission had been a bust. Diana sensed that Brian was almost glad, at least relieved that he had been unable to pin anything on his surgical idol.

He had been drawn over to the far wall, where Harley had displayed some of the mementos of his military service: the I Corps shield mounted on a walnut plaque; an aerial view of the field hospital at Phu Bai; photographs of Harley ceremonially shaking hands with village chiefs; an elaborate framed testimonial from the men of the Third Division. Against the wall was a small table. It almost looked like a dictionary stand. On it was a green marine helmet inside a Lucite display case. The helment was dented and marked by the impact of glancing bullets. And stenciled onto the side was the message DON'T SHOOT ME. I'M THE DOC!

Diana watched Brian from a respectful distance. She had always been amazed and, she had to admit, incensed that he could be as nostalgic about his time in Vietnam as she was about her days with the movement that had wanted to bring him home. Now, for some reason, she found it strangely touching.

Next to the display case was a flagpole, topped by a brass eagle, bearing a battered and frayed Stars and Stripes. The flag had obviously flown over some military installation under siege. "The medical unit at Phu Bai, I'll bet," said Brian. "They located it right next to the airstrip, and it was forever getting shelled. Big mistake."

The eagle standard had a wide, majestic wingspread. Its head was turned fully to the side, as it appears on national crests. It was perched boldly atop a sphere that looked like a cannonball.

"That's a pretty fearsome-looking bird," Diana said.

" 'Proud' is the word you're searching for," Brian said.

"I'd hate to be grabbed by those claws."

Brian smiled. "They're called talons in the business."

"Especially the ones sticking out from each foot. Talons, you say?"

"I did say, didn't I?" Brian said. They looked at each other. "Eagle's talons."

It was as if a lightning bolt had just struck the room.

He grabbed the top of the flagpole and pulled it over on its side. He and Diana knelt on the floor and studied the standard closely. Three of the talons on each foot wrapped tightly around the cannonball. The fourth protruded aggressively outward. Brian played around with both of them, fiddling and twisting and pulling. Nothing happened with the right one. As he clutched the left between his thumb and forefinger, it seemed to give a little, then visibly moved.

Diana jumped back in surprise.

"The sinister talon is what the Latins called the one on the left," Brian said, "the one that holds the arrows or weapons of war."

He continued twisting. It was screwed into the eagle's foot at the point where the feathers begin, covering up the seam in the metal. It took about thirty turns before the brass talon came loose. Brian held it in his hand.

He peered into the hole it had left in the standard. There was an edge of something sticking out. He reached in with two fingers. Carefully he drew out a small wad of paper, onionskin, it appeared to be, yellowed and shiny with age. Diana held her breath.

The paper crackled as Brian unfolded it. Dark, straight lines were ingrained where it had been creased. It was a single sheet, typewritten on an old, uneven manual. From the lightness of the print, the ribbon must have been almost as old as the machine.

At the top of the page in underlined caps was printed:

EYES ONLY!!   DO NOT COPY!!   DO NOT SAVE!!
PROJECT RATSBANE

And underneath appeared two lists in succession:

DELIVERY FORCE

Abraham, Pfc. David M.	2187365
Craig, Cpl. Maxwell J.	6807193
Dantley, Pfc. Timothy S. B.	8840372
Davis, LCpl. Radley J.	1249684
Fine, Cpl. Harold A.	3068246
Fletcher, Pfc. Arthur M.	5862182
Hardesty, Sgt. Samuel (NMI)	7523653
Jacobs, Cpl. Harold A.	4150027
Jefferson, Sgt. Tyrrell L.	5546852
Lofton, Pfc. Anthony R.	7523043
Moreland, Cpl. Roger T.	9135543
O'Brien, SSgt. Matthew T.	1153524
Santoya, Pfc. Luis J.	2933410
Schuyler, Lt. Christopher P.	2289745
Shapiro, Pfc. Nathan S.	1565147
Washington, Pfc. Maurice (NMI)	2555798

COUNTER DELIVERY FORCE
Bui Minh Cau
Dang Duc Hoa
Duong Thi Bac
Hoang Thanh Tinh
Nguyen Tien Truong

"Look at the names on the first list," Diana said. "All the dead marines, the two guys we were able to locate from Jill's list, and the others that we couldn't."

"Plus two more," Brian said. "We'll have to check into those. But there's no question, we were on the right track."

"And Harley was right in the middle of it."

"I'm afraid so." Brian took the Olympus XA clamshell camera from his breast pocket and opened the cover. He carried the sheet of onionskin over to the desk and laid it down under the lights. He leaned over above it and positioned himself so that he could get the page full frame in the viewfinder. He snapped the shutter, then took several more pictures for safety. He brought the paper back over to the flagpole standard and photographed it again next to the brass eagle and the separated talon, in case he ever had to prove where he'd seen the evidence. Then he stepped back so that he could get a good portion of the room into the frame to provide the necessary context. He closed the camera's cover and put it back in his pocket. Then he folded the paper back up the way he had found it and inserted it back in the base of the standard.

As he was screwing the talon back into position, Diana asked, "Why would anyone hold onto that kind of incriminating information?"

"Probably to protect himself," Brian responded.

"But it's done just the opposite here," she said.

"You notice he didn't leave it in the safe or anywhere a routine burglar would be likely to look," he replied. "What we've just done isn't part of anyone's standard operating procedure. But betraying coconspirators is. I don't know who he was working with on this Project Ratsbane, but with this kind of nasty business, there's always a good chance one fall guy is going to be selected to take the rap. This is obviously an official document. There are serial numbers next to each name which Harley obviously didn't make up on his own. This is his insurance if the shit ever hits the fan."

"Ratsbane. Isn't that a rat poison?"

Brian nodded. "Arsenic trioxide."

Diana shuddered. "What a disgusting name."

"But a fitting one. The end result wasn't any too palatable."

"So you think Harley really was working for the enemy."

"I do," Brian said. "But one thing bothers me."

"What's that?"

"The name itself. Why would the North Vietnamese have an English code name, and why would they have access to American serial numbers? More to the point, why would they even need or want them?"

"You've got me," Diana said. "But it probably means Harley wasn't acting alone."

"It most definitely means that," Brian told her. He righted the flagpole and restored it to its original position. "Project Ratsbane was an inside job."

Diana placed her hands firmly into the pockets of her hooded sweatshirt, as if for security. "Brian," she said, "when I asked you back in Atlanta whether we could trust anyone in authority, you said we would have to. Did you have someone particular in mind?"

Brian held onto the flagpole and stared back at her, as if plumbing his own mind to recapture his thought processes. Or maybe he was just fearful of his own response.

"I do now," he said quietly.

HAVANA, CUBA

Keeping the patient still and comfortable posed little problem. The genuine doctors to whom Goncharov's team had turned him over saw to that. He was growing stronger and had tolerated the journey well, considering he had made it unconscious in a furniture crate ostensibly carrying the belongings of a departing Soviet diplomat.

Goncharov had made a point of looking in on Moreland. Certainly he had to make sure these Cubans knew what they were doing. But he had also developed a certain attachment to the comatose man they had smuggled out of the United States and down to the closest secure and "friendly" medical facility. Or perhaps it was just that he was proud of the flawlessness with which the mission had been carried out and thought of Moreland as his trophy. In any event, his evaluation of the importance the committee placed on this particular prize was confirmed when he stepped from Moreland's room into the hall to see Anatoly Nikolayev approaching him. If the deputy chief of Directorate S would bring himself all the way from Moscow for this exercise, it confirmed all the stories he had been hearing about the importance of the project.

"Ah, Comrade Goncharov." Nikolayev greeted him. "Excellent. Let me first of all congratulate you on a first-rate delivery." Goncharov nodded his head humbly in appreciation. "You will join us now. We are about to be briefed."

There was no one else with the deputy chief. Either he was speaking in the institutional "we" or was purposely making a magnanimous display of including Goncharov. Like everything else about this line of employment, it came down to a matter of interpretation.

Nikolayev led the way into the radiology department. There they were met by a man who introduced himself as Dr. Tomás Gutiérrez. Goncharov was surprised by his youth and good looks, but his eyes burned with the fire of scientific adventure.

Once inside the room, Nikolayev and Goncharov switched from Russian to Spanish, which presented a problem for neither of them.

Gutiérrez had put up what seemed like an endless number of X ray films attached to light boxes lining an entire wall. On the table in the center of the room were brown envelopes containing additional films. And next to them in a large, well-organized stack rested a computer printout. But it was not one of the type Goncharov was familiar in his work. Rather, the top sheet bore a set of wavy lines and looked like nothing so much as a weather map.

The doctor acknowledged Goncharov with a formal nod, but it was clearly Nikolayev to whom he was speaking. "We have done extensive analytical studies on the patient," he explained. "We began with a full-body CAT scan, which was followed up by regional radiographic tomograms of the entire chest, torso, and pelvis. I am sure you will appreciate the fact that the interpretation of these studies was made more difficult as a result of the subject's recent wounding."

"I can well appreciate that fact," Nikolayev said to him. "And I am sure you have solved the problems posed by the crime with admirable ingenuity."

Gutiérrez seemed to take no notice because he went on explaining. "Metal of any sort, whether it is from grenade shrapnel or rifle shot, tends to scatter the radiation waves directed at it. Positioning becomes all important."

Typical Cuban, Goncharov thought. *He has to blow his own horn even after someone else has done it for him.*

"I am sure your explanation is quite complete and fascinating," Nikolayev stated, "but I am sure it is also far over my simple head. Also, I am most anxious to learn of your results, and my time in your beautiful country is unfortunately most limited."

The doctor finally picked up on the fact that he was trying the foreign dignitary's patience. "Yes, of course, Comrade," he said. "What it comes down to is this." He motioned the two men over close to the light box and directed their attention to one particular series of studies. "We were able to locate and identify thirteen individual fragments of shrapnel. They cover a range from the middle of the sternum up here, all the way down to the mid-thigh area of the left leg. Each one of these situs was then carefully screened to see if the particular fragment was the one we were looking for."

"And?" Nikolayev prodded.

Gutiérrez shook his head. "Unfortunately there is no reasonable possibility of any of these fragments' having a hollow center as you described."

"You are sure of this?"

"Comrade, our diagnostic facilities at this institution are every bit as advanced and our staff as well qualified as what you would find in the finest such institutions in the United States and the Soviet Union. As we were asked to undertake this examination, I had assumed that—"

Nikolayev took a step forward and seized the Cuban's hand in both of his. "Please, please, Doctor, I did not mean to imply any lack of faith on our part or to cast any question over your fine institution. To be sure, we have the utmost respect for you and your staff or else, as you have so astutely pointed out, we would not have brought our most sensitive work to you. I was asking more in the scientifically rhetorical sense only."

Goncharov tried to keep his reaction to himself.

"As I was saying, Comrade," Gutiérrez continued, "we have effectively ruled out the possibility of a hollow-center shrapnel fragment residing within the body of the subject."

Nikolayev shot a glance at his intelligence operative. "Is it possible we have the wrong man?"

"That is an extremely doubtful possibility," Goncharov told him.

"This is as I thought."

"But this is what you should know," Gutiérrez went on. "You see this lesion here?" He pointed his finger at a specific spot on one film. "This is an area of fresh wounding, just above the surface of the liver, obviously arising from the shotgun injury. However, the scar tissue formation is such that it indicates a larger cavity than would be caused by a shotgun pellet. I think it more than likely that the surgeon who operated actually removed a fragment of the approximate size and mass you have specified."

"The surgeon in question was Commander Thorpe," Goncharov said.

"Yes, of course," said Nikolayev. "It all stands to reason." He clasped his hands firmly behind his back and paced off to the other side of the room, where he could be alone with his thoughts. He stood there for a long time, not saying anything, facing out the window. When he returned to the other two men, the expression on his face suggested that there would be no further need for discussion. Nikolayev had been told what he needed to know and had made up his mind accordingly.

Accordingly Gutiérrez's usefulness to him was now at an end, so Nikolayev now turned his full attention to Goncharov and began once again speaking in Russian. The Cuban appeared somewhat miffed by the sudden dropping of deference, but the two visitors paid him little heed. "This was always a very real possibility," the deputy chief commented, "though I thought this exercise was worth the effort. I still do. Anyway, it confirms something for us and tells us something else we wanted to know."

"Quite so," Goncharov said.

"Now, as to the matter of the disposition of the subject."

Goncharov had known this issue would soon have to arise. "An injection would be the simplest and least traumatic method," the operative said.

Nikolayev smiled benignly. "I was actually thinking that we might restore him to his natural setting if you think such a maneuver to be feasible."

Goncharov's face lit up. "I should think it would be," he declared. "Removing him from his original location was the challenge. Bringing him back would present no unusual difficulties." He was pleased and surprised by his superior. How much more bureaucratically simple it would have been for him simply to order Moreland's termination now that he had served his purpose. But because the patient had been unconscious during the entire exercise, there was no real reason to get rid of him. It was no more than a matter of common decency. But as Goncharov knew from a lifetime of professional experience, common decency was the rarest and most uncommon of traits for those in power. "We will arrange for him to show up in the charity ward of Bellevue Hospital in Manhattan. His wife will then be alerted to where he can be found."

"Sounds like a fine plan." Nikolayev chuckled. "Because by now I am certain our brothers on the other side have noticed him missing. His resurfacing should provide a bit of a shock, and when they reason out where he's been, I'd say a nasty shock. Letting them know from time to time that we are one step ahead of them tends to force their hand, I have found. And as long as we can stay one step ahead, the game will have to come to us."

Goncharov should have known that the deputy chief's motivation would have been other than purely compassionate.

"Well," Nikolayev said in a hearty voice, clapping Goncharov on the shoulder, "now that we know what we know, we will have to pursue this matter through other channels."

22

Staying at the apartment was out of the question, Brian had decided. Even coming back to Washington was risky enough in itself. But what had to be done next could be done only from here.

He had checked them into one of the string of anonymous little 1950s-style motels along Route 50 that adjoin Fort Myer. They registered under made-up names and brought only enough luggage to suggest two people just passing through. Almost everyone else was either a midwestern tourist who couldn't manage the expensive lodging downtown or a lover or family visiting a soldier at the base. No one paid much attention to anyone else. It wasn't that kind of place.

Brian wouldn't take a chance on the phone in the room. Instead, he made his calls from the phone booth at the end of the parking lot. It was one of those old-style metal-framed glass boxes with the folding glass door that afforded a degree more privacy than the modern plastic hoods that have largely replaced them. Flies and mosquitoes swarmed just outside at head level, and the round white light fixture on the ceiling was blackened wherever moths had made suicidal dive-bombing runs. The cobwebs looked old enough to qualify for historic preservation and shimmered in the early-evening semitropical heat. As he dialed, Brian thought of Diana in the room watching one of the zillion cable television channels heralded on the motel's neon sign. He sure knew how to show a girl a good time.

He called Gregory at home. "Where are you?" the radiologist inquired.

"It's better if I don't say," Brian answered, and on matters of personal safety, Gregory was only too happy to defer his friend's judgment.

"Now that I've got you here, Jill's gone to work on those other two names you asked about—Fine and Santoya, the marines who didn't kick out of the computer for our control group."

"Right. What did she find out?"

"They both were listed MIA. Later it was confirmed they'd both been taken prisoner."

"So was Roger Moreland."

"That's right," Gregory said. "The difference was that Moreland got out alive. Santoya and Fine didn't."

"I see," Brian said quietly.

Neither he nor Gregory said anything else for a while, as if observing a moment of silence in the two marines' memory. Then Gregory ended it by saying, "Let me tell you about that little stopper from the fragment chamber. I had our best pathology guy look at it. I didn't tell him what it was or where I'd gotten it. And he was interested as it turned out because he'd never seen anything exactly like it."

"So what is it?" Brian asked.

"We ran it through all the neat tests," Gregory reported. "It appears to be some sort of organic compound."

"Organic?"

"Yeah. Definitely carbon-based. The spectrometer told us that. But a very dense material. Denser than human tissue, and it won't break down the same way either. It's almost like that first artificial skin material the air force was experimenting with several years back. You probably remember—the stuff that wore like iron but didn't really behave like skin. At any rate, my guess is that this is based on the same research."

"So is this material porous?"

"Not under any circumstances we've been able to duplicate so far."

"But if the capsule has a stopper rather than a hermetic seal, it has to be so the stuff inside can get out," Brian reasoned.

"I was thinking the same thing," said Gregory.

"That's the first step of logic. And the second is, if the stopper is made up of some organic material rather than a metal or a polymer, it has to be that it's supposed to interact with something under certain circumstances—for the purpose, I would assume, of letting whatever's inside out."

"Excellent analysis. I agree completely. But we saw what was inside Radley Davis's capsule. Water. H_2O."

"I know. I haven't figured that one out yet," Brian said. "But we also know what was inside Roger Moreland's capsule. And we have to assume the same thing was inside Sam Hardesty's."

"And all the others?"

"And all the others."

"And someone out there is very nervous about them."

"Yes," said Brian. "That is, someone in addition to us. Which leads me to my next request, my next two requests actually."

"Anything, dear boy."

"First of all, can you have Jill cover me for a while longer?"

"We'll try." Gregory sighed. "But there comes a point when even the computer starts getting suspicious."

"I know, I know," Brian said. "Just try to bear with me a little longer. Put me on sick leave if you have to. Just try not to call too many people's attention to it."

"If anyone can do it, it's the snake charmer of the computer age. When you get to that level, though, these things are no longer simply mechanical procedures. I hope you realize, Brian, I'm selflessly going to have to perform extra-special fancy tonight to put her in the proper mood of inspiration."

"If you perform one-tenth as well as the reports you're always giving me, I'm sure it'll be enough to make the angels weep."

"Brian, the navy's faith and investment in you have not been misplaced, and if I were with you there, wherever you are, I would pinch your cheek with warm delight. You're a poet, if not a scholar. And I'm gratified to see you can appreciate that like yourself, I am eternally willing to sacrifice myself for the sake of others. Now, what is the second task my master wishes?"

"I'm coming into Bethesda tomorrow," Brian told him. "Don't tell anyone, and if I'm seen, I'll say I'm there just to check the mail or something. I'm coming for only a few minutes and for one reason. That is, if you can arrange something for me."

* * *

For Lieutenant General John Winthrop Blagden of the United States Marine Corps, early morning was usually the only quiet time, before the crises of the day began in earnest. He arrived at the Pentagon most mornings at six, took forty-five minutes of vigorous exercise in the basement gym, showered, dressed, and was seated in his office by seven. The next hour was the critical one, the one in which, left undisturbed, he could expend the serious, concentrated thought that had become a luxury since he'd moved to this five-sided bureaucratic jungle and that would be impossible once the endless parade began just outside his double mahogany doors.

His secretary, Miss Thornton, had been well schooled in the distinction between an ordinary cause for interruption during this hour and an extraordinary one, the first being absolutely intolerable and the second requiring some degree of personal initiative on her part. And the consequences of being wrong, she had discovered, were never pleasant. So Blagden knew that something extraordinary was taking place when from the corner of his eye he saw her standing in his doorway, waiting to be recognized, at 7:38 A.M.

He looked up from his desk. "Yes? What is it?" he said tersely.

"General, a call just came in from Bethesda Naval Hospital," Miss Thornton reported. "About the tests you had done there. They want to do some follow-up."

"What kind of follow-up?"

"They didn't say. Just that it was of a delicate nature and that they would like you to come back over as soon as possible. They'd like it to be today."

Blagden thought for a moment and sighed. His mind considered the various possibilities, just as he had been trained to do in somewhat different circumstances. What sort of follow-up could possibly be of a "delicate nature"? In his younger days, that term used to refer to some condition implying sexual compromise. But no longer. They must have picked up something serious on one of the tests and must want to tell him in person. But if that were what it was, for someone of his rank they would probably just send someone over to his office and tell him right here. Still, what other possibility was there?

Well, if that was what it was or if it was something else, there was nothing he could do about it. When, at the age of nineteen, John Winthrop Blagden had decided to make his career as a marine, he knew he would be facing many situations which were legitimately worthy of serious worry and fear. He also knew at that same formative age that worry and fear would beneficially affect the outcome of none of them. If anything, they could only diminish his clearheaded effectiveness to deal with the concrete aspects of the challenge when called upon to do so. So whenever the uncomfortable sensations arose, young Blagden practiced the willful act of banishing them from his consciousness until though they remained, they were no longer a force to be contended with. And whatever happened would happen on its own. Just like this business this morning. Until he learned its exact nature, it required no further expenditure of thought or action.

"Clear away the first block of time you can." Blagden calmly instructed her, as if he were still giving commands on the battlefield as in the old days.

"I already have," Miss Thornton declared. "The driver will be here to pick you up at oh-nine-thirty." She handed him a sheet of notepaper embossed with the three silver stars of his rank. "This is the room number you're to go to."

"Very well," John Winthrop Blagden said, and went quietly back to his work.

BETHESDA, MARYLAND

John Winthrop Blagden proceeded through the lobby of Bethesda Naval Hospital, up the elevator and directly to the room Miss Thornton had specified. Along the way he was met with all the deference he took for granted. Once at his destination, he was met by a nurse whose name tag proclaimed that she was J. Timberlake (a civilian), who told him the doctor would be right with him. If the general wouldn't mind, would he please go into the examination room and make himself comfortable?

Should he remove any of his clothing? Blagden asked her.

"Not unless the doctor asks you to do so," Miss Timberlake replied, and closed the door behind her, leaving him by himself in the confining room.

Here, away from his desk, cut off from his environment, Blagden finally found it impossible to restrain his thoughts. If it turned out to be something that couldn't be taken care of, he would face it. He would face it because there was no choice, just as he had faced everything else. Everyone must face it eventually, soldiers often earlier than most. And never in his life, as he thought back on it, had he ever turned away from anything. If it were to be the worst case, he hoped only it would be something that wouldn't be wasting or drawn-out or rob him of his dignity. As he waited for the doctor to arrive, he thought of Charles I in the Tower of London, awaiting his execution at the hands of Cromwell, requesting an extra shirt to brace himself against the damp morning air, lest the crowd mistake his shivering for a last-minute loss of nerve.

The door at the other side of the room opened. A man of medium height and dark blond hair wearing a white lab coat came in. He looked vaguely familiar, but Blagden couldn't quite place him. Perhaps he had seen him many years before.

"General Blagden, I'm Commander Thorpe. Brian Thorpe. Thank you for coming here."

"The question is, Commander, should I be thanking you," Blagden said tersely.

"I'm sorry to have had to bring you here under these circumstances, but I felt it was the only way." Blagden nodded stoically. Brian observed the downcast turn of the general's mouth and knew instantly what it meant. "I also want to apologize for any mental anguish my request to see you might have caused. I knew that was a possibility but saw no secure way around it. But let me assure you, sir, that there's nothing physically wrong with you, certainly nothing I'd know about."

Blagden let out a pent-up sigh of relief, then looked immediately perplexed.

"I had to talk to you, sir," Brian went on, "and this was the quickest, most efficient, safest way of getting to you."

Blagden continued staring at him, his stone-cold noncommittal stare. Finally he said, "Are you really a doctor?"

"Yes, sir, I am," Brian replied. "A surgeon here at Bethesda. But before that I was a medical corpsman with the Seventh Amphib. I was at Eagle's Talon." First test, he thought.

Unblinking, without a hint of false emotion, Blagden said, "Not many of you boys made it back."

"No, sir. Not many of us did."

"Then for that at least, Commander, I owe you something." He took another long pause. "Now, does this meeting have anything to do with that?"

"In a way, I suppose it does." Second test. And this was the critical one. This was where he laid the big chips on the table. It was a calculated risk, he knew, opening up to Blagden like this. But it was a risk that had to be taken. And Brian had done his best to throw the advantage in his favor by playing on his own court where he could better control the situation.

"General Blagden, does the name Calvin Chandler Harley mean anything to you?"

Blagden regarded him impassively. "The surgeon from Stanford. He was one of our division medical officers."

"That's right," Brian said. He removed the five-by-seven photograph from the pocket of his lab coat, wiped away the lint with his sleeve, and handed it over to Blagden. "This is a picture of a document I found in Dr. Harley's possession."

Carefully, meticulously, he searched Blagden's face and bodily movements for reactions, for any nuance that would indicate his true feelings and perceptions.

Blagden scanned the photograph. His face turned instantly grim and, if Brian was not mistaken, lost a touch of color. "How did you come by this?" he asked.

"It's a long story," Brian said, and gave him the short form of it. The general listened, silently and somberly. Hardly a muscle twitched during the narrative. Brian remembered many things about his commanding officer during that year at the DMZ. The thing he remembered most clearly was his iron self-discipline. Apparently he had been remembering correctly.

"Then it's true," Blagden finally said, raising his head, as if looking back into his own memory.

"What's that?" Brian asked.

"We'd heard rumors about this before. Back at the time. Good rumors. Strong sources. But since nothing ultimately came of it, I was always inclined not to believe them."

"I'm not sure what you're referring to, sir."

Blagden looked him squarely in the eye. "Can you come to my office at the Pentagon tomorrow morning—say, oh-seven-hundred?"

"Yes, yes, of course," Brian replied.

"No, you'd be too obvious then. Better make it oh-nine-thirty. Then it'll just look like a routine meeting. Do you have a medical bag?"

"Yes."

"Bring it. I'll tell my secretary your visit has to do with this medical follow-up, and I don't want it on the log." He took another scrutinizing glance at the photograph, then looked up at Brian. "You showed me something I hadn't seen. Now I want to show you something that presumably you haven't seen. Then we'll talk. Just the two of us."

Purple called from a phone booth outside the Little Tavern on Wisconsin Avenue. He dialed the number that only twelve people in the world knew, that was not written down anywhere. He punched in his scrambler code and waited until he heard the confirming beep.

"We've placed Thorpe again. At the naval hospital."

"Very good," Michael Swansea responded. "I suppose it was natural he would come back to a predictable location. A man can veer from routine only so long, even as extraordinary a man as Thorpe."

"Should we take him out when he leaves the building?" Purple asked. "We're in good position here for an auto accident. We could get him just as he comes out of the grounds onto the main highway."

"I've never been partial to crashes," Swansea said. "We weren't terribly successful the first time we tried it with Dr. Thorpe. It's more difficult than most people realize to kill a man that way, and the 'weapon' is too easily traced. But that's not the point. If we decided to carry it out, I trust you and your people implicitly to carry it out with efficiency and precision. The point is, I'm afraid, that Thorpe has eluded us and been out of our care for too long a unit of time now. We don't know where he's been, what he's found out, or who he's talked to. And we can't afford to take him out without knowing that. Remember, he is merely incidental to our singular goal of *controlling the situation.* So stay on his trail, follow him, and let's see where he goes."

"Absolutely," Purple said.

"Oh, and good work," Swansea said. "I don't think this situation is going to get out from under us." It was one of the few compliments Purple ever remembered coming from him.

Thorpe did not stay at the hospital long. He came out shortly after Purple returned to his observation post and drove off with a short, overweight, and curly-haired man the satellite chart had identified as Cheever, Gregory, M.D.

Swansea—still formally referred to as Contact by his agents—had always taught that human beings are creatures of habit, and cognizance of that fact can aid immeasurably in analyzing and anticipating their actions. They will tend to do things the same way each time. And if they do not, there will be a reason. Nothing in the universe, Contact asserted, happened at random. If Thorpe followed his normal pattern—the one established before his recent flight—the vehicle would turn left onto Jones Bridge Road, then right onto Connecticut Avenue and straight on south into the District.

But this was not the course he followed today. Instead, the car came out the main gate, near the flagpole shaped like a ship's mast, and turned left onto the Rockville Pike. From there the vehicle proceeded south only a few blocks to the Medical Center Metro stop. It pulled to a stop near the station entrance, the passenger door opened, and Thorpe got out. He exchanged a few words with the driver, Cheever, waved, then walked across to the escalator as the car drove off.

"He's gotten out of the car," Purple spoke into the microphone he picked up from the chase car's dashboard. "He's taking the subway home," he reasoned. He opened his D.C. resource book and consulted the Metro time chart. Medical Center to Van Ness-UDC. Red Line. No transfers. Time, assuming no wait for train. "Be prepared to pick up the tail between the Van Ness station and his apartment house in nine minutes," he ordered.

Purple couldn't figure out why more than an hour later Thorpe still had not been sighted coming out of either entrance to the Van Ness station. The only logical conclusion was that he must not have gone home.

It was a good bet that Contact would not be pleased.

ARLINGTON, VIRGINIA

"This could be a trap," Diana said. She watched from behind as Brian put on the tie of his uniform in the bathroom mirror.

"It could be," Brian said in acknowledgment.

"Why couldn't he have just told you what he wanted to when you got him to the hospital yesterday?"

"He said he had something to show me."

"But that means he's got you on his turf now, not yours. You're totally unprotected there, Brian. There's nothing you can do."

"I hardly think he's going to try to assassinate me in the bowels of the Pentagon. This isn't Dzerzhinsky Square."

"Who knows what goes on there?"

He turned to her. "I forgot who I'm dealing with. Who knows what evil lurks in the big bad Defense Department?"

She placed one hand hard on his shoulder and the other on her own hip. "Come on, Brian. I'm being serious. You won't let me breathe one word to my people at the centers, yet you're spilling your guts to some hard-ass marine general that you'd never even talked to before yesterday."

"It's different," Brian replied dispassionately. "Blagden was my commanding officer. He was the CO for all the marines on our list."

"So? We still don't know anything about him. We don't know if he can be, as you so quaintly put it, trusted. Has it ever occurred to you that he may be the one behind all this?"

"Of course, it's occurred to me," Brian stated. He began to pack his medical bag with routine supplies. Its inside was empty and lined with dust. In his current work he hardly ever used it.

"This man was a marine colonel," Diana continued, "a man who led other men into battle to die in an unjust and ultimately meaningless war. This was the perpetrator of Eagle's Talon. The *last* person I'd trust would be a member of the oppressor class." *How quickly and easily the ringing block phrases of the old mind-set could reassert themselves*, she mused.

How quickly and easily the old stridency filters up to the surface, Brian thought. *Once mastered, it's never to be forgotten. The next phrase out of her mouth is going to be "baby killer."* He remembered that it was the first thing he'd been called when he got back to the World after returning from a year over there as a medic. Just as he left Travis Air force Base, a girl about the age Diana would have been at the time, carying a protest sign of some sort, shouted it at him from behind the chain-link fence.

Well, it wasn't for nothing that it came back to me, Diana told herself. *We thought what we thought and did what we did to change the world, didn't we? What we were going for back then was the lasting effect. And damned if some of us didn't achieve it.*

"And yet you're still going to confide in him," she said disparagingly.

"We don't have any choice. Blagden was at the center of things," he replied. "He was the one with the overview. He's the only one who can put the information together for us so we can use it." He took a pause and let out the full volume of his breath. "So we have to trust him. At least up to a point."

"And what if it is a trap? What if he's the one who killed all the marines?"

"I seriously doubt that."

"But what if he is?" Diana pressed on. "What if he's setting you up?"

"I'll try to be careful."

"You'll try to be careful!" she repeated. "You're just one guy, Brian. He's about to be the fucking general of the Marine Corps. All the president has to do is sign the papers. He's got incredible resources behind him, plus ... if he knows what's really happening and you don't, that puts him at the advantage. He may be just trying to find out what you know, and then you'll walk out of there and—bang!" She was beginning to have a hard time keeping her vehemence from slipping into tears.

"It's a risk we have to take," he stated definitely. He came around and positioned himself beside her so he could wrap his arms around her waist. "I haven't mentioned your name in his presence. As far as I can tell, he doesn't know you exist."

"So what are you saying?" she asked.

He faced her and placed his hands squarely on her shoulders so that he could keep her there, looking at him. "You know what I'm saying. If anything happens to me, it's up to you."

"But we already know from the attack on Sharon that *someone* knows about me, someone with the power to get to anyone he needs to. What if that someone is Blagden?"

"If for any reason I don't come back—not that I'm expecting it—that should confirm that. Then you call Hugh Stanway. He'll give you whatever help you need." He arranged the supplies he'd been loading and snapped the medical bag shut.

"B-but, B-Brian," she stammered, "why do you have to go? Why do you have to do it like—like this?"

"I have to," he told her. "It's the only way to find out what we need to know."

"You're the one who keeps telling me how critical time is."

"I know. It is." She pulled him tight and put her head against his chest. "But this is too risky."

"It's a calculated risk." He angled her chin with his hand and kept her looking at him. "You know what a point man is?"

"I—I think so."

"Back in Nam on any patrol there was always a point man. Someone had to do it. Sometimes it was me. Someone always has to walk point to let everyone else know if there are any minefields up ahead."

There was something strangely incongruous to Brian about John Winthrop Blagden's office. It was wood-paneled and high-ceilinged and cavernous. There was a private waiting room out-side where he'd sat facing an ageless secretary for several long minutes until, with no visible cue, she had suddenly risen from her desk and conducted him into the inner sanctum for his audi-ence with the general, who in turn had nodded to him and then waited until they were alone to say anything.

But sitting in the overstuffed colonial wing chair, studying the wall of photographs and certificates and testimonials behind the imposing walnut desk in the tastefully indirect lighting and ab-sently pressing his shoes into the ostentatiously deep-piled car-pet, Brian had the feeling he was on an elaborate stage set that didn't remotely fit the actor. The only prop that felt right in the entire room was the green metal helmet, similar to the one he'd seen in Harley's house, that was lying on the end table next to the luxurious sofa. That had some relationship to the real Black Jack Blagden, the one Brian remembered in open-collar fatigues and dusty combat boots, in an "office" that consisted not of a corpo-rate suite but of a field tent and a map-covered folding table.

Then, when Blagden's secretary closed the huge double doors behind her and he confronted his former commanding officer alone on his own territory, Brian felt as if he had taken one crucial step farther in his journey of no return.

"If the subject arises later on," Blagden said quietly, "this meeting will be described as a personal medical discussion, which, in fact, it is. That is because I do not have sufficient confidence at this time to speak of this to anyone inside the traditional channels. And I will assume your word of honor as a soldier to do the same."

"I understand," Brian said.

Blagden's close-cropped hair was now the steel gray of raw shell casings. Other than that, he had changed remarkably little over the years. Perhaps that was why he seemed so out of place in this environment. The word that always came first to Brian's mind when thinking about him was "solid." Everything about Blagden was solid. But he looked stiff and uncomfortable in the regulation green marine tunic. And the ribbons arranged in a deep block across the left side of his chest were merely abstractions of real places and events, some of which Brian had been to and remembered.

With no small talk and without further discussion, Blagden handed a two-page stapled document across the desk. Both pages were photocopies. The first Brian recognized as Vietnamese. It was typed on an ancient typewriter with several broken letters and bore a case officer's receipt stamp and initials. The second page was in English, bearing both the case officer's stamp and the translator's name and classification.

"This document came to me in 1969, in the field, shortly before Eagle's Talon," the general explained. "It appears to be the second or third page of something, but we don't have the rest. I saved it, as you can see. I never showed it to anyone else, but I carried it with me in my personal files everywhere I went, through every command. I thought about it often but never did anything about it because I didn't know what to do. But it has silently plagued me all those years. And I had no idea what it meant . . . until yesterday."

Brian glanced first at the Vietnamese copy, to see if he could make anything out of it with the few words and phrases he still remembered.

"There was a translator's report along with it," Blagden continued, "saying that he believes the Vietnamese version itself to be a translation. It apparently bears none of the normal rhythms of formal Vietnamese construction or phrasing. The translator states that the grammatical arrangements and usage are typically Russian. As you read on, you will understand the significance of this observation."

Brian folded over the first sheet and scanned the second, containing the English translation:

Demonstration trials (translation approximate) have verified a mortality rate of 100%. With exponential transmission from those originally infected, actual *field* (translation approximate) results should be close to or equal that number. Within seventy-two hours of the first transmission of the PRIMARY AGENT, the projected effect should be achieved.

When the PRIMARY AGENT has reached the appropriate level of saturation in the target population, the COUNTER DELIVERY AGENT will be introduced through the repatriation of the CARRIERS. Owing to the specific nature and placement of the capsules within their bodies, interaction with the PRIMARY AGENT should be nearly instantaneous and neutralize the PRIMARY AGENT before it can cause them ill effects. The effects of the COUNTER DELIVERY AGENT itself to the——(number deleted before receipt) CARRIERS will be limited to standard influenza symptoms which should not hamper their effectiveness.

It is anticipated that equilibrium state between the two competing viral strains will be accomplished within an additional——(number deleted before receipt) days, assuming normal migratory patterns of the CARRIERS. During this time the mortality rate will drop off along an exponential curve, and will continue until the COUNTER DELIVERY AGENT has superceded the PRIMARY AGENT within the totality of the remaining population.

Brian laid the pages down on the edge of the desk and looked up.

"As you can imagine," said Blagden, "as soon as I read this, it scared the shit out of me."

Brian nodded.

"All I knew was that the enemy had worked out a germ warfare offensive that they seemed pretty confident would be a hundred percent effective. When it was coming, under what circumstances, our people had no idea."

"And nothing else turned up?" Brian asked.

Blagden shook his head. "One thing did. A map with coordinates marked off that made it pretty clear this offensive was to be directed in the northern region of I Corps and probably the Third Marines in particular. But beyond that, nothing. A total void. The CIA cranked up the network, strong-armed its indigenous assets, put the word out to anyone it could get hold of. The bucket came up dry each time. So I sat and I waited and I held my breath. Nothing happened. Could be a fake, I thought, intentionally leaked to us. It wasn't likely the North Vietnamese had this kind of scientific capability."

Brian nodded his agreement with the assessment. He had thought the same thing.

"Traditional psychological warfare, the intelligence boys figured. When you haven't got the guns, often the next best thing is to make your enemy think you do."

Brian nodded again.

"But about the same time a highly classified CIA report was forwarded to me. It said that the Soviet Union had tremendously stepped up its biological weapons R and D, and had built two new secret plants, one not far from Moscow at Zagorsk and the other at Sverdlovsk. I'll never forget those two names. Now the Soviets couldn't do anything directly for all the obvious practical and diplomatic reasons. But their North Vietnamese clients would have been the perfect ones to test out some of the product for them under actual field conditions. At the same time, this leaves the Russkies themselves with complete deniability when anyone rattled the Geneva Convention. And since their strategy in Southeast Asia was to wear us out and sap our national will and let us bleed ourselves dry, it didn't hurt them any to attach one more leech.

"So we—I, specifically—sweated for quite a while till long after Eagle's Talon. But you hear a lot of things about what the other side is trying to do, especially in wartime. And after a while you realize that nothing's happened, and you begin to relax about it. I figured that despite that document fragment and the CIA report, it was all a sham; there was no 'primary agent' and I could stop worrying." He sighed and looked straight across the desk at Brian. "But from what you told me yesterday, I see I was wrong after all."

Brian asked, "How many people knew about this?"

Blagden shrugged. "I don't know. It was a CIA operation so there's no way to be sure. Agency people tell you only what they think you have to know. And the only reason it came to me at all was that it seemed to be directed at my unit. I would assume that someone above me—a general at divisional level—was also told. But that's purely conjecture, and line colonels aren't supposed to deal in conjecture. My only discussions were with the agency liaisons. No one else in the corps ever talked to me."

"And you never suspected Harley?"

"No," Blagden replied adamantly. "There was never any reason to, with what we knew. You have to remember, we had no idea what the method of transmission was supposed to be. It wasn't spelled out in the document. The most likely thing would have been spraying from planes, we thought, some giant crop-dusting operation. It never occurred to us they would use American troops and implant these things in their bodies, same as the 'Counter Delivery Force,' which we figured must be ARVN POWs they planned to release." Then, almost as an afterthought, he added, "Harly was saving lives for us. That was the only thing I thought about him."

Brian had said very little so far. He had been listening carefully, feeling out this war hero who had once been his commanding officer and who now, at the president's pleasure, was about to take over the entire Marine Corps. He was trying to separate out the myth of Black Jack Blagden he'd carried around all these years so that he could accurately distil his own pure impressions. More than anything else, Brian knew, it was critical that he come away with a reliable sense of the man.

"And before yesterday," he asked, "you hadn't heard about the recent deaths of any of the marines from the unit?"

"No." Blagden shook his head. With his hand he indicated the walls around him. "I'm afraid that in this splended fortress we're cut off from most of the truly important intelligence, at least the intelligence that makes us human."

Brian almost felt sorry for Blagden. The tough, brilliant field strategist had been promoted, it seemed, into a fancy, ceremonial bureaucrat.

"But quite clear, from what you tell me," the general continued, "is that one of the marines must have found out about Ratsbane. And whoever was behind it has been taking no chances with the rest." He looked straight at Brian. "Or anyone else who may be on to it." He drummed his fingers, briefly and impatiently, on the polished desk surface. "Let's not mince words here. We're both military men. We both know strategy. Someone, most likely an agent of a foreign power, has proved he is very serious about this. And we both know that until we have the big picture, anyone remotely associated with this remains in danger."

The image of the paper-bound bureaucrat rapidly faded from Brian's mind. "My thinking exactly, General," he stated, staring straight at him.

Blagden picked up the document that Brian had left on the

desk and returned his gaze. "Well, Commander Thorpe, you're a doctor. How do you analyze this?"

"That's a tough one," he responded, then stared up at the ceiling for several seconds of silent speculation. "Immunology is extremely complex, and it's far from my field." He knew he was already out of his depth. He also wasn't sure how much he wanted to say. He wished he had Diana here with him as a balance. He stuffed his hands into his pockets and stretched his legs, extending them far out in front of him. He remained silent for a long time as Blagden's unwavering gaze bore down on him.

But in the end he did speak, verbalizing the struggle in his own mind to see if he could make sense of the sketchy evidence. "Well," he said, "this counter delivery agent would seem to be some substance that counteracts or somehow, as they say, neutralizes the original virus."

"A vaccine?" Blagden questioned.

"No, I wouldn't think so," Brian responded, searching his face for telling reaction. But there was none. "If they came up with an agent that neutralizes the virus, then technologically I would assume they had a vaccine, too." He pointed to the clipped papers. "But this doesn't describe a vaccine, which would have to be administered *before* the virus infected the host to be effective." He pulled his legs back in and sat up straight in the wing chair.

"I see."

Brian watched as Blagden picked up a letter opener in the form of a small samurai sword. He slid it out of its ornamental case and, with the edge of the gleaming blade, scratched the bristly gray hair behind his ear. "Well," he said, "with what we know and what we don't know, I suppose the next question is where do we go from here."

With a sense of relief that they had finally reached a commonality of purpose, Brian said, "I agree, sir. That is the question."

Blagden put down the letter opener and, as he shifted his weight, crossed one leg over the other. The muscles were still tight and solid. "Any ideas, Commander?"

Brian pulled his chair up and, even so, leaned in closer to the front of the desk, his forearms resting on his knees. He weighed his answer carefully before he spoke. "Personally, General, I'd like to find out who is behind this and get to him before he gets to me and the people close to me."

"I can certainly appreciate that," Blagden commented. "And believe me, I feel for what you've been going through."

Barely focusing on the response, Brian's mind flashed to images of Katie and Diana and even Lizzie, then moved out in concentric rings to take in his parents, his brothers, Gregory, and Jill. For his entire adult life he had had little trouble facing the idea of his own mortality. He had trained and conditioned himself for it and had gotten used to thinking of himself as the sacrificial offering for any group that included him. But the idea of any harm coming to those he loved, especially because of something involving him, shook the foundations of his world. If that happened, he knew that the rest of his own life would become nothing more than a quest for revenge.

"But I'm afraid there's an even larger concern," he stated. "We've got the potential for a major epidemic on our hands. There were seventeen names on the list I found in Harley's house. Two died as POWs. Six more are recently dead. Then there's Moreland, the shooting victim in New York that I took the last capsule from. And there's Dantley in West Virgina we can put our hands on quickly if we have to. But we have utilized all the resources of the military computer network, and that leaves six still unaccounted for. If even one of them is alive and the contents of the capsule he's carrying around inside him gets out and there's no available antidote, it could actually kill everyone in North America within a matter of weeks."

"That is indeed a sobering thought to contemplate," Blagden sardonically commented. He paused for a moment, then said, "Assuming we were able to locate each of these six, as, by the way, I doubt we could do, there really isn't any assurance that they are the only ones carrying this Ratsbane agent or that additional stocks aren't being maintained somewhere else, is there?"

Brian shook his head.

Blagden tapped the end of the letter opener on his desk blotter. "So as long as we know that this virus exists without any known antidote, we can never feel secure. Am I correct in my logic?"

"If we can get hold of the remaining capsule that we know of, we could submit it to the experts at the Centers for Disease Control for analysis to try and come up with a vaccine," Brian said.

"And what would be the chances for success?"

"Hard to say, since we don't know anything about the virus's makeup. Our sample was destroyed before we could analyze it under an electron microscope. Some viruses have never proved vulnerable to vaccines. But even under the best of circumstances, with luck riding completely on our side, it would take two years to come up with a vaccine and then six months to produce it in large enough quantities to immunize the entire country, not even thinking about Canada and Mexico."

"Then I think we both know the only alternative," Blagden stated with finality. In the heat of crisis Blagden's instincts were purely functional, Brian realized. It was the mark of a first-rate commander. "Unfortunately for us, you and I are the only ones who know about this. And since we don't know who we're facing, we can't take a chance on alerting anyone else in a position to help. We don't know where the weak spots are. That puts a heap of responsibility on our two sets of shoulders. And it all comes down to this: Wherever they are, we've got to get our hands on one of those counter delivery folks."

Neither man spoke for several minutes. Finally Blagden leaned back in his chair, swiveling gently from side to side, grazing the point of the letter opener under the ridges of his fingernails. The image was almost homespun. It might have been a move calculated to throw him off guard, Brian thought, or to take some of the edge off his wariness.

"Since our meeting yesterday morning I've looked up your service record," Blagden announced. "In strictest confidence, of course. You told me you had been a medic. You didn't say you were also a SEAL."

"That was a long time ago," said Brian.

Blagden nodded. "Perhaps. But I don't consider that particular specialty so much a job description as an approach to life and its challenges. From what I've seen, both of you and your kind, I don't think I'd be far off to suggest that you possess a certain resourcefulness and a sense of responsibility that are beyond the experience or comprehension of the vast majority of people."

Brian said nothing. But the idea seemed to come to the two of them simultaneously, the way two field commanders, cut off from each other in the heat of battle, can conceive of the same plan and move their forces in concert without ever communicating. Was it at all feasible? he wondered. Could it possibly be done? A thousand questions of strategy, reconnaissance, logistics, converged at one point in his brain.

"As I'm sure you can appreciate," Blagden went on, "I am somewhat hamstrung by my position here. A general's powers, though great, are severely circumscribed. And like a preacher's wife, he operates in a fishbowl. Any order I give is instantly public knowledge. Under normal circumstances, this is the kind of thing that should be turned over to the military intelligence authorities. But quite clearly whoever is behind this has extensive access to classified information, command structure, everything. We don't know how high this goes. Whatever's going on here, this could be the military version of Watergate. So I can't take a chance on bringing any of the inside people or organizations on board."

Brian nodded his agreement with the logic.

Blagden fixed him once again in his gaze. "You're not on the inside. At least not in the sense I'm talking about. You can operate independently, without alerting anyone."

"Up to a point," Brian said.

"And one of the things I can do, though, is cover for you, fix it administratively so that you're not missed for a while."

Brian wasn't sure he liked the sound of that.

"I can also provide you with some degree of financial backing without raising any eyebrows. And upon the completion of the mission I will see to it that in some form you receive the recognition and rewards you deserve."

"What about the people who are trying to kill me?" Brian asked.

"I don't know who they are. Neither do you. But your little sojourn will give me some chance to do some personal digging. Once we find out who they are, we can deal with them more effectively. Plus, once we've recovered one of the counter delivery capsules, we can go after them without pulling any of our punches. We can let the chips fall where they may, knowing that our adversaries no longer have the big threat to hold over us."

There was a certain logic to it, Brian had to admit.

"Once the antidote, or whatever it is, is safely in hand, we don't have to worry about who knows what or who's on to us. At that point we track them down and let them have it with both barrels." His mouth formed a calculating smile. "Ultimately, it would seem, this is the most direct avenue to your own salvation."

Brian resisted the impulse to get up and pace.

Blagden must have sensed from his eyes that Brian had accepted the possibility of attempting this and was trying as subtly as he could to keep him on the reservation. "Of course, the risks would probably be substantial." Blagden looked to his visitor for reaction.

Brian took a moment to answer. "This all would be contingent upon being able to identify and locate one or more of the names on the counter delivery list and then to get to that person quickly. Otherwise, we haven't got a prayer."

"Yes, of course. But I wouldn't be surprised if some discreet inquiries to the agency, properly phrased, might render the information we need without tipping our hand. That is something else I can do that you cannot."

"I'd feel more secure if we had some independent confirmation," Brian commented.

"So would I. Unfortunately we're in a bit of a bind. The best source for independent confirmation would be Dr. Harley. He's the only one we can identify with some assurance who knew fully what was going on. But we can't touch him at the moment. If he has been working with the enemy, the minute he gets the least little bit suspicious of someone breathing down his neck, he'll be on the next plane to Guy Burgess's flat in Moscow, after first tipping off his masters that you've fingered him."

Brian had thought of that. Like everything else, it all came down to a matter of trust. "I could recruit whoever I felt I needed?" he asked.

"I don't think this is the type of thing you could pull off on your own, even with your resources," Blagden answered. "But if I am not mistaken, SEAL training stresses independent thought and judgment. I would rely completely on yours." Then he added dryly, "I wouldn't have any other choice."

"Give me a number where I can call you," Brian said.

Blagden scribbled the numerals on a blank sheet of notepaper. He handed it to Brian.

Brian rose to his feet and extended his hand across the desk. Blagden stood and reached over to take the proffered hand.

Brian saluted, waited for Blagden to return the salute, then picked up his medical bag and strode quickly and silently out of the office.

23

They were alone in the cabin of the Gulfstream jet; by Brian's reckoning, somewhere over the fields of Kansas. The two pilots were hidden away in the cockpit and had left them alone since shortly after takeoff. Even the flight attendant normally assigned to the plane had been told to stay home this trip.

The plane's interior space consisted of two facing couches with deep, swiveling lounge chairs on either end. A bulkhead behind them separated a small office area with a desk and another chair. And in back of that, toward the rearmost section of the craft, was a small but well-stocked galley. Anything they wanted would be there, they were told, and they should just help themselves.

The decor throughout the plane was designed to create a restful and soothing environment. The colors were subdued, and the materials soft and inviting. Diana felt relaxed, safe, and secure in this cocoon, the safest she could remember feeling since this whole business had begun.

Brian wore a blue blazer and had loosened his tie. He sat in one of the lounge chairs, cradling his second neat Glenmorangie against the occasional turbulence. He hated to think of a drop going to waste. Diana had on her traditional traveling outfit of light sweater and skirt, the one that didn't wrinkle much. Her shoes were somewhere in the cabin, she thought, and she had stretched out the full length of one of the couches.

"I could get used to this kind of luxury," she said. "I can't get over it: a private plane sent especially to carry us across the country."

Brian moved over next to her on the couch. "Didn't I say, 'Stick by me, baby, and you'll go places'?"

She smiled at him and stretched her trim legs out over his lap. "I wasn't sure exactly what you had in mind." With the gentle rush of the jet stream outside the window and the quiet intimacy within, Diana felt removed, almost objective about the situation that brought them here. She began to feel as if she could separate it out in her mind, an interesting medical problem but one happening to someone else.

"So what do you think?" Brian asked, concerned that he had described the meeting to her completely and accurately.

"I agree with you," she said. "That document doesn't sound as if it's talking about a vaccine." She entwined her fingers behind her head. "A vaccine is either a dead or live, attenuated form of a virus that stimulates the immune system to produce protein molecules called antibodies, which bind onto the virus's own protein coat to neutralize it. Then the white blood cells can engulf and destroy it."

"I remember that much from med school," Brian said.

"And my guess from what we've seen and what you found out is that this counter delivery agent must be some greatly attenuated form of the original virus or something very structurally close to it. Think of either the Sabin polio vaccine, which is a laboratory-attenuated form of the live virus, or the smallpox vaccine, which gives the patient a case of the mild cattle disease cowpox and in the process gives immunity against the deadly smallpox. In any case, the one that document described must be of the same antigenetic strain so that it can afford immunity against the original virus inside the fragments."

"Okay, I'm with you so far, but here's the part that's thrown me. A vaccine offers only prophylactic protection, right? Once you get polio, for instance, the vaccine wouldn't help you."

"Right."

"But this document Blagden showed me specifically said that the new agent would interact with the original virus and neutralize it inside the carrier's body. Once the original virus infects the carrier's body, how do they figure the second virus is going to protect the carrier and kill off the original one?"

"That is a tough one," Diana replied. She crossed her legs tightly over Brian's lap and closed her eyes in concentration. She tried to think of everything she knew about virology, like a computer spitting out random bits of information by the thousands until it finally comes up with the one nugget it needs. She knew she would have to think creatively, fitting together disparate concepts, shaping them into a unified theory which explained the seemingly unexplainable.

She ruminated for several minutes. Then she opened her eyes, swung her crossed legs back onto the floor, and stood up. She paced over to the window and gazed for a while at the brownish gray plains passing beneath them. It took a little while longer to be sure she had her logic straight. She held onto the top of the bulkhead as she slowly spoke.

"The late sixties was when scientists first started playing around with the genetic components of viruses, so God knows what they came up with. And we know very little about what the Russian scientists were up to at that time. They may have known exactly what they were doing, or they may have stumbled onto something. But my guess would be that the second virus was cultivated with what we would call a particular tropism, or biochemical attraction, for the material of the stopper. You said that the stopper to the capsules we found was made of some sort of organic material."

"That's right."

"Well, let's say this is a kind of biochemical 'lock and key' situation."

"How do you mean?"

"I'm not exactly sure how it would be triggered. Wait a second now. Okay, say the Ratsbane virus infects the body. Initially it's going to be only a few viral particles. But if this organic material of the stopper is specifically sensitive to that particular virus, it may have been designed so that upon interaction with the virus, the body's complement system disintegrates it and releases the contents—the countervirus—into the body."

"All right. But still, how does that counteract the effects of the first virus?"

"The countervirus is probably packed into its capsule in tremendously greater density, so that millions of the countervirus particles are released to overwhelm and outnumber the original virus. It must have the ability to bond onto the original virus's protein coat and prevent it from entering the cells to reproduce, which means it can use those same cells to reproduce itself. And since it is a variant of the original virus, it should be just as contagious, so it spreads—harmlessly—to everyone the carriers come in contact with. And then it disseminates exponentially from there, until everyone left alive in the so-called target population is immunized."

"Brilliant," Brian said, gazing up at her. "Neat, self-contained, and scientifically elegant."

"Within its own terms, yes," Diana said.

"Why couldn't the Americans think up something like that?"

She grimaced. "We did enough over there as it was."

"So you're finally willing to chalk one up to the friendly Commies then."

She reached over for the sofa cushion to bash him with, but it wouldn't come loose. Instead, she stuck out her finger and held him under the chin, forcing his attention to her. "Like yourself, Dr. Thorpe, I am a scientist. And though, admittedly, I have strong and deeply held political views, I endeavor to keep them separate and distinct from my scientific observations."

"Forgive me," Brian said.

She pushed her finger farther up under his chin, making him rise slightly from the couch. "I'll consider it," she said, reveling in her little display of control.

She let him go, and he slumped back into his seat, picking up his drink from the side table. "But one thing about that, Brian," she said. "If it is the Russians behind this, with as much as we know now, why can't we, or General Blagden, just confront them openly?"

"It's not that simple, I'm afraid. Blagden's right. It is a very delicate issue. The evidence against them is all circumstantial. It would be easy for them to deny. And at the same time, if they wanted to, they could still release the virus through some well-constructed cover. Or they could be backing some international terrorist group. Or worse still, some client government of theirs might have gotten hold of it and themselves given it to terrorists. I can think of ten countries right away that'd jump at the chance. No, I'm afraid the only real solution is to get that countervirus capsule, and get it fast."

"Well," she said, indicating their close confines, "that's why we're here." She sat down opposite him but squirmed around restlessly, unable to come up with a comfortable position. Brian watched her with amusement. "How much longer do we have up here?" she asked.

Brian glanced at the steel Rolex on his wrist. "About two hours."

"I'm getting bored," she said, continuing to squirm.

"I can see that."

Suddenly an idea lit up her face. With the grace of a cat, she slipped down off the cushiony couch. Tigerlike, on all fours, she came across the aisle and knelt in front of Brian. As she looked up at him with her large eyes brimming, she purred, "Have you ever made love in an airplane?"

"I think it's one experience I've missed," he told her.

"Well?"

"What makes you think I'm in the mood?"

"I can put you in the mood," she said, and unzipped his fly.

"You're sure?"

"Sure."

"What makes you think so?"

She reached into his pants and closed her fingers hard enough to make him jump. "What was that quaint little expression you boys in uniform used to use? 'When you've got 'em by the balls, their hearts and minds will follow!'"

BIG SUR, CALIFORNIA

For several miles away on Highway 1 they could see Hugh Stanway's house, perched on an outcropping above the Pacific as if it had grown there.

Diana had come this way often when she'd been at Stanford and in the Public Health Service. To her the Big Sur coast was the perfect meeting of land, sky, and water. For as many miles as she could see in either direction, the green sculptured slopes of the Santa Lucia Range swept down for nearly 1,000 feet to reach their sharp, crooked fingers out into the ocean.

They were driving Stanway's green Range Rover, which had been left for them at the Monterey Airport. In addition to its standard four-wheel-drive capability, the vehicle had been specially converted for expedition use by Overland, Ltd. of Hampshire, England. Diana leaned her head as far out the window as she dared and cast her eyes down to the serpentine shoreline, where the sea was always white and foamy against the jagged rocks. She followed the endless swirls outward, away from the beach, where they gradually turned a deep azure blue. The color grew progressively deeper as the waves were lost beyond the misty horizon that went on without interruption all the way to China. Above, the sky was of a slightly paler blue, as if consciously choosing not to deflect attention from the coast or from its own puffed cotton clouds.

Though she had been through here many times and had marveled at the houses dotting the primeval coastline, Diana had never known anyone fortunate enough to live here. They turned off the narrow highway where the pine trees parted. They found themselves on a one-lane ridge down the crest of the hillside. Just beyond the tire rims the earth fell off steeply on either side. Diana was glad Brian was driving.

Hugh Stanway's house was an A-frame with a soaring roofline of weathered cedar and walls composed of large expanses of glass. It perched on the edge of one of the sweeping Big Sur cliffs. From Diana's vantage point it didn't appear that the rugged, angular structure was terribly large. But even from the road it was easily the most exciting house she had ever come across. Even more than the houses on the other side of the road, higher in the mountains, this one seemed to emerge organically out of the promontory it obstinately hugged. The house at once embodied, through its own apparently precarious existence, the intersection of all the elemental hazards of California life: rampaging forest fire, sudden rock and mud slides, earthquake, thunderstorm, and ocean gale.

This, Diana thought, *is what a SEAL who's made a lot of money does with it.*

They parked the car in the second slot of the garage that had been chiseled out of the cliff. The first slot was occupied by a gleaming metallic brown Rolls-Royce Corniche convertible. A discreet crest bearing the *Men of Action* logo adorned the door.

"There must be a lucrative market for mayhem," Diana commented.

"You should know there is."

Brian picked up their two small suitcases. Together they headed down the stone path into the tropical garden that led to the front door. Diana was the first to see the tall, robust figure emerge into view from the other side. He wore tan khakis and a matching bush shirt with epaulets. Brian spotted him.

The two men approached with measured stride. Wordlessly they threw their arms around each other and slapped their hands hard enough to hurt on each other's shoulders. Diana stood back, silently, as if she would like to fade away for a time. She didn't want to take anything away from the reunion by her presence.

"It's been too goddamned long, you old water rat!" Stanway bellowed. He gazed at Brian, beaming. "So you still have your blond hair and blue eyes and farm boy good looks. I swear, you could have modeled for cornflake ads. And I know that you still have your SEAL tattoo!"

Diana looked at Brian quizzically. She watched them both with fascination, and the emotion she observed in each pair of teary eyes she could describe only as one of love.

Then Stanway turned away from Brian. His reaction to her was not quite so elevated or sublime, she decided.

"And this is Diana," Brian said.

When she was finally introduced, she gazed into those same eyes that a moment before had held such love for Brian, and she could tell he must be speculating what she'd look like naked and posing for one of his violent "action" pictorials. She found it amazing. Back in college, she couldn't have stood even to be around a man like this, and now he was becoming their partner in this bizarre quest.

He stood back for a moment to take her in. "Diana, goddess of the hunt," he proclaimed. "Well"—he slapped Brian on the shoulder and squeezed Diana's hand hard—"let's get to hunting!"

Inside, a short stone hallway led in one direction to the two bedrooms and in the other to the great room—the kitchen, dining area, living space, and den that composed the primary part of the house. There the roof slanted on either side all the way from the oak floor to the triple-story ceiling, which was inset with glass at its peak. The two gable walls were entirely of glass and hummed as the sea wind roared up against them. Each one offered the glorious view of thirty-five miles of untampered California coastline.

They lounged in front of the towering stone hearth, drinking Stanway's expensive brandy. The sounds of the evening were starting to assemble. Chirps, hums, and buzzes surrounded them, hidden in the shrubs and trees just outside the house.

"I wanted to thank you for sending your plane out for us," Brian said.

"Yes, that was extremely gracious of you," Diana added, but the words sounded forced and inappropriate as she heard herself saying them.

"Don't worry about it," said Stanway. From him it sounded like an order.

He stood up and warmed his hands in front of the fire. "So . . . you've obviously gotten bored playing doctor and yearn for the life of action"—he eyed Diana suggestively—"though if this is who you're playing with, I can't see how you could be bored."

"It has nothing to do with that," said Brian.

"Then let me get this straight. You want to stage a raid into Vietnam to capture one of five men who no one's heard from in a decade and a half and bring him back unharmed with the intention of operating on that person and taking a metal capsule out of his gut. Am I stating this fairly?"

"That's essentially it," Brian answered.

"You are, of course, aware that we lost the war and that as a result, Vietnam is currently in the hands of a less than friendly power."

"That had crossed my mind."

"And that you're talking about going into a place where there aren't going to be any standing resources to rely on?"

Brian took another sip of his brandy. "Probably so."

"Who's going to finance this thing?"

"Blagden said he'd try to get me some funds."

"Is he going to get you personnel, too?"

"No."

"Okay, let me ask you another. How much time would we have for planning, training, and recon?"

"Realistically?"

Stanway nodded.

"None."

Stanway tossed off the remainder of his drink in one gulp and swallowed hard. "Great. I see you've thought this out very carefully."

Brian rose and came over to stand next to his host, resting his hand on the roughhewn stone of the chimney. "You know I haven't thought it out carefully, Hugh. I haven't thought it out at all. I know it isn't very practical. But I also know it's something that's got to be done." He leaned over and rested his hands on the back of an easy chair. "And that's why I came to you."

Stanway stared at him for a long time before he spoke. "You're serious, aren't you?" he said at last.

"I'm afraid I have to be."

Stanway crossed over to a bar near the hearth. It was a massive piece of wood, made from an eighteenth-century campaign chest. He refilled his snifter to twice its original contents. "I'm touched, Thorpe. I really am. And you know I'd do anything I could for you, and I know you'd do the same for me."

"But?"

He sat on the bench in front of the fireplace, facing Brian and Diana. He rested his hands on his knees. "Thorpe, over the years, we've learned to play high-stakes poker with very few chips, you and I. But you know there's a reason the SEALs were the most effective unit in Vietnam. And it has nothing to do with that 'hold your hand over the flame' macho horseshit we thought we could impress the *jeunes filles* with." He continued looking straight at them, almost staring them down. "There's a reason why not one SEAL was ever captured during the entire war. It's because we were the best, because we knew and understood our capabilities, and because unlike the poor suckers in the army and marines, we didn't get into situations without a firm idea of what we were trying to do."

As Stanway spoke, a montage of images—memories that twenty years later could still make his mouth dry like shedded snakeskin and the hair stand up on the back of his neck—came rushing back to Brian. There had been the time shortly after they had arrived in-country when their team was ordered by some jerk-off lieutenant to attack a secluded hamlet where a detachment of Vietcong was reputed to be hiding out. There'd been no reliable recon. No one from the field had thought it through. It had looked like a real fishing expedition, designed to make some rear-echelon colonel look good on the body count reports. Stanway had been a chief petty officer back then.

"We don't attack targets like that," he had calmly explained.

"It's not a request; it's an order!" The exasperated lieutenant had erupted.

Stanway had remained unfazed. "You haven't given me a good reason why I should risk fourteen of the best-trained men in the world to take out fifty average VC ruffians." In any other unit that kind of insubordination would have earned him a court-martial. But the idiot lieutenant had been smart enough to know one thing: not to mess with the SEALs.

The best-trained men in the world. It wasn't a phrase any of them had ever used lightly. They'd paid too dearly for that. Brian remembered the day he'd reported to basic underwater demolition school at Coronado. A blue sign at the entrance had welcomed them to the amphibious base with the message PRIDE AND PROFESSIONALISM PREVAILS. Inside, the pride of heritage had been immediately evident all around him. All the streets were named for celebrated naval campaigns: Attu, Guadalcanal, Tarawa, Kwajalein, Inchon. Then he remembered something else. A hundred and sixteen men had reported with him to BUD/S. Twenty-six weeks later thirteen had earned the right to call themselves SEALs. And in those six months they had learned to stretch their resources and endurance beyond even the limits of the imagination. "A man is capable of about ten times as much physical output as is usually thought," the manual had said. Inspite of that, most of the guys Brian knew had been, like him, far from being physical supermen. Most would have rated themselves about a seven out of ten. On average, few of them could have beaten on a marine on points.

But there'd been something in their heads that made them different, something no one had ever quite been able to describe that made them go on when all sense and logic told them to quit. Just to make it to the first cut, they had to run through fourteen miles of soft sand and deep mud in full field packs with live ammunition exploding around them. They had to paddle inflatable rafts upstream fast enough to beat their instructors cruising alongside in power boats. They were tested on their drownproofing techniques by being thrown into the ocean with their hands and feet tied. And after the first four weeks the initial phase of training wrapped up with "Hell Week," a full-scale island attack that demanded and consumed everything the recruit had to give, then demanded twice as much again. During the entire seven days of nonstop physical action and unrelenting mental stress, no one in Brian's team had managed to steal a cumulative seven hours of sleep. No meal that week had lasted more than three minutes.

Then there had been the private demons to overcome. For some guys it was the lonely claustrophobia of deep-water diving at night. For others it was the constant pain and fatigue. Brian had always had a fear of heights. He didn't know where it had come from, maybe from growing up in Indiana, where there wasn't any height to speak of. Whatever it was, it terrified him. When they got to the army jump school at Fort Benning, he couldn't sleep for days. The first time he had to hang out of an airplane going hundreds of miles an hour as the wind tore into his hair had set his heart pounding uncontrollably in his chest. By the end of a week of static line parachuting, he knew he had finally slain his inner dragon, just as the others had eventually mastered theirs.

No wonder, he supposed, that each of the men who finally made it had come away with an incredible confidence in his own capabilities and an unwavering respect and trust in the other members of the team. The idea had been to produce not well-developed bullet stoppers who would march into death unquestioningly but resourceful, independent thinkers—men who could operate with initiative and creativity, even if cut off and alone, under the most trying of conditions.

"If the tire goes flat during a mission and you don't have a spare, you go creative." That was the way they used to describe the difference. And on top of all that, each SEAL had to be able to speak at least one foreign language. In Vietnam days this usually meant French. Then they were taught the intricate principles of Hwarang-Do, the Oriental martial art which emphasizes the offensive, aggressive use of bare hands, knives, clubs, or whatever happened to be available. SEALs got very good at improvisation.

No wonder, he supposed, they all had thought they could do anything.

Brian sat down again and slouched into a casual position. Diana was next to him sitting up, too rigidly, he thought, obviously out of her element.

"All right, I understand where you're coming from, Hugh," he said. "And it all makes sense; I can't deny it. The whole thing doesn't make any sense. But just for the hell of it—so I can make my own decision—if you *were* going to try something like this, how would you pull it off?"

Stanway went to the wood rack and came back with two good-size oak logs. Diana winced as he laid them directly on the burning pile with his bare hands. "Well . . . as I said, we have no resources over there. It's a totally hostile environment. So the key is speed and execution." He looked up toward the glass insert in the roofline, as if he might draw inspiration from the stars. "Westerners stand out there like a boil on a stripper's ass. So the first thing you'd have to do is recruit at least two Vietnamese peasant types living outside the country who could infiltrate a day or so ahead. I'm sure the CIA has lists. Then you'd take a squad of about four of your own men in."

"How would we do it?" asked Brian.

"Your best bet would be a night drop. Insert into a rural area as close to your target as possible. The Viets meet you with, say, motorbikes. Remember, this all has got to be done at night, when your ugly Caucasian faces aren't obvious. If we assume there are no unusual circumstances to be considered, the snatch itself starts out as a standard inland demolition raid. The four guys surround the perimeter, take out guards, and move in. You have claymores available for diversion but hope like hell you don't have to use them, 'cause you'll make enough racket to wake up Ho Chi Minh. Then you get to your target, get him bound and gagged real good, then move out again. The Viets meet you at the perimeter with two or three hay wagons. You get inside, they take you as far as the nearest frontier or realistic landing zone, and you extract by chopper." He raised his refilled glass and pointed it in Brian's and Diana's direction. "To your very good health."

"One other consideration, Hugh."

"What's that?"

"We've got to try to do this dry."

Diana wrinkled her nose in confusion. "What are you talking about? You mean, go in sober?"

"No. He means no blood," said Stanway.

"I thought you SEALs maimed and pillaged wherever you went," Diana replied sarcastically. "I thought it was a point of honor."

"*Au contraire.*" Stanway grinned with pride. "You must have been talking to the Green Berets."

Diana grimaced.

"The best SEAL ops are the ones when no one even knows you've been there," Brian added. He turned to Stanway. "So that's how you would do it," he said.

"*If* it could be done at all," Stanway said.

"I understand. Sure. Let me think a minute. May I have another drink?"

Stanway refilled his glass.

"These other guys I'd need. You'd know where I could pick them up?"

"I could put you in touch with some people."

"Uh-huh. Hmm. And even if we could locate this carrier fairly accurately, you still don't think there'd be much chance of success?"

"It would have to be pulled off like clockwork. No screwups, no hesitation. And if you're still in-country by sunrise, you're all dead men."

"Yes, yes," Brian said. "I can see what you mean. So you wouldn't want to try something like this?"

"It wouldn't be my choice of mission, no."

"But . . . you're more tied into this stuff than I am. So if I did decide to go ahead with it, and if I could locate the capsule carrier, could I ask you to make some of the necessary . . . arrangements?"

Stanway set his glass down on the bar. "You're really going to go through with this, aren't you?"

Brian nodded. "And I know it isn't for you. But whatever help you could give me, I'd certainly appreciate."

The two men stared at each other for what seemed to Diana like several minutes. The wind off the ocean seemed to grow louder to fill in the silence. Finally Stanway picked up his glass again, turned, and slung it into the hearth. It shattered against the jagged rock, making Diana jump from her place. "Fuck yourself, Thorpe!" he roared. "You know I'm not going to let you go in there on your own. You're good, but you aren't *that* good. If you're that determined to get your ass shot off, I'm going to be there to watch it happen."

"Then you're in?"

Stanway returned a sour expression. "Don't give me any of your shit, blondie. And don't think you've been playing to my ego. I've always been able to see through you. You know I'm in. You knew it right from the beginning."

Brian fell silent. As he had throughout their friendship, he knew now better than to try to thank him.

"Two things, Thorpe," he added.

"Anything you say, Hugh."

"Number one, I finance this mission. This is our show, and we take no outside advice or government blood money. Number two, If we get out of this alive, or even if we don't, I get exclusive rights to the story."

Brian broke out in a broad grin and lifted his glass in salute. "You got 'em, chief."

There was another long silence, broken finally by Diana. "I can't believe we're actually going to Vietnam!" she said in amazement.

"*We're* going to Vietnam." Stanway corrected her. "*You're* staying right here under armed guard until we get back."

"But—but that's not fair!" She looked to Brian for support, but he only nodded his assent to Stanway's decree. "I won't do it!" she said insistently.

"It's not a question of fair," Brian said sharply. "And you *will* stay here if we tell you to, even if I have to tie you. It's the only way we can be sure you're safe."

"You'd like that, wouldn't you?" she retorted.

Brian pursed his lips in exasperation. "We're talking about a secret paramilitary operation into a hostile country. You aren't trained or in any way equipped to participate. You'd be a tremendous burden."

"I would not be!" Diana folded her arms across her chest and pouted. She was emphatically opposed to the idea of anything that violated her ideal of pacifism. But she also knew she wasn't suited to the role of Achaean woman, waiting patiently for her warrior to return from the bloody fields of Troy.

Despite Diana's own discomfiture, the agreement on the mission seemed to lift the blanket of tension between the two men. They spent the rest of the evening raising their glasses and reminiscing about the old days, while Diana kept to herself, curled into a ball at the end of the couch. Much as she hated to admit it, the more she heard about their times together in the filthy, steaming jungles, the more she had to conclude that Brian and Hugh were right: She wasn't equipped for it. But that didn't mean she couldn't be resentful just the same. And if it did, she didn't care. And she still hated the idea of being held prisoner.

Later that night she lay in bed next to Brian, staring up at the darkly glimmering shapes the moonlit ocean projected onto the ceiling. "How come when people like Hugh say how much they hate war, you just don't believe they really mean it?" She sat up and clasped her hands around her knees. "When he was describing all the killing, it wasn't horror. It was more like melancholy, melancholy tinged with nostalgia."

"It's a complex set of emotions," Brian responded. "I don't know if I can explain it to you. The war was rotten, and everything that happened there was rotten." He thought about the unconscious nineteen-year-old marine who'd been medevacked with a live three-inch-long mortar shell buried in his skull. The neurosurgeons were afraid the shell might explode in the OR if they tampered with it. After some agonized but quick discussions back and forth, they called the bomb disposal unit, which took him out into a field, attached plastic explosives to his scalp, and detonated. There wasn't much left when they came back from the bunker to clean up.

"But you're still glad you went," said Diana.

"But I'm—I'm not completely sorry I went."

"And you're not sorry you're going back."

"No, that's not true. I'm too old for this kind of nonsense. Plus I'm nervous about it. We aren't as prepared as we should be, and we're out of condition besides." He turned to her. "But why do you get such a warm glow when you talk about taking over buildings and pelting cops with bricks and bottles?"

"It's not exactly the same," she protested. "That was the era of 'Make love, not war.' And you know which side I was on."

"Maybe we all were excessive back then."

"Maybe so." She hesitated for a moment, then said, "But I'll bet you've killed more people than I . . . loved."

Brian looked at her dubiously. "I hardly think so. You've been reading too many comic books."

"You SEALs must have been mean mothers."

He laughed, then evaluated this, nodding and arching his eyebrows. "I'd certainly lock up my daughter when guys like us were around."

Diana laughed, too. She couldn't believe this coming from him. Whatever he was, a wild hellion he was not. But then she considered the conversation of the evening and recalled the interaction between Brian and his old comrade. There was a whole side of him that she really didn't know, that she never really could know without going through the same crucible of experience. She thought back to the tavern in Montana. She had not been watching someone in his first bar fight.

"Something I've never asked you," she said. "Why did you become a SEAL?"

In one form or another how many times had he asked himself the same question? He turned over onto his side and propped his head on his bended arm. "It's like when you asked about having any fond memories of war," he said. "I'm not sure I know the answer. All I can give you are abstract concepts."

"You mean, like duty, honor, country?"

"I guess. But I don't think I was focusing on things like that back then. It was probably more of direction, purpose, belonging."

"There are easier ways to belong, Brian. Look what I did."

"I was in college for two years before I joined the navy. I guess at that age you can go with either side. I wasn't all that impressed with what I saw on the other side."

"But you were with the military, at least with the SEALs."

"With the SEALs I guess it was the sense of belonging to something where everyone else had proved the same intense level of commitment you had."

"And it was the commitment itself that was important, rather than what it was directed toward."

Brian shrugged. "I thought so at the time."

"And now?"

"And now it's a habit. Just like yours."

"There's another thing," she said. "After your SEAL tours, after finishing college, I never understood why you went back to Vietnam voluntarily as a medic."

"Neither did Lizzie."

"And yet you married each other anyway as soon as you got back home."

"Yeah. Life is like that."

"And now you're forty-two years old and you're still prepared to go out there and risk your life for something that isn't even your responsibility, that just fell in your lap."

Brian didn't respond.

"Does it have anything to do with meeting the middle-aged crisis head-on?"

"I don't think so."

"I knew a guy once who parachuted out of an airplane on his fortieth birthday just to prove he wasn't getting old."

"That's a good way to *insure* you'll never get old," Brian commented.

"But isn't that part of it?"

"Not for me. I told you that I *was* too old for this. I've already proved everything on that score I care to."

Maybe that finally had something to do with the SEAL mystique, Diana thought. "Then tell me the truth. Why are you doing this?"

"Because I can't see any way out," he said flatly. "I don't know how to say it plainer than that. There are certain things you do, not because you want to, or even want to prove yourself trying, but because you won't be able to live with yourself afterward and think of yourself as the same kind of person if you don't."

"What's it like, getting ready for a mission?" she asked.

"A lot of work."

"No, I mean, emotionally."

"I'm not sure I remember."

"I can't believe that's the kind of thing you ever forget."

"I can only tell you what it was like back then."

"That'll do."

He wasn't quite looking at her and not quite looking away. He was focused somewhere in the dark middle distance. "Well," he said, "when you're planning, the fear comes in for the first time and it just sort of lingers, stays with you, holing up in some small corner of your brain. Then you get on the boat, or the plane, or sometimes even the truck. And then the op starts, and you're so preoccupied with what you're doing that the training takes over again. You become a problem solver, and if there's any room left over in your brain, it isn't devoted to being scared anymore, but to something that just keeps saying, 'Please God, don't let me fuck up.'

"Then the action begins, and you don't think of anything . . . until there's a lull, even a tiny lull. That's when the panic hits you. You start sweating. You have trouble breathing. And you don't see how you can go on. You're sure you're going to throw up or shit in your pants, and you're sure that everyone else can look at your face and see exactly how you're feeling. And they can, too."

She asked in a hushed voice, "Then what happens?"

"Then, all at once, you somehow click back into what you were conditioned and prepared to do. It's like a reflex, and suddenly you're very grateful for all the agonies of training because you realize that it's the only thing getting you through.

"Then the mission's over. You get back into a sanitized area, and you think about what you've done. That's when the fear comes back and the cycle starts again. If you'd had a bad op or something about it's been unsuccessful, the fear intensifies. And if you've personally had something happen to you during the operation, it can become terror, awesome terror. That's what you work in inside until the mission."

Underneath the blanket Diana could feel the perspiration forming around her own sensitive areas. "Thank you for sharing that with me," she whispered. A kind of desperate love she'd forgotten she was capable of flooded through her. She laid her head back down on the pillow and waited for the intensity of the moment to pass. It took a long time before it did, and in that time neither said anything.

With time, finally, to think and consider, Brian reflected on how he felt about going back to Nam. Back to that bloody, leech-infested mudhole. Because no matter what the country had since become, he knew that was how he would always think of it. This would be his fourth trip—two SEAL tours and one as a medic. He remembered his last time back, talking in a Dong Ha bar to a SEAL he'd served with, who was on his fifth tour in-country. "I'm starting to get nervous this time around," the guy had told him. "Comes a point when the law of averages starts catching up." That was the last time Brian saw him. Now he was no more than a memory and a name on the black granite wall.

You've done your flirting with the odds, too, he told himself. Maybe he should forget about this. Fate is only so forgiving. Then he reflected on the alternative. It wasn't as if he'd asked for this plum assignment or that he'd be safe and sound just sitting here. If he didn't go, the odds would inevitably catch up with him, and soon . . . along with everybody else.

Diana broke into his morbid brooding. "Do you ever think about what it would have been like to go into private practice?" she asked.

"Not very often," Brian answered.

"Have a nice, secure practice in the big city, maybe one of

those East Fifty-seventh Street groups in Manhattan. You could have been taking out gallbladders. I could have been treating pompous society ladies with the sniffles, rake in the cash, have partners to cover, not have people shooting at us or trying to rape me or put bombs in your car. You know, that sort of thing."

Brian laughed. With his free hand he tenderly brushed back her long dark hair. "You know, if I'd met someone like you earlier in my life, I might not have gone off to war."

"I wish I could believe that. You probably would have hated me and everything I stood for."

"You may be right." He tossed it off lightly, continuing to stroke her silky hair.

"Anyway, I'm glad I didn't know you back then."

Brian's smile faded. "Why is that?"

"Because I would have worried for you. The way I'm worried for you now." She rolled over onto her side and buried her face in his shoulder.

Brian gripped the side of her head and pulled her close. At one time, a time that now seemed very long ago, he had comforted himself with the belief that this stage of his life was behind him. Now he had begun to suspect it never would be.

The Big Sur house seemed altogether different after dark. The magnificent landscape had vanished into blackness, giving Diana the sensation of floating through ether as she drifted off to sleep. She didn't dream that night.

The blackness was still enveloping them when the loud crack sounded.

Brian awoke instantly and was instantly alert. Diana awoke slowly, her face puffy from sleep and her eyes unfocused. Brian bolted up from the mattress, instinctively ready to spring.

Hugh Stanway, fully dressed, stood in the doorframe. The door was touching the wall and still shuddering slightly from the force with which he had flung it open. When his presence in the room finally registered on Diana, she quickly pulled the blanket up over her breasts.

Stanway didn't bother apologizing for the intrusion. He took it all as a matter of course. "I just got a phone call," he announced. "The Vietnam mission is off."

Brian looked at him attentively, an expression of perplexity beginning to show on his face. "What's happened?"

"My people have located one of the carriers on your list. Nguyen Tien Truong. He's in Paris. That's a whole new can of worms. We have to start planning first thing in the morning."

Diana shot up in bed onto her knees, the blanket not quite keeping pace. "I'm going with you!" Her tone was aggressively insistent, but her bright blue eyes were wide with pleading.

Brian and Stanway exchanged glances.

"You have to take me with you!" she went on, her eyes darting from one of them to the other. "You can't deny a girl a trip to Paris!"

24

It was a vestige left over from his young manhood. The night before any critical mission Brian had always had two dreams. In one, the operation would go well, and he would rise to the challenge facing him. In the other, it would fall apart, and he would fail his own image of himself. The actual missions, when they happened, were often no more vivid in real life than the twin visions of triumph and despair which had preceded them. So that whatever chanced to happen in this uncertain and capricious universe, Brian Thorpe was psychically prepared.

Reveille was at 0600 or, by Diana's bleary-eyed calculation 6:00 A.M. The sun was still low in the sky and shimmered on the calm surface of the Pacific like a sheet of silver. She thought she'd slept an actual total of maybe forty-five minutes since they'd been awakened in the middle of the night. Her hair still in tangles and wearing Brian's C-4 shirt and her own hiking shorts, she stumbled into the kitchen, where Stanway was serving a breakfast of mountain trout, thick slab bacon, and huge buttermilk biscuits. He and Brian seemed full of unnatural morning cheer, and her first instinct was to bite off the head of anyone who so much as offered her a "good morning." But she was sufficiently coherent to sense that she'd pay for any emotional indulgences. These men perceived that she was still earning her right to be among them.

"She looks like she gets dangerous around feeding time," Stanway commented.

Never corner a hungry bear, Diana remembered from Montana, *because there's nothing it can do then but attack.* She stifled the urge to respond and instead smiled back as sweetly as her morning face would permit.

She attacked everything set out on her plate. She knew it wasn't ladylike to eat with such abandon, especially this early in the morning, and for a little while she tried to rein herself in. But the strain and the fatigue and the combination of the sea breeze with the cool, crisp mountain air had made her ravenous. And as she finally looked up from the last of her fish, she was sure she detected admiration on the faces of her two companions. It dawned on her that every minute she was being tested and evaluated.

"I see you approve of the chow in this outfit," said Stanway as he tossed his dishes onto the wooden drainboard.

She swallowed the last bite and wiped her mouth. "Yes. Thank you. It's very good." There was no reason she couldn't be gracious and polite.

"Good. Now that you've got your strength, let's go to work! We've got too much to do." He raised his open left hand. She thought he was going to slap her on the shoulder the way he did with Brian. She tried not to cringe. Instead, he put his hand on the middle of her back and guided her into the hallway, with Brian following right behind.

At the end of the hallway was a circular staircase that Diana hadn't noticed before. Stanway led them both down and into a room with no windows. She hadn't realized there was a floor below the main one. Then, from the one unfinished wall, she could see that the room was below the groundline and had been carved out of solid rock. It looked nothing like the rest of the house. Bright fluorescent lights were recessed into the acoustically tiled ceiling. There was a heavy oak table in the center of the room. A pin map of the world covered one wall.

"I call this the situation room," Stanway explained. He gave them a brief tour, supplemented with commentary primarily aimed at Diana. "Special operations aren't like normal military exercises and can't successfully follow the normal command structure. Unfortunately there's no such thing as a foolproof mission. But the way to raise your odds is that the man who plans and organizes the mission also leads it. He's the one who has to make all the split-second decisions, based on firsthand input, not transmitted reports. That's the extra measure of safety and precision we work with."

"What Hugh's telling you," said Brian in translation, "is that he's in charge. As I keep telling you, this isn't a game. Once we're in the field, you're allowed to voice your own opinion, but voice it short and sweet, and do what you're told."

"Yes, sir." She saluted. Brian swatted her playfully on the backside in response. But she was suddenly seized with the dynamics of her current situation. Once you were placed in a certain environment, it was amazing how quickly you could become conditioned to taking orders, she thought. Hers was not the only mass movement of the sixties. She was finally beginning to understand how the army had gotten all those kids to become cannon fodder.

Stanway turned his attention to Brian. "I'd prefer to do this op with SEALs. Since for obvious reasons we can't, I'll take the next best thing: former SEALs like you."

As if on cue, there was a knock at the door. "Enter," Stanway ordered. Two men appeared. Diana wondered how they had gotten into the house. The first thing she noticed, for some reason, was that they both were wearing star sapphire rings identical to those that Brian and Stanway wore.

Before she had time to wonder about anything else, the two of them had embraced Brian and hugged him tight. It was a replay of his reunion with Hugh Stanway.

"God, it's been too long!" Brian said. That seemed to be the prevailing sentiment among reunited SEALs.

They both were quite attractive, she thought, probably in their early forties and about Brian's height and build. One had green eyes, a strong, triangular-shaped jaw, and moderately long, wavy brown hair. The other's hair was clipped into a neat, moderate-length Afro of the kind not seen too much these days. He had the kind of rugged, angular good looks that reminded her of Huey Newton at the height of his Panther days. It made her nostalgic—in the same strange way, she guessed, Brian and Stanway had been about the war. She casually wondered how this man would look in a black beret.

"Lest the racial and ethnic stereotypes be perpetuated," Stanway went on, "let me now assure you that the SEALs are an equal-opportunity employer." He indicated the first man, standing right next to him. "Epstein, here, is Jewish."

"I see," Diana responded, not knowing what else to say.

"And Rowland, here, is black."

"I kind of guessed that," she said.

"I told you she was bright," Stanway said to the newcomers.

"Hi. Mark Epstein." The first man extended his hand. "And this is Ernest Rowland."

"Pleased to meet you," Rowland said, offering his hand.

"The pleasure is mine," Diana said.

"These guys both served with us," Brian told her.

"I can tell you're surprised to see a black SEAL," Rowland said.

"There aren't many of them," Epstein added. "You see, they do fine in the Green Berets and the Rangers. But for some reason, when they get underwater, most of the brothers be sinkers."

"Whereas my friend Epstein comes from the long, proud tradition of great, famous Jewish swimmers and jumpers," Rowland declared. "And my people generally do better during the training."

"Oh, yeah? Why's that?" Epstein asked him.

"Because we're more used to putting up with shit than white folk."

Diana smiled. In strange way, with the addition of these two, it was starting to be like the old days. Then she began to wonder where they'd come from. Where do you get men like this on such short notice, men with these skills, willing to risk their lives out of loyalty to someone else?

Stanway seemed to anticipate her question. "In the real world one of these guys is an accountant."

Diana looked to Epstein.

"No," Stanway said. "You see, even you liberals are prisoners of preconceived mind-sets." Diana shifted her gaze to Rowland, who flashed a grin at her. "He's my personal accountant," Stanway continued. "And since he got out, Epstein has owned and run a printing business in San Francisco. Among his many other clients is *Men of Action*."

So this is how it's done, Diana said to herself, though she wasn't surprised. That sense of loyalty and interdependence extended even to here. Whenever possible, on whatever level, deal only with the people you know you can trust. It was a creed they all lived.

"I asked Rowland to pick up some ordnance maps of Paris and surroundings," Stanway said. He spread the first one out on the table. "Before we do anything else, let's get oriented."

The three other men gathered around him. Diana followed.

"Not you."

Her feelings were instantly stung. She felt just like the "different" kid at school who can't achieve acceptance, no matter what she does. She blinked back her first tears. But as she looked at him, Stanway's expression was not domineering, nor was it unkind.

"We can't make up completely for thirty-five misspent years in twenty-four hours, but I want you to read and study this. There'll be a quiz at seventeen-thirty. Passing is ninety-nine percent. If you fail, you don't get dinner."

He handed her a thick, oversize tan paperbound volume. The heavy black lettering on its cover spelled out:

UNITED STATES NAVY

SEA-AIR-LAND FORCES

COMBAT MANUAL

(*Use Restricted*)

The sacred text. Her first step into the brotherhood. She opened the cover and scanned the table of contents. "Do you have one of these?" she asked Brian.

"Somewhere," he replied. "Only I'm sure Hugh's is the latest edition. In fact, I think he wrote part of it. But unlike him, I haven't needed mine in a while."

She ignored this and said, "You never showed it to me."

"For what purpose? You've proved yourself capable of getting into enough trouble on your own."

With mock solemnity, Stanway said to her, "Keegan, you're neither an officer nor a gentleman. But you've got to swear on your word of honor that if you ever go back to taking over buildings or protesting against the United States government, you'll never use any of the techniques you learn here."

"I swear," she answered, and impulsively kissed him on the cheek.

"Well, that's going to shoot command discipline all to hell," Epstein remarked.

Diana retired to the corner to immerse herself in the manual while the four men stood around the table. "Anything you don't understand in there or any questions you have, just holler," Stanway told her.

"Thanks," she said. And after a little while she called over, "Will we be carrying guns?"

"You mean rifles and/or sidearms?" Stanway said gruffly.

She couldn't tell if he was being serious. "Yes. I'm sorry. What's the difference?"

"Big difference."

Brian, Rowland, and Epstein all grinned in anticipation as Stanway pointed down near the crotch of his trousers and recited the age-old marine DI's rhyme:

This *is your rifle, and* this *is your gun.*
The one is for killing; the other's for fun.

The four men waited for her reaction.

She swallowed the feminist torrent that came immediately to mind. She wouldn't give them the satisfaction. "You guys are a real stitch." It looked as if there were a little more to being part of the circle than she'd originally thought.

"To answer your question," Stanway said, "we will have the benefit of armament, but we dearly hope not to use it. Now, back to the book," he commanded.

She buried her nose in the text. Without looking up, she overheard the leader saying, "On that issue Thorpe has stated his preference that this be a dry op. Forgetting the moral considerations as we must at this stage of planning, I am inclined to agree with him. Even if we could muster sufficient firepower to blast our way out, this isn't an analogous situation to Nam or any other war zone. We can't call in choppers and blow anyone away. Working clandestinely in a friendly country places us under certain constraints. Any overt incident blows us out of the water. We don't want anyone to know we've been there till we're out."

He walked over to a flip chart on which he'd drawn a time line down the side of the first sheet. Along the top axis he'd written each of their names. "I will arrive at Le Bourget on a private plane, with the announced purpose of raising funds overseas. The rest of you will travel commercially, two to Orly and two to Charles de Gaulle. You'll each have one stopover on the way. Epstein will use his Swiss passport. No one, least of all the French, questions the Swiss. Rowland will carry a Belgian passport. Keegan carries her passport with her, so she'll use her own. Thorpe doesn't, which is just as well, because I don't want him traveling under his own name. He's been the point man, and someone could recognize him. Instead, we'll have false navy orders made up for an assumed name and give him enough fake identification to verify it. Epstein, make sure you get a photo of him this afternoon."

"I could get court-martialed for this," Brian said.

"Not if they don't find out," said Stanway. "And if they do, you'd better hope your buddy General Black Jack Blagden is on the level and can pick up the pieces."

They worked through until lunch, which they ate out on the deck, overlooking the Pacific, 600-odd feet below. There was a thick beef stew made with giant fresh vegetables that looked as if they'd been picked that morning. Diana couldn't figure out where all the food was coming from. Did Stanway have a cook hidden away somewhere? Knowing him as she was beginning to, she did not find that beyond the realm of possibility. Who knew who—or what—else he had hidden here? Yet it all seemed unreal. In this idyllic setting, with the blessings of nature so evident all around them, it was hard for Diana to remember that they were planning what amounted to an international kidnapping. The adventures of Diana among the trained killers.

Every time she'd opened her mouth to ask a question, she'd weighed her words carefully, lest she appear to the others as the outsider she actually was. But now was a good time. Everyone seemed pleasant and jovial. It was a welcome break from the relentless pressure of the situation room.

"You've been doing a lot of planning," she said. "Are we going to do any physical training or practice, too?"

"What do you have in mind?" Rowland asked. "Rappeling into the ocean with grappling hooks?"

She smiled innocently. "I don't know. Maybe."

Stanway looked up from his stew. "There's too little time to take care of every contingency. We have to spend whatever time we have planning. Also, I don't want to take a chance destroying the fragile confidence of these aging gentlemen. At one time they were all highly trained. I hope that when push comes to shove—

and I guarantee you, mateys, it will—it'll all come back to them."

"What about me?" Diana asked.

Stanway leaned back on the bench that ran the length of the deck railing. He gazed up at the hills beyond the highway and looked completely comfortable slouching against the hard cedar slats, completely in his element. "Back in World War Two, for some of the missions behind enemy lines, the only way to get the commandos in was by night parachute drop. Now I don't suppose you've ever parachuted—"

Diana shook her head no emphatically.

"—but I can tell you that a night drop, particularly in hostile, unfamiliar territory, is one of your more arduous tasks in the sphere of military science. Anyway, after they'd trained a bunch of these guys who'd never jumped before, they started compiling statistics. And they found that a novice's chance of some injury on a first jump was about fifty percent. Over two jumps it rose to about eighty percent. So they decided the odds were better overall if the first jump was the real thing." His gaze traveled down from the hills and fixed on Diana. "Does that answer your question?"

"I think it does," she said nervously. She was glad that at least she'd kept up with her running.

In the afternoon the focus in the situation room shifted to the specifics of their target. Diana, Brian, and their two companions sat in a row of folding chairs. Stanway dimmed the lights and turned on a slide projector. A fuzzy image appeared on the screen at the end of the room. It was a newspaper photograph, not in sharp focus, and made blurrier by being blown up many times. Diana had to concentrate hard on taking in the entire image, or the component dots that made it up threatened to take over.

"This is the only photograph we could locate of Nguyen Tien Truong." Stanway lectured them. "Unfortunately it's about ten years old, taken from a Parisian newspaper." It showed a slim, benign-looking man in his early to mid-forties. He had a high forehead and heavily lidded eyes, as if already weary of the ongoing struggle.

While the others stared at the screen, Stanway briefed them from a sheet of typed notes. "In a way Truong was an extraordinary choice to be one of the carriers in that his political orientation was always questionable."

"How do we know this?" asked Rowland.

"Company documents," Stanway replied. "One of my sources over there briefed me early this morning. The agency has a long file on him. He comes from a prominent Vietnamese Catholic family and was well educated. He learned to speak several languages. Ostensibly, according to the records, Truong was a prosperous restaurateur in Saigon with ties to the South Vietnamese and Hanoi governments. However, he was also known to be an independent. He served a brief jail term in 1962 for activities opposing the Diem regime. It's not clear how or why he got out. There were also strong rumors that at the time of our interest—namely, the late sixties—he was a counteragent for the North Vietnamese. These rumors were never confirmed, but it's likely neither side trusted him for very long because around the time of Ratsbane there are reports of his being briefly in both North *and* South Vietnamese prisons."

"Figure that one out," Rowland said.

Stanway continued. "Shortly before the fall of Saigon—six days, to be specific—Truong smuggled himself out of the country. The first conclusion the agency came up with at the time was that he had been found out by the Thieu regime, which by this point was understandably paranoid, terrified, and vindictive as hell, and that he was escaping for his life. This being the case, though, the logic was that he should have surfaced in the North or come back to Saigon after the Communist victory, as so many of the underground people did. This never happened, though.

"There is a period of almost two years that is unaccounted for, and the next place he's known to have turned up is Paris. Paris is a natural magnet for Vietnamese expatriates. It's a beautiful, cosmopolitan city, and they can feel at home in the French culture, which was ingrained during centuries of colonial rule in Indochina. Also, the French are known to be tolerant of minorities and easily accepting of differences among people."

Stanway clicked the projector. A second image appeared on the screen: a building façade, three stories high, with a glass-fronted ground floor and a bright awning. Café tables and chairs were crowded onto the sidewalk in front. This image was also in black and white, but much brighter and sharper than the first photograph. "This picture is more recent. It was taken the day before yesterday at my request and transmitted by wire to my office in San Francisco. It's a restaurant Truong owns and runs, called La Fin du Tunnel, or the End of the Tunnel."

"Guy's got a great sense of humor," said Epstein.

"It's located on the Île Saint-Louis, not far from Notre Dame Cathedral. The establishment is known to be a meeting place for Southeast Asian refugees and expatriates of all political stripes. It's quite possible that he's using his place and influence to organize something from the outside, much the way Ho Chi Minh did when he was haunting the Left Bank in the 1930s."

"Maybe that's our key," said Brian.

"That's what I'm thinking," replied Stanway. "Whenever you find a weak spot, exploit it for all it's worth."

By dinnertime Diana was again famished. Porterhouse steak, baked potato, broccoli, and garden salad had been laid out on the antique refectory table in the dining room. Each piece of china bore the crossed-swords logo of *Men of Action*. But as she approached the table to pick up her plate, Stanway put his hand on her shoulder to stop her.

"Not so fast."

"What's wrong?" she asked, suddenly alarmed.

"The quiz."

"Oh, Jesus. You're not serious, are you?" She looked for support to the other three, who were trying mightily to keep straight faces.

"I can't afford not to be serious when lives are at stake," Stanway replied. "And I can't afford to tolerate insubordination."

Diana sighed and blew a bothersome wisp of hair away from her face.

A few minutes later the four men were seated on both sides of the table with their heaping plates in front of them. Diana stood at the end with her feet apart and hands clasped behind her back, like a schoolgirl put on the spot or a doctoral candidate defending her dissertation.

Stanway motioned to Brian. "Professor . . ."

Brian looked squarely at Diana, doing nothing to alleviate her awkwardness. "What is the prime SEAL mission?"

"To get behind enemy lines, disrupt operations and communications, gather intelligence, and organize resistance."

"What are the method and technique when facing a larger unit?" asked Epstein.

"To combine superior training and discipline with the element of surprise to hit a much larger unit, annihilate or deplete its ranks, and then withdraw before a greater enemy response can be organized."

"What are the four key components of hand-to-hand combat?" Stanway called out. He wasn't using any text for reference.

"Making use of any available weapon, attacking aggressively by using your maximum strength against your enemy's weakest point, maintaining your balance and destroying your opponent's balance, and using your opponent's momentum to your advantage."

"Very good!" exclaimed Rowland.

She breathed a sigh of relief.

"During an inland demolition raid what are the important factors in stalking a sentry?"

Diana closed her eyes in concentration for a moment and silently counted off on her fingers. "Get as close as possible to the sentry before attacking him; kill him swiftly and silently before he has the opportunity to alert others."

Rowland and Epstein broke out in spontaneous applause. Brian came over and kissed her.

Holy Christ, she couldn't believe she was actually saying this, talking about hand-to-hand combat and taking out sentries. What would the Diana of the movement days have said? Of all the topics Stanway could have selected, she knew he'd carefully chosen these questions for just such an effect.

He handed her a loaded dinner plate. "Congratulations, Keegan. We might just make a killer out of you yet."

Diana wasn't quite sure whether to swell her chest with pride or go drown herself in the Pacific.

Long after dark, when they were alone in their room, Diana said to Brian, "How could you let him put me through that humiliating ordeal?"

"You wanted this, baby," Brian said. "No one forced you. And if you want something, you've got to be willing to pay the dues. Anyway, you earned Hugh's and everyone else's respect, so what are you complaining about?"

"There's got to be a more dignified and humane way to do it," she replied.

"There isn't any," he told her.

She realized she had been concentrating so intently all day on the details of the mission that she'd completely blocked out the deadly, devastating virus and the reason for the trip. When it came back to her, she involuntarily shuddered. Brian held her hand in his.

"Are you glad I'm going along?" she asked.

He stared moodily into space. "Objectively I still think it's dangerous, foolhardy, and stupid."

"Okay then. Subjectively."

"Subjectively ... I'm very glad," he said. He hugged her to him and held her, as if he could not bear ever to let her go.

He fell asleep before she did. She looked at him awhile in the flickering half-light. He seemed almost as peaceful as a baby. He had been through this before. So had all the others, all the others but her. She began thinking about what Brian had said the night before—the emotional stages you go through preparing for a mission, identifying each one in her mind. Her mouth was dry. Her tongue felt like sandpaper. She bit her lower lip. She turned onto her side and put her hand comfortingly between her legs. And for the first time in her life Diana Keegan thought she knew what real fear was all about.

In the morning Epstein and Rowland were gone. "They've taken off already," Stanway explained. "We'll all meet up again over there." He picked up his custom-made leather rucksack. "Well ... strap your brass balls on, and let's get at it." Diana and Brian picked up their bags.

Stanway led them out through the underground tunnel to the garage. They went over to the Range Rover.

"No," said Stanway. "We'll take the Rolls. We might as well go in style."

They climbed in, Stanway in the driver's seat and Brian in the seat next to him, Diana in the rear. She all but sank into the luxurious tan Connolly leather. This supreme luxury seemed such a crazy anomaly when she thought about what they were setting out to do. Stanway brought the engine to life and backed the large vehicle nimbly out of the gravel driveway.

Once on Highway 1, he immediately put the top down and

pressed the accelerator pedal to the floor. Diana could feel the wind whipping her hair about her face and whistling past her ears. She should have known Stanway would drive like this. She only hoped they'd make it to Monterey, much less to France. Brian didn't seem to mind. *This must be another thing he's used to*, she thought.

Stanway himself didn't seem troubled either. She sensed that once he could become active and get on with it, he banished all his fears and doubts to a remote region of his brain.

Instinctively he confirmed this for her. He deftly pulled the car out of a high, steep hairpin turn and opened up the throttle on the brief straightaway.

"Lafayette, here we come!" he yelled out with all the exuberance of a child.

25

It was the best time to work, late at night, when it was finally quiet. Of course, the shop never really shut down, and activity never completely halted. But most of the support staff had gone home, and the endless round of meetings and interfaces had temporarily stopped. And it was better than the postdawn early morning, when all those eager-faced young analysts scampered into work, to be the very first on their corridors to behold the overnight cable traffic, as if this somehow put them a leg up not only on the rest of the world but on all the other eager-faced analysts trying to push their interpretations before their stern-faced branch chiefs.

Michael Swansea sat at the desk and stared at the single-page list in front of him. It was the original of which Calvin Harley had been given a copy. In retrospect, Swansea wished he could have controlled all the tangible evidence. But then he always did.

With a blue pencil he had checked off the various names and organized them into the proper categories. Abraham, Fletcher, Jacobs, O'Brien, Shapiro, Washington: unaccounted for, despite Swansea's best efforts. Craig, Davis, Hardesty, Jefferson, Lofton, Schuyler: dead. Dantley, Moreland: accounted for. *Strange about Moreland. He just disappears. Then ten days after the shooting he turns up in the charity ward of Bellevue. No one, including the staff, has any idea how he got there. Created quite a stir for a while. Better lie low on him for a while; the exposure's too great at the moment. Dantley is contained, off by himself. Not likely to cause any problem. More important to deal with Thorpe first.*

Then there was the Counter Delivery Force. That was a tougher one. You had to expect that, though. They weren't our own people, and the control over them to begin with was tangential at best.

Ever since Thorpe began closing in on the puzzle, Swansea had been crunching those five names through every available data bank in the entire intelligence community. He'd gone through the deputy director of administration to get the highest priority; he hadn't wanted to do that. And then he'd gone outside the agency itself; he wanted to do that even less.

No one had any idea where these five people were today . . . if they were, today, anywhere at all.

Finally, this morning, a teletype printout had been left on his desk. It was a standard response to a request for information he'd filed with Interpol. He'd made it all seem routine, sending in about sixty names to the locator section at world headquarters in St.-Cloud, outside Paris. Most of the names he'd submitted were people he already knew about, and he quickly dismissed them. And of the five counter delivery carriers, Interpol had no line on four of them. But on the fifth he struck gold. Nguyen Tien Truong, according to the last sighting, was right there in Interpol's backyard, right there in Paris. Swansea wouldn't have been surprised if after talking to Blagden, Thorpe was on his way there right now. That is, if he'd been able to locate Truong. If Swansea, with all the resources at his disposal, had been unable to locate any of the others, there was no reason to conclude that Thorpe could either. And the odds were long that he wasn't even as far along as Swansea on Truong. But the odds weren't long enough, not for this kind of work. If Truong had surfaced, it was possible that Thorpe could find out about him. And then there were the reports he'd been getting from Background. If the Soviets got a handle on this thing, they'd blow it clear out of the water. Since Afghanistan they'd been looking for something like this to take the international heat off them. And ever since that meeting with Background at Dulles Airport, Swansea knew he'd been racing against time.

He picked up the secure phone and dialed Amber. It wouldn't

matter whether he was home or not. Wherever he was, the sig-
naler would go off and he'd call back within minutes.

And he did. "What's up?" he asked his chief without bothering
with time-consuming preliminaries.

"You've been working hard lately," Swansea told him, "and I
think you could use a change of pace. So you and I are going to
take a little trip to Paris."

MOSCOW, USSR

Anatoly Nikolayev was sitting at his desk when Goncharov
knocked and entered.

"We've had a communication from the Paris office," the operative reported. "Commander Thorpe has arrived in the city."

"Very good," Nikolayev responded. "And do we know for a
fact that this Mr. Truong is also in the city at this time?"

"Yes, it has already been confirmed. I will be leaving to go
there myself this evening."

"Excellent." He tapped his desk surface once with satisfaction.
"Then everything is falling into place. And has Commander
Thorpe made any attempt to contact or ... abduct him?"

"No," Goncharov stated. "Mr. Truong is still moving about
freely." He waited for his superior to continue, but when Nikolayev just remained thinking, he asked, "Would you like *us* to
pick him up?"

"No, there's no point to that. The situation is under control.
Time is on our side, I am content to sit back for a little while and
let Thorpe do our dirty work for us. And when he has done the
hard part, that is when we will move."

PARIS, FRANCE

She hadn't been to Paris since she was seventeen, fresh out of
high school and aching for romance. It was the last summer of her
girlhood, the last summer before the world turned serious.

The first place she'd gone was the Montmartre, which was
supposed to be arty and bohemian and nothing at all like Briarcliff Manor. She was not disappointed. On the steps of Sacré-
Coeur that very afternoon, she had met a French boy her own
age. His name was Marcel. And every night for the rest of her
stay they met there, high on the hill, holding hands, watching the
sun go down and turn the buildings a glowing reddish gold, then
gazing out over the rooftops at the shimmering lights of this most

magic of cities. She knew that once she left, she would never see Marcel again and their poetic interlude would be nothing but a bittersweet memory. But Diana had been a romantic, and this was how these things were supposed to be. You were supposed to find; you were supposed to love; you were supposed to part; you were supposed to cry. She had been so happy then, she thought her heart would break.

Since then she had grown up and grown older. And so, she thought, had the world. She had traveled all over it for the CDC, but Paris was still magic. And that was why, venturing out after a few hours of overcoming jet lag, her first stop was once again the steps of Sacré-Coeur. From far away the six conical domes of the gleaming white basilica beckoned her like vision. Coming back here and remembering, she could almost become the dewy-eyed seventeen-year-old again, at least for a little while.

Hugh Stanway had told her she was free to wander randomly about the city, pretending to be a tourist, visiting the places tourists are supposed to visit. If anyone was following her or tracking their movements, he wanted to now about it before they moved in on their "target."

"Go wherever you like," he had instructed her. "And don't worry about keeping in contact. Epstein and Rowland will be trailing you."

As well as anyone else who happens to be trailing you, he added. Just to be on the safe side, he had made her unbutton her blouse and planted a homing device in one of the cups of her bra. Stanway's probing fingers made her feel awkward, and the tiny metal disk was cold and uncomfortable next to her skin. But she decided to take both in stride. If she were going to play commando, she'd have to learn to put up with a lot of things.

She stayed at Sacré-Coeur almost an hour. Then she took the *métro* from Place de Cliche to Cité, with transfers at St.-Lazare and Chatelet. She liked the trains. They were clean and quick and crowded. This was the original *métro*, the one for which Washington's subway was named. And it was pretty much the way she remembered it. You could get within a few blocks of just about anywhere in the city on it. But no matter where you wanted to go, you had to transfer two or three times to do it.

She came up the steps into Île de la Cité, the island in the center of the Seine that is the original city of Paris. She walked to the center of the Place du Paris and gazed for a time at the perfect

Gothic façade of Notre Dame. From time to time, out of the corner of her eye, she caught a glimpse of either Rowland or Epstein, lurking somewhere along the periphery of the crowd. She hadn't gotten to know either one of them well yet, but she had decided she liked them both immensely. They were strong and capable and had well-developed senses of humor. And she admitted to herself more admiration than understanding of two men who would leave the security of their jobs and families and risk everything for a comrade they hadn't seen in years.

She made a complete circuit inside the cathedral. Despite the gawking crowds, it was still possible to get a sense of the awe and mystery that medieval man yearned for and sought to attain with these incomparable temples of faith. She wished her own faith could be both as soaring and as solid.

She crossed over the Pont St.-Louis to the island of the same name. The tourists in their shorts and T-shirts and polyester disappeared. She passed by row after row of beautiful seventeenth-entury façades, the wrought-iron balconies and tall brick chimneys hearkening back to a more stately and elegant time. She saw Rowland rounding the corner.

It didn't take her long to find La Fin du Tunnel. It looked just as it had in Stanway's photograph, only in living color. With its deep blue window shutters and bright yellow awning, it was even more charming and evocative of a life-style she had once yearned to be part of.

She sat down at one of the small round tables outside. A white-aproned waiter came over and asked in French what he could bring her. With her preparation for her "mission," she had become hypersensitive to every conceivable contingency. That was one question she was not prepared for and it caught her flat-footed.

"Oh, ah, let me see . . ." But she was in the heart of Paris, sitting at an outdoor café She decided she wanted whatever Hemingway would have had. "*Un moment . . .*" She asked for the only Hemingwayesque thing she could think of. "*Un daiquiri, s'il vous plaît.*"

The waiter gave her a questioning glance. Then he shrugged, a tacit comment on her taste, perhaps, replied, "*Eh bien,*" and was off.

As soon as he was gone, before her drink arrived, Diana got up and went inside the restaurant with the ostensible purpose of visiting the ladies' room. Actually, after all this walking she did have to go. But the main purpose was to "case the joint," as Stanway had instructed her.

"Notice everything you can," he had said, "particularly possible escape routes. Is there a back alley? Are there untended doors or windows? What about access from an adjoining building? A basement or cellar? What about an attic? Find a way to get us out of the building unseen, and we'll take it the rest of the way."

Inside, Diana found the place quite charming, an interesting mixture of *la belle époque* and Left Bank bohemian, just what she would have sought out during her last trip to Paris. But despite the typically Parisian decor, she could see that the influence and bitterness of a Southeast Asian expatriate were very much in evidence. Just beyond the entryway a large framed poster proclaimed:

I believe there is light at the end of what has been a long and lonely tunnel.

—PRESIDENT LYNDON BAINES JOHNSON, 1966

Diana smiled. There was a good chance she and Mr. Truong were going to share a certain outlook on things.

By the time she returnd to her table, the daiquiri was waiting there for her. She took a tentative sip. The other tables were beginning to fill up, and strains and snippets of French conversations floated by her in the air. She remembered enough of the language to pick up references to music, the theater, politics, literature. Some of the conversations were animated. Others became downright heated. It was wonderful. A cross section of French café society. And she was actually sitting here in the midst of it, on an island in the middle of Paris! Just beyond the ring of tables young lovers held hands and kissed, mothers strolled along, pushing prams, cyclists rode by with long loaves of French bread clamped to the backs of their bikes. She could hear the low-pitched horns of the *bateaux mouches*, and through an angle between the buildings down the street, she could even catch a glimpse of the long, fat boats slowly gliding through the Seine. Everything was as it was supposed to be. Atlanta, Washington, even Big Sur seemed a lifetime away. She had to struggle with herself to keep sight of why she was actually here.

She sat for a while just taking in the scene, pretending she was waiting for her rendezvous with Papa and Scott and Gertrude and Alice. She glanced at her watch. They couldn't fail to show up, she thought, joking with herself.

At her final sip of the daiquiri the waiter returned. "*Voulez-vous un autre?*" he asked.

"*Non, merci. Mais parlez-vous anglais?*"

"*Oui, un peu.*"

"Could you tell me if Mr. Truong is here, please?"

"You wish to see him?"

She nodded.

The waiter left without saying another word. She waited, not knowing what would happen next.

A few minutes later Nguyen Tien Truong came to her table. He was considerably older than the fuzzy newspaper picture she'd seen. His skin was more wrinkled. He had less hair, and his eyelids were even heavier. But this was definitely the same man.

"I am Nguyen Tien Truong," he announced with effusive cordiality. He put his heels together and bowed his head slightly in greeting.

This is really him, Diana thought. As Hugh would say, the "target." Her heart quickened. She was afraid she would start babbling, as she often did when she was nervous. *Don't jump the gun in your excitement*, she cautioned herself. *Take it step by step, according to plan.*

"How may I be of service?"

She caught herself staring too hard, as if she could gaze right through his sallow skin to the capsule planted somewhere inside. "I'm—I'm most pleased to meet you." She had recovered. "You have a very lovely establishment here."

Truong said effusively, "The lady is most kind to say so. And might I have the pleasure of knowing your name?"

"Diana Lane." Brian and Stanway had decided it was better if she used her real first name. Being inexperienced in subterfuge, they told her, she couldn't be counted on to react instinctively to a made-up name. In a time of stress this could give her away.

She extended her hand. Truong took it, held it cordially for a few seconds, then gave it back to her.

"I'm pleased you could enjoy our hospitality and our beautiful city on such a splendid day, Mlle. Lane. I've always enjoyed Paris this time of year, with the flowers in bloom, before the heat and the humidity become too oppressive. Ever since I was a young man, I remember coming here and . . ." He winked. "But I go on too long, as it is all too easy to do in the presence of such a beautiful young lady." It was obviously an act with him, Diana decided, certainly not reserved exclusively for her.

She beckoned him to sit with her, but without seeming impolite, he remained standing.

"Tell me, how did you happen to stop at our café? If it were on the Left Bank, the Champs-Élysées, one of the areas young intelligent, sophisticated people are known to frequent, I would just attribute it to our good fortune. But here, as we are . . ."

"That relates directly to the nature of my visit," she said. "I'm hoping you can help me."

"If it is at all possible, you can be assured that I will do my utmost." He was still practically bubbling over with goodwill.

Diana hesitated for a moment, then said, "I have been informed that you have been known to make your restaurant . . . convenient to certain people who might be in need of—"

Truong stiffened almost imperceptibly. He recovered his effusive manner almost immediately. "Perhaps you would like to accompany me to a—a more private setting." With a wave of his hand he indicated the interior of the restaurant.

"Thank you." Diana rose and silently followed him. They passed the bar and the dining room, each looking more familiar to her on this second pass by. Again she tried to take in the entire scene.

Next to the kitchen entrance at the end of the corridor was another door. Truong pushed it open and went through. Diana was about to follow him when she felt two sets of hands stopping her from moving. Her pocketbook was jerked from her hands.

A stab of panic shot through her. Instinct told her to struggle, to scream. But no, that was wrong. She suppressed it and held her breath until she was trembling.

One set of hands held her rigidly by the shoulders from behind. The other set belonged to a young Oriental man—also Vietnamese, she supposed—who was crouched in front of her and had begun roughly patting her down, from the ankles on up. When his hands reached up inside her skirt, she froze, needing every ounce of restraint to keep from bolting away in revulsion. He took his time inching his fingers up her legs. She had the feeling this exhibition was as much to frighten and intimidate her as to uncover any secret—and unlikely—cache of weapons. She casually wondered, if it came to that, whether she'd be able to use anything she'd learned from the SEAL manual in a situation like this. Could she aggressively attack, using her maximum strength against her enemy's weakest point while maintaining her balance and using her opponent's momentum to her own advantage? She seriously doubted it. So she continued smiling icily at her examiner. He continued up her torso, and when he had completed the frisking, he nodded to his companion, indicating that she was clean. He smiled back at her and motioned for her to go through the doorway Truong had just entered. The second man smiled and gave back her handbag.

She let out her breath and paused for a split second to recover her form. She was getting it from all sides today. Hugh's fiddling inside her blouse now seemed no more than a clean-hands check in nursery school. Oh, God. She'd forgotten about that. What if this Oriental capo had been even more adventuresome and had discovered the homing device? That would have blown the entire mission. Plus God knew what they would have done to her. She could feel the perspiration beading around her hairline and hoped it wasn't too obvious.

The room to which Truong had guided her was small and rather plain, compared to the rest of the establishment. There was a simple wooden table with chairs around it, an old sofa, and a bureau that didn't go with the rest of the furniture. There was a window in the center of one wall, but it was boarded up.

"I'm sorry to have had to put you through that little indignity," Truong said solicitously. "But a stateless person such as myself can never afford to be too careful. Had you been carrying a weapon, for example, it would have gone quite badly for you." He made this last statement without ever losing his ambiguous smile. Diana didn't need him to go into details.

"So . . . welcome to my humble office," he said.

She glanced around the room. "I was noticing, as I was having my drink, such a lovely view you have outside. A pity you can't enjoy it yourself in here."

"It is a pity," he replied.

"And even your window is boarded up, I see."

"Were it not, it would do me little good," he said. "When the building was first constructed, I understand that it looked out over a courtyard for horses and small wagons below the level of the street. Now, I'm afraid it leads only to the sewer."

"The famous sewers of Paris," Diana said.

"The same. I wanted to plaster it over, but the municipal people insist it must remain to give them access." He shrugged good-naturedly. "What is a humble proprietor to do who depends on these people for his licenses?"

Diana herself shrugged in sympathy.

Truong sat down at the table and motioned her to do the same. "Now, what may I do for you?"

She came right to the point. "In the circles I travel in, you have been known to offer temporary haven to certain people."

Truong nodded noncommittally, waiting, in no seeming hurry, for her to elaborate.

"I'm sure you don't know who I am," she said.

"No, that is true." He smiled again, as if to make a show of taking in her beauty. "Unfortunate but true."

"I'm a doctor now, back in the United States. But at one time a number of years ago I was deeply involved with the underground movement in the United States against the Vietnam War." *Stick to the real story as much as possible,* Stanway had counseled. *Less chance to trip yourself up that way.*

She continued in a hushed voice. "I have a friend who is wanted by the authorities for certain things they say he's done—the bombing of a military training building at a university; the robbery of several banks. He has had to be underground more than ten years." Though well rehearsed, she tried to make her narrative sound rambling and disjointed. "Finally he has left the country. He heard of you, of this place. We both did. I have not seen him in those ten years. But I desperately want to see him now. If things work out, maybe we will be back together again, who knows? He is afraid to meet me in any public place. He is afraid of who might be watching him. But he says he will meet me here, that he has heard you are friendly and supportive of people in his—in his situation." She stared at Truong imploringly. "I hope that what they say is true. His name is—"

Truong waved his hand in front of her. "I need not know his name. At least I need not know his true name. It is better for all, better for me if I do not. Tell me only, how will he make himself known to me?"

"He will call himself Peter Quint, and he will ask for you as I did." She looked at him again and managed to squeeze a tear out of her large blue eyes. "Then you'll do it?"

"I am to provide only the meeting place and act as go-between for the two of you?"

"That's all."

"There will be no involvement from these authorities of whom you spoke?"

"None. I promise."

"There is little I can do for you in my position, despite what you might have heard. But I will provide a meeting place. That is perhaps not too much to ask of any sympathetic person. And what you have heard about me is true in one respect. I have been given certain favors in my own life. And I wish to repay those favors in whatever way I can."

She reached across the table and placed her hands on his. "Oh, thank you," she cried. His hands were moist and clammy. "And please," she added, "we can trust you to say nothing of this to anyone?"

"You have my word of trust. Now, when shall I expect this Peter Quint?"

"It should be anytime now," Diana said. "Maybe today. I hope by tomorrow. I will return this time tomorrow afternoon."

He took her hand again in his. "I will look forward to it. And to making the acquaintance of Mr. Peter Quint."

Hugh Stanway had set up headquarters on a side street near the Étoile, in a building occupied by a small French film company that had done a feature for him on the Foreign Legion. It was one of those typically Parisian structures, built around a small stone-paved courtyard. Large wooden double doors in the blank façade provided the only access to the street. The film company had only four full-time employees, and as it happened, they were completing another assignment for the Men of Action Film Division in Algeria.

Before any of them did anything else, Stanway had Diana draw a floor plan of the restaurant while it was still fresh in her mind. He had already obtained detailed municipal maps of the city, which he correlated with her drawing. Then the five of them sat around a conference table, and Diana related the particulars of her conversation. Epstein and Rowland reported that she had not been followed.

"He'll be expecting you to use the name Peter Quint," she told Brian. "And the cover stands just as we agreed on it. Any time tomorrow after dark will be fine."

"Good," Brian replied. "I don't think we should wait any longer than that."

"I agree," said Stanway.

Diana would have much preferred to have it all happen this first day, to get it over with. But Hugh and Brian had decided it was more important to hide the sense of urgency and create a level of trust. That way Truong was less likely to react suspiciously. "Oh, and he'll have you frisked," Diana added.

"I figured as much," said Brian. "When you come back tomorrow, will he frisk you again?"

"I don't think so."

"Can we take that chance?"

This prompted a good deal of debate around the table. Stanway had his own opinions. Despite the fact that he was the titular leader of this operation, it had always been SEAL policy to hear out all quarters whenever possible before arriving at a conclusion. The discussion lasted about ten minutes. The fact was, everyone admitted, they couldn't go in there completely empty-handed, and the instrument under consideration was both small and narrow. In the end it was decided that Diana was well enough endowed that her bra still provided the best possible hiding place.

"I suppose that's intended to be a compliment," she commented dryly.

"All right, so we meet in this back room of his," Brian went on. "Unless he decides to walk out willingly, we've got to get him out of there. And we can't just saunter out the front door. We've just got to disappear, so that nobody knows we're gone."

"What's the access?" asked Stanway.

"It's one of those long, narrow buildings, and the door's at the end of a corridor that runs the entire ground-floor length," Diana reported. "And it's right next to the kitchen, where there's a continual bustle of activity." She shook her head. "I'd say that's out of the question."

"What are the alternatives?" he asked. "What about other doors or windows?"

"No other doors. And only one boarded-up window."

"Do you know what's on the other side?"

"Yeah, he told me. The sewer."

Stanway and Epstein immediately shifted to the public utilities schematic map. "Okay, I found it," Epstein called out. "It looks about two to three hundred feet long."

Stanway tapped the map with his finger. "That's our extraction point then."

"Where does the sewer lead?" Brian asked.

"Right into the Seine."

Diana stuck out her tongue. "Yuck! So it's *Les Misérables* time."

"If we have to," Stanway replied. "By the way, what can you tell me about what's covering the window?"

"Wooden boards, just like on an abandoned building."

"Nailed shut or screwed?"

"Nailed, I'm pretty sure."

"Be very sure."

Diana closed her eyes a moment and tried to visualize the entire room. She opened them again. "I'm very sure."

"Good. Make a note of that," he said to Rowland.

"I've already got it down," Rowland replied.

"Okay, this looks like a possible Chapter Four situation," Stanway said, referring to the SEAL manual shorthand. "Epstein, you get the Emersons ready. The rest of you, get a good night's sleep. You're going to need it."

Everyone had got up from the table and begun filing out of the room when Stanway added, "Oh, and Keegan . . . congratulations. You did good today."

Michael Swansea climbed up the steps of the American Embassy on the Avenue Gabriel. Behind him stood the gray obelisk of the Place de la Concorde and, beyond it, the Tuileries Gardens and the massive, embracing expanse of the Louvre. But Swansea's interests were other than sightseeing at the moment. The sooner he could get in and out of here, the better.

He presented his cover identification to the marine at the reception desk in the lobby. The CIA was accommodated under differing departmental designations at the various embassies and consular offices throughout the world. At this particular installation at this particular time his contacts would be located in the Economic and Political Office.

He went up to the third floor and presented his credentials. The receptionist directed him back to the Special Interests section. Behind that department's locked door he told the deskman that he needed a secure line. The duty officer accommodated him immediately without asking for details or corroborating data. As a matter of policy, Covert Action personnel were not to be questioned.

Once in the soundproofed booth with the door tightly shut, Swansea dialed in the code for the deputy director of operations' direct line. Swansea gave his own code to the first voice that came on the line. The second was that of the man he wanted to talk to.

"I'm in Paris," Swansea explained. "I need a status report. "Last name: Stanway. First name: Hugh. He is under an occasional services contract. He is here in Paris at the moment according to a flight·plan his pilot filed. I need to know if he is currently on agency business."

The DDO would be one of the few people with access to this information, Swansea knew, and the only one authorized to give it out. And Swansea was one of the few people not directly involved in any possible operation authorized to receive it. He also knew that the DDO would not want to know what he intended to use this information for. The entire concept behind CA was that it was handled independently of the traditional reporting structure. That assured flexibility on the one end and deniability on the other.

"Hang on a second," the deputy director said. Swansea could hear him punching in names and codes on his desk console. There was a low churning, whirring sound. Finally he said, "No. He's not doing anything for us right now. The last assignment I see here was about eighteen months ago."

"No possibility that anyone else in CA is using him?" Swansea questioned.

"That's correct," the DDO said.

"Thanks for your time," Swansea said.

"That's what I'm here for."

And now he knew what Stanway was here for, Swansea said to himself as he replaced the phone in its cradle. He would somehow have to get to the target before Stanway did. And that wouldn't be easy, Swansea knew, because Hugh Stanway was a pro.

This time she hadn't bothered sitting at one of the outdoor tables and going through the ritual of ordering a drink. Instead, she went directly inside the restaurant, where dinner was in full swing, and told the maître d' she'd like to speak with Mr. Truong. The imperious-looking Frenchman had raised his eyebrows slightly, evaluating her, and when she stood her ground and returned his gaze, he'd said, "*Un moment*," and gone down the corridor into the back room. He came out a few moments later and signaled her in that direction.

The frisking wasn't as complete this time. It was more perfunctory, to let her know they were still taking precautions, she supposed, and there was no overt attempt to intimidate her. She was wearing slacks today and the patting down was confined to the outside this time. And she wasn't carrying a handbag, so that the second Oriental honcho had little to do.

Inside the back room Truong was sitting at the table. Everything seemed the same as it had been the day before. She made a quick show of glancing around the room, put on her most concerned expression, and said, "He isn't here? I was sure he'd be here by now."

"No, mademoiselle. I have yet to hear a thing. Are you certain he is still coming?"

"Yes," she said with a touch of desperation in her voice. "I'm sure of it."

Truong shrugged. "If he comes, then we will welcome him. If he does not, then . . ." He shrugged again and gave her a curious half-smile. "In the East we learn to let things unfold at their own rhythm."

Diana nodded to this. "I know he'll come here tonight," she said. "May I wait here for him?"

"As you wish. You will excuse me, though, if I resume my working. I have accounts to balance. I am not good with numbers, but alas, I trust no one else here to do it for me." He opened the top drawer of the bureau. She half expected him to take out an abacus and flip beads back and forth. Instead, he brought out a pocket calculator, and she privately chastised herself for this racial stereotype.

"Would you like me to wait somewhere else while you work?" she asked.

Truong waved his hand in front of her. "That will not be necessary. You will not bother me."

Or else he wants to keep me where he can see me, she thought. She sat quietly across from him, letting her eyes drift idly about the room. When they lit on the boarded window, she checked again to make sure she had reported it accurately to Stanway. Yes, she had. Nails, not screws. Thank goodness.

They continued sitting in silence, Truong apparently deeply engrossed in his accounts, Diana deeply engrossed in nothing. The longer she sat like that, the more she had to think about all the things that could go wrong. What if something happened to Brian? What if he never showed up? How long should she stay? Would they let her leave? Was Truong on to him? Was it possible that he might listen to reason? And even in the most extreme sense was what she was proposing reasonable?

About twenty-five minutes later there was a knock on the door. Truong stood up and crossed from behind the table. He opened the door, and the man who had frisked Diana was standing there. He stepped aside, and Brian came in. His clothes were slightly disheveled and his hair was mussed. Obviously they'd done a good job frisking him, too.

"I presume we are having the honor of Mr. Quint," Truong said.

Brian nodded tentatively, as if he were still cowed by the ordeal of the frisking. Diana couldn't remember the last time she'd been so glad to see someone. She started to mumble something but then let her glistening eyes say it for her.

Brian and Diana locked eyes from across the room. They ran for each other. She threw her arms around his neck. He embraced her tightly around the waist and lifted her off the floor. They hugged and kissed the full ten years' worth, making every second count, making every moment real. Diana held on to him as if she would never let him go, as if she had done so once and seen what the results had been. Of all the parts she had to act, this was by far the easiest.

"I didn't believe it was possible." She wept, still clutching tightly to him.

"I told you it would happen," Brian whispered. "I told you to believe me."

Truong watched the reunion discreetly. Then, when the lovers had had sufficient time to catch their breaths and come back down to more practical considerations, he said, "I'll give you some time to be by yourselves." He put his hand on the doorknob to open it.

"No, please," Brian stopped him. "Please stay. What I have to say concerns you, too. We need your help."

Truong regarded him quizzically. Without saying anything, he crossed back behind the table and reclaimed his seat.

Good, they'd gotten through that stage convincingly. Diana looked intently at Brian. The next step would be critical.

"Mr. Truong, I'd like to talk to you about your time in prison," Brian said, "in North Vietnam." That was the plan, Diana knew. Throw him off-balance. Don't give him time to think.

Truong's sallow face drained of all color. "What is going on here? What is the meaning of this?" He stood up.

"Please, hear me out," Brian said. "As I said, we need your help. Thousands, maybe millions of lives are at stake, and you are the only one who can save them."

"I don't know what you are talking about," Truong said tensely. "I am sure we have nothing to talk about."

"Please allow me to explain."

Truong listened in stunned silence as Brian described the capsule implanted in his body.

"This is nonsense," Truong said. "I tell you, I have no idea of what you speak."

"I assure you we wish you no harm. Your political views, whatever they are, are of no interest to us. But please, you must go with us."

"Go with you where?" Truong asked, as if the mere suggestion was the utmost of absurdities.

"Back to the United States. To Atlanta, Georgia. For only a few days. For the surgery. I know this is asking a lot, but there really isn't any other way."

"The war is over. Let it stay that way."

"I wish we could," Brian responded.

"I will have no part of this!" he declared.

"Mr. Truong, I'm afraid I don't have time to argue with you."

It had been decided during the final strategy session the night before that they would have only a very few moments to introduce the subject of the capsule to Truong and make one good stab at trying to convince him to cooperate. If it didn't seem to be working right away, they would shift to the second plan. There was always a chance that with extensive explanation, conversation, or pleading, they could get him to go along. But that was not a risk they felt they could afford to take. The longer they delayed without real hope of his cooperation, the greater his opportunity to resist, call out, or summon his henchmen. That was why they had worked out the timing so precisely.

Brian glanced at this watch. "I'll ask you one more time, Mr. Truong, will you help us?"

The Vietnamese spun on his heels until he was facing Brian directly. "How many times have people asked for my help? What has it ever gotten me? Where is my country now, I ask you? What has become of it? No!" he shouted as he slammed his fist on the table. "The answer is no! You have both betrayed my confidence. Now get out! Leave!"

Brian glanced at his watch again and hung his head sadly. "All right, I'm sorry. I did my best." He turned to Diana accusingly. "I told you he'd never go for it."

Diana looked back to him pleadingly, then turned to Truong as if he still might reconsider and save the relationship. But Truong merely glared coldly at both of them, waiting for them to get out of his sight.

Brian put his hand on the doorknob, then turned to face Truong. "Thank you for your time," he said, and behind his back he turned the key in the door to the locked position.

Pushing off his left foot, Brian charged across the room. In one leap he had Truong from behind, one hand cupped over his mouth, the other across his chest and pinning both his arms. He struggled furiously, but Brian held him tight.

Diana quickly reached into her blouse and withdrew the thin plastic syringe. She plucked off the cover as Brian pulled Truong's right forearm out straight in front of him. Diana grabbed it firmly at the wrist and jabbed the bare needle its full length into the brachial vein in Truong's arm. She congratulated herself on hitting the vein the first time. She hadn't always been able to do that in med school. She pressed the plunger home as the sodium Pentothal coursed into his system. Brian held him rigidly for another few seconds. Then he collapsed like dead weight in Brian's arms.

Diana replaced the protective cover on the syringe and put it back into her bra. They both had been careful not to leave their fingerprints on anything and had agreed there was to be no physical evidence left at the scene.

Brian checked his watch one more time. Just as he did, they saw the nails holding the window boards in place pushing outward, one by one. They clattered to the floor. Once the top board fell, Brian went over to help pull the lower ones off.

Rowland and Epstein climbed through the opening, wearing black wet suits under the SCUBA gear. They carried three sets of Emerson bag and vest assemblies in a utility case. The one they strapped on the unconscious Truong had a full face mask with the regulator built in. When it was secure, they helped Brian and Diana into their gear.

"Everything all right?" Epstein asked Diana, helping her adjust her mouthpiece for testing. She nodded.

"As soon as Truong's employees notice he's missing, there'll be a police alert for both of us," Brian said. "So let's get out of here quickly."

Rowland gave him the thumbs-up. Carrying the utility case, he led the way back out the wall opening, with Diana right behind him and Brian and Epstein carrying Truong.

The area outside the window was a bricked space, only about four feet high and seven feet long, before it emptied into a round hole that led to the sewer. Rowland jumped down the hole, waiting to receive Truong from the other two men.

"I got to tell you," Epstein said, "this place really is to puke from."

Diana glanced at the drying crud, not quite identifiable, that clung to his wet suit from the journey in and was afraid she might demonstrate her agreement.

"You had to swim in the swamps of the Rung Sat," she heard Brian saying to Epstein, "where whatever the bats and pythons don't get, the leeches will. Forget the bats and alligators; even the ants are poisonous over there. And you're complaining about slogging through a sewer?"

"I was young and stupid then," Epstein replied, "like we all were."

"And a famous, *classy* sewer like Paris's at that!"

Classy sewer, indeed, Diana thought as Rowland hurried them along down the hole. The unconscious Truong became her Marius, and she could easily conjure up the image of the unrelenting Javert, close on their heels. And like Valjean's, their ultimate destination was the Seine.

They found themselves in a narrow tunnel. The stench was overwhelming. Diana had to breathe through the mouth just to keep from passing out. Several times she felt the gorge rising in her throat. If she got out of this alive, she didn't think she would ever eat again. There was practically no light. The flowing sewage at their feet was almost knee-deep and so dark and thick that nothing could be seen below its surface. That was okay with her. She didn't even want to think about what was in it. Little shapes slithered along the walls. She wished she were wearing a wet suit like Rowland and Epstein. She was thankful she'd at least worn slacks and pumps today.

As they slogged through the muck, Rowland shone a penlight on a laminated card on which he'd marked the escape route with a grease pencil. "Okay, there should be a turnoff in about forty feet," he stated.

They pushed on. The flow became heavier and deeper. It was lapping up toward their waists. Epstein and Brian changed their grip on Truong to a dead man's carry. The sounds of labored breathing bounced off the close arched walls.

Underwater something furry brushed up against her ankle. She nearly jumped out of her skin. She wanted to scream and to cry, and she wanted to be somewhere—anywhere—else.

Brian said, "Are you okay?"

She nodded that she was. If she tried to talk, she knew she'd come apart. She just hoped she could make it the rest of the way.

"Just a little farther," he told her, giving Truong a laborious heave.

"This is it," Rowland announced. He stood in place and directed the flashlight's beam into the black connecting tunnel. Diana waited for Brian to go ahead. She didn't want to be the first. She watched him drag Truong and saw that he was actually stepping up and out of the water. This connecting tunnel must be an air shaft or some sort of access way. When she realized that, she scrambled up the ramp and out of the sewer tunnel as fast as she could. Her legs were freezing from the wetness as the small band set off down the new passageway. No one said anything, as if they all were trying to conserve their energy for what they knew lay ahead.

Another couple of minutes in the same direction, and a glimmer of light flickered in the distance. "That's it!" Diana called out joyfully. "That must be the light at the end of the tunnel!"

"So is that what we were looking for all those years?" Epstein asked.

"If only LBJ could be with us now." Diana said.

"There were a lot of times back then we wished he were," Rowland offered. "Despite what Epstein tells you, we've got plenty of experience in sewers."

The tunnel ended up at a hole in the stone retaining wall that surrounded the Île St.-Louis. Rowland stuck his head out to make sure they couldn't be seen from any passing boats. In the dark of night it was difficult to judge, but Diana figured the drop to the river to be about fifteen feet. The water was absolutely black. Rowland opened the utility case and handed out the swim fins. He kept it open so that it would sink quickly. Then he threw it into the water to judge the drop. Brian and Diana threw their shoes in. "Everybody ready?" Rowland asked.

They all adjusted their mouthpieces and opened the valves. Epstein fitted the face mask securely on Truong's head.

Rowland and Epstein stepped out of the tunnel and plunged into the water. It was Diana's turn next. In the split second before she stepped off, she reflected that this was only her second time with scuba equipment. The first had been in Jamaica during a vacation her second year in college. She didn't know if that counted.

Well, the longer she thought about this, the harder it would be. Just like going off the high dive for the first time. She took one step and then another, and by the third she was walking on air.

She lost her stomach on the way down. No, she knew right where it was—up under her chin. She hit the water with a loud splash and plummeted down several feet before the natural buoyancy brought her back to the surface. She looked up and saw Brian holding Truong under the armpits, lowering him down as far as he could. Then he let him go. Rowland and Epstein rescued him as soon as he hit the water. When the way was clear, Brian jumped in after him and swam back to the group.

They formed into a small circle, treading water to stay afloat. Rowland clipped a long nylon line onto a band around his wrist. He pulled it out to the next clip, which he attached to Diana, then the next to Brian, and the final one to Epstein, both of whom were responsible for carrying Truong. Without a connecting line under the dark, unfamiliar water, there was too great a risk of separation.

The Emerson is a closed-circuit breathing system designed to keep the swimmer from being detected. It utilizes 100 percent of the gas media so that no bubbles are produced and is used extensively for underwater demolition work in harbors, where bubbles rising to the surface would instantly give away a diver's presence and position. The system's limitations on depth and the relatively short canister life presented no problems here. Once they were in the Seine, no one would spot them. No one, Diana realized. No matter what happened. All they had to do was get to the next bridge. But they had to do it on their own.

Despite her running and conditioning, despite the fact that they were moving with the flow of the river, Diana had forgotten what hard work swimming can be, especially in the dark, in cold, black, dirty water with God knew who already pursuing them. It was incredible to her that she was actually swimming in the Seine. Fully dressed. This river sure lost its romance in a hurry when you were about to drown in it in the middle of the goddamned night.

It was like swimming through ink. She fought with herself not to panic. That would only fatigue her more. It couldn't be that much farther. She had to make it. They all did. Think how much harder it must be for Brian and Epstein, who were dragging another body in addition to themselves. In spite of their burden, both of them kept swimming up next to her, pulling her along. That helped somewhat. It gave her the courage to go on. But if this was what being a commando was all about, you could shove it. And she was sure that if it weren't for the nylon lifeline connecting her to the others, she would die right there.

Everything in her ached. All her muscles begged for release. How did people swim the English Channel? Why would anyone want to? These mindless questions formed a rhythm of their own in her brain, mercifully taking the place of all rational thought. *Just keep going. Don't stop. Don't think. Just keep going.*

Finally she saw it. They were there—the embankment under the Pont Sully. It was quiet and eerie, and the shadow of the massive iron bridge kept it pitch-dark. She looked up the eight feet to ground level. During the day the promenade would have been crowded with painters and strollers and sunbathers and lovers. Now it was deserted except for the occasional derelict and drunk. And Hugh Stanway. Stanway was right there. Thank God. What if he hadn't been? She didn't even want to think about it.

He threw a line down into the water. It had a large loop at the end. Rowland grabbed it and handed it across to Diana. She held on for dear life as Stanway began hoisting her up out of the water. He was incredibly strong. She felt secure again. Only when she was up on the embankment did she realize that the other end of the line was attached to a power winch on the bumper of Stanway's Land Rover.

She threw her arms around him, and instantly she began sobbing uncontrollably. She sobbed from the cold and the fright and the exhaustion and from the exhilaration of having pushed herself beyond the limits of her imagination—just like a SEAL. He helped her off with her equipment and threw a blanket around her.

Within three minutes everyone else was up on the embankment. There was a brief round of hugging and handshaking. Then they all piled into the car. Stanway looked over his shoulder at Truong and asked, "Does he need another shot yet?"

"I think he's still good for a little while," Brian replied from the back.

"Good," the leader retorted. "Then let's get the hell out of here." He gunned the Land Rover into a U-turn, raced up the earthen ramp that led to the embankment, turned onto the Quai St.-Bernard, and disappeared into the Parisian night.

"I want one person with him at all times," Stanway directed when they had returned to headquarters. "We'll drink a toast when we're airborne. But now let's all get some sleep. By now they probably know Truong is missing, and this town is going to be crawling with cops. I want us out of here first thing in the morning, as soon as it doesn't look suspicious to be flying out."

Brian and Diana discussed the medical implications, and decided Truong could remain drugged until they got him onto the plane. Then they'd make a second stab at convincing him to go along with them, and if they couldn't, they'd give him another shot when they were ready to land in Atlanta.

Rowland took the first watch with Truong. They kept him in

the little room near the front gate so that they could get him back into the car in a hurry if the situation arose. The rest of them roomed across the courtyard, in a suite of apartments on the second floor.

Diana went right to sleep. And four hours later she didn't stir as Brian arose to relieve Rowland on the watch. He ambled quietly down the stairs, crossed the deserted courtyard, and rapped on the door. Rowland opened it. Truong was still laid out on the cot, his breathing rhythmical and even. Brian listened to his chest with a stethoscope and was satisfied that he was tolerating the medication and the stress.

"How we doing?" Brian asked.

"Tight as a drum," Rowland answered, and yawned. He handed Brian the Smith & Wesson 9mm. "See you in the morning."

"Yeah, see you." He put his arm on Rowland's shoulder. "Good mission, Ernie. Good mission all the way around."

She was awakened by the commotion.

It was already light out, and at first Diana thought it was the trashmen banging the cans against their truck or the side of the building. But something didn't sound right. She opened her eyes, looked over next to her, and saw that Brian wasn't there. A stab of panic pierced through her. Then she remembered he had taken the second watch. But the panic wouldn't go away. They'd all been sleeping in their clothes that night, so she hastily pulled her shoes on and ran down the stairs and into the courtyard.

When she got to the opposite side, Stanway, Epstein, and Rowland were already there. They were standing outside the door to Truong's room. The door was open.

"They've taken them," Stanway said tersely.

The stab of panic turned itself into the eruption of a volcano. "Who did?"

"We don't know."

"When?"

"Just now. That's what we all heard."

"How did they find this place?"

"We don't know. There are always sources."

"What did they do?"

"They've taken Truong."

"And Brian?"

"And Brian." His face was ashen. She noticed in her brief moment of lucidity that this was the first time she had ever heard Stanway call him by his first name.

Then it hit her like a hammerblow. They'd taken Brian. It had finally happened. The fear that had been with her so long that she'd stopped thinking about it. That's what had done it. She'd let down her guard and look what had happened! A cry began forming deep in her gut, and by the time it reached her constricted throat, it had become a low, moaning wail.

"All right, Diana. Stop!" Stanway ordered sharply. "That's not helping anything." It was the first time he'd ever called her by her first name. He looked ready to slap her back to her senses. He didn't, but she thought it might have been the greater kindness if he had.

With supreme effort she managed to pull herself together, barely together. She gazed out the open gate to the entrance to the courtyard. The street was already alive with morning sounds. Merchants were opening their shutters across the street. Somewhere out there the people who'd been after them all along, the people who'd attacked Sharon and shot Moreland and switched Hardesty's insulin and all the other things were racing off with Brian.

"What do we do now?" she asked, her voice teetering between despair and hysteria.

"We improvise," Stanway declared. "That's what we've been trained for. If the tire goes flat and you don't have a spare, you go creative."

He looked to Epstein and Rowland and in a firm voice said, "It's time to go creative."

26

They had been riding for more than an hour, zigzagging back and forth through the streets of Paris to make certain they weren't being tailed. There had been two car shifts to make doubly sure, accomplished with the no-questions-asked aid of other Covert Action personnel in the area, and each time Swansea himself had taken the wheel. He felt most secure when he was in control.

They were on the highway north of the city now, past St.-Denis and on the road to Roissy. The car they'd ended up in was a BMW 5-Series with back doors that opened only from the outside, keeping their reluctant passengers secure. Swansea was confident he could outrun anything short of a Ferrari in that. And even Hugh Stanway wasn't likely to come after them in a Ferrari. As it turned out, he hadn't come after them at all, and now it was too late. He'd lost too much time. The abduction had been effected with surgical precision, just the way Swansea liked. The entire operation had taken less than a minute.

He allowed himself a brief lapse into humor when he thought about surgical precision, glancing into the rearview mirror to see the surgeon sitting behind him in the rear seat. A trickle of blood from the altercation had dried on the corner of his mouth. A large bruise was forming just below his eye. Amber, facing to the rear and sitting diagonally across from Thorpe in the front, never took his .38 Colt Special off him. Truong, next to Thorpe and out like a light from whatever Thorpe had shot him up with, required no special attention.

What a stroke of good fortune to get both of them together. After the way things had been going up till now, this made it all a lot easier. They'd get Thorpe to the safe house for debriefing, pharmacologically induced if necessary, find out what he knew and whom he'd told it to; then his body would be discovered the next day in a wrecked car on the way to the coast. It would take the naval authorities a long time to figure that one out, though his blood alcohol level at the time of the crash would make it a little clearer.

Truong would be even easier to write off once they'd been able to operate on him. With his checkered background no one would even wonder that he'd suddenly disappeared. Fifty different sources could be responsible for that. Swansea only hoped Truong hadn't shot his mouth off to Thorpe or Stanway yet. But since they'd obviously had to give him the Mickey Finn, it was likely they hadn't been able to interrogate him yet. Not that he'd know that much to begin with. But once he came out of it, he and Thorpe could have started comparing notes, and between them, they might have had enough information to put things together.

Okay, that exposure had been eliminated. But there was still a potentially greater threat. It seemed to Swansea that Thorpe and General Blagden were on the verge of a beautiful relationship. Whatever was happening there, the time for idle rumination was past. They had a time bomb on their hands, and Swansea now trusted no one other than himself to defuse it.

The BMW raced on toward Roissy.

Since they'd picked him up, Thorpe had refused to say anything. Now, as Swansea glanced back, he continued sitting there tight-lipped and sullen, the good soldier to the end. He was apparently playing the good doctor, too. When they'd broken into the room where Truong was being held, Thorpe had had the opportunity to get a shot off that could have taken out one of Swansea's men. But Thorpe hadn't taken it, afraid of hitting Truong, who was in the path.

There was no question in Swansea's mind. He had a lot of respect for Thorpe. It was too bad that in war it was often the best who had to be sacrificed.

Out the window, he heard something back behind the car. A

high-pitched two-note whine. In the rearview mirror he saw a Peugeot police car. Swansea glanced at the speedometer. He was doing more than a 100 kilometers an hour. He eased off on the accelerator pedal to slow down gradually. Pumping the brakes would have lit up the rear brake lights and been obvious. He glanced in the mirror again. The police car had its flashing lights on.

Oh, shit, Swansea thought. He knew what the gendarmerie could be like. The love of uniforms and procedure without the German sense of efficiency. Out loud he said, "Son of a bitch!"

"You want to try to lose them?" asked Amber.

"No. The last thing we want to do is call any more attention to ourselves. You know the French. If we try to get away, they'll make it a point of honor to catch up with us. And if we get this made into an incident, it opens up everything. If they stop us, just smile." He spoke to Brian. "And I trust I don't have to remind you to behave yourself if we're stopped. Don't try anything stupid and heroic. You say one word, and not only are you a dead man, but so is Truong. And once he dies, as you know, the stuff in the capsule dies with him."

The police car sped up alongside the BMW, waving it over onto the shoulder of the highway. At these speeds it took several hunded feet to coast to a halt.

There were two policemen in the front seat of the Peugeot, one white and the other black. There was a blond woman in the back. And even from such a casual glimpse Swansea could see that she was stunning.

Both officers got out of their car and paced over to the BMW. They stared at it for a while, and the white officer wrote down the license number in a small notebook. The black officer walked over to the driver's side and said, "*Parlez-vous français?*" He spoke with an odd accent that made Swansea think he was probably an immigrant from Algeria.

"Ah, no," Swansea replied. "English."

"From England?"

"American."

"Very well. I will try to speak to you in English. You were going one hundred and twenty kilometers per hour. The speed limit on this road is ninety."

Swansea didn't think he'd hit more than 105, tops, but thought it wise not to argue. "I'm sorry, Officer," he said. "We're in a hurry to catch a plane. If you'll just write out the ticket . . ."

"Not so fast," the officer interrupted. "There was an incident in the area not long ago and—"

Oh, shit, Swansea thought again. *Stanway actually reported it to the police.*

"—and your vehicle matches the description—"

But we were in a Citroën at that point, he said to himself.

"—a shooting . . ."

Thank God. It was something else. Now all he had to do was convince them he was not their man and they could get out of here.

The policeman stepped to the side so he could see into the back seat at an angle. "You all are going to the airport?"

"Yes, that's right," Swansea responded impatiently.

"Charles de Gaulle?"

"Right."

"A fine airport, though I found it confusing the first time I was there."

"Yes, I did, too. But I've been there several times since then and— Look, Officer, we really are in a hurry."

He stared into the back for an uncomfortably long time, then said, "The Oriental gentleman does not look well."

"He is sleeping. He has a heart condition and is not up to the rigors of traveling," Swansea said.

"I could radio for an ambulance."

"It's really not necessary. I've traveled with him before. I know how to take care of him. It's only important that we get to the airport."

The policeman sighed apologetically. "I'm afraid I will have to call this report in on the radio before I can let you pass."

Enough of this shit already, Swansea decided. He opened the door and got out of the car. "Sir," he said in his most authoritative tone, "this is a matter of international security." He pulled out his wallet and opened it. "We both are with the American Central Intelligence Agency, and we cannot afford to be detained."

"Oh, I see," the policeman replied. "Then we will expedite this business with extreme speed and efficiency." He spoke to the other policeman in French. "Albert, remove the girl from the car. I want her where I can see her."

Albert opened the back door of the Peugeot and harshly ordered the woman to get out. She grudgingly complied. She was heavily made up and had on a shiny white blouse at least three sizes too small, which was opened more than halfway down to reveal her enticing breasts. Her bra was also obviously tight to make them look larger. She wore a black leather miniskirt that just barely covered her crotch and knee-high white patent leather boots. The second officer positioned her near the front of the BMW, instructing her to place her hands on the front fender where he could see them. When he took his hand away from her arm, she defiantly stepped up and rested her foot on the car's bumper, bending her leg into a right angle, hitching her short skirt up in front to expose her black satin panties. She glared at the gendarmes sullenly and made no move to assume a more modest position.

"She was picked up for solicitation," the first policeman needlessly explained. "Look at the way she taunts us! I know what I would like to do to her! We were on our way back to the station when we received the radio call. It is a never-ending struggle," he said philosophically, "just as it must be in your own country. You round them up; you take them to the jail; their pimps come and bail them out; they are back on the street. Over and over and over."

"Yes, I can well sympathize, but we're in a terribly great hurry," Swansea said.

"Of course you are. Forgive me. Could you also have your associate step out from the car and show me his identification as well? I hope that will be the last remaining step. Also, I would like to see your driving license. An international one is not required. An American license will be quite sufficient."

"Is this all necessary? We're to be given special—"

"Alas, it is," the officer said apologetically. "Now if the other gentleman will come over here, we will have you on your way in moments."

Amber got out of the car, came around, and presented his ID. While he waited for the policeman to examine it, he tried not to stare too intently at the hooker.

"Will you come this way, please?" the officer said, leading them the few feet back to the police car. The second man squinted at the driver's license and the agency ID cards, then leaned inside the car and picked up the radio microphone from the dashboard. "This won't take a minute," he told them.

Swansea and Amber were growing more fidgety by the second.

As the officer began speaking French into the microphone in great detail about the unusual situation he and his partner had come across, the blond woman bolted for the BMW, jumped into the driver's seat, threw the car into gear, and peeled away.

"Jesus Christ!" Swansea yelled.

"*Arrêtez-vous!*" the first officer screamed while the other one threw up his arms in amazement.

"Why weren't you watching her, idiot!" the first officer shouted in French. "Why do you think I wanted her out of the car?"

"How could I watch her?" the second one said. "I was making the radio report."

"I don't care who was watching her!" Swansea shrieked. "Stop her!"

"Yes, of course. We will. You may have no doubt about that! Give me the radio, swine," he commanded. He babbled into the microphone all the details of the car snatching. "We will follow right away. Right away. Another police car will be along shortly to pick you up."

"What? That's no good," Swansea protested. "We must go with you."

The policeman shook his head emphatically. "Impossible. Please wait right here until the car comes. Please tell the officer everything you saw. We will need a full statement. Now we have not a minute to lose!"

Both officers jumped into the Peugeot simultaneously and sped off after the stolen BMW, leaving Swansea and Amber standing dazed by the side of the highway.

The two cars pulled up onto the edge of the tarmac, next to Stanway's jet. The engines were already running. He was standing on the stair ladder waiting for them. Diana stepped out of the BMW and immediately ripped off the tight blond wig, which was starting to give her a headache.

"It was amazing that you thought to bring disguises," she said with admiration.

"SEALs, like Boy Scouts, are always prepared for any contingency," said Stanway.

Rowland and Epstein got out of the Peugeot and opened the

back door of the other car for Brian. Together they carried Truong up the airplane steps.

"I monitored the whole thing on the radio," the mission leader stated. "You all were brilliant!"

"Do we have to leave the uniforms?" Epstein asked.

"No, I think my friends in the department can absorb the cost," Stanway replied, "as long as we leave the car before my friend's shift is over. Don't want to get anyone in trouble." They all laughed. "I told them where to pick it up." He turned to Brian. "Like I always tell you, Thorpe, it's good to have friends you can count on, especially at such short notice." He held him by the chin to examine the facial injuries.

Brian loosened his belt and extracted the homing disk that was attached to its inner surface. He handed it to Stanway.

"Thank God for that," Diana said. "Otherwise, we never would have found you." She threw her hands around his neck and pulled him to her. He reached one hand under her short skirt and made her jump with surprise.

"If I decide to slap you, it's going to be on the side with the bruise," she warned.

They all got onto the plane. The last one up pulled up the stairway and closed the door. When they were settled in and ready for takeoff, Diana asked Brian, "Well, were you scared? Tell the truth."

"Of course, I was scared," he said offhandedly. "But I had faith that you'd figure out a way to rescue me. By the way, that was some pretty fancy driving back there."

"Thanks. That's one of the two things today I don't want my mother ever to find out about." She glanced down at her provocative attire and reacted with a grimace. "But I guess every girl fantasizes about being a prostitute once in her life. Well, now I've got it out of my system."

She excused herself to go to the head to take off her garish makeup and change into something more practical for traveling. When she returned to her seat next to Brian, Ernest Rowland came over and told her to stand up. Stanway and Epstein stood behind him.

Diana did as she was told. Rowland was holding something small and shiny. It looked like a brass pin of some sort. When he came closer, she recognized it as the eagle with anchor, trident, and flintlock of the SEAL insignia.

"Hold still," he ordered her. Then he pinned it onto her shirt, just above the breast pocket. "You've earned this," he said. "We all think so."

She looked down at the badge. The she looked at the four men, who had formed a circle around her. She looked down at the badge again. Wordlessly Diana hugged every one of them in succession, then again, one at a time. Then, as the inner circle closed around her, once again she cried.

WASHINGTON, D.C.

The hut was constructed of bamboo and thatch, just like the hooches they'd known in Nam. From Sylvester, West Virginia, they had brought the materials one night and put it together on the grass just beyond the sidewalk on Constitution Avenue, right next to the Vietnam Veterans Memorial. And when it was finished, Timothy Dantley had climbed inside, his buddies standing a continuous vigil outside, pledging to all the world to remain there until one of two things happened: The disgraceful insensitivity of the government toward the Vietnam veteran was redressed or he was carried out feetfirst. He had already tried everything he could think of to call attention, and nothing had worked. So now he had decided to stage a fast, right here next to the memorial, where no one could ignore him.

It had been five days now, and Tim Dantley was determined that he would not eat again until those in high places finally heard his voice.

ATLANTA, GEORGIA

The abduction of Brian and Truong turned out to be a bit of luck, the way Hugh Stanway saw it. During the forced confusion surrounding the "speeding" incident Epstein had managed to snap off a photo with his spy camera, which Stanway was able to identify as Michael Swansea—code name Contact—a deep-cover operative whose very existence was known to only a handful within the entire intelligence establishment. As if to confirm this very point, Rowland noted that the name did not correspond to the one on the official agency ID he'd presented.

"There's no way we can pin this on him," Stanway said. "But let's say we've got him neutralized for the time being."

They had taken Nguyen Tien Truong to Emory University Hospital, only a short walk from CDC headquarters. With the capsule safely in their control, Brian agreed to let Diana give an expurgated briefing to Herb Secrest, which had the twin effect of placing the Emory facilities completely at their disposal and getting her suspension lifted. Herb seemed both shocked and genuinely moved by Diana's narrative, which she cut short when she felt an awkward apology coming on. He assured her he would remove from her file the letter of reprimand that had accompanied the suspension and replace it with a letter of commendation and a recommendation for the Public Health Distinguished Service Award.

The reunion with Sharon was joyous and emotional. The two women had come to realize how much they meant to each other, and Diana promised her roommate that "sometime soon, when we're both good and drunk, I've got one hell of a story to tell you." It was Sharon who suggested that it would be terrific if they started living together again.

Just to make sure there were no further incidents at the hospital Stanway, Epstein, and Rowland made sure the "patient" was never alone as Brian prepared for the surgery. The repeated doses of sodium Pentothal had long since worn off, and despite assurance that he would be returned as good as new as soon as the operation was completed, Truong was not overly pleased by his circumstances. This became particularly evident during the series of X rays and CAT scans necessary to determine the exact location of the capsule in his body.

The timing of the surgery was most critical. Since it had been determined that under normal circumstances the countervirus capsule could not live away from its host, a "body surrogate" had to be established in a CDC lab that would provide the virus with the proper environment while it was cultured and reproduced. A transport medium made from Truong's own blood was created for the move from the hospital to the lab.

While he was waiting for all the elements to come together, Brian phoned Gregory in Bethesda.

"I'm still working on the capsule for you," Gregory reported. "I haven't given up."

"And what have you got?

"Well, it's interesting, Brian. Once we knew the stopper was made of some organic compound, I thought it would be a pretty simple matter to figure out what it was designed to react to." He paused for emphasis. "That turned out not to be the case. We tested it against all the normal stuff we could think of, threw in everything but the laboratory sink, but there was never any reaction. Nothing worked. I was about to throw in the old towel.

"Then I started thinking about the case histories we had to work with. Now we've only got one example where the capsule actually did erode and open up."

"Sam Hardesty, in Montana."

"Exactly. So I said to myself, what do we know about him? Well, the main thing was that he was in a diabetic coma when he died, a state of ketoacidosis."

"So you think that had something to do with it?"

"It sure seemed logical," Gregory said. "I went down to the animal lab, implanted the capsule and the remainder of the stopper in a dog—in the liver, just like in our marines—and tried to create an artificial diabetic state. We pumped him full of sugar, got his blood level way over five hundred."

"What happened?"

"Not a goddamned thing. I was really depressed, plus I was starting to feel guilty about what I'd done to the dog for no results. So next I thought about trying insulin. But then I remembered that Hardesty had no insulin in his body at the time, only the sterile water they'd switched on him. That's what must have made him go into the coma. That one was definitely out.

"I was about to give up again. Then I thought: *What's actually happening in diabetic shock?*"

Brian thought for a moment. "Well, when the body can't break down its own sugar for energy, it starts manufacturing ketones as a substitute."

"Right you are! Ketones. So I pumped our four-legged friend full of beta-butyric acid—about a hundred times the normal level for a start. And you know what happened?"

"I have great faith that you'll tell me," Brian said.

"That little stopper dissolved away like my willpower when I see a chocolate cake."

"So the stopper material reacts to a dramatic rise in the ketone levels, even as low as ten times normal."

"Brian, it was right there under our noses."

"But why would they design something that reacts to ketones? How were they going to get the levels up high enough in those marines to make any difference? They certainly couldn't induce diabetic shock the way you did with the dog."

"Search me," Gregory said. "Anyway, that's your answer."

"Thanks," said Brian. "You've done terrific work."

"And when do we get to see you up North?"

"Soon. Very soon."

"Good. Can't wait. Jill sends you a great big kiss."

"And you can give her a great big one back for me."

"You know I will."

WASHINGTON, D.C.

The television news trucks all were assembled in readiness; the local stations, cable, even the networks were there. They'd been tipped off it was coming.

A fairly good size number of people had gathered on the sidewalk, though as one commentator using them as a backdrop for his broadcast had pointed out, it was probably the presence of the television equipment, more than the event itself, that had attracted the crowd. They watched as six District of Columbia policemen carried Timothy Dantley feetfirst out of the bamboo hut that had been his home for ten days and placed him in the blue and white paddy wagon.

As the door slammed closed, there was a chorus of jeers and boos from the crowd, many numbers of whom were dressed in jungle fatigues, as Dantley was. The police authority on the scene explained it away by saying that this was not an arrest, and despite the fact that he had been placed in a lockup van, Dantley was not being taken to jail. Rather, he was being removed to a Veterans Administration hospital, where he would be kept under "protective confinement and observation" for his own safety and welfare. The removal, it seemed, had little to do with the public embarrassment his presence here had caused governmental and military authorities.

Then was he free to leave the VA at his own discretion? the woman from ABC asked.

That would be determined by the staff at the hospital in close consultation with the appropriate officials, the police spokesman said.

And who were these "appropriate officials"? the reporter asked.

The spokesman did not know.

And would an attempt be made to force-feed Mr. Dantley at the hospital during his protective confinement?

The police authority's understanding was that there would be.

ATLANTA, GEORGIA

It was the evening before the surgery. On her way home Diana met Brian in the hospital's radiology reading room. The light box covering one wall was entirely taken up with Truong's films. The plain X rays had been arranged across the top row. The CAT scan tomograms accounted for the bottom two.

"It's in the liver, just like the others," Brian reported. "Superior lateral portion of the left lobe." He pointed with his pen to one of the views. "Look at cut two-oh-four here. You can see its position."

"A tough procedure?" Diana asked.

"Not too bad. More complicated than the one I did on Radley Davis, I think. But we should be in and out of there in two, two and a half hours."

"You're sure you're up to it with all the strain you've been through lately?"

"I'm up to it," Brian replied. "I'm anxious to get back to the operating room. The more important question is: Are your friends across the way up to handling the capsule once I get it for them?"

"There won't be any trouble with that. These people are the best in the world."

"They'd better be."

"You ready to come home?" she asked.

"In a little while. You go without me. A surgeon should always talk to his patient the night before surgery. I want to see Truong."

"This isn't exactly a normal situation," Diana commented. "He's not exactly in here of his own free will."

"I know. But that doesn't mean I can't observe the rules of common decency." He kissed her once on the lips. "I promise I won't be long."

"Okay, see you soon."

When Brian got to Truong's room, Rowland was sitting in the visitor's chair, staring intently at the patient. For a moment Brian had an uncomfortable sense of déjà vu. The last time he had taken over the watch from Rowland both he and Truong had been kidnapped. "I just want to spend a few minutes with him," Brian said. Rowland nodded with understanding and left the room.

Brian took the chair he had vacated and brought it up close to Truong's bed. The Vietnamese followed him with his eyes, saying nothing. His resignation over his condition had not altered his hostility.

"How are you feeling tonight, Mr. Truong?"

"Better than I expect to be feeling tomorrow at this time, Mr. 'Quint,'" he replied acidly.

"I apologize for everything that's happened. I wish there were some other way. And Dr. Keegan has spoken to some of her associates. They've assured her that the government will do whatever is possible to compensate you."

"That was very generous of Dr. 'Lane.' Perhaps this time they will not let us down and abandon us, as they have in the past. But why should I believe that? Why should I now have trust in your government that betrays my homeland and makes me flee for my life? Nothing you say will make any difference to me."

Brian couldn't blame him for feeling this way. The Vietnamese had been jerked around by one side or the other for hundreds of years. *And now, when the guy thinks he's finally bought himself a little peace, this ghost comes out of his past and tells him he's been the victim of some horrible North Vietnamese plot while they held him in prison.*

Brian said, "I just wanted to go over the surgical procedure with you, reassure that it's not a risky one, and see if you have any questions I can answer for you."

Truong shook his head. "Perhaps you are forgetting that I have already had this operation once—to place the capsule inside—though at the time I thought I was being operated on to repair my wounds."

"No, I'm not forgetting that," Brian said wearily. "I just

thought it was important to let you know that everything's going to be all right."

Truong regarded him with skepticism. "That is the precise same thing your people said to me the first time," he replied sardonically, "just before your Dr. Harley performed the surgery."

Brian felt his heart turn over in his chest. "Dr. Harley?" he stated slowly.

"Of course. Who else would have done it?"

"But you were in a North Vietnamese prison?"

Truong smiled malevolently. "Not when I had my wounds. At that time I was in a *South* Vietnamese prison. No matter what a person did in those days, it could end one up in jail . . . or dead. You could be both a freedom fighter and imperialist running dog at the same time. You see, perhaps, why I left when I could."

"But you mean to tell me you were operated on by Americans . . . in South Vietnam."

"This conversation is growing tiresome."

"You're sure about these facts?"

"Doctor, I am an educated man. I know English spoken when I hear it. I saw, I observed. I heard your 'great leader' speaking to the doctor. The doctor was timid, hesitant. But the commander said this would help quickly end the war. They thought I was only a humble peasant. He did not know I understood the English he was speaking."

"My leader?" Brian continued, trying to make sense of his confusion. "You mean President Johnson?"

"Of course not." Truong spit back the words at him. "I mean, the leader of the doctor who did the surgery on my wounds—the leader of the marines."

"Do you remember anything about him?"

He regarded Brian as if he were stupid or had just delivered the ultimate insult. "I remember everything about him: what he wore; how he looked; the name upon his uniform."

"And that name would be?"

"Colonel John Blagden."

TYSON'S CORNERS, VIRGINIA

The last formal meeting between the two men had taken place on the edge of the airstrip one cold and rainy dawn in 1970, as units of the Third Marine Division prepared to leave Dong Ha. Neither man, by personality, was much given to emotional demonstration. But as they solemnly shook hands and surveyed the fields of frosty mud they were leaving behind, each recalled a sense of completion without fulfillment. It was, for both of them, the end of a mission that had become their responsibility by default. Because neither those above them who'd been asked for their policy or those below them who'd been asked for their lives had ever had a clue to what it was all about.

Now, more than fifteen years later, John Winthrop Blagden sighted down the length of the massive regional mall and surveyed the seemingly solid mass of frenzied Saturday morning shoppers. He was wearing civilian leisure clothes in a successful effort to look like any one of the thousands of retired military personnel who had made their final home amid the colonial charm and commercialized blight of suburban Virginia.

"So, is this what we fought to preserve?" Michael Swansea asked as they casually came together and melded into the crowd.

"The eternal question of democracy," Blagden commented. That was it for the formalities of greeting. With one great "magnet" department store at their backs, they slowly sauntered down the mall in the direction of another.

Without introduction Blagden turned to his companion as they walked and said, "So I see you've resurrected Ratsbane."

"Not by choice," Swansea replied.

"What happened?"

"Swansea stopped in front of the video store. "Look, Jack, I agreed to meet you out here if that's what you wanted. But I thought we'd agreed that the less you knew about this, the better. That was the whole idea behind having someone from the other side of the agency handle the details for you."

"But people have died," Blagden stated rigidly. He glanced around self-consciously.

"People always die in war. As a general you should know that. It's one of the unfortunate side effects."

"But this isn't war any longer. It hasn't been for more than ten years."

Swansea picked up his pace, making sure that no one in the crowd heard any extended fragment of the conversation. "Isn't it war?" he asked challengingly. "What has changed to make it *not war*, other than the incidental fact that we no longer have ground troups in Vietnam? Has anything been resolved? Have we made our statement? Has the enemy been checked? Is the empire any safer? In one way or another we're still fighting the same battle and will be for a long time to come."

They had made a good pair back then, Blagden realized. It had been a war with no parameters, no ground rules, no defined objective from the bozos in Washington, no clear-cut enemy, and no dependable ally. The hard-assed military strategist teaming up with the geopolitical theoretician spook. It had taken that uncomfortable combination to make any sense and progress there at all.

"You told me the capsules would go inert after six or seven weeks," he said.

"We thought they would. That's what the Chase Corporation scenario said. You read it before you approved the plan. But when we found out they didn't, we couldn't just sit by and let nature take it's course now, could we? No one's quite sure why the virus stayed active, although Harley has some ideas." He regarded Blagden with regret. "I was trying to insulate you from all this, especially in your new position. How did you find out we'd reopened the file?"

Blagden remained silent.

"Must have been Thorpe. We hadn't figured on someone like him getting involved . . . and getting this far."

"You obviously hadn't planned on a lot of things." He didn't look at Swansea. "I assume you were responsible for the deaths of the marines from my unit."

"What is it they say, Jack? It's a dirty job, but someone's got to do it."

Blagden's expression made it clear that he failed to see the humor. "You'd better tell me exactly what happened."

"The less you know, the better," Swansea said. "If the proverbial shit ever hits the equally proverbial fan, it's your distinguished face that's going to get splattered. You can get your ass hauled before some congressional oversight committee; I can't. I haven't asked you to get involved, Jack. As far as you need be concerned, Ratsbane is a dead issue. Better leave the dirty work to me, just like in the old days."

"I want to know what happened," Blagden quietly demanded.

"I hope we both don't live to regret this." Swansea sighed. "I know I already have."

"Tell me."

The man known as Contact took a deep breath and stared idly into the window of the sporting goods store for several long seconds. He continued looking into the glass as he spoke. "A couple of months ago—actually it's been a little more than that by now—one of the men from the original delivery force named Anthony Lofton stopped in at Stanford to see Harley. He was some sort of traveling salesman and was having gut pains and such, and since he was in the Bay Area, he went to see a doctor he knew and trusted."

Blagden was amazed that not a touch of irony had entered Swansea's tone of voice.

"Harley immediately suspected what it might be. Pain from shrapnel fragments years later is not uncommon."

"Yes, I know," Blagden told him.

Swansea resumed walking, pointing in the direction of the next big department store. "In what I gather was a fairly simple operation, Harley took out several fragments from Lofton's body, including the one he knew contained the Ratsbane capsule." He turned briefly to his companion. "I can still stop at any point, and this conversation never happened. Beyond this, it gets ... unpleasant."

"Go on," Blagden directed.

"Though he tries to convey a somewhat different image in the operating room, Calvin Harley is, by nature, a rather cautious man. As a result, he took the capsule in question, and under completely secure laboratory conditions, he opened it and tested the contents." Swansea let an uncomfortable pause fill the air between them. "He discovered that the Ratsbane virus was still alive. That's when he hit the panic button."

"And he called you?"

"He called me. We suggested he get Lofton back for follow-up surgery, during which the patient would unfortunately expire on the operating table. But Harley refused on 'ethical' grounds. That's the trouble dealing with doctors—they're so fucking squeamish."

"So instead?"

"So instead we sent people down to L.A. to mix it up with Lofton for a while, get to know his habits, where he hung out. Since he turned out to be a frequenter of bars, the task was not overly complex. Many 'influencing' substances can be casually introduced into beverages which, in toxicology studies, will give the appearance of inordinately high blood alcohol levels."

"And that's what happened to the others."

"More or less. The ones we could still locate. One by one, over time, so as not to arouse any undue suspicion. The ones with the highest profiles—like Roger Moreland—we preferred to wait on until they could be handled with some delicacy. But sometimes, as you know, the exigencies of the situation require quick and decisive action that can force one into unpleasant compromises."

Blagden found Swansea's connotation for the word "unpleasant" both strange and unnerving. "Did you have to kill them?" he asked through clenched teeth.

Swansea shrugged. "We thought so."

"It could have been handled differently. Why didn't you just round up all the people and operate on them?"

Swansea's expression bordered on bemusement. "And tell them what? That we had turned them into walking time bombs and now we wanted to undo the damage?"

"Something like that," Blagden said.

"Actually we thought of that. For a while we strongly considered it. Admittedly it would have been the humane thing to do. It's nice and clean and symmetrical . . . in theory. But in practice the risks were too great. As a student of war, Jack, you've read Clausewitz. You know what he says separates the game from the real event. It's the friction—all the little minor incidents and irritations that accumulate and eventually destroy you. Can you imagine trying to operate on eight or more men—all of them civilians now, by the way—without telling them what you're going in for? You'd have to make something up and make it stick and then go through their own personal doctors and families and all that and not screw up once. Or the other alternative: take them all into our confidence; tell them what we did to them, what we put inside their bodies, and now we want to take it back out again. Can you conceive of the hue and cry! What do we do—make each of them promise not to tell? We might as well take out an ad in the *New York Times*. The protest over Agent Orange becomes a Sunday school picnic by comparison. That's before we even start talking about the world community. Once it gets out over there, we're dead. Not just you and me, Jack. The whole fucking country. Then what did we fight for?" He paused, as if preparing a summation. "All in all, I considered this an acceptable sacrifice."

An acceptable sacrifice. Those words had come back to haunt him. In his worst nightmares, and there had been plenty of them, he never thought it could come to anything like this. "You didn't have to kill them," Blagden said insistently.

Swansea put his hands in his pockets and looked down at his feet as he walked, as if he had nothing better to do in all the world than kill a Saturday morning at the mall. "I knew you'd react that way. But really, Jack, what's the difference? You were willing to sacrifice them, too."

Blagden grasped him by the arm. It was a gesture of frustration, of desperation, he realized. And it was the first time they had touched at all since Dong Ha. It all had seemed so clean at the time, so simple. "Yes, but there was a war on then," he said.

Swansea looked up from his feet and over to Blagden. "We've been through that already." Then, as if to cushion the remark, he added, "Don't get me wrong. I admire you for the distinction you make. But we really have been through it before. It comes down to the difference in orientation between you and me. You are a soldier, and I am a spook. You have been conditioned to think of war as an instrument of national will, a discrete time and place and state of being, with specific goals and objectives and rules. I have been conditioned to think of it as an ongoing situation which changes only in terms of specifics. And for that reason, I suppose, I can be somewhat more sanguine about finishing up an unpleasant job once it has been started."

"I don't need you to lecture me!" Blagden snapped.

Swansea continued, seemingly oblivious of the rebuke. "The other consideration is that you are—shall we say—hamstrung by your leadership position as far as taking any protective action is concerned. I am not."

Hamstrung. Another word he'd used in relation to himself. But coming from Swansea's mouth now, it seemed a critique, almost a taunt.

This time it was Swansea who placed his hand on his companion's arm. For a moment he even seemed unaware of the crowds of shoppers buzzing around them both. "Look, Jack, don't play coy with me. I've arranged things up to now to give you deniability, but we're both in this together. We're *all* in this together. So don't go bringing the world down in flames around you for some misguided principle of honor."

Blagden begrudgingly relented. Swansea was right. At least up to a point. And Blagden told himself he must have realized this all along. Otherwise, he would have told Thorpe everything he knew and made it easier on both of them. But that would have been the end—the end of his career and everything he'd worked for. There was still a principle of honor at work here. But it was a larger, more universal one. And Blagden accepted the fact that he would have to sublimate himself to it, just as he had forced others to do in the past. Life is full of compromise. And at this point there was no other choice.

"How much does Thorpe know?" Swansea asked, testing him.

"Enough," Blagden replied.

"You didn't spill to him, did you?"

"I considered it . . . but no."

Swansea looked visibly relieved. "What about the details of the project?"

"No."

"Has he traced it to Harley?"

"Yes."

"Is he going to try to talk to him?"

"I don't think so."

Swansea rubbed the back of his neck as he thought. "Okay, good. But just in case, we've got one of two choices with Harley. Either we've got to put him on ice until we can deal with the situation as a whole, or we've got to give him a cover that will hold solid enough to make him feel secure in keeping his mouth shut."

"Needless to say, I would prefer the latter," Blagden states.

"So would everybody." Swansea dismissed him. "We'll see what we can do. But if we have to implicate him, that's what we'll do." He thought for a moment. "I presume you showed Thorpe Document C."

"I did," Blagden said.

"I assumed you would if it came to that. I'm glad we generated that cover. I wasn't sure at first. There were too many elements of the truth in it. But it turned out to be the right thing. I always believe in having documentation for your fallback positions." He motioned Blagden to continue walking.

They strolled past a central plaza. It had been a long time since he'd been here, but Blagden remembered that there had once been a large fountain here. The mall's developers had apparently removed it to accommodate a larger number of people in front of the shops. Fountains do not contribute to sales.

Blagden shifted his tone to something casual, hoping to get

Swansea in one of his more unguarded moments, if there was such a thing. "According to the Chase report, I thought a stockpile of the countervirus was supposed to be maintained."

"It was. But only for a while. Once they didn't think they needed it anymore ... You know, no sense keeping evidence."

"So there is none of the countervirus still in existence other than what's inside the five carriers?"

"That's right," said Swansea.

"And no more of the vaccine developed at Fort Detrick?"

"Same thing. It was all destroyed when the operation was shut down over there. No one thought we'd ever need it again."

"I guess not." Blagden reflected somberly. He looked Swansea squarely in the eye. "What do you intend to do about Thorpe?"

"Please don't ask. Leave yourself the deniability."

"I'm not going to let you free-lance this thing anymore."

Swansea pulled him to the side, close to a shoe store window where they'd be out of the direct flow of traffic. "I hope you're not thinking of anything foolish, Jack."

"I don't think I am," Blagden answered decisively.

"I hope you're not in danger of losing your nerve at this late date."

"I am more concerned with you having lost your soul," the general rebutted.

A rueful smile touched Swansea's lips. "A soul is a nice and pleasant luxury," he said. "But unfortunately it's never been coin of the realm, and you've got to be willing to surrender it if the situation arises, same as a passport or driver's license." He placed his hands in his pockets and continued walking. "Sometimes it's the only moral thing to do." They hadn't gone more than two windows when he added, "I hope I can count on you the same way. For everyone's sake, don't worry about what I'm doing."

Blagden said nothing. They passed the window of a travel service. "I understand Paris is quite lovely this time of year," the marine general said as he strolled off on his own.

28

WASHINGTON, D.C.

Visiting hours at the hospital were over, and the attendant in the lobby told the three men they'd have to come back tomorrow. But they told her they were Tim Dantley's best friends; they were the ones who'd stood the vigil by his hut. They'd thought it over and wanted to try to convince him to start eating before the force-feeding began in the morning.

The attendant thought she recognized them from the newscast. She called upstairs to the ward, explained the situation, then told them they could go up if they stayed only a little while. They thanked her and asked which way to the elevator. She pointed and watched them walk off. All three were wearing sweat socks and tennis shoes and carried large gym bags. They looked as if they had spent more time playing basketball than worrying over his condition.

When they got off the elevator and presented themselves at the nursing station, the chief nurse directed them down the hall to the patient's room. There was a large, muscular orderly sitting on a folding chair outside in the hall, looking bored. He looked as if he hoped the patient would try to bolt, just to give him something to do.

The three men went into the room, made their respectful greetings to the weakened patient, then closed the door behind them for privacy. As soon as they did, they each opened their gym bags. Two of them pulled out matching M-16s, kept clean and functioning ever since Vietnam. The third took out a Remington M 700 bolt-action rifle with telescopic sight. They all put on M1955 flak jackets and grouped their ammunition cache into the center of the room. The man with the Remington established himself next to the window, while the ones with the M-16s took up positions next to the bed and by the door.

The one next to the bed looped the rifle strap around his forearm, then came over and put his other hand on the shoulder of the man lying in the bed. "Ain't nobody going to make you eat if you don't want to," he said.

Timothy Dantley nodded weakly.

ATLANTA, GEORGIA

Brian walked back to Diana's apartment in a state of shock. His worst fears had been confirmed, the ones so vague and unthinkable he had never permitted himself to voice them, not since this whole wretched mess began.

There had been so little that was positive to cling to from that time, so little of lasting value other than such abstract ideals as responsibility and honor. Now they sounded like no more than hollow clichés.

So Ratsbane was an American project. And John Winthrop Blagden was a traitor. Or else he had somehow taken leave of his senses during his command. Either way he was a threat.

And he was about to become the commandant of the Marine Corps.

Brian felt his stomach heave. As soon as he finished the surgery tomorrow and delivered the antivirus capsule safely into the hands of the CDC, he would have to confront Blagden. How, he wasn't sure. Whether anyone would believe him he didn't know. But he had the evidence now, and he would use it. He had to.

Diana had been right all along. Blagden was the enemy. It was still unbelievable. Black Jack Blagden, hero of I Corps. He must have been the one responsible for the killing of the marines, for all the other deaths and attempts. He would go on trying to kill them until Brian did something about it. And this Michael Swansea must be his personal henchman. Vietnam had been crawling with CIA men in those days, Brain recalled, especially where Brian had been.

Brian opened Diana's apartment door, not knowing how he was going to face her. He'd always found the antiwar people so smug and arrogant in their moral self-righteousness. And though he'd come to love Diana more than anything, he knew that just below the surface she was still as much a radical as he was still a soldier. She was not the one to give him aid and comfort as his last illusions from that time crumbled around him.

When he came into the living room, she was sitting cross-legged on the sofa, watching television, something he almost never saw her doing. Actually, "watching" was not an accurate description. "Transfixed" was a better one.

"Hi," he said dispiritedly.

"Hi," she replied without taking her eyes off the screen. She didn't even seem to notice his despondency. Well, he knew how much emotional support and understanding he could count on tonight.

She stood up, still without averting her eyes from what she was watching. "Come over here."

"What is it?"

She pointed to the screen. "Tim Dantley."

Brian was suddenly alarmed. "What about him?"

"He staged a fast near the Vietnam Memorial. After six days the police took him to the VA so they could force-feed him. Then just tonight three of his friends went up to his room with rifles, and they're holding off the world."

Brian came over and stood in front of the television next to Diana. The reporter, bathed in floodlight, was standing outside the main entrance to the Veterans Administration Hospital. Police and military vehicles filled the driveway behind him. Clearly the place was an armed camp.

Brian listened in stunned disbelief as the correspondent detailed the situation: "As you can probably see behind me, the hospital has been cordoned off, and patients in nearby rooms have been moved to safety. We understand a SWAT team has been called in. As you've heard by now, the three gunmen entered the hospital about an hour and a half ago, carrying gym bags, according to the attendant on duty in the lobby. These bags concealed not only weapons but apparently also a large amount of ammunition and enough food—in the form of K rations, incidentally—to wait out a prolonged siege. A negotiating team that specializes in these armed standoffs has been brought in and has apparently established telephone contact with the room. The gunmen have made no demands, other than to stress that they are not, repeat not, holding Mr. Dantley as a hostage. Rather, they say they are simply preventing the hospital staff from ending his hunger strike against his will. If he wants to eat, or leave, or whatever, they say they will not stop him. In fact, they say they will accompany him out of the building and provide safe passage. But so far there's been no word that anything of the sort is in the offing. In fact, there's been no movement here on either side since the beginning of this incident. We'll be standing by throughout the night to bring you reports as events warrant."

"How many days did you say he's been fasting?" Brian asked.

Diana finally looked at him. "Six. Why?"

"Holy shit," he said quietly. His face turned white. He looked stricken.

"What is it?"

"Diana, what happens during starvation?"

She looked at him quizzically. "Well, the body goes through its sugar and its stores of fat. Then it starts metabolizing protein to keep itself alive—"

"Creating an elevated level of what?"

Her mouth dropped open. "Ketones. Oh, God, Brian."

"Ketones," he repeated. "Just like in diabetic coma. And Gregory said that the capsule stopper eroded at ten times normal levels."

"And if Dantley's capsule ruptures . . . Brian, he's in the middle of a crowded hospital, and no one can get to him."

"I know. Okay, listen, Call Herb Secrest. Tell him I'm not going to do the operation on Truong, but they've got to get someone else to do it—tonight. Don't wait till morning. They've got to get that antivirus cultured as quickly as possible. Then tell him to call the Public Health Service in Washington. If that hospital floor hasn't been evacuated already, make sure it is now."

"Right." She dashed over to the phone, rang up Herb at home, and urgently explained the situation.

As soon as she put down the receiver, Brian picked it up again. He called Stanway, who had ensconced himself at the Peachtree Plaza. Stanway answered gruffly.

"Hugh, it's Brian."

"This better be important, Thorpe, because I am at the moment exercising my gonads for the first time since you descended on my ocean paradise."

"It is, Hugh. Can you get your plane ready to fly to Washington tonight?"

"Absolutely necessary?"

"Absolutely necessary."

"Meet me at Hartsfield Airport in an hour."

When Brian hung up, Diana asked him, "What do you want to do now?"

"It's not what I want to do; it's what I have to do. We have to operate on Dantley as soon as we can; get to that capsule before the stopper erodes. If we don't, and the antivirus hasn't been cultured and released yet, we're looking at a million deaths ... to start with."

"You don't have to tell me," she said grimly. "But how are you even going to get to Dantley?"

"I'm going to have to go through friends in high places," Brian replied caustically. Then he took out his wallet and pulled out the slip of paper bearing the unlisted home telephone number of John Winthrop Blagden.

WASHINGTON, D.C.

Goncharov had just arrived in town that day, but Andrey Stoltz asked him to come to his office in the embassy for a debriefing that evening.

Since they both worked for the committee, there was no need to waste time exchanging pleasantries, even after so long an absence. Stoltz knew Goncharov must be fatigued and so did not want to take up any more of his time than was necessary. Stoltz motioned for Goncharov to sit wherever he'd be most comfortable.

"I understand the mission in Paris had to be aborted at the last minute," Stoltz reviewed.

"Correct," Goncharov said. "It was well planned and on track. Commander Thorpe's group performed superbly, did everything we could have asked of them. Then our friends from the agency managed to get into the act and snatched the bait right out from under us."

"But I also understand that the 'bait,' as you call it, was subsequently regained."

"That is also true, Comrade. But by then there was no time to organize an alternative strike. They were out of the country within the hour."

"Yes, very unfortunate," Stoltz said. "But the reason I called up here tonight is this: Despite the unfortunate slipup, Moscow still thinks we can avail ourselves of the opportunity that has been presented. Though you were traveling all day, I assume you have been apprised of the drama currently playing itself out at the Veterans Administration Hospital."

"Yes, I have."

"I have just received a report that Commander Thorpe has unexpectedly departed from Atlanta and is on his way here."

"And the two events are related?"

"Moscow has reason to believe. What else would make Thorpe rush to Washington, unless Mr. Dantley was one of . . . those affected?"

"The same personnel will be working on our behalf?"

"That is my understanding," Stoltz informed him.

Goncharov stood up, knowing the brief meeting was at an end. "That being the case," he told his superior, "we will be ready."

29

Brian tried to catch a few hours of sleep on the plane.

When it was on its final approach path into Washington, the pilot received word to divert from National Airport to Andrews Air Force Base. There a military staff car met the plane on the runway and brought Brian directly to the VA Hospital. Diana and Stanway followed separately.

John Winthrop Blagden was standing at the joint military-police command center that had been set up in the lobby when Brian arrived. In spite of the hour, he wore his full uniform with general's stars and ribbons, lest anyone mistake him for a mere mortal.

"This is Commander Brian Thorpe—Dr. Thorpe," he said to the captain in charge of security. Brian caught the name James Lindsay on his tunic. The hospital's chief of medicine, Dr. Howard Meridor, was also there. "You're to give him whatever he needs and wants," Blagden said. "Please alert your entire staff."

"I understand," Dr. Meridor replied. He waited for Brian's first request, but Brian merely stood there amid the turmoil, for a long time, his eyes riveted on Blagden.

"I owe you an explanation," the general said.

"I'm not the one you owe," answered Brian.

"Sir, Commander, what can we do for you at this point?" Captain Lindsay asked.

Brian turned to Meridor. "I want an OR readied. Essential personnel only. Anesthesiologist, scrub nurse, and your most senior surgical resident."

"Certainly," the doctor relied. "When would you like to begin?"

"As soon as I can convince the patient."

"Sir, things are at a very delicate stage," Captain Lindsay said.

"We don't have much time."

"They've threatened to kill anyone who comes within sight of the door."

"I'll have to take that chance."

Lindsay glanced quickly around the assemblage. "Come with me, please," he said.

Brian followed silently. Lindsay led him down the corridor, turned the corner and into one of the elevators. The door closed. Inside, Brian saw it was an automatic car but was being tended by an armed, helmeted MP.

When the door opened again, Brain saw that police had taken over the nurses' station. Snipers in blue flak jackets were pressed into doorways all the way down the ward. The officer sitting behind the counter said, "We called into the room and said you were on your way up to talk, but they said to stay away. These are all Vietnam combat veterans, sir. They know their business. I'd take them at their word," he advised.

"Which room is it?" Brian asked.

"Four-oh-two east." He pointed.

"Have you got a bullhorn or anything?"

The officer handed one over.

For a crazy moment Brian felt like the cop in all the old gangster movies, shouting for George Raft or Edward G. Robinson to throw down his weapon and come out with his hands up. He pressed the button on the bullhorn's handle and said, "Tim, it's Brian Thorpe. You remember me. I'm coming in to see you."

A strong voice that wasn't Dantley's called from down the corridor, "Stay away!"

"I'm sorry," Brian responded. "I can't. If you'll let me in, I'll explain why."

"If you come any closer here, we'll blow your fucking head off!"

"I'd really prefer you didn't," Brian announced back. "I'm coming now." How do you reason with men who are already willing to die? "I'll approach with my hands up."

He handed the bullhorn back to the officer at the desk, took a deep breath, and stepped around the corner. With his hands raised, he walked slowly down the hall, one pace at a time. From the corners of his eyes he could see the snipers readying their rifles into position.

The barrel of another rifle stuck out from the door of Dantley's room. Brian recognized it as an M-16. The same voice called out, "We told you! One more step, and you're dead."

Brian continued walking. "I'm unarmed. My hands are in the air. I'm completely defenseless. I have nothing to do with the VA or the cops or the negotiating team or anybody. And I was with Tim in Nam." He didn't know if that would cut any ice, but he figured it couldn't hurt.

The rifle coming out from Dantley's door drew aim on Brian's head. His heart was pounding so hard it made him tremble. He continued walking. He heard the ominous click of the rifle's safety.

He continued walking. Suddenly he was in the room. All three weapons were trained on him. But he was in the room. And he was still alive. He gazed down at Dantley, lying in the bed. He was pale and thin and wasted. His skin disease was even worse than when Brian had last seen him. But there was still that burning determination in his eyes that no amount of fasting or hardship or deprivation was likely to erase. This, he realized, was the type of marine he remembered. This was the type of man Black Jack Blagden had betrayed.

"Tim, I'm not here to force you to eat. I'm not here to ask you to give up your principles. I understand what you're doing and respect why you're doing it. But there's something you *don't* understand. And you've got to let me explain it to you."

"What are you doing here?" Dantley rasped. His lips were cracked and bleeding.

"You have to let me operate on you. Tonight. Right away."

Dantley's half-closed eyes grew wide with amazement. His mouth actually formed into a smile. "I—I think you must be crazier than they say I am."

His three buddies said nothing. They watched and listened warily, their rifles still trained on Brian's head.

"Can I tell you the story?"

Dantley raised his shoulders slightly in an approximation of a shrug. "You're here. Talk."

"We have to talk alone. Your friends are going to have to step out into the hall."

"You *must* be crazy," the one nearest the door exclaimed. "The minute we step out of here, those SWAT boys are going to blow *our* fucking heads off." He said to Dantley, "This is a trick. Don't listen to him."

"Look, I know there's no reason to trust anyone after what's been done to you," Brian said. "And even more's been done to you than you know. That's what I have to tell you about. And when you've heard me out, I hope that somehow you'll find it in yourself to trust me. Because there's a whole lot riding on it, Tim. More than you could possibly know. We know about Agent Orange. We know about all the other outrages. Don't let them do it to you again, Tim." There were tears flowing down Brian's face. "Just don't let them do it."

He stopped to catch his breath. His eyes darted among the three standing men. "All right, how about two of you go into the hall? I promise nothing will happen. And just to make sure, the third one can stay in the bathroom as insurance. If anything happens out in the hall—anything at all—he can shoot me."

The gunmen seemed to consider this. Brian turned back to Dantley. "Tim, Radley Davis came to me awhile ago. That's what started all this for me. I know he was a friend of yours. He told me the story I'm about to tell you. I let him down. And he's dead because of it. Please, please let me make it up to him ... through you."

Dantley raised his head weakly so he could look squarely at Brian. He seemed to evaluate him for some time. Then he motioned to his buddies. "Do like he says."

They exchanged glances among themselves. Brian picked up the telephone. He was automatically connected to the command center in the lobby. "Two men are coming out into the hall," he said. "Nothing is to happen to them. Leave them alone. Either of them gets the least bit spooked, the third one kills me and anyone else he can take with him. Understood? Good. And another thing. If Dantley agrees to come out of here with me, nothing happens to his three friends. Nothing. They walk away as if it never happened. No cops, no charges, nothing. That's the deal, and I want your answer right now." He waited about ten seconds. "Good. We have an understanding." He put down the phone and nodded to the three men. Warily two of them began making their way out into the hall. The third one eased into the bathroom and closed the door.

Fifteen minutes later Brian Thorpe wheeled Timothy Dantley's bed down the corridor toward the elevator.

Brian hurried into the scrub room to prepare for the operation. John Winthrop Blagden appeared in the doorway. He sat down on the bench opposite the washing facilities and watched as Brian removed his running shoes and then stripped off his shirt. "I guess by now you know," the general began.

"Know what?" Brian retorted.

"About what I did."

"That you betrayed your country?"

Blagden seemed stung by the words. "No, sir," he stated emphatically. "You may, if you wish, interpret that I betrayed the trust of certain of the men under my command. But everything I did was always with my country's greatest interests at heart. Were that not the case, I couldn't sit here facing you. It's important to me that you understand this."

Brian stepped out of his trousers and tossed them in one of the open lockers. "It would take a rather twisted logic to convince me that helping the enemy wipe us out with germ warfare was in your country's greatest interests," he said bitterly.

"What are you talking about?"

"That you ordered the Ratsbane virus implanted in the bodies of marines in your unit."

"That much is true, I'm afraid."

"So they could then infect all the rest of the Americans and South Vietnamese." He slipped on the bottoms of his surgical greens.

Blagden regarded him grimly. "Please bear with me a moment while I set you straight."

Brian paused a moment in his ritual. He knew he could tear this man limb from limb with his bare hands right now if he wanted to. And one part of him very much wanted to.

"What I told you in my office about the Soviet biological warfare threat was true," Blagden said. "A CIA report did come down in the late sixties detailing their renewed interest and research. So in response to this, our own scientists at the Army Medical Research Institute at Fort Detrick, Maryland, began gearing up, too. Ratsbane was one of the things they came up with. I'm not a scientist, and I'm not a doctor, but I understood it to be a genetically manipulated virus combining strains of rabies, smallpox, and a couple of other things I'd never heard of, thrown in to make it work terrifyingly fast. I first found out about it in a Chase Corporation scenario."

The Chase Corporation. The sophisticated California think tank whose members spent much of their time coming up with intellectual "scenarios" for the soldiers to test out with their bodies and blood. Every once in a while Brian had run into a "Chaser" over there. You could always tell who they were. They looked as if they were attending an international chess match rather than a war.

"Now, put yourself back in 1969, when you were with my unit. It had been a long, grim, ugly war up to that point. That's no flash to you. The way we reacted to Tet, it was obvious we'd lost our stomach for the whole thing. Then, when the Pentagon began pulling the marines out in late '69, that was it. You could see that meant there was no more realistic expectation of victory. It would become nothing more than an expensive holding action to save military face and political ass. It was going to take years more and get thousands and thousands more people killed. And for nothing. For absolutely nothing. Once we had lost the will to win, every death after that point was a wasted, needless, obscene death, in my opinion." He looked Brian straight in the eye. "That's why I did it."

Brian pulled on the shirt of his scrub suit. He grimaced. "Did what?"

Blagden hadn't moved from his place on the bench. "Decided to implement Ratsbane. It was one of several scenarios Chase came up with. But the brass rejected it, afraid of what the politicians and the media would do with it. So I implemented it on my own authority, without consulting or informing my superiors, using only the covert action CIA men in my region for support. I figured that unlike the generals or the politicians, they weren't accountable to anyone."

"What did you do?" Brian wanted to know.

As Brian relaced his running shoes, Blagden spoke haltingly, his voice even, but as though each memory was a painful struggle. "There were all kinds of variations in the Chase report—dropping canisters from airplanes, poisoning the drinking water, that sort of stuff. None of them seemed very practical, and they all included unacceptable potentials for detection. This one didn't.

"From my own unit, the Seventh Amphib, Calvin Harley and I identified a profile that we called the delivery force. These were men who'd been wounded by shrapnel to a degree which required surgery but which would return them to combat duty in relatively short order. Harley implanted the capsules while the men were in for their shrapnel surgery, so they never knew what was being done. The Ratsbane capsules were hidden inside specially machined shrapnel fragments. The virus was supposed to remain vital for about six or seven weeks. If nothing happened after that, it was supposed to go inert, to die.

"We knew from intelligence reports and the testimony of American POWs who'd escaped approximately where the prison camps were in the area. We knew they were far away from any of our own installations but close to Vietcong training areas and North Vietnamese population centers." Blagden took a deep breath and frowned. "We also knew from firsthand testimony that POWs were having a real rough time of it. Aside from all the interrogation and brainwashing and physical abuse, they were also subjected to starvation-level diets."

It came to Brian like a bleak inspiration. "Which would raise the ketone levels, erode the stopper, and release the virus—" Sweat beaded on his forehead and ran down his face. He felt himself growing suddenly nauseated.

"—into the enemy population," Blagden completed the thought. "And since the virus kills so quickly, the distances from the population centers would preclude any carrier from bringing it back to any friendly peoples. Once the host dies, the virus dies with him, which makes the disease self-limiting.

"Then, of course, there were other protective measures. At a certain point we had these counter delivery carriers—that much of the fake document I showed you was true—who would be introduced into the target population to counteract the original virus. North Vietnamese prisoners of war whom we'd had to operate on for battle injuries were selected, just like our guys. Harley operated on them, too. At a certain point after the disease had reached predetermined devastating levels, the POWs selected as counter carriers were to be released. Eventually they'd meet up with the original disease and start 'infecting' the remaining population with the new, harmless virus. In a short time, the second strain would have taken over, and Ratsbane would be dead, having done its job for all of us, and all evidence erased from the face of the earth."

Blagden took a long pause. "This was a last-ditch stab at ending the war . . . winning the war . . . at a very small cost in American lives. In almost ten years, we hadn't been able to win the war through military means. This was a chance to win it in *ten days* through 'natural causes.' "

Brian walked over to the sink and stepped on the foot pedal. "So you purposely sent men off to be captured."

"No. But I knew that in certain types of engagements there was a high possibility of capture of a given percentage of the men."

Brian released the pedal, and the water stopped. "Eagle's Talon." He practically whispered the name.

"Eagle's Talon," Blagden repeated.

"Then Eagle's Talon wasn't a tactical mistake as we'd always thought. You knew it would be a massacre."

"I had an idea." The general sighed.

"The only tarnish on a brilliant military reputation. And it was all a setup."

"Those are not the words I would use. I sent my men in there with a specific military objective in mind. And in a certain circumscribed way that objective was achieved. Three of the seventeen carriers were captured."

"Fine, Moreland, Santoya," Brian said. "Only Moreland made it back. And then you tried to kill him." He resumed lathering his hands, as if he could somehow scrub the memory away.

"I had nothing to do with that. I give you my word of honor. What we have to do in war and what we choose to do in peace are two different matters. I don't know how to make you believe it, but it's true. I had nothing to do with any of those later deaths. I was as appalled as you were when I found out about them."

Brian turned around and looked at Blagden over his shoulder. "And what about the others?" he asked harshly. "What about all the other carriers—the ones who managed not to be captured or killed?"

"Well, as I said, there was a fail-safe built in. Anyone who wasn't captured and subjected to starvation within those six or seven weeks would be okay. The virus inside their capsule would die and whenever they were X-rayed later in life, the capsule would just show up as one more fragment of shrapnel. Since the chances of anyone's putting all the men's X rays together was impossibly remote, no one would notice that all the capsules happened to be in the same location in the liver."

"But evidently the capsules didn't go inert."

"Some did, I understand."

That must have been what had happened with Radley Davis, Brian thought, the one who brought him into all this. It seemed like such a long time ago.

"You're the doctor, Thorpe. You have to remember that when all this work was going on, genetic recombination was in its infancy. In fact, most scientists today would be shocked to find out how advanced the work going on at Detrick was in those days. But I'm told that one of the primary interesting properties of most viruses is their capacity to mutate."

And some of this one mutated into a virus with an unpredictably extended life by going into a dormant state, to be revived by contact with the bloodstream, Brian reasoned. And how could the Detrick researchers recognize that they had a mutation on their hands? Chemically and genetically it would have appeared the same as the original strain.

"And after all that it didn't work," he declared.

"It did, actually," Blagden said. "In a very limited way. We got back an intelligence report from an isolated POW camp of a disease outbreak whose description matched the Ratsbane symptoms. There were aerial and infrared reconnaissance photos. Absolutely horrific. Bloated, rotting bodies all over the ground. And those were mostly the North Viets. Our guys would still have been inside huts. Incredible contortions. Did you ever see any of the pictures of Jonestown? The same kind of thing, only worse. But the area was so remote that the disease just didn't travel. We received word shortly after this that both Fine and Santoya were dead. Roger Moreland had already escaped.

"When I thought about those photos of that fifty-man compound and then thought about the same thing in New York City, or L.A., or wherever, I knew I had to send you for that countervirus."

Blagden now looked at Brian as if he were imparting an article of faith. He spoke in a low, insistent voice. "Needless to say, if the world community found out about this, they'd have our nuts. The prohibition against any type of germ warfare is the most sacred tenet of the Geneva Convention. The images of the doughboys choking on phosgene and mustard gas in the trenches of Ypres are still powerful. So whatever you may think of me, you cannot reveal what you've just heard."

"And if I decide to, you'll have me terminated," Brian said tauntingly.

"No," Blagden said. "Despite what you might think, that's not the way I operate. You have the story. You're on your own." He watched Brian turn and go quickly toward the swinging door. When he was almost there, the general said, "Just another minute, Thorpe."

Brian turned back around.

"What's your beef with me specifically ... other than your delicate, wounded sensibility?" He seemed suddenly less reflective, more combative, the Black Jack Blagden Brian had always known.

Brian stopped and looked at him, holding his hands in the air to avoid contamination. "How could you do it?" he asked simply. "I just don't understand how you could send loyal, innocent, unsuspecting men to their deaths?"

"How could I send men to their deaths? I don't know. But every combat commander since the beginning of history has sent men to their deaths, and the only valid measure of their individual morality under the circumstances was how much they hated themselves for doing it. We call it a sacrifice. We sacrifice some— we hope—to save many others. When Eisenhower sent the troops out to storm Normandy Beach, he knew a large number of them weren't coming back."

"No, this is different," Brian said.

Blagden continued. "What is the damn difference, Thorpe? Was it that I didn't play by the rules? No one played by the rules in Vietnam. For ten goddamned years our bosses thought they were fighting the fucking Battle of the Bulge, while these little slant-eyed ghosts in black pajamas were running around, setting up bamboo traps to rip our balls off. I sacrificed a handful of men in hopes of saving an entire army ... plus the national honor of the the United States. Okay, it didn't work. In retrospect, with the benefit of twenty-twenty hindsight, we pose all the correct and proper questions. But at the time we seldom have the whole picture to work from. We go on impartial or incomplete information and instinct and what seems right at the time. It turns out I made a mistake. But those could have been the best damn odds of that whole lousy war."

Brian remained rigidly still. Blagden took a step closer to him and said, "Let me remind you of something most people have conveniently forgotten or never knew in the first place. We in the field were given the responsibility and the blame but none of the power. The politicians had the power but wanted none of the responsibility. War is an endgame play. You can't get caught up in arbitrary rules. We just talked about honor. But there is no honor in war, only results. We thought we'd figured out a way to end the war with American lives *and* American honor intact, with the people who knew what they were doing exerting the power, while the people who didn't could avoid the responsibility. And given the same situation, if I had it all to do over again, I would. What has happened since then, in civilian life, that is a different story. I would not have condoned the killing of my men, no matter what the cost. That is not the way things are done."

"And yet you were willing to lie to me," Brian said accusingly. "You purposely led me to think it was a North Vietnamese plot."

"That's true," Blagden said. "The damage was done. I wanted to contain it as best I could . . . for my sake, and everyone else's. But not at the expense of endangering the country or anyone in it. And that's why I pushed you to do something I couldn't do—go after the counter delivery agents, even though I knew it might ultimately come back to me."

A torrent of responses, of conflicting sensations and emotions cascaded through Brian's mind. He opened his mouth to speak, then closed it again without having said anything. He took a step toward Blagden, then another one back away. Finally he said, simply, "I have to get to my patient."

"Yes—yes, you do," Blagden impassively remarked, and watched him stride out of the scrub room.

30

The entire area inside the surgical suite was blocked off. The viewing gallery was empty and locked. No one but those involved was anywhere around. If contact was necessary, an intercom had been set up to communicate with a new command post in the office of the suite. When Brian entered the operating room, the surgical team was already in place, waiting. So were Hugh Stanway and Diana, standing away from the table, garbed in scrub suits.

"What are you doing here?" Brian addressed them both.

"We're staying with you," Stanway declared.

"Both of us," she said.

"I specifically stated that I wanted as few people in here as possible," said Brian. "Only essential personnel."

"We decided we're essential personnel," said Stanway.

"Yeah." Diana winked above her mask. "The anesthesiologist is here to keep the patient asleep. I'm here to keep you awake. If you look like you're nodding off in the middle of the procedure, I'll just pinch you. Someplace interesting," she added.

This was just exposing two more people to the danger, Brian knew, two more people very close to him. But there was no time to argue with them. And maybe it was only that he was facing the need for extreme concentration while entering the stage of extreme fatigue, but Brian found himself deeply touched by their gesture. Both of them wanted to share the risk with him. Brian held his hands up for the scrub nurse to glove him, then stood rigidly as she tied the dull green gown around him.

Two orderlies, accompanied by the anesthesiologist, wheeled Dantley into the operating room. Brian, the resident, and the scrub nurse helped them transfer him to the table. To save precious minutes, the anesthesia had already been started. The anesthesia equipment and regulating gauges were on a wheeled cart that followed Dantley into the OR. The metal box in which the capsule was to be sealed stood in easy reach next to the instruments.

In his physically wasted condition Dantley was not a good candidate for surgery. Under normal circumstances he should have had two or three weeks to recuperate before going under the knife. But now there was no choice. An IV dextrose solution was all they could manage at this point to help him along. Also, there had been no time for X rays or CAT studies or physical examination. Every other capsule had been in the same place in the liver. Brian hoped Dantley's was no exception. Other than when he acted as trauma surgeon in the emergency room, Brian had never gone into an operation winging it.

He took a deep breath, and when he was sure his head was reasonably clear, he called for the scalpel.

This procedure was by now very familiar. He was thankful, at least, for that. He dictated into the overhead microphone: "I'm making a midline incision directly below the xiphoid process. This is being carried down through the various subcutaneous layers. When we reach the peritoneum, we will open a longitudinal hole to expose Glisson's capsule. The diaphragm itself will help stanch the bleeding."

Meticulously Brian pulled the thin membrane away to expose the liver itself. It was enlarged and yellowish brown. Brian added alcohol abuse to the list of Dantley's other problems. Unless—unless this was also related to the effects of Agent Orange. Brian felt guilty for having jumped to the first conclusion.

When he had the liver's left lobe firmly in his grip, Brian studied the surface for any swellings or scar tissue formation that would help him determine the exact placement of the capsule. Without X rays he had no other markers to go on.

It wasn't long before he found his spot—a slight protrusion that looked almost like the stitching on a football. He cut carefully into the outer surface of the organ. He held his breath as he probed with the tip of the scalpel.

Then he felt it, the resistance of metal touching metal. He called for a needle. The scrub nurse slapped one into his up-turned palm. With the needle in one hand and the scalpel in the other, Brian delicately splayed the liver tissue apart so he could reach the fragment. He was without the magnifying lenses he normally kept around his neck when he operated at Bethesda, so he called for a standard magnifying glass to confirm the frag-ment's orientation and positioning.

With one hand still on the scalpel, he held the glass close to the surface of the liver and squinted into the surgical field.

What he saw made his blood freeze.

He addressed the resident next to him. He strained to keep his voice steady. "Give me the box."

The scrub nurse handed it to resident, who held it open for Brian.

"No, give it to *me!*" he ordered.

The resident quickly handed it to him.

"Now get out of here!" Brian shouted abruptly. "Get out of here, all of you! Right now!" He shoved his hands quickly into the surgical wound. Blood spurted all around him.

"What is it?" Diana called out from the back of the room.

"The capsule stopper's already started to disintegrate! Get out! Everyone!"

The scrub nurse and the resident backed away from the table.

"I can't leave," the anesthesiologist protested. "What about the patient?"

"Start bringing him out," Brian said. "By the time he's fully off the gas, I'll be through. This is going to be the fastest close in surgical history. Turn the gauges toward me. Then all of you, get the hell out of here!"

Stanway grabbed Diana by the arm and roughly yanked her out through the double doors. She landed painfully on her knees on the other side.

Brian spoke into the second microphone, the one for the inter-com that connected them with the office in the surgical suite. "Shut the air off!" he directed. "Reverse the ventilation. Do whatever you have to, but keep the air in here from getting out!" Brian set the metal box on the edge of the operating table. He dispensed with surgical protocols, instead trying to saw the fragment loose with the scalpel while holding the liver in place with his other hand. When enough of the binding tissue had been cut away, he ripped the shrapnel free. He wiped the blood away from it with a gauze and deposited it in the metal box and placed the top on it. Brian began furiously stitching up the wound, just as he would have done in a battlefield hospital.

He looked up to make sure everyone else had left the room.

Hugh Stanway was standing there next to him.

"Hugh, get out of here! Didn't you hear what I said?" He pulled the surgical thread tightly through the lacerated tissue.

"Give me the capsule," Stanway calmly said.

"The stopper's started eroding," Brian yelled desperately. The front of his surgical gown was covered with Dantley's blood. "The virus could be loose any second." Why wasn't Hugh leaving? This wasn't the time to play hero. He didn't understand the enemy.

"Give me the capsule," Stanway repeated.

Brian ceased his stitching a moment. He looked up at Stanway incredulously. Then he spoke into the intercom again. "Hugh's coming out right now. Put him in an isolation suit right away."

He had the liver itself stitched. Now he had to close up the incision. He glanced at the anesthesia gauges to make sure Dantley was getting the proper supply.

Stanway took a step toward him. "I want that capsule."

Brian held up his hand to keep him away. "Stand back! I'm telling you! Don't come any closer."

Deliberately, Stanway stepped over to the intercom microphone and ripped it out of the wall. "Brian, give me the capsule. I need it for my clients."

Brian looked up again. "Your what?"

"It's just between us. Don't worry. No one else is going to know. You're a partner with me. Somehow the capsule will get lost in the shuffle of the lab, and nobody will be the wiser. You'll make enough off this to spend the rest of your life on the beach in Tahiti."

He couldn't afford to divert his attention from the patient, but Brian reacted to Stanway's words as if they were hammerblows. He forced himself to continue concentrating on the surgery. He reached to the instrument table for the tape he would use to secure the box closed. Even after that they would place it in a uranium carrier before risking a move. Without taking his eyes from the surgical field, Brian said, "What are you talking about?"

"My clients need the capsule. They've known about it all along, but they needed the proof. They want to demonstrate it under controlled conditions to prove to the world what the United States has been doing behind everyone's back. It's a real coup. Should take some of the heat off them for the poison gas in Afghanistan, too."

Brian stared at him incredulously. "The Russians?" he gasped. "You've been working for the Russians."

"Only this one assignment. It's no big deal. Just hand over the capsule, and we'll both be rich. It's perfect, Thorpe. Russia gets what it needs—the propaganda. The United States gets what it needs—the antidote. And you get what you never knew you needed, which is about a million dollars! I know what your concern is. You want to protect the public against this killer epidemic. Great! I'm with you, and Brian—we got the Truong capsule, and now we've done it! This is another matter now, a political one. And in a way this protects the public, too. Because once it's revealed publicly, the chances of anyone's risking it again go way down. So think of this as a public service."

Brian quickly tied off a bleeder. Then he shifted his gaze to Stanway, utterly stunned. They both had become part of some bizarre dream. This was a man he'd more than once been ready to die for. "I can't believe it. I can't believe you'd betray your country, your friends. After all we've been through, after all we've done. . . ."

"We were going to turn the other capsule over to them in Paris, too," Stanway went on. "But then the agency boys came in and fucked that one up. They were the ones who tried to kill you, Thorpe, not the Soviets. How does *that* make you feel?"

"But your own country, Hugh . . . You're a Communist." He folded the flap of skin and muscle back into place.

"I am not," Stanway answered with annoyance. "This was a contract, same as I'd do for Angola or South Korea or our own CIA. It's all the same. I'm an *individualist*, just like you. that's what *Men of Action* has always preached. Survival of the fittest."

"What about your service? Didn't being a SEAL mean anything?"

"It meant everything, Thorpe. And one thing the SEALs should have taught you is that you rely on yourself and the others like you. The only thing worth fighting and dying for is yourself and the people who mean something to you."

Brian leaned over Dantley's body and tried to close the cavity. "But what about . . . ?"

"What about any of it, Thorpe? Maybe the country didn't learn anything from Nam. But those of us who were there should have. It isn't worth putting yourself out for anything other than your own personal interests. If they happen to intersect with the leader's interests, fine. But was it worth fifty-seven thousand American boys dying in Nam? For what? Did all those others die before them in World War Two so the highways could be glutted with BMWs and Toyotas? President Reagan laid a wreath at an SS military cemetery and said these people were victims of the Nazis! Come off it, Thorpe. None of it makes a fucking bit of sense. Don't hide behind that silly cloak of patriotism. 'Patriotism is the last refuge of a scoundrel.' Samuel Johnson said that."

"I can't believe I'm hearing this," Brian murmured again.

"Once you get up to a certain level, all the countries are the same anyhow. It's just one corporate CEO talking to another. Face it, the American president and the Soviet premier have more in common with each other than you did with all the marine grunts you took care of in Nam. Well, no matter, as it turns out. Now that we've turned up the antidote, all's well that end's well."

He was working too fast, too distractedly. He had sewn through to the fascia. He broke the thread with his fingers and began again. "Why'd you do it, Hugh? You're a self-made millionaire. The money can't mean anything to you."

"Why do we do any of this?" Stanway replied. "Because of the adventure. Because we're 'men of action.' Because we're above the petty political demarcations set up by lesser men for their own benefit."

Brian was trying hard to keep the hysteria out of his voice. "How long have you been involved with Ratsbane?"

"Ever since you first called me about that fragment. When I couldn't find out anything, I called my Soviet contacts to see what they knew. They got right back to me, then hired me for the case. I knew you'd come back to me for help. And I knew that *you knew* that once you did, I wouldn't let you down."

Brian quickly thought back over Stanway's involvement. He'd trusted Hugh at every stage. And at every stage he'd played right into his hands.

"They uncovered the first evidence back in Vietnam itself. The North Vietnamese took an empty capsule out of a dead POW named Fine, who'd been in a camp that had come down with some horrible plague they'd never seen before. There were no survivors—prisoners or guards. The North Viets called it the Corporal Scourge affair. They handed it over to their Russian masters, who licked their lips at it. But they could never get any further evidence. Until now."

Brian was still standing above Dantley's prostrate form. Stanway came over and put a hand on his shoulder. "Now come on. Stop playing hurt. Give me the box, and let's get out of here."

Brian stepped in front to block Stanway's path. "I can't let you take it."

Without warning Stanway lunged at Brian and grabbed for the box. The two men fought for it. Brian got hold of it, but Stanway tackled him around the knees. The box flew from his hands and crashed to the floor. As it did, the impact knocked the lid off. Brian had not had the opportunity to tape it shut. The fragment skidded across the room.

"Oh, God, Hugh!" Brian gasped. "You just killed all three of us."

Suddenly Stanway charged Brian. Brian instinctively stepped to the side and Stanway landed on Dantley's chest, pushing the body halfway off the table. The surgical instruments clattered to the floor. Dantley gave out a moaning gasp. Then he was silent.

Stanway turned around and lunged for Brian again, burying his fingers in Brian's throat. Brian kneed him in the groin, stunning Stanway enough to break his grip.

The two men exchanged blows, Stanway connecting with a right uppercut to Brian's jaw, Brian returning with a solid crack to Stanway's chin. Stanway reached for the capsule again. Brian wrestled him to the floor.

The principles of Hwarang-Do that both men had been taught emphasize the quick and aggressive use of any available weapon. Stanway spied the surgical instruments scattered on the floor. He nimbly bent down and reached for the largest scalpel he saw.

He approached Brian from a low crouch. He thrust the scalpel up toward Brian's throat. Brian jumped back, but not before the blade grazed the surface of his skin, drawing a thin bead of blood across his neck.

Stanway leaped forward and thrust the weapon forward once

again. This time Brian formed his hands into a V in reaction. With his own arms fully extended, he was able to stop Stanway's forearm. As he blocked the thrust, he took a short crow hop to the rear to keep his midsection out of the range of the knife. Instantly he spun around and grasped Stanway's wrist tightly with both his hands, pivoting to his left on the ball of his left foot. At the same time he raised his opponent's knife hand and stepped directly beneath his arm. From that position, bending at the waist, he snapped Stanway's arm forward and downward simultaneously, then drove him to the ground with a radical whipping action.

Hurt but not stopped, Stanway searched the floor, then scrambled over and reached for the scalpel again. But the distance was too great. As he came up this time, Brian was ready to kick the weapon out of his hand.

The scalpel flew across the room. Both men darted for it. Brian got to it first. He fixed it securely in his grasp. Ducking out of the way, Stanway came at him. Brian anticipated the evasive move. When Stanway bent over into a crouch in front of Brian, the scalpel was waiting for him. It glided easily into his heart without touching bone.

The fragment was lying on the floor just beyond Stanway's outstretched hand. Brian retrieved it and held it to his eye, squinting. It was his worst fear. It had happened. The impact of hitting the floor had dislodged the eroding stopper. The disease was loose and by this time had undoubtedly found its way into the one living host left in the room.

Brian staggered away from the corpse and collapsed on the floor in exhaustion.

A long time later, when he opened his eyes, he looked up and saw Diana watching him from the glassed-in viewing gallery above. Tears were running down her face.

31

She felt completely, utterly helpless. And as the hours drew on toward morning, the helplessness was replaced by bitter, dry, gnawing despair. She sat in the first row of the viewing gallery, her fingers gripping the front railing, her chin resting on her hands, and stared. Brian lay on the floor, his eyes closed, one knee flexed, his chest rhythmically rising and falling with each labored breath. The already decomposing bodies of Tim Dantley and Hugh Stanway flanked him on either side.

She thought about the symptoms that any minute now would begin presenting, graphically, horribly. She imagined the viral particles invading the cells of Brian's body, taking over, converting each one into a miniature biological factory of death. She knew she couldn't stand to watch his final agonies, but she also knew she couldn't bear to leave him.

When he saw that the capsule stopper had already eroded, he had purposefully sacrificed himself to save her and the others. It was like a soldier intentionally throwing himself onto a grenade to save his buddies. And whatever else he was, Diana knew that Brian was a soldier. As she watched him behind the glass and thought of what he had done, her mind was brought back to a passage from the Bible, something that didn't happen to her much anymore.

"Greater love hath no man than this, that a man lay down his life for his friends."

This was only the most recent—and last—time Brian Thorpe had been willing to do that. Images passed through her mind as if it were her own life coming to an end: Montana, Atlanta, Washington, California, Paris. She'd thought she'd lost him there. She couldn't go through it again.

It was tragic, just thinking about it. Even after he had died, it would be hours, no, probably days, before they could open up the doors and take the three of them out. The virus in Tim's and Hugh's bodies was undoubtedly dead by now. But they would have to wait considerably longer to make sure the disease Brian had contracted had completely died.

Gregory Cheever came by. He and Diana embraced each other and cried together until all the tears were gone.

The hospital people had rigged up some kind of new intercom to take the place of the one that Stanway had ripped out. Somehow they'd managed to patch it through the tape recorder mike hanging from the ceiling above the operating table. Dr. Meridor handed her the microphone. It was awkward. She had to press the button in each time she wanted to talk.

This was torture. She wanted to hurl the microphone through the glass. If only she could touch him. She yearned to cradle him in her arms just one more time.

Brian finally opened his eyes and propped himself up to a sitting position. Painfully he slid himself over so he could lean against the wall. He saw that Diana was still there.

"I want you to go," he said.

"I won't," she replied.

"I don't want you to see me how I'm going to be."

"I can't leave you," she responded, and found more tears she didn't know she had. "I don't want to stay up here. I want to come in there and be with you."

"Don't even talk like that."

"I don't want to live without you."

She thought she saw Brian give her a slight smile. "That's a beautiful sentiment. But it's stupid."

"No, it's not!" She sobbed. She stood up. "I'm coming in." Gregory held her in place.

"I'd let you do it, but you can't open the door," Brian said.

"There's a chance some of the virus could escape." He smiled weakly again. "So I've got you."

The smile quickly faded, and he grew serious. "Diana, listen to me. We've just fought a battle together. We won. It's too bad that we all didn't make it back. But we won; that's the only important thing."

"It's not the only important thing to me."

"Please go away now. Please."

"I can't leave you."

"Yes, you can. You have to." He closed his eyes in weariness, then, in a little while, opened them again. "I wish we could have spent our lives together. But—but just remember ... I love you, Diana."

She turned her head away from the glass and buried it in Gregory's arms.

Brian Thorpe didn't know how long he'd been asleep when he heard the sound that woke him. When he closed his eyes and drifted off, he hadn't expected ever to awaken again. He had hoped only that he would go in his sleep, without the agony that he now knew was in store for him.

He searched the operating room for the source of the sound. It was the door. Someone had opened it! Maybe someone in a radiation suit was coming in with a syringeful of barbiturates. About 500 milligrams ought to do the trick. That would be the easiest way to go.

The doors swung open. Calvin Chandler Harley walked in.

Brian's mouth dropped open. "What are you doing here?"

"I came as soon as I could," the surgeon announced. "As soon as I heard."

"Now you're going to die!"

Harley gave him a bemused smile. "No, I'm not. And neither are you."

"What are you talking about?"

"How do you feel?"

Brian stopped to consider this odd question. "Okay ... so far."

"There's a reason for that." Harley walked over and leaned casually against the operating table. He looked regretfully at Tim Dantley's body, stiffened by rigor mortis. He bowed his head in silence for a moment. Then he explained. "Whatever you might think about the wisdom of Ratsbane, whatever we all might think about it with the benefit of hindsight, we did understand the deadliness of the viral agent we were dealing with. That's why I insisted that anyone who had access to the field hospital at Phu Bai while I was doing the implants—that means doctors, nurses, *medics*—all receive the vaccination against the virus. We didn't tell any of them, of course. I think we said it was for cholera if I'm not mistaken." He walked over and rested his hand on Brian's shoulder. "You did valuable work getting that countervirus capsule back to protect the rest of the population. But in your particular case you'll die of old age before Ratsbane will get you."

"The president wants to meet with you tomorrow," Gregory triumphantly informed him as he greeted Brian outside the operating room door. "Something about a promotion and a medal. The medal will have to be given in secret, though. None of this can get out."

"I'll give him an earful," Brian responded darkly. "But tell him to try to make it in the afternoon. I'll be busy in the morning."

"Oh, yeah? Doing what?"

"I intend to pay a brief visit to a certain gentleman in Langley," he said ominously. "My last act as a SEAL."

Gregory asked him, "How does it feel to come back from the dead?"

"It feels great," Brian responded idly. At least that was how it was supposed to feel. But it didn't feel that way. No, not at all did it feel that way. Maybe it was that he was too tired to think. Maybe he'd been through so much that he could no longer feel anything. No, that was wrong, too. Because he was definitely feeling something now.

Emptiness. Everything was gone. He was overwhelmed by a sense of loss as he had never known.

Worse than he'd had in Nam. An all-embracing feeling of loss over everything in creation. Loss of his people and loss of his trust. His medical hero, Harley. His military hero, Blagden. Rad Davis, all the other men, the marines . . . Tim Dantley.

"I couldn't even save him," Brian said.

"You tried," Gregory told him. "It was Stanway who killed him. You did everything you could. Even at the risk of your own life you stayed with your patient. No one's ever going to forget that. And they also won't forget that in the end he died for something. He wanted people to understand, and now they will."

And Hugh Stanway. Oh, God, Hugh. "I killed Hugh Stanway."

"No, Brian. He tried to kill you. You tried to save him, just as you tried for Dantley."

Still, he felt a hollowness within his soul that he did not think would ever leave him. So much had been taken away that there could be no way left to close the agonizing void, to fill the emptiness of his life.

"It's over, Brian. Come on, let's get out of here," Gregory said. He clapped a hand across Brian's back and guided him in the direction of the recovery room. It was a large space, large enough to accommodate several patients at the same time and all the equipment needed for their care.

When he came through the door, Diana was standing there, waiting . . . waiting for him.

They stood there, both holding their ground, and gazed at each other with looks bordering on amazement, as if they were discovering within each other some new form of life. She didn't say anything. Neither did he. But then, as she rushed toward him and they threw themselves into each other's arms, Brian Thorpe felt the emptiness begin to close with the tears of mystical, wordless, all-knowing passion.

The door at the opposite end of the room opened. Knowingly Diana took one discreet step away. Brian looked up to see what it was.

Katie.

She was dressed in a blue sailor suit and white knee socks. With her little hands outstretched she raced across the floor and hurled herself into his arms. "Daddy, Daddy, Daddy, Daddy!"

He swept her up, high into the air. His tears came in a torrent as his kisses smothered her eyes and nose and mouth and golden yellow hair. "Oh, Katie, Katie, Katie. I've missed you so much!"

She grasped him with one arm around the neck. He supported her firmly with a forearm under her bottom. He felt the smooth, soft skin of her exquisite doll's face against his cheek, and he sensed the emptiness vanish completely with the radiant magic of childish laughter and delight.

Brian looked from the one woman in his life to the other. He was beaming as he said, "Katie, this is Diana. Diana, this is Katie."

Diana took the beautiful smiling child into her own arms. She turned her so that they were face-to-face, and she said, "Hello, Katie. I've been wanting to meet you for a long time."

EPILOGUE

BLAGDEN TO LEAVE MARINES

In a surprise announcement, Pentagon sources today revealed that Marine Corps General John Winthrop Blagden is resigning. Blagden sent his letter of resignation directly to the president, who, according to a White House spokesman, accepted it "with regret."

The timing of the announcement was peculiar. At the time of the resignation the president had on his desk Blagden's nomination to become commandant of the Marine Corps, which is the highest post in that branch of service and one of the four Joint Chiefs of Staff.

Blagden, whose nickname of Black Jack is said to derive from his legendary battlefield exploits, is regarded as one of the great military strategists of modern times. He most recently distinguished himself while serving as a colonel with the Third Marine Division during the Vietnam War, though his reputation there suffered, according to some experts as the result of his role in the infamous Eagle's Talon raid, where a large part of Blagden's Seventh Amphibious Unit was killed, wounded, or captured.

There was no official explanation cited for the sudden and unexpected resignation. Sources close to the general cited "personal reasons," and calls to Blagden's Pentagon office as well as to his home in Arlington were not returned.

2812-25A
22-24